D-P Filippi, J. Etienne & Silvio Camboni

gregory and the gargoyles

book 1

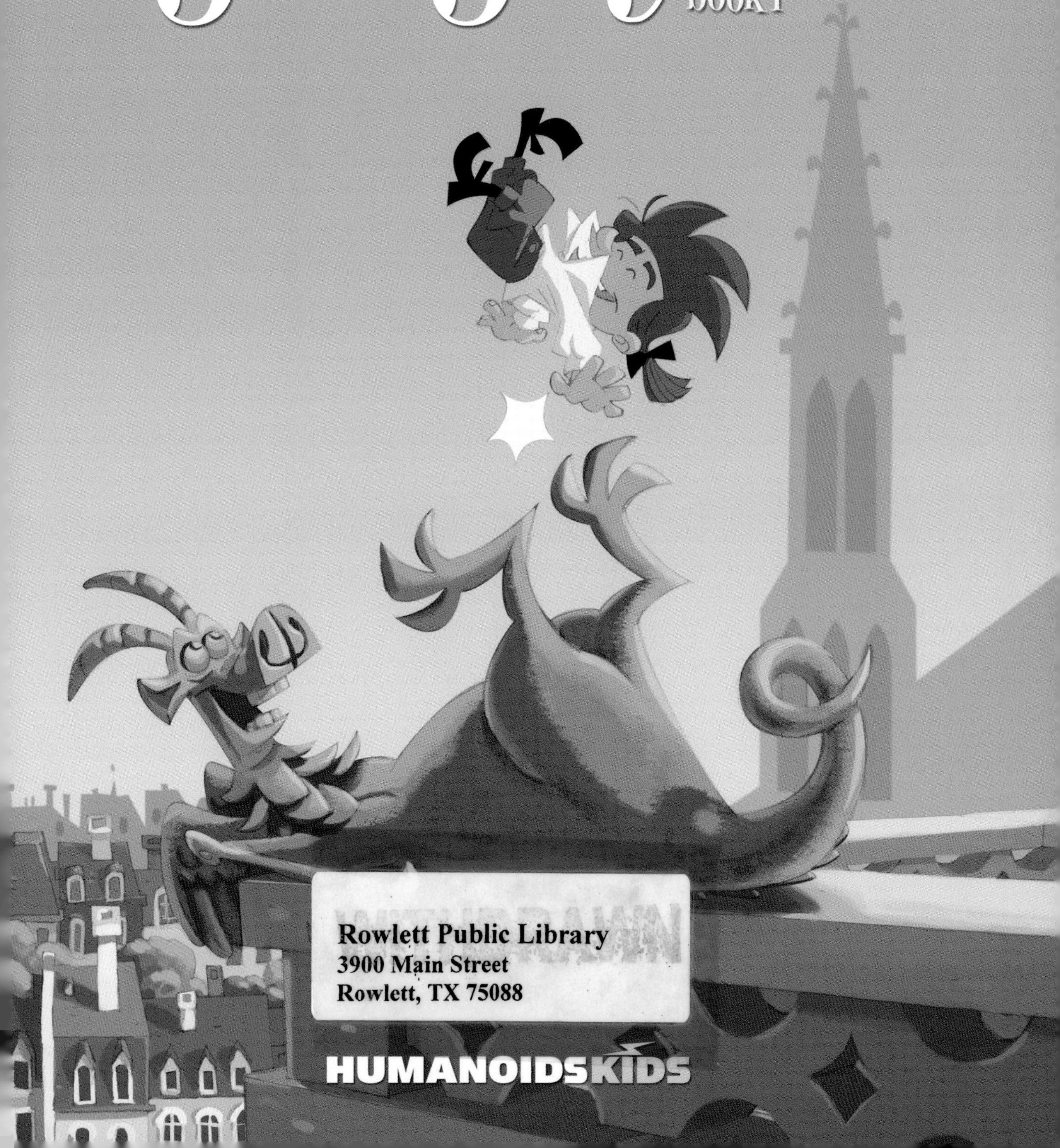

HUMANOIDS KIDS

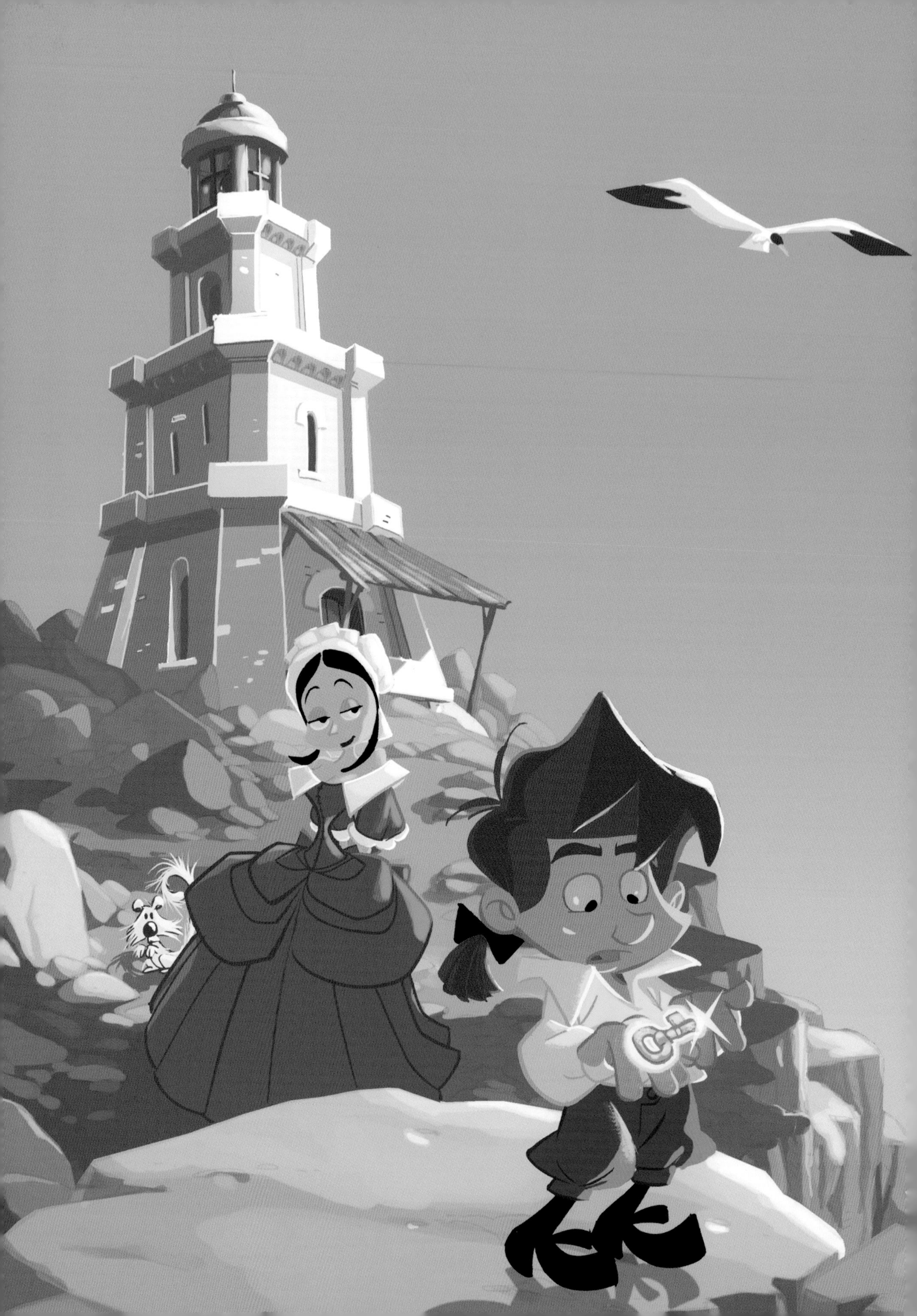

D-P FILIPPI
WRITER

J. ETIENNE
(COVER, PAGES 4 TO 50)
SILVIO CAMBONI
(PAGES 1-3, 51-96)
ARTISTS

J. ETIENNE
(PAGES 5 TO 50)
CHRISTELLE MOULART
(PAGES 51-96)
COLORISTS

ANNA PROVITOLA
TRANSLATOR

JERRY FRISSEN
SENIOR ART DIRECTOR

ALEX DONOGHUE
& TIM PILCHER
U.S. EDITION EDITORS

FABRICE GIGER
PUBLISHER

Rights & Licensing - licensing@humanoids.com
Press and Social Media - pr@humanoids.com

GREGORY AND THE GARGOYLES: BOOK 1
This title is a publication of Humanoids, Inc. 8033 Sunset Blvd. #628, Los Angeles, CA 90046.
Copyright © 2017 Humanoids, Inc., Los Angeles (USA). All rights reserved.
Humanoids and its logos are ® and © 2017 Humanoids, Inc.

Originally published in French by Les Humanoïdes Associés (Paris, France).

ALSO BY D-P FILIPPI:

MUSE
ISBN: 978-1-59465-038-3

JOHN LORD
ISBN: 978-1-59465-183-0

MARSHALS
ISBN: 978-1-59465-140-3

HALLOWEEN TALES
ISBN: 978-159465-654-5

ALSO BY J. ETIENNE:

BRUSSLI: WAY OF THE DRAGON BOY
ISBN: 978-1-59465-150-2

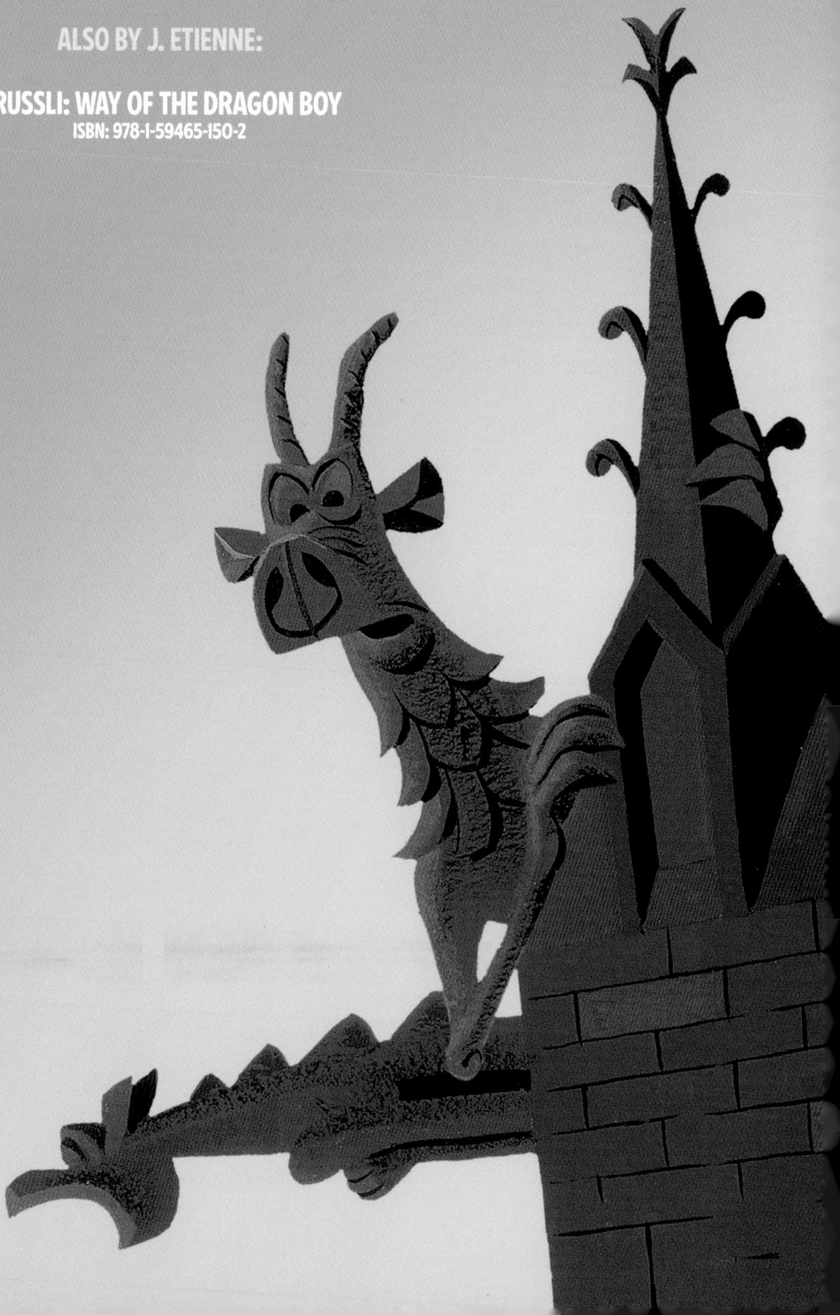

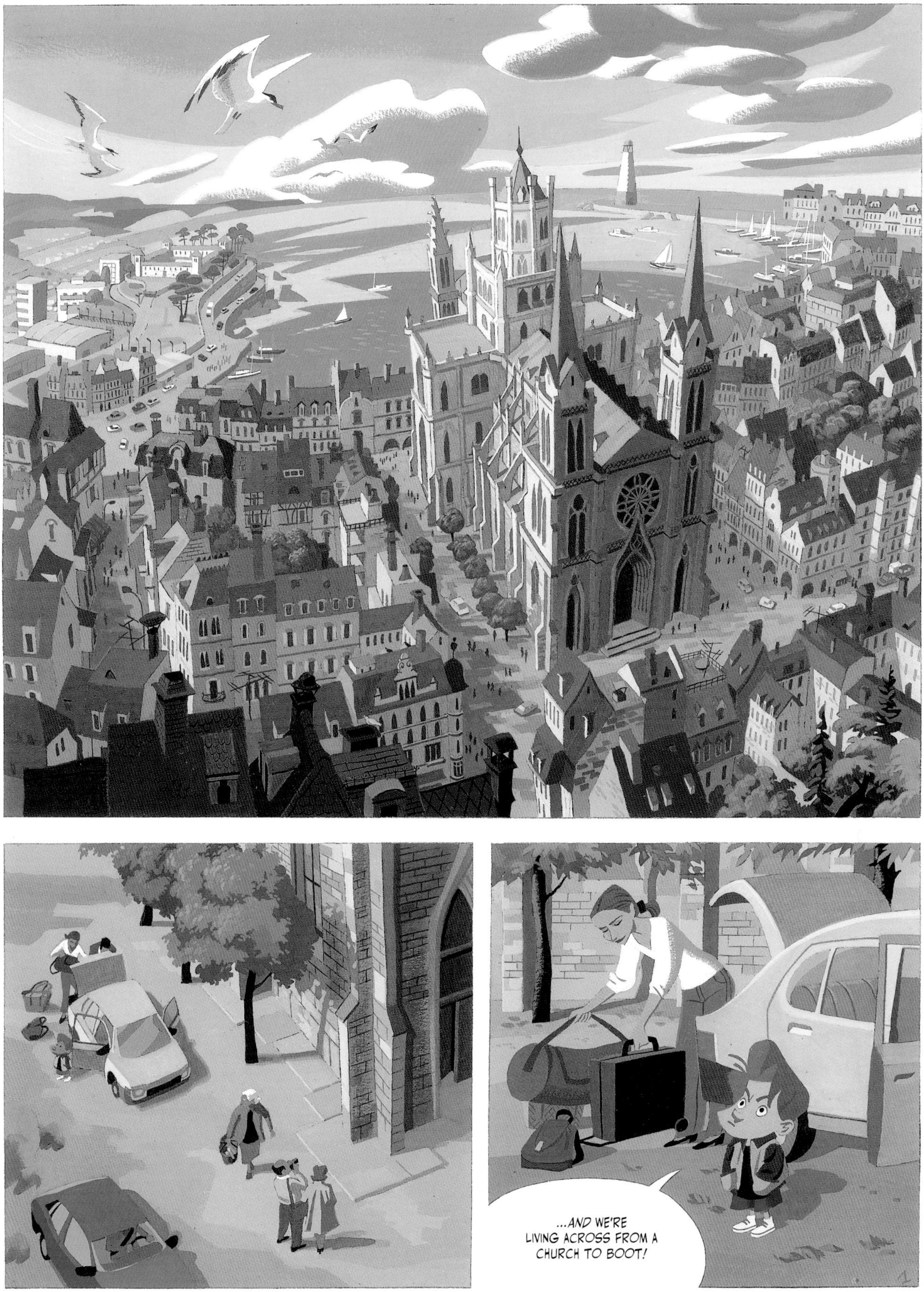
...AND WE'RE LIVING ACROSS FROM A CHURCH TO BOOT!

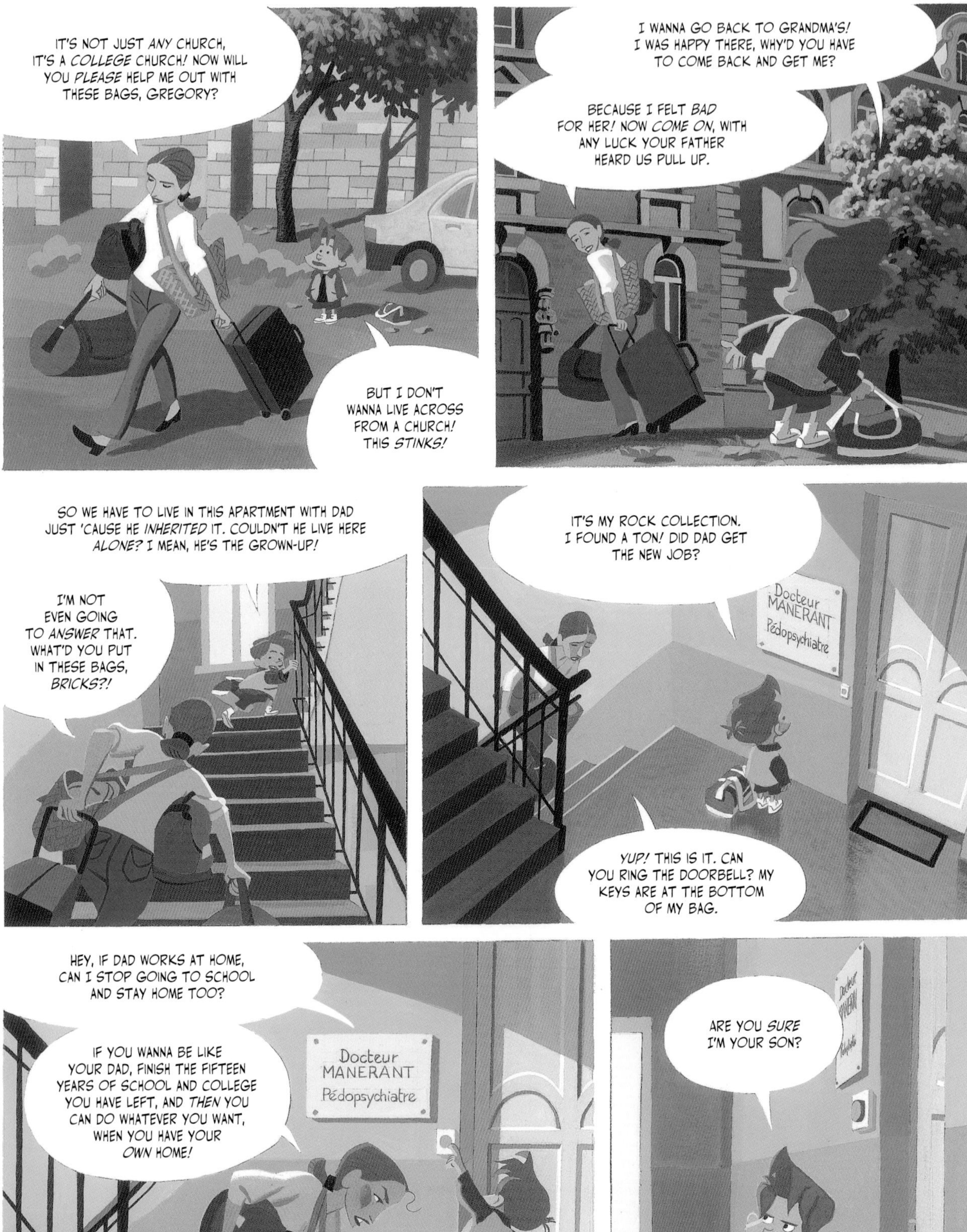
IT'S NOT JUST ANY CHURCH, IT'S A COLLEGE CHURCH! NOW WILL YOU PLEASE HELP ME OUT WITH THESE BAGS, GREGORY?
BUT I DON'T WANNA LIVE ACROSS FROM A CHURCH! THIS STINKS!
I WANNA GO BACK TO GRANDMA'S! I WAS HAPPY THERE, WHY'D YOU HAVE TO COME BACK AND GET ME?
BECAUSE I FELT BAD FOR HER! NOW COME ON, WITH ANY LUCK YOUR FATHER HEARD US PULL UP.
SO WE HAVE TO LIVE IN THIS APARTMENT WITH DAD JUST 'CAUSE HE INHERITED IT. COULDN'T HE LIVE HERE ALONE? I MEAN, HE'S THE GROWN-UP!
I'M NOT EVEN GOING TO ANSWER THAT. WHAT'D YOU PUT IN THESE BAGS, BRICKS?!
IT'S MY ROCK COLLECTION. I FOUND A TON! DID DAD GET THE NEW JOB?
Docteur MANERANT Pédopsychiatre
YUP! THIS IS IT. CAN YOU RING THE DOORBELL? MY KEYS ARE AT THE BOTTOM OF MY BAG.
HEY, IF DAD WORKS AT HOME, CAN I STOP GOING TO SCHOOL AND STAY HOME TOO?
IF YOU WANNA BE LIKE YOUR DAD, FINISH THE FIFTEEN YEARS OF SCHOOL AND COLLEGE YOU HAVE LEFT, AND THEN YOU CAN DO WHATEVER YOU WANT, WHEN YOU HAVE YOUR OWN HOME!
Docteur MANERANT Pédopsychiatre
ARE YOU SURE I'M YOUR SON?
2

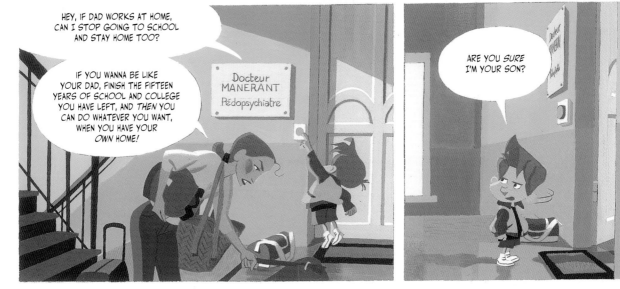

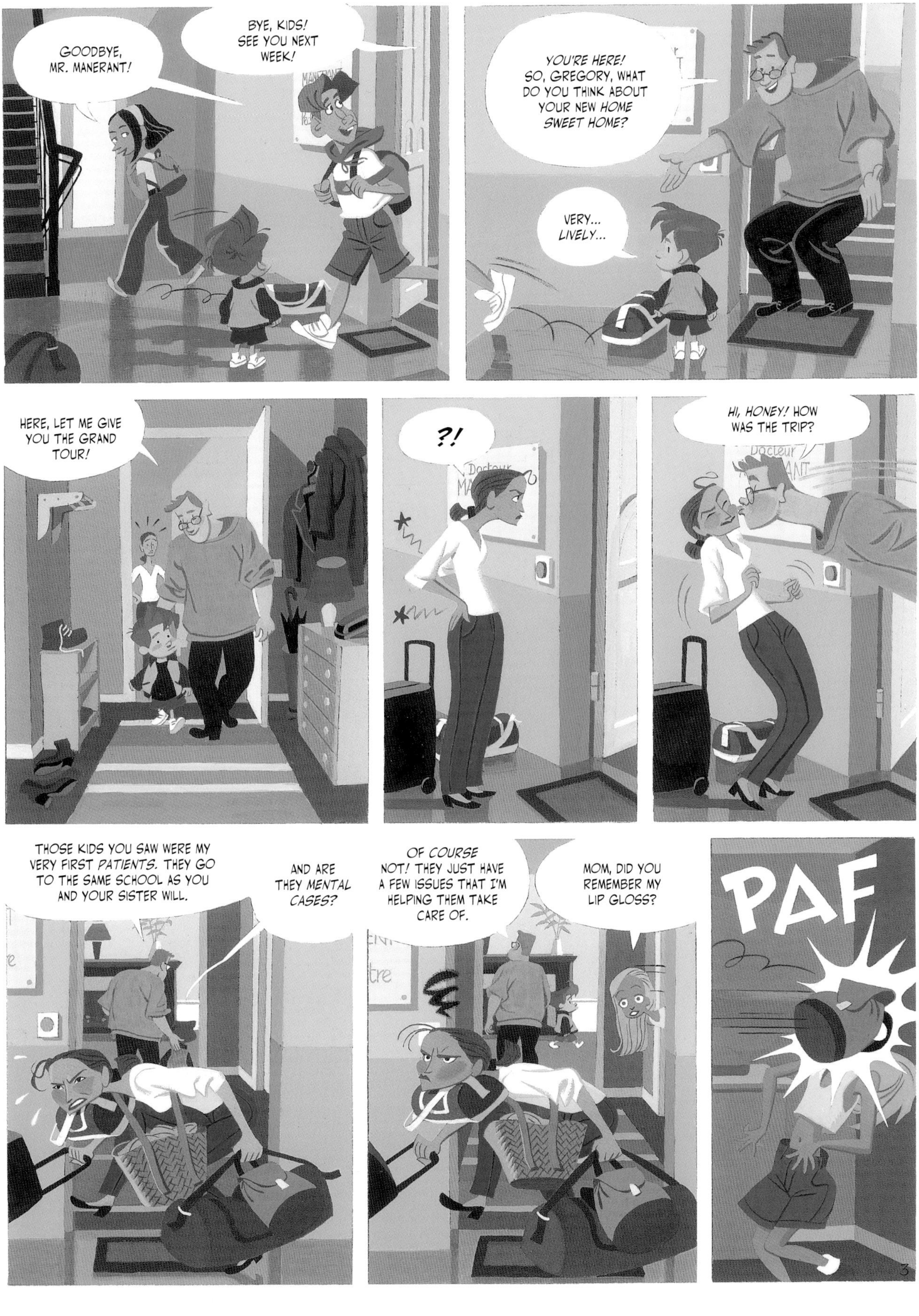
GOODBYE, MR. MANERANT!
BYE, KIDS! SEE YOU NEXT WEEK!
YOU'RE HERE! SO, GREGORY, WHAT DO YOU THINK ABOUT YOUR NEW HOME SWEET HOME?
VERY... LIVELY...
HERE, LET ME GIVE YOU THE GRAND TOUR!
?!
HI, HONEY! HOW WAS THE TRIP?
THOSE KIDS YOU SAW WERE MY VERY FIRST PATIENTS. THEY GO TO THE SAME SCHOOL AS YOU AND YOUR SISTER WILL.
AND ARE THEY MENTAL CASES?
OF COURSE NOT! THEY JUST HAVE A FEW ISSUES THAT I'M HELPING THEM TAKE CARE OF.
MOM, DID YOU REMEMBER MY LIP GLOSS?
PAF

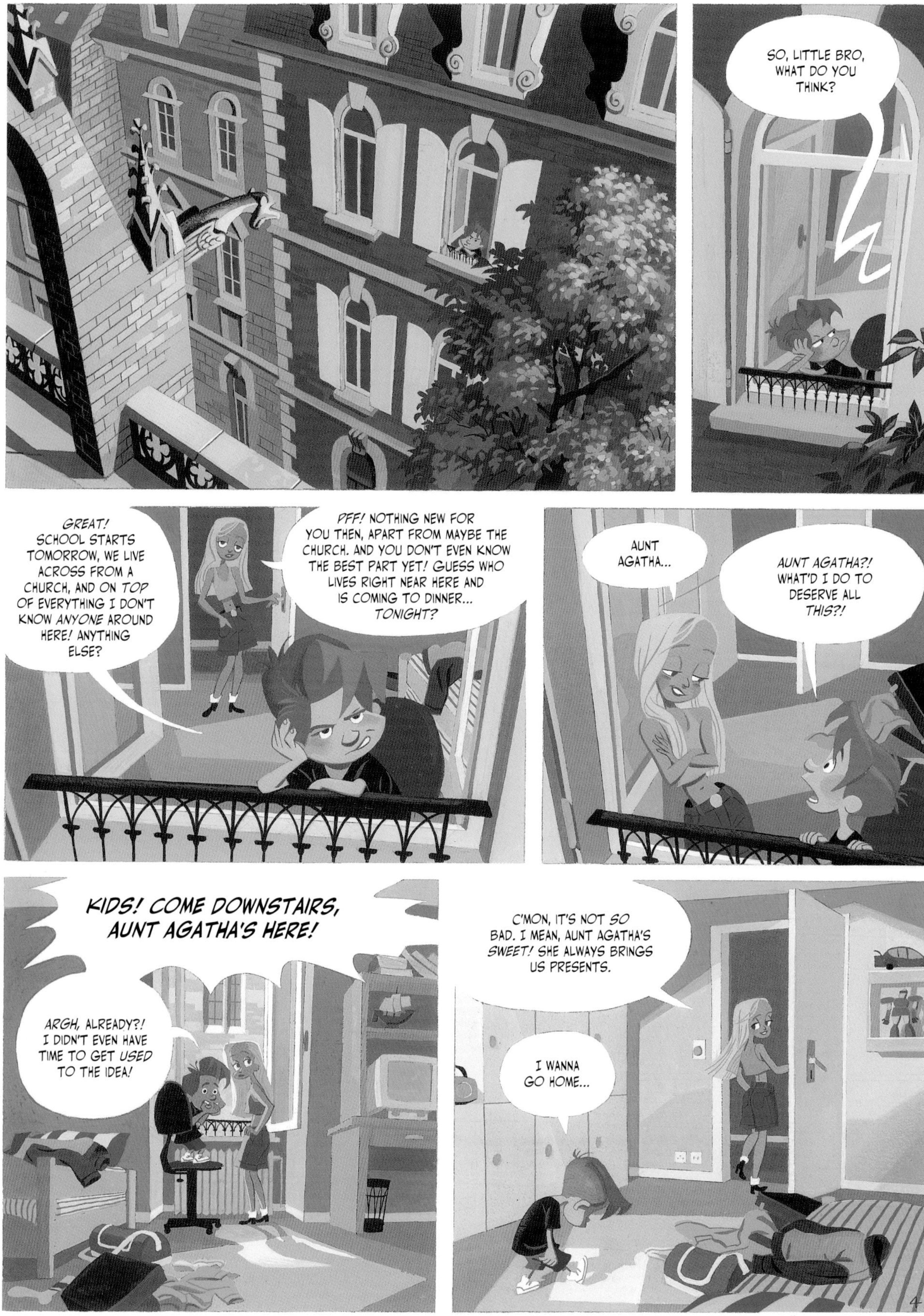
SO, LITTLE BRO, WHAT DO YOU THINK?
GREAT! SCHOOL STARTS TOMORROW, WE LIVE ACROSS FROM A CHURCH, AND ON TOP OF EVERYTHING I DON'T KNOW ANYONE AROUND HERE! ANYTHING ELSE?
PFF! NOTHING NEW FOR YOU THEN, APART FROM MAYBE THE CHURCH. AND YOU DON'T EVEN KNOW THE BEST PART YET! GUESS WHO LIVES RIGHT NEAR HERE AND IS COMING TO DINNER... TONIGHT?
AUNT AGATHA...
AUNT AGATHA?! WHAT'D I DO TO DESERVE ALL THIS?!
KIDS! COME DOWNSTAIRS, AUNT AGATHA'S HERE!
ARGH, ALREADY?! I DIDN'T EVEN HAVE TIME TO GET USED TO THE IDEA!
C'MON, IT'S NOT SO BAD. I MEAN, AUNT AGATHA'S SWEET! SHE ALWAYS BRINGS US PRESENTS.
I WANNA GO HOME...
4

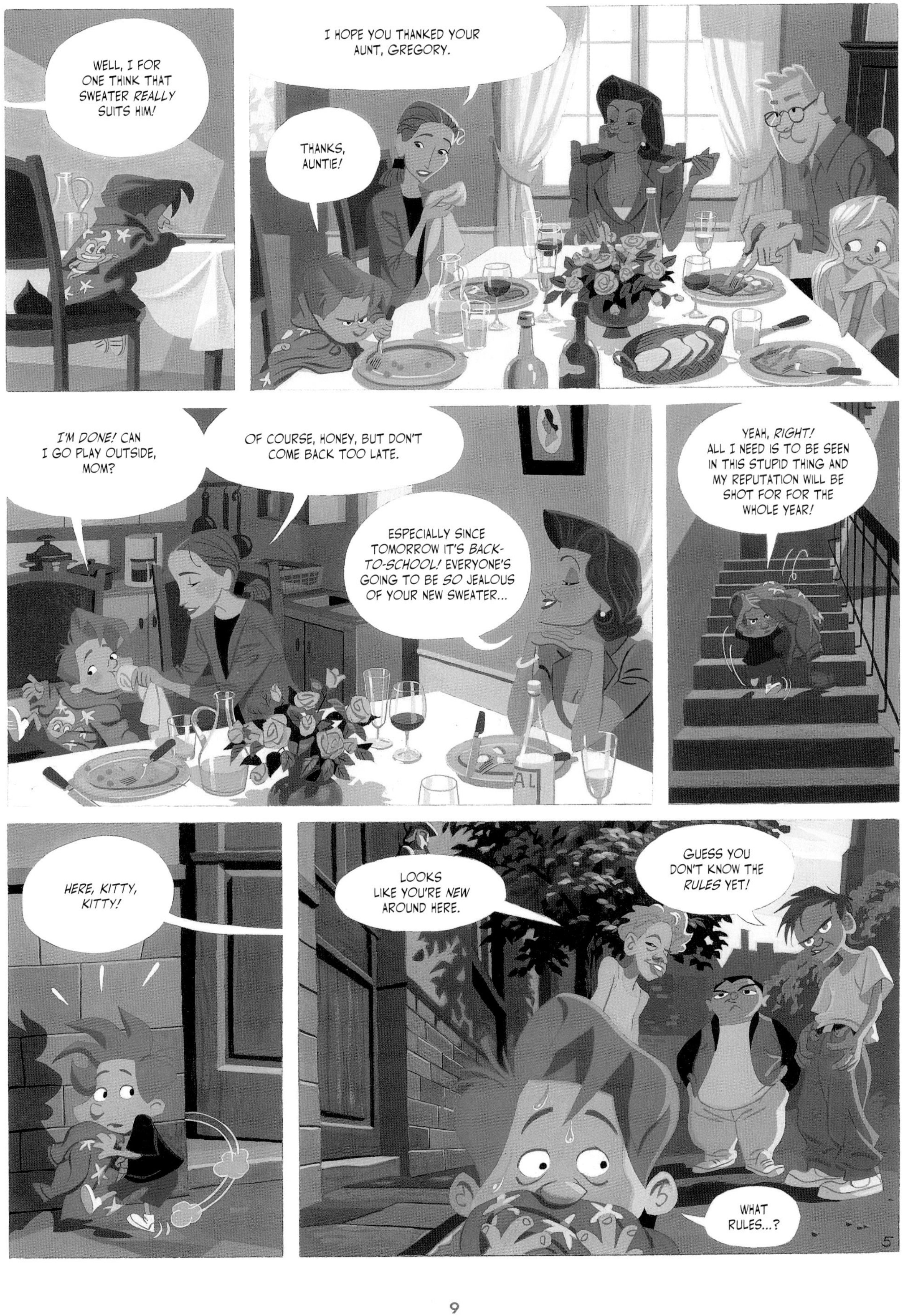
WELL, I FOR ONE THINK THAT SWEATER *REALLY* SUITS HIM!
I HOPE YOU THANKED YOUR AUNT, GREGORY.
THANKS, AUNTIE!
I'M DONE! CAN I GO PLAY OUTSIDE, MOM?
OF COURSE, HONEY, BUT DON'T COME BACK TOO LATE.
ESPECIALLY SINCE TOMORROW IT'S *BACK-TO-SCHOOL!* EVERYONE'S GOING TO BE *SO* JEALOUS OF YOUR NEW SWEATER...
YEAH, *RIGHT!* ALL I NEED IS TO BE SEEN IN THIS STUPID THING AND MY REPUTATION WILL BE SHOT FOR FOR THE WHOLE YEAR!
HERE, KITTY, KITTY!
LOOKS LIKE YOU'RE *NEW* AROUND HERE.
GUESS YOU DON'T KNOW THE *RULES* YET!
WHAT RULES...?
5

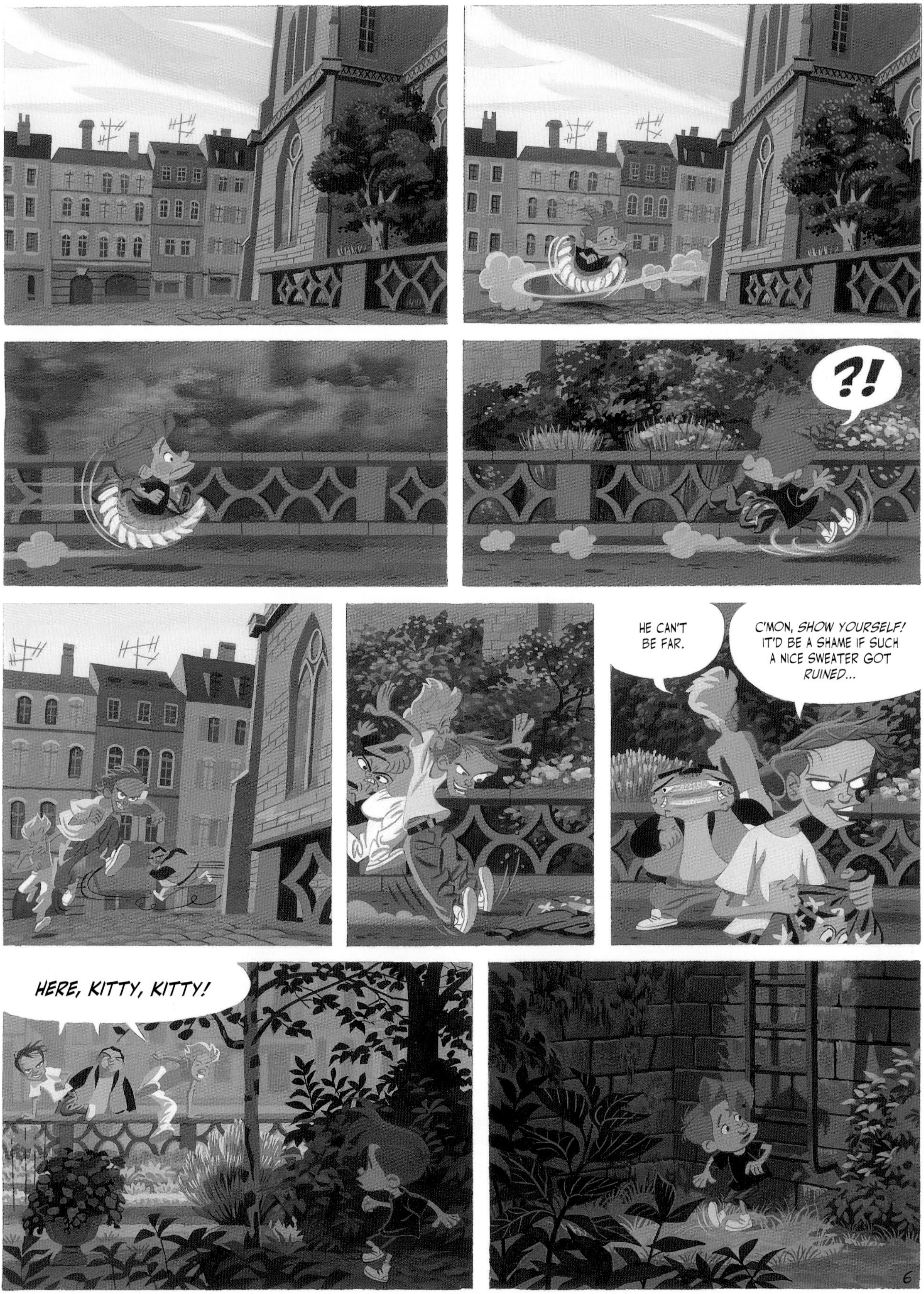
?!
HE CAN'T BE FAR.
C'MON, SHOW YOURSELF! IT'D BE A SHAME IF SUCH A NICE SWEATER GOT RUINED...
HERE, KITTY, KITTY!
6

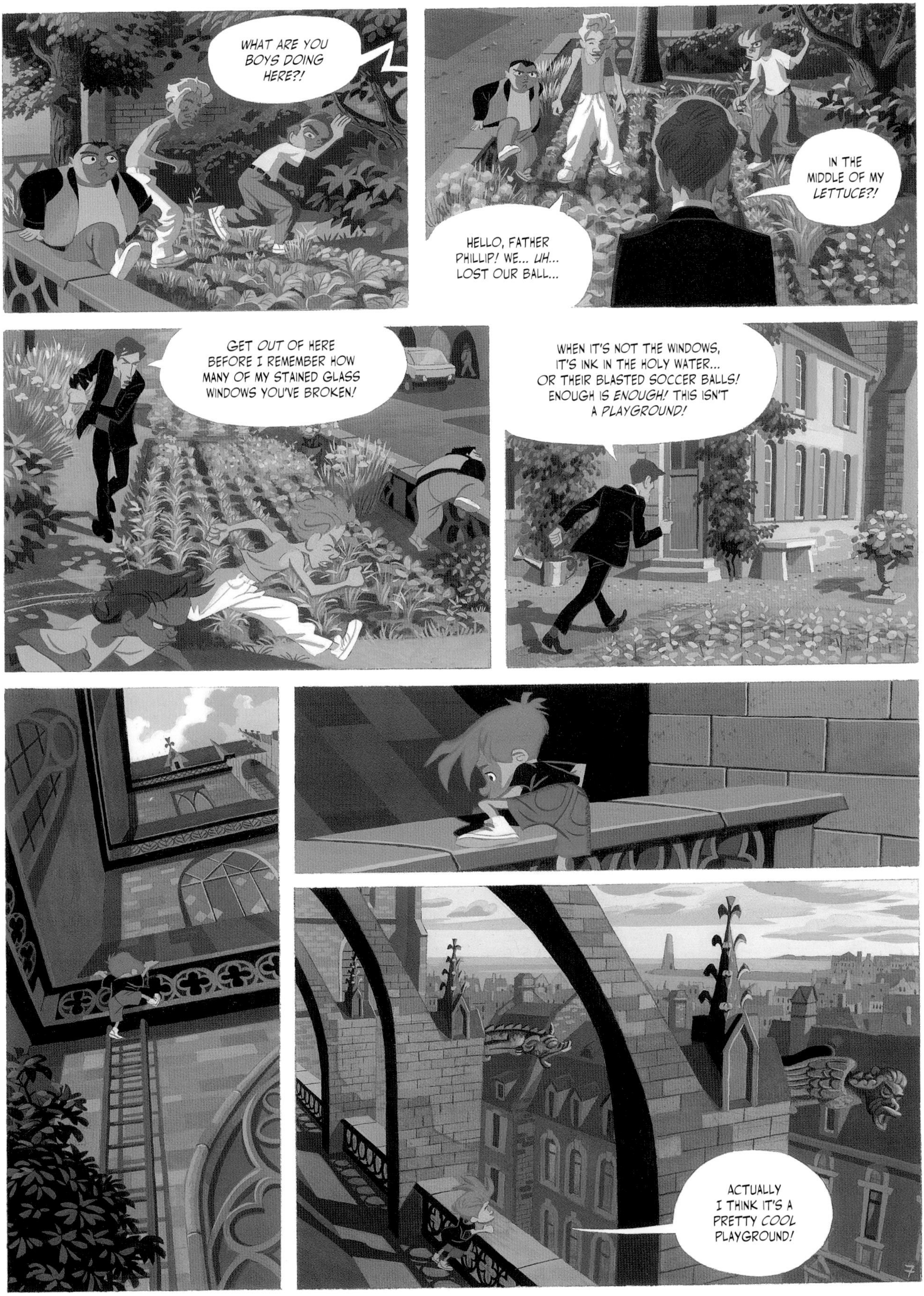
WHAT ARE YOU BOYS DOING HERE?!
IN THE MIDDLE OF MY LETTUCE?!
HELLO, FATHER PHILLIP! WE... UH... LOST OUR BALL...
GET OUT OF HERE BEFORE I REMEMBER HOW MANY OF MY STAINED GLASS WINDOWS YOU'VE BROKEN!
WHEN IT'S NOT THE WINDOWS, IT'S INK IN THE HOLY WATER... OR THEIR BLASTED SOCCER BALLS! ENOUGH IS ENOUGH! THIS ISN'T A PLAYGROUND!
ACTUALLY I THINK IT'S A PRETTY COOL PLAYGROUND!

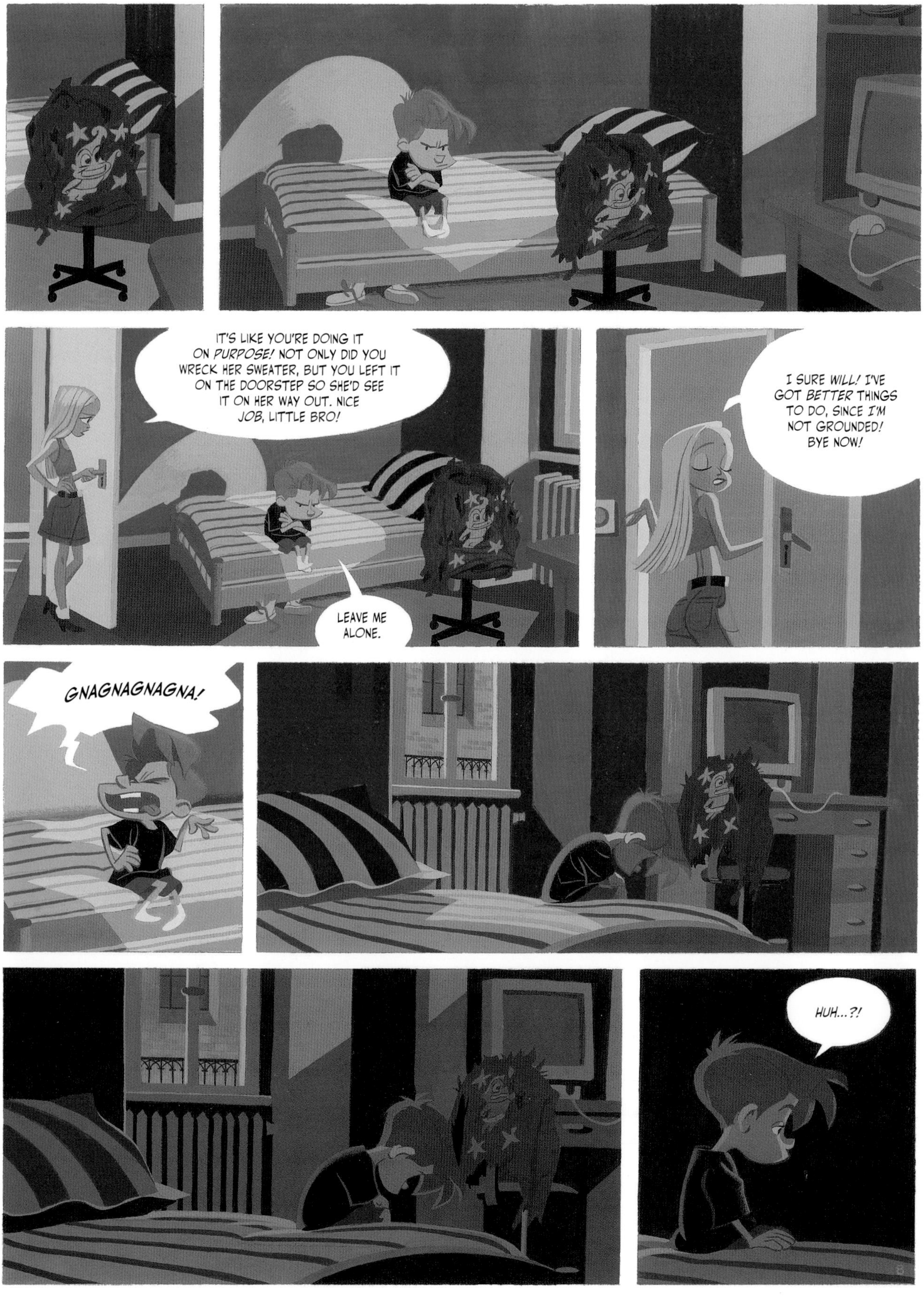
IT'S LIKE YOU'RE DOING IT ON PURPOSE! NOT ONLY DID YOU WRECK HER SWEATER, BUT YOU LEFT IT ON THE DOORSTEP SO SHE'D SEE IT ON HER WAY OUT. NICE JOB, LITTLE BRO!
LEAVE ME ALONE.
I SURE WILL! I'VE GOT BETTER THINGS TO DO, SINCE I'M NOT GROUNDED! BYE NOW!
GNAGNAGNAGNA!
HUH...?!

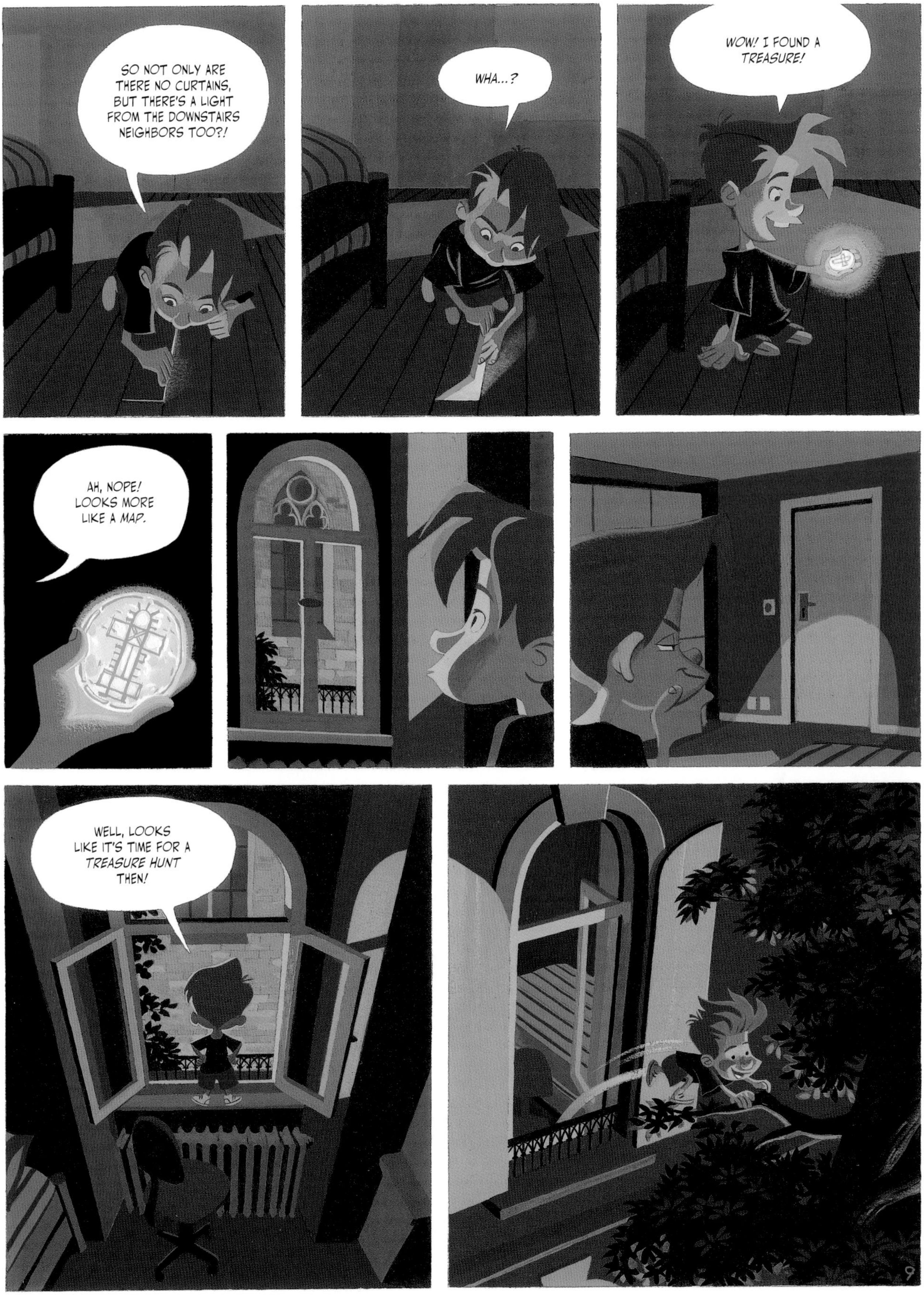
SO NOT ONLY ARE THERE NO CURTAINS, BUT THERE'S A LIGHT FROM THE DOWNSTAIRS NEIGHBORS TOO?!
WHA...?
WOW! I FOUND A *TREASURE!*
AH, NOPE! LOOKS MORE LIKE A *MAP.*
WELL, LOOKS LIKE IT'S TIME FOR A *TREASURE HUNT* THEN!
9

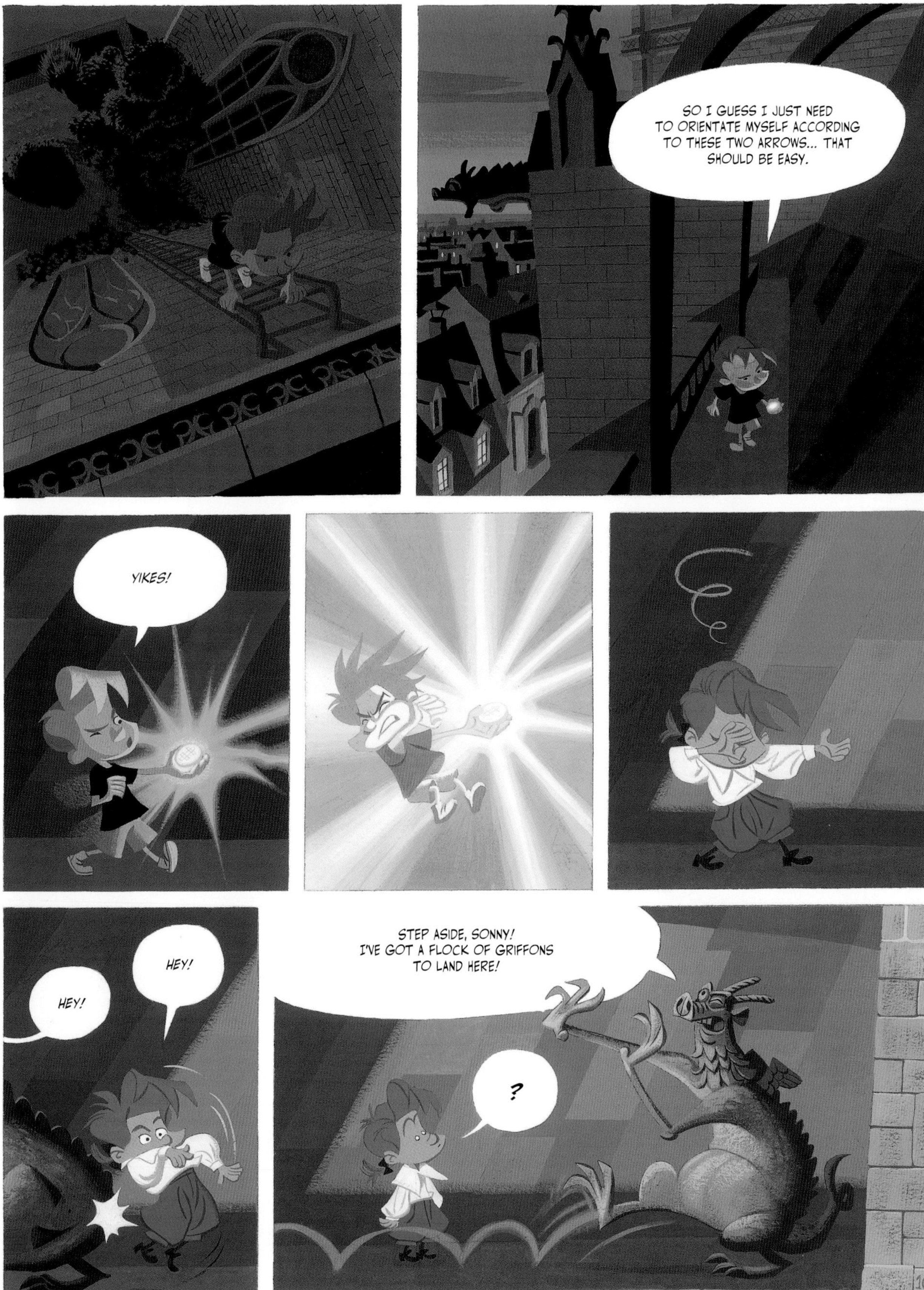
SO I GUESS I JUST NEED TO ORIENTATE MYSELF ACCORDING TO THESE TWO ARROWS... THAT SHOULD BE EASY.
YIKES!
HEY!
HEY!
STEP ASIDE, SONNY! I'VE GOT A FLOCK OF GRIFFONS TO LAND HERE!
?
10

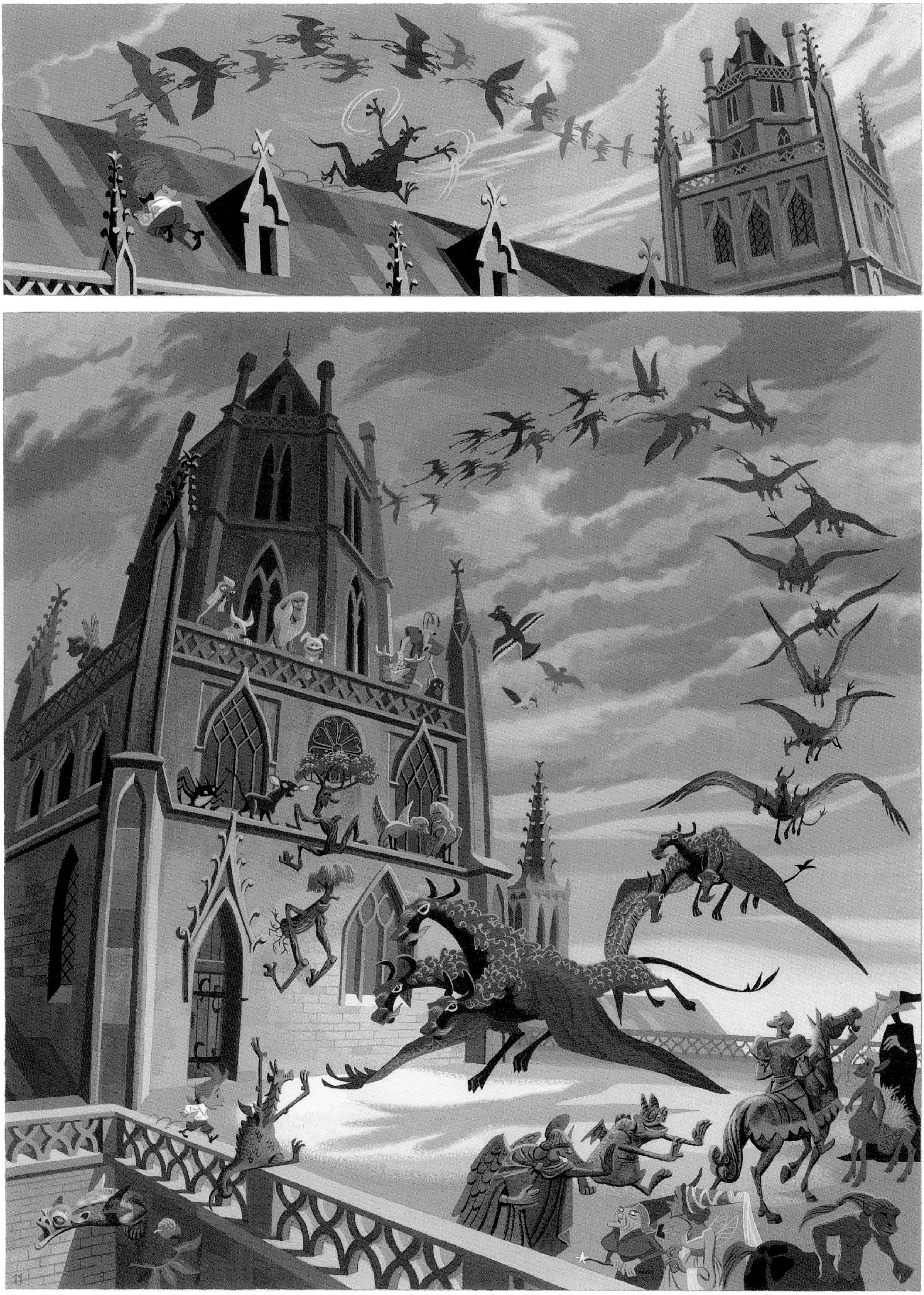

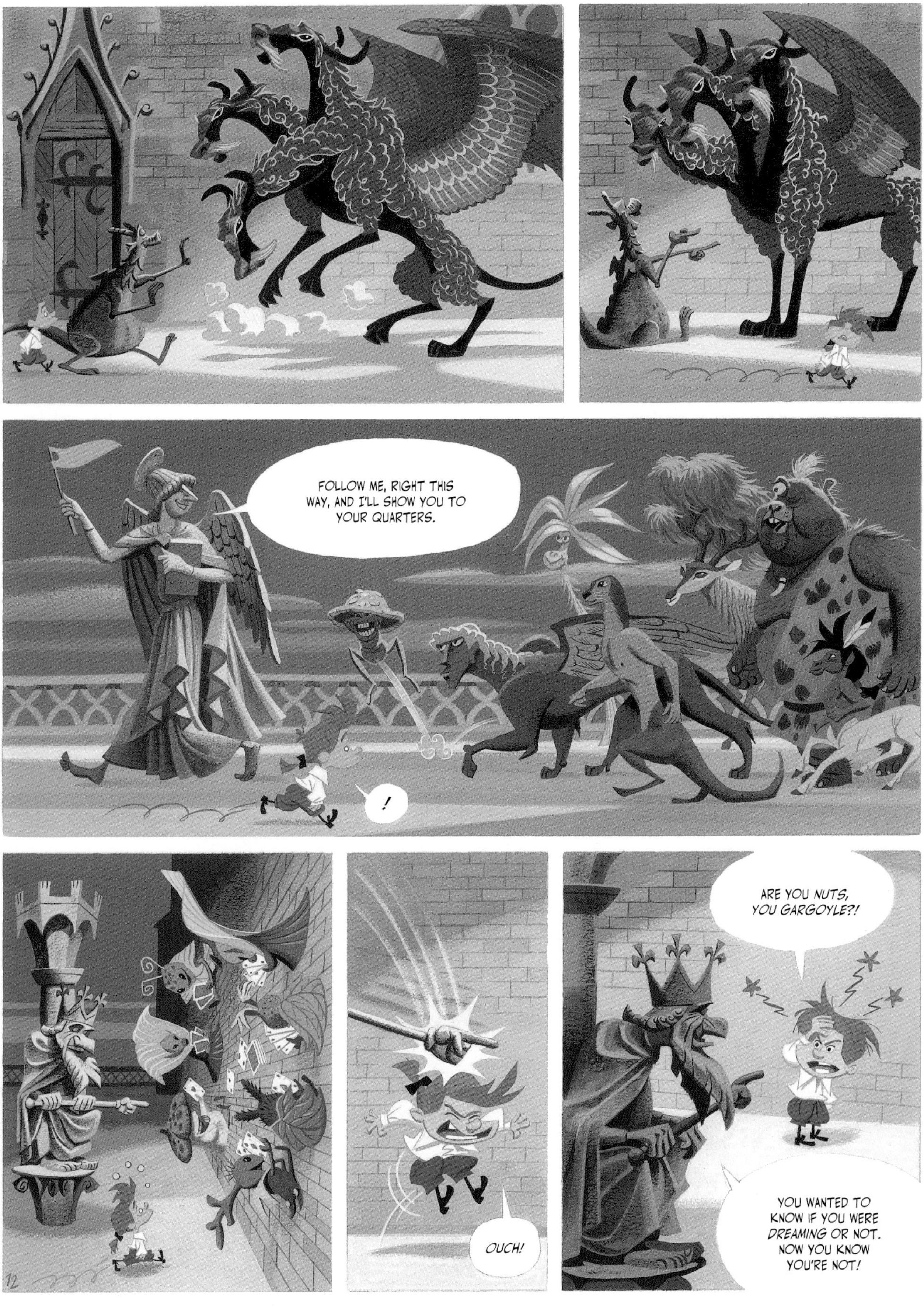
FOLLOW ME, RIGHT THIS WAY, AND I'LL SHOW YOU TO YOUR QUARTERS.
!
OUCH!
ARE YOU NUTS, YOU GARGOYLE?!
YOU WANTED TO KNOW IF YOU WERE *DREAMING* OR NOT. NOW YOU KNOW YOU'RE NOT!

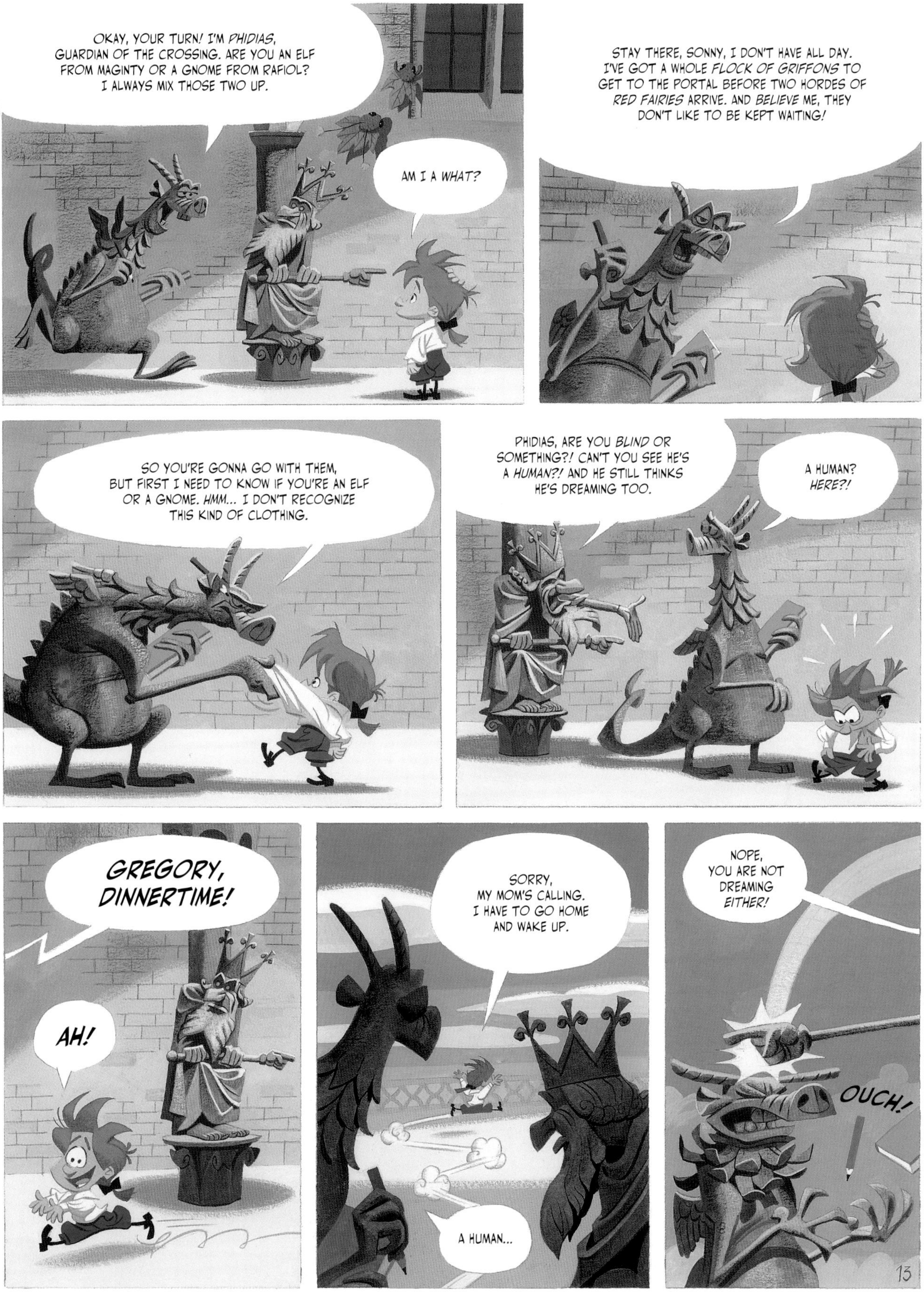
OKAY, YOUR TURN! I'M PHIDIAS, GUARDIAN OF THE CROSSING. ARE YOU AN ELF FROM MAGINTY OR A GNOME FROM RAFIOL? I ALWAYS MIX THOSE TWO UP.
AM I A WHAT?
STAY THERE, SONNY, I DON'T HAVE ALL DAY. I'VE GOT A WHOLE FLOCK OF GRIFFONS TO GET TO THE PORTAL BEFORE TWO HORDES OF RED FAIRIES ARRIVE. AND BELIEVE ME, THEY DON'T LIKE TO BE KEPT WAITING!
SO YOU'RE GONNA GO WITH THEM, BUT FIRST I NEED TO KNOW IF YOU'RE AN ELF OR A GNOME. HMM... I DON'T RECOGNIZE THIS KIND OF CLOTHING.
PHIDIAS, ARE YOU BLIND OR SOMETHING?! CAN'T YOU SEE HE'S A HUMAN?! AND HE STILL THINKS HE'S DREAMING TOO.
A HUMAN? HERE?!
GREGORY, DINNERTIME!
AH!
SORRY, MY MOM'S CALLING. I HAVE TO GO HOME AND WAKE UP.
A HUMAN...
NOPE, YOU ARE NOT DREAMING EITHER!
OUCH!
13

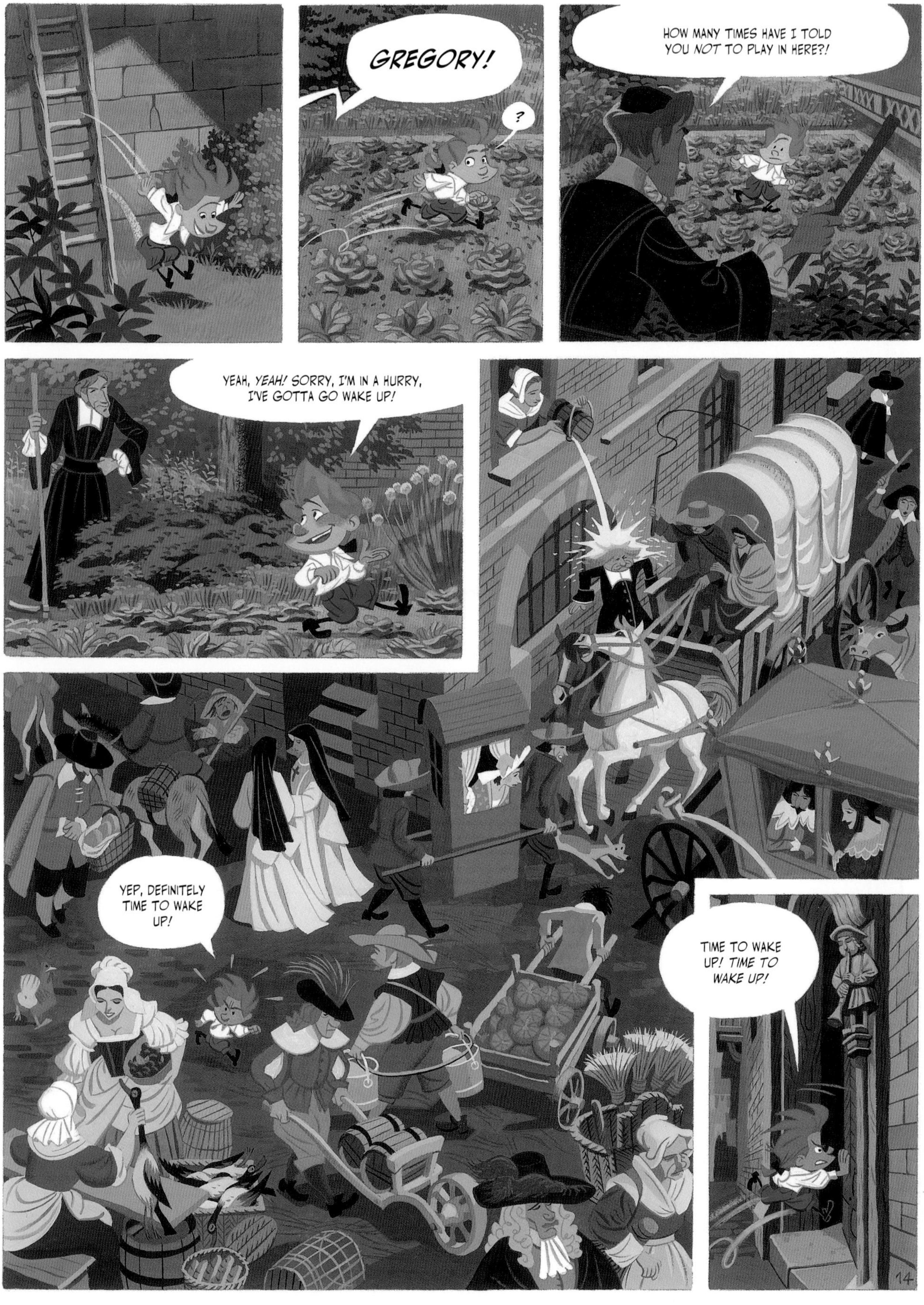
GREGORY!
?
HOW MANY TIMES HAVE I TOLD YOU NOT TO PLAY IN HERE?!
YEAH, YEAH! SORRY, I'M IN A HURRY, I'VE GOTTA GO WAKE UP!
YEP, DEFINITELY TIME TO WAKE UP!
TIME TO WAKE UP! TIME TO WAKE UP!
14

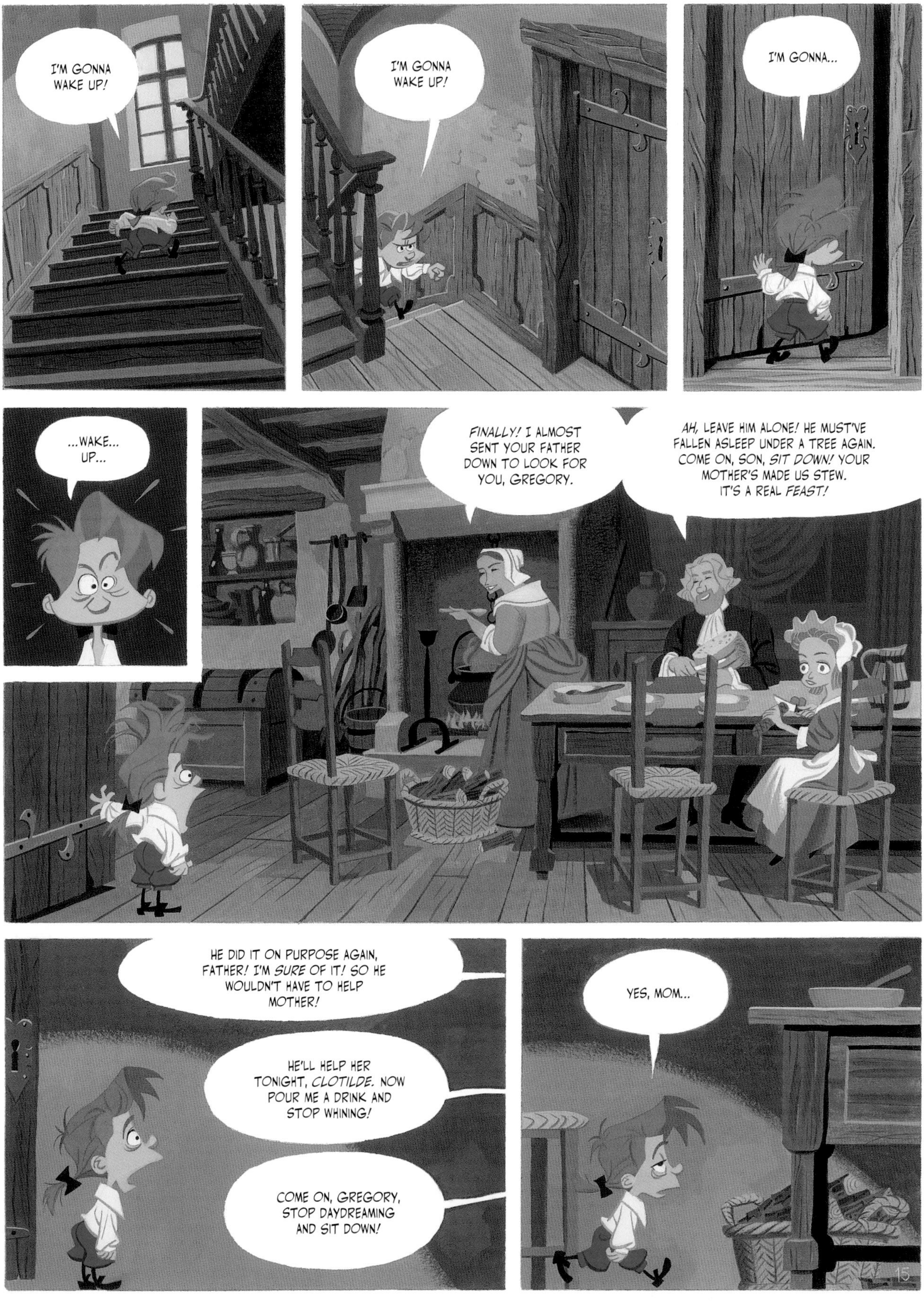
I'M GONNA WAKE UP!
I'M GONNA WAKE UP!
I'M GONNA...
...WAKE... UP...
FINALLY! I ALMOST SENT YOUR FATHER DOWN TO LOOK FOR YOU, GREGORY.
AH, LEAVE HIM ALONE! HE MUST'VE FALLEN ASLEEP UNDER A TREE AGAIN. COME ON, SON, SIT DOWN! YOUR MOTHER'S MADE US STEW. IT'S A REAL FEAST!
HE DID IT ON PURPOSE AGAIN, FATHER! I'M SURE OF IT! SO HE WOULDN'T HAVE TO HELP MOTHER!
HE'LL HELP HER TONIGHT, CLOTILDE. NOW POUR ME A DRINK AND STOP WHINING!
COME ON, GREGORY, STOP DAYDREAMING AND SIT DOWN!
YES, MOM...
15

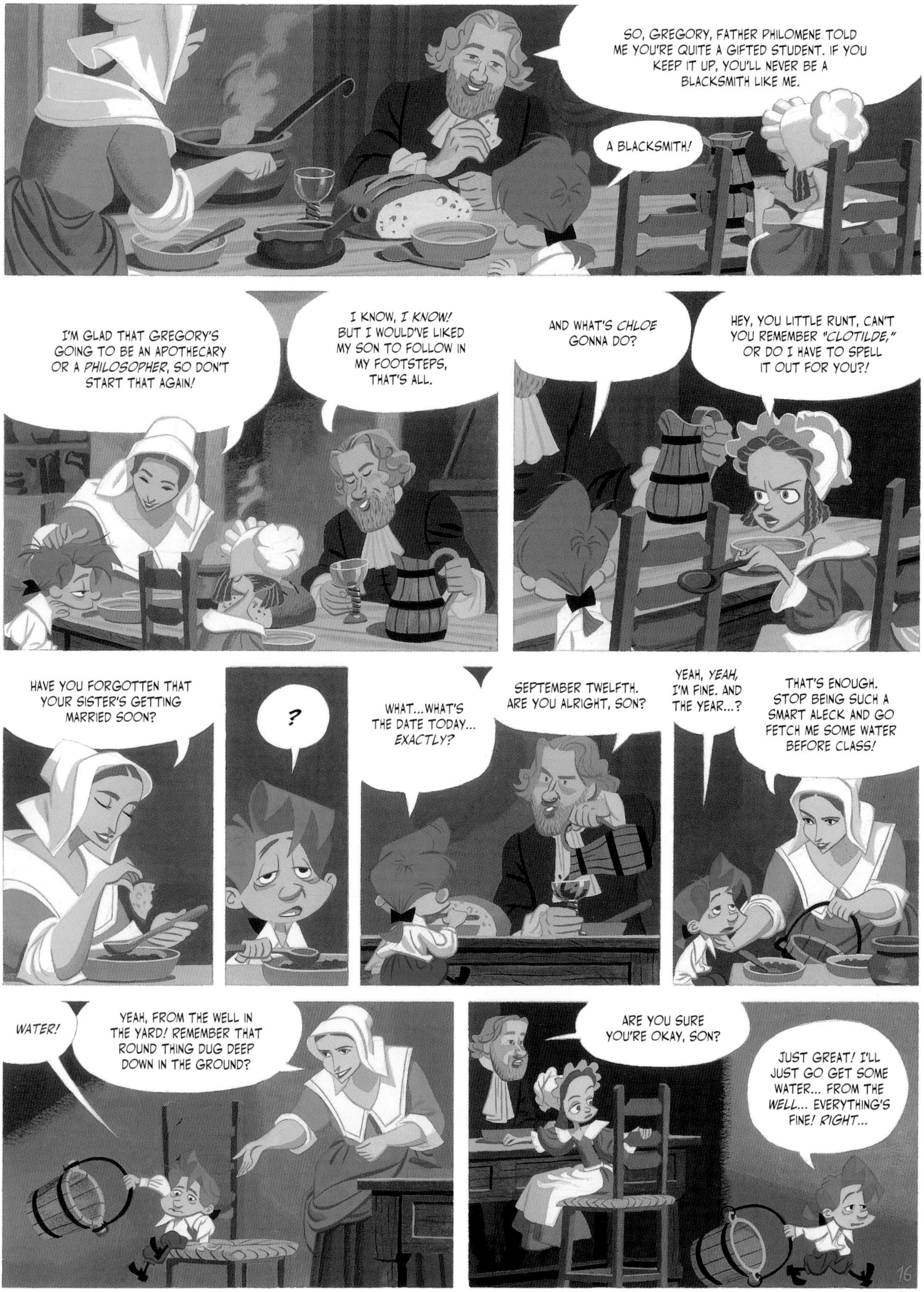
SO, GREGORY, FATHER PHILOMENE TOLD ME YOU'RE QUITE A GIFTED STUDENT. IF YOU KEEP IT UP, YOU'LL NEVER BE A BLACKSMITH LIKE ME.
A BLACKSMITH!
I'M GLAD THAT GREGORY'S GOING TO BE AN APOTHECARY OR A PHILOSOPHER, SO DON'T START THAT AGAIN!
I KNOW, I KNOW! BUT I WOULD'VE LIKED MY SON TO FOLLOW IN MY FOOTSTEPS, THAT'S ALL.
AND WHAT'S CHLOE GONNA DO?
HEY, YOU LITTLE RUNT, CAN'T YOU REMEMBER "CLOTILDE," OR DO I HAVE TO SPELL IT OUT FOR YOU?!
HAVE YOU FORGOTTEN THAT YOUR SISTER'S GETTING MARRIED SOON?
?
WHAT...WHAT'S THE DATE TODAY... EXACTLY?
SEPTEMBER TWELFTH. ARE YOU ALRIGHT, SON?
YEAH, YEAH, I'M FINE. AND THE YEAR...?
THAT'S ENOUGH. STOP BEING SUCH A SMART ALECK AND GO FETCH ME SOME WATER BEFORE CLASS!
WATER!
YEAH, FROM THE WELL IN THE YARD! REMEMBER THAT ROUND THING DUG DEEP DOWN IN THE GROUND?
ARE YOU SURE YOU'RE OKAY, SON?
JUST GREAT! I'LL JUST GO GET SOME WATER... FROM THE WELL... EVERYTHING'S FINE! RIGHT...
16

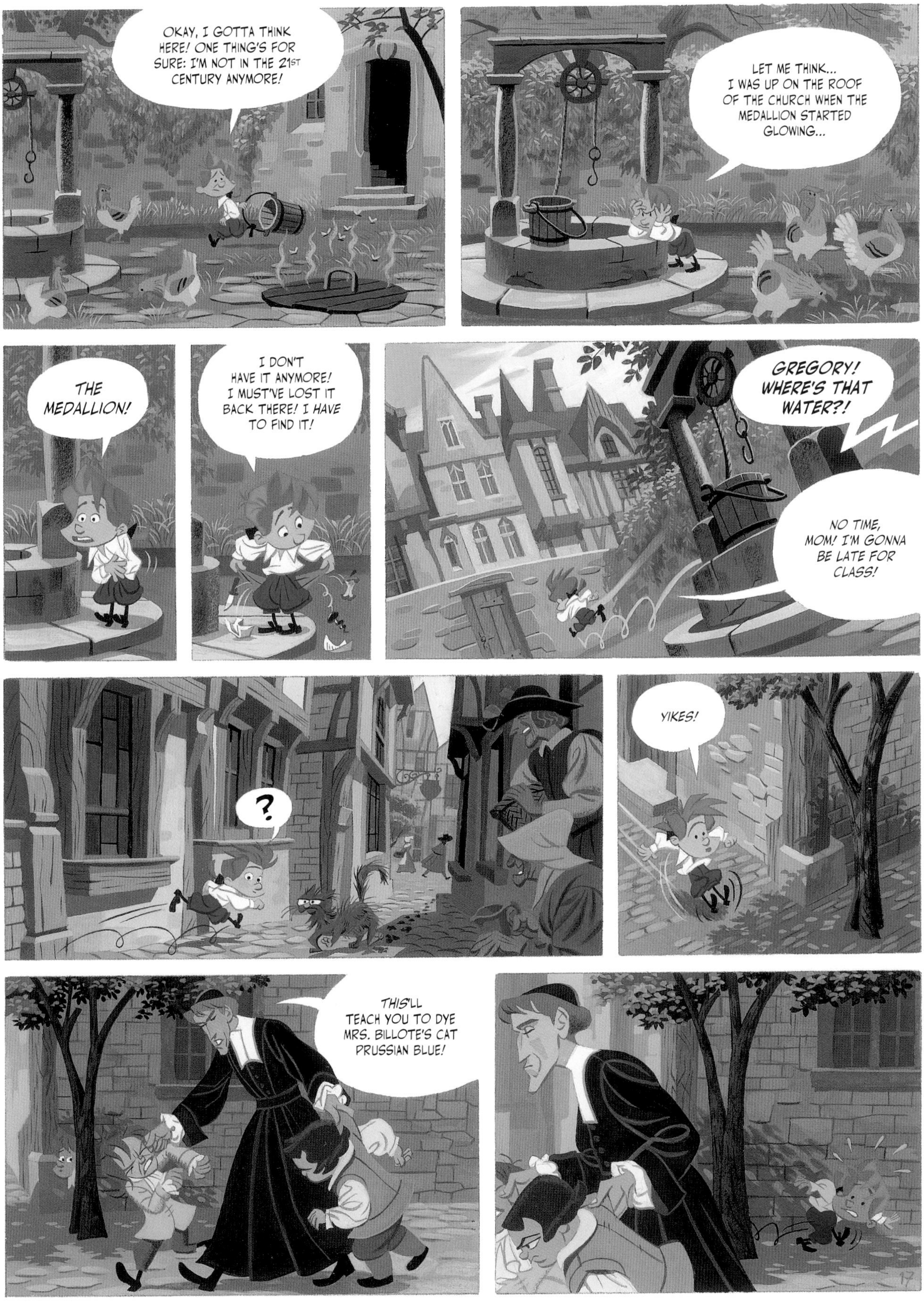
OKAY, I GOTTA THINK HERE! ONE THING'S FOR SURE: I'M NOT IN THE 21ST CENTURY ANYMORE!
LET ME THINK... I WAS UP ON THE ROOF OF THE CHURCH WHEN THE MEDALLION STARTED GLOWING...
THE MEDALLION!
I DON'T HAVE IT ANYMORE! I MUST'VE LOST IT BACK THERE! I HAVE TO FIND IT!
GREGORY! WHERE'S THAT WATER?!
NO TIME, MOM! I'M GONNA BE LATE FOR CLASS!
?
YIKES!
THIS'LL TEACH YOU TO DYE MRS. BILLOTE'S CAT PRUSSIAN BLUE!

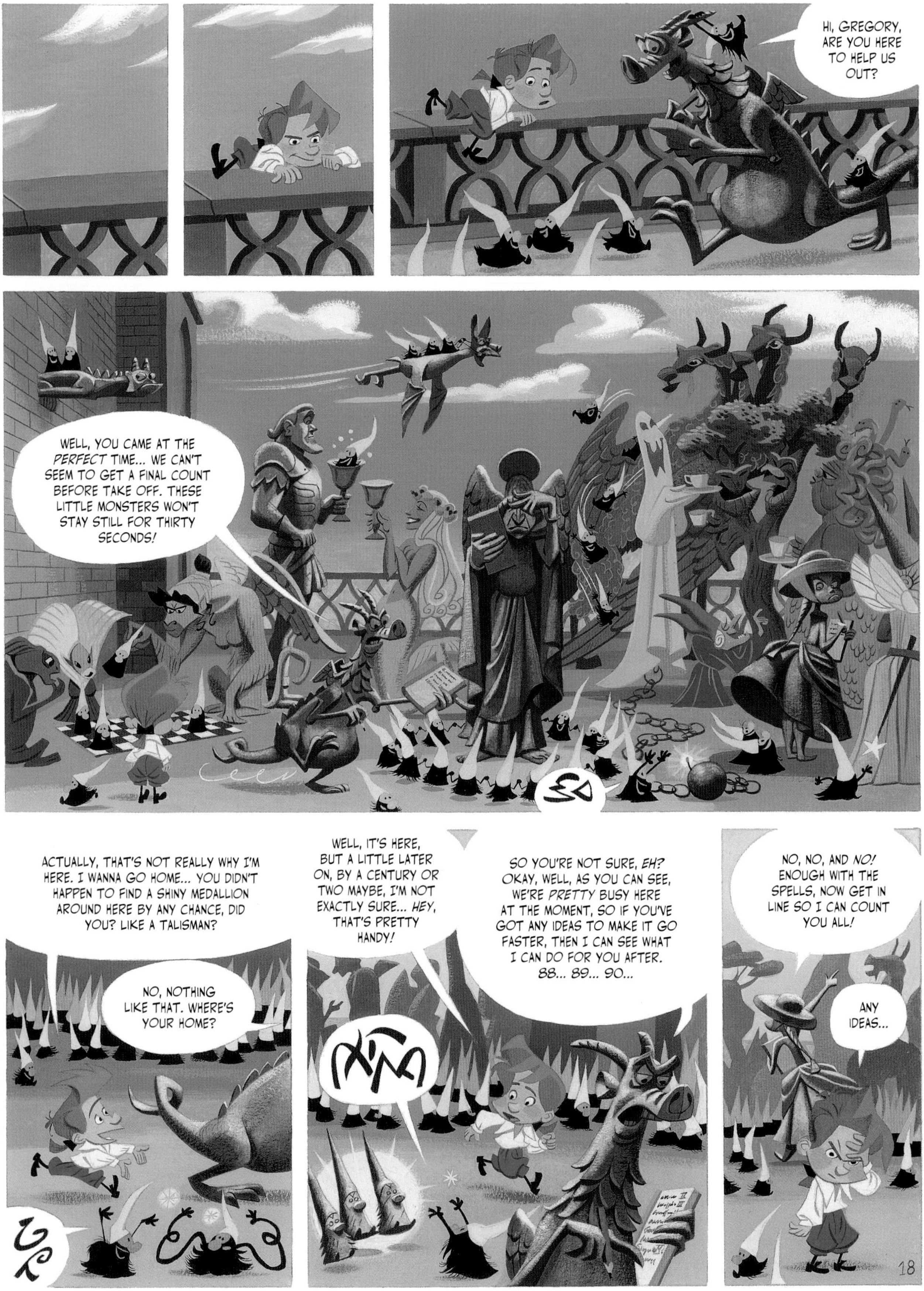
HI, GREGORY, ARE YOU HERE TO HELP US OUT?
WELL, YOU CAME AT THE *PERFECT* TIME... WE CAN'T SEEM TO GET A FINAL COUNT BEFORE TAKE OFF. THESE LITTLE MONSTERS WON'T STAY STILL FOR THIRTY SECONDS!
ACTUALLY, THAT'S NOT REALLY WHY I'M HERE. I WANNA GO HOME... YOU DIDN'T HAPPEN TO FIND A SHINY MEDALLION AROUND HERE BY ANY CHANCE, DID YOU? LIKE A TALISMAN?
NO, NOTHING LIKE THAT. WHERE'S YOUR HOME?
WELL, IT'S HERE, BUT A LITTLE LATER ON, BY A CENTURY OR TWO MAYBE, I'M NOT EXACTLY SURE... *HEY,* THAT'S PRETTY HANDY!
SO YOU'RE NOT SURE, *EH?* OKAY, WELL, AS YOU CAN SEE, WE'RE *PRETTY* BUSY HERE AT THE MOMENT, SO IF YOU'VE GOT ANY IDEAS TO MAKE IT GO FASTER, THEN I CAN SEE WHAT I CAN DO FOR YOU AFTER. 88... 89... 90...
NO, NO, AND *NO!* ENOUGH WITH THE SPELLS, NOW GET IN LINE SO I CAN COUNT YOU ALL!
ANY IDEAS...
18

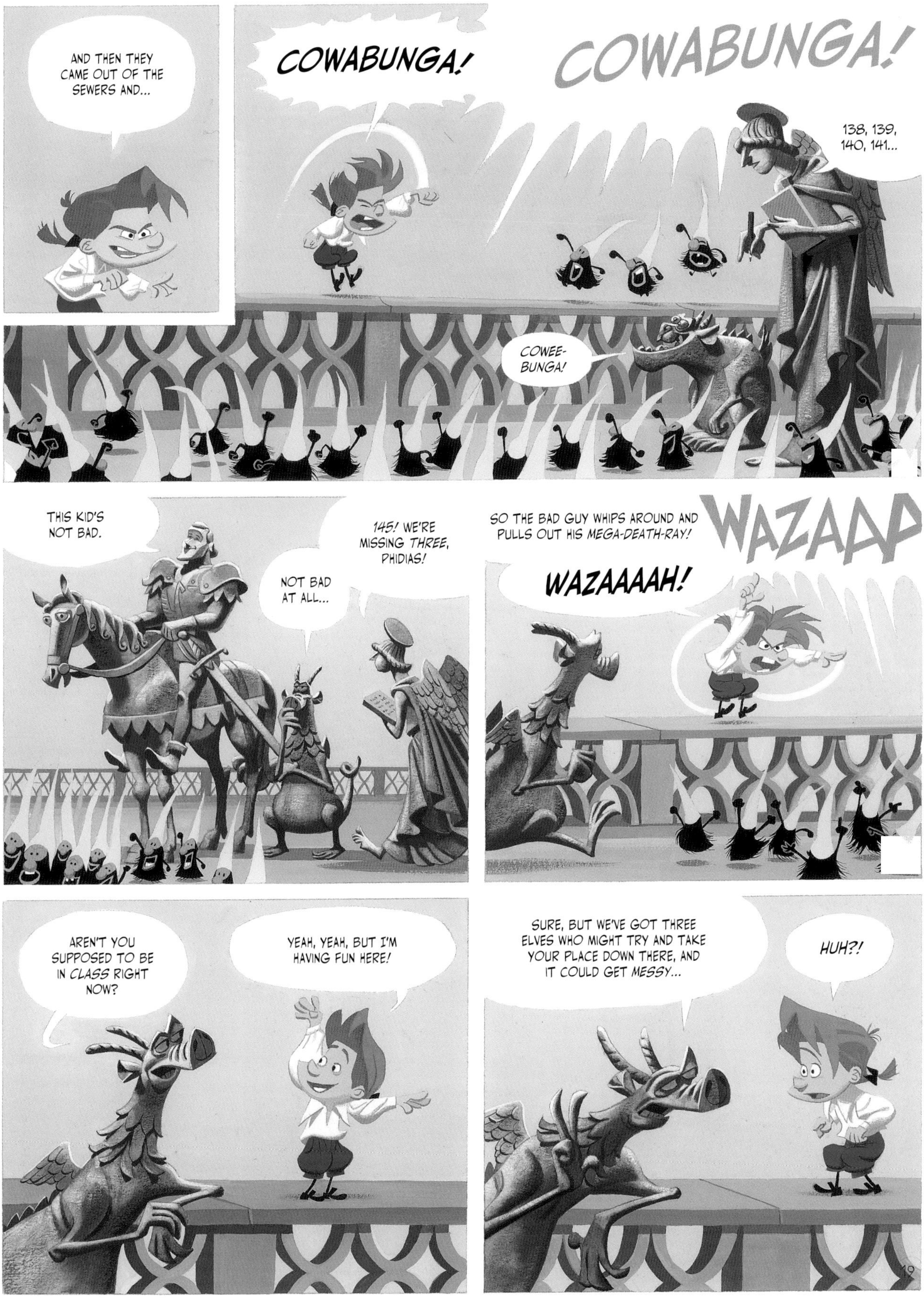

AND THEN THEY CAME OUT OF THE SEWERS AND...
COWABUNGA!
COWABUNGA!
138, 139, 140, 141...
COWEE-BUNGA!
THIS KID'S NOT BAD.
NOT BAD AT ALL...
145! WE'RE MISSING THREE, PHIDIAS!
SO THE BAD GUY WHIPS AROUND AND PULLS OUT HIS MEGA-DEATH-RAY!
WAZAAP
WAZAAAAH!
AREN'T YOU SUPPOSED TO BE IN CLASS RIGHT NOW?
YEAH, YEAH, BUT I'M HAVING FUN HERE!
SURE, BUT WE'VE GOT THREE ELVES WHO MIGHT TRY AND TAKE YOUR PLACE DOWN THERE, AND IT COULD GET MESSY...
HUH?!
19

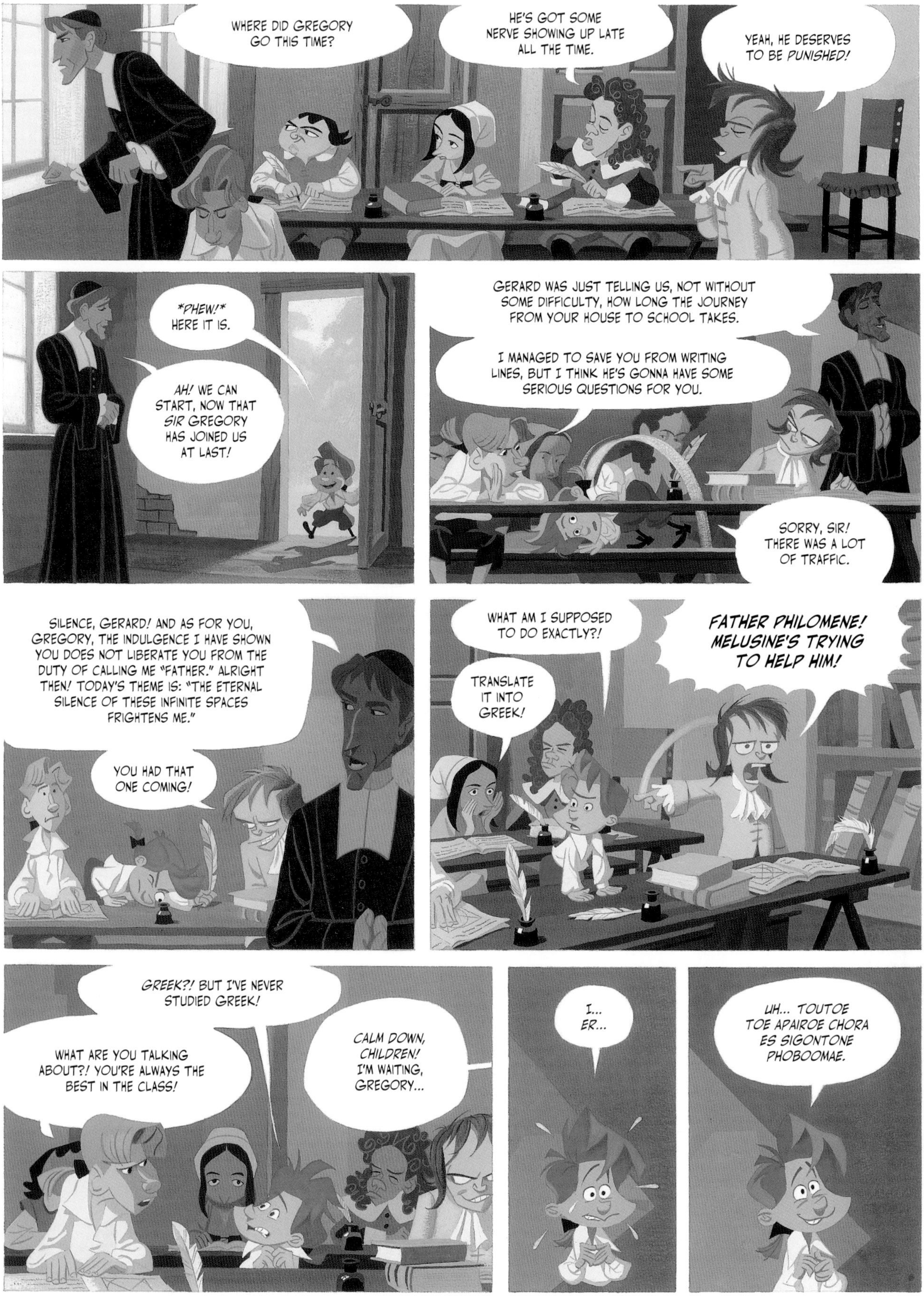
WHERE DID GREGORY GO THIS TIME?
HE'S GOT SOME NERVE SHOWING UP LATE ALL THE TIME.
YEAH, HE DESERVES TO BE PUNISHED!
PHEW! HERE IT IS.
AH! WE CAN START, NOW THAT SIR GREGORY HAS JOINED US AT LAST!
GERARD WAS JUST TELLING US, NOT WITHOUT SOME DIFFICULTY, HOW LONG THE JOURNEY FROM YOUR HOUSE TO SCHOOL TAKES.
I MANAGED TO SAVE YOU FROM WRITING LINES, BUT I THINK HE'S GONNA HAVE SOME SERIOUS QUESTIONS FOR YOU.
SORRY, SIR! THERE WAS A LOT OF TRAFFIC.
SILENCE, GERARD! AND AS FOR YOU, GREGORY, THE INDULGENCE I HAVE SHOWN YOU DOES NOT LIBERATE YOU FROM THE DUTY OF CALLING ME "FATHER." ALRIGHT THEN! TODAY'S THEME IS: "THE ETERNAL SILENCE OF THESE INFINITE SPACES FRIGHTENS ME."
YOU HAD THAT ONE COMING!
WHAT AM I SUPPOSED TO DO EXACTLY?!
TRANSLATE IT INTO GREEK!
FATHER PHILOMENE! MELUSINE'S TRYING TO HELP HIM!
GREEK?! BUT I'VE NEVER STUDIED GREEK!
WHAT ARE YOU TALKING ABOUT?! YOU'RE ALWAYS THE BEST IN THE CLASS!
CALM DOWN, CHILDREN! I'M WAITING, GREGORY...
I... ER...
UH... TOUTOE TOE APAIROE CHORA ES SIGONTONE PHOBOOMAE.

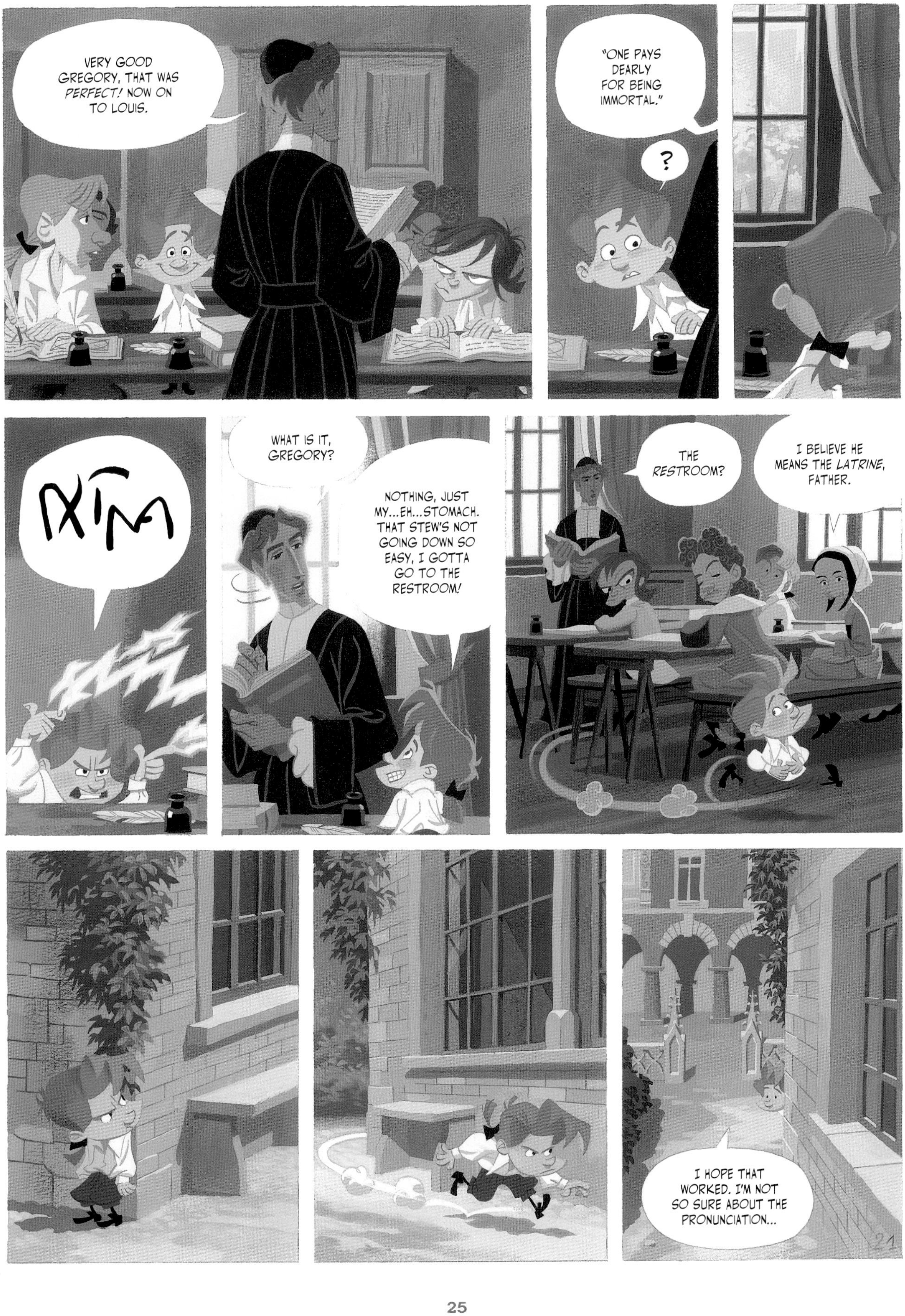
VERY GOOD GREGORY, THAT WAS *PERFECT!* NOW ON TO LOUIS.
"ONE PAYS DEARLY FOR BEING IMMORTAL."
?
WHAT IS IT, GREGORY?
NOTHING, JUST MY...EH...STOMACH. THAT STEW'S NOT GOING DOWN SO EASY, I GOTTA GO TO THE RESTROOM!
THE *RESTROOM?*
I BELIEVE HE MEANS THE *LATRINE*, FATHER.
I HOPE THAT WORKED. I'M NOT SO SURE ABOUT THE PRONUNCIATION...

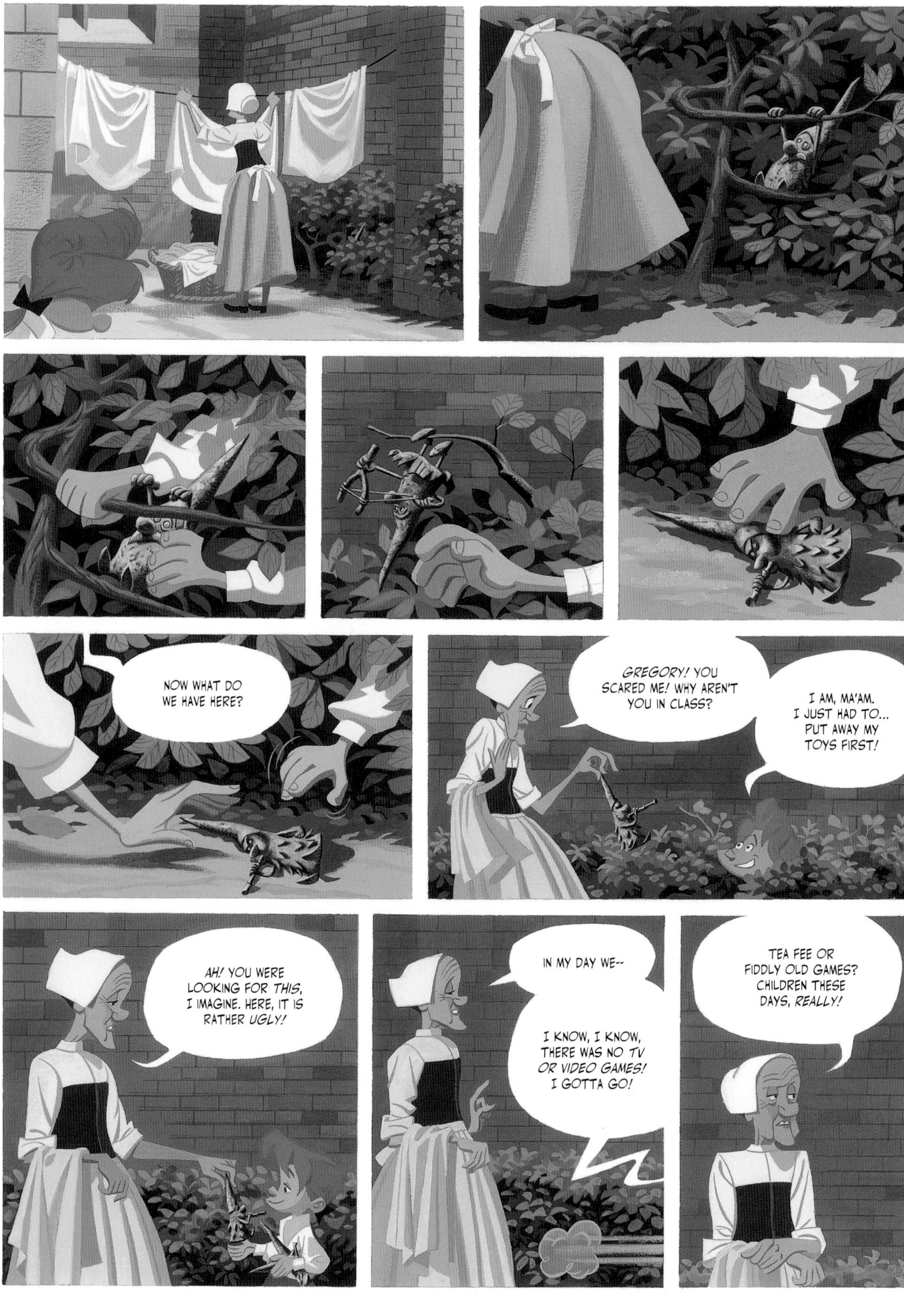
NOW WHAT DO WE HAVE HERE?
GREGORY! YOU SCARED ME! WHY AREN'T YOU IN CLASS?
I AM, MA'AM. I JUST HAD TO... PUT AWAY MY TOYS FIRST!
AH! YOU WERE LOOKING FOR THIS, I IMAGINE. HERE, IT IS RATHER UGLY!
IN MY DAY WE--
I KNOW, I KNOW, THERE WAS NO TV OR VIDEO GAMES! I GOTTA GO!
TEA FEE OR FIDDLY OLD GAMES? CHILDREN THESE DAYS, REALLY!

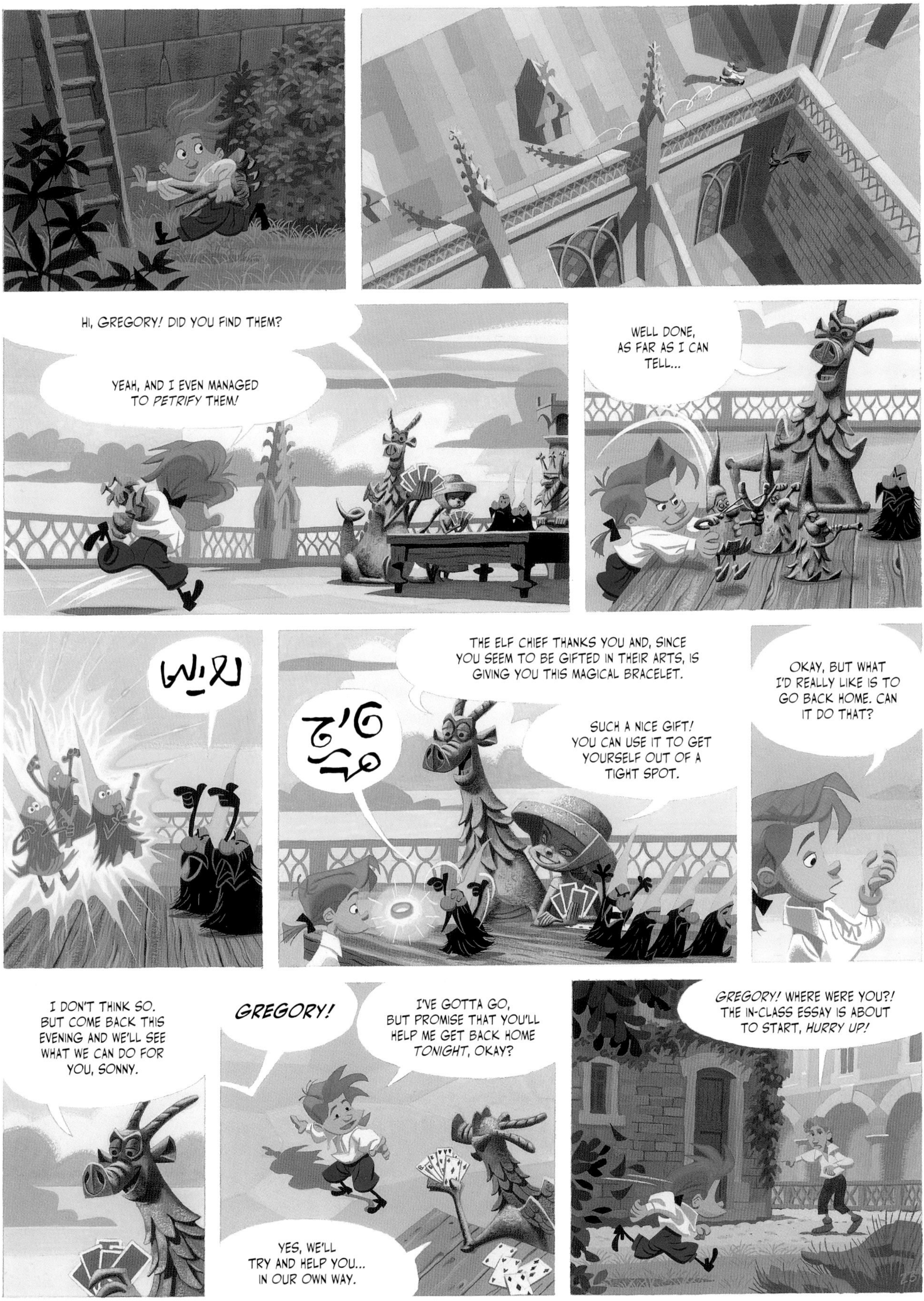
HI, GREGORY! DID YOU FIND THEM?
YEAH, AND I EVEN MANAGED TO *PETRIFY* THEM!
WELL DONE, AS FAR AS I CAN TELL...
THE ELF CHIEF THANKS YOU AND, SINCE YOU SEEM TO BE GIFTED IN THEIR ARTS, IS GIVING YOU THIS MAGICAL BRACELET.
SUCH A NICE GIFT! YOU CAN USE IT TO GET YOURSELF OUT OF A TIGHT SPOT.
OKAY, BUT WHAT I'D REALLY LIKE IS TO GO BACK HOME. CAN IT DO THAT?
I DON'T THINK SO. BUT COME BACK THIS EVENING AND WE'LL SEE WHAT WE CAN DO FOR YOU, SONNY.
GREGORY!
I'VE GOTTA GO, BUT PROMISE THAT YOU'LL HELP ME GET BACK HOME *TONIGHT*, OKAY?
YES, WE'LL TRY AND HELP YOU... IN OUR OWN WAY.
GREGORY! WHERE WERE YOU?! THE IN-CLASS ESSAY IS ABOUT TO START, *HURRY UP!*

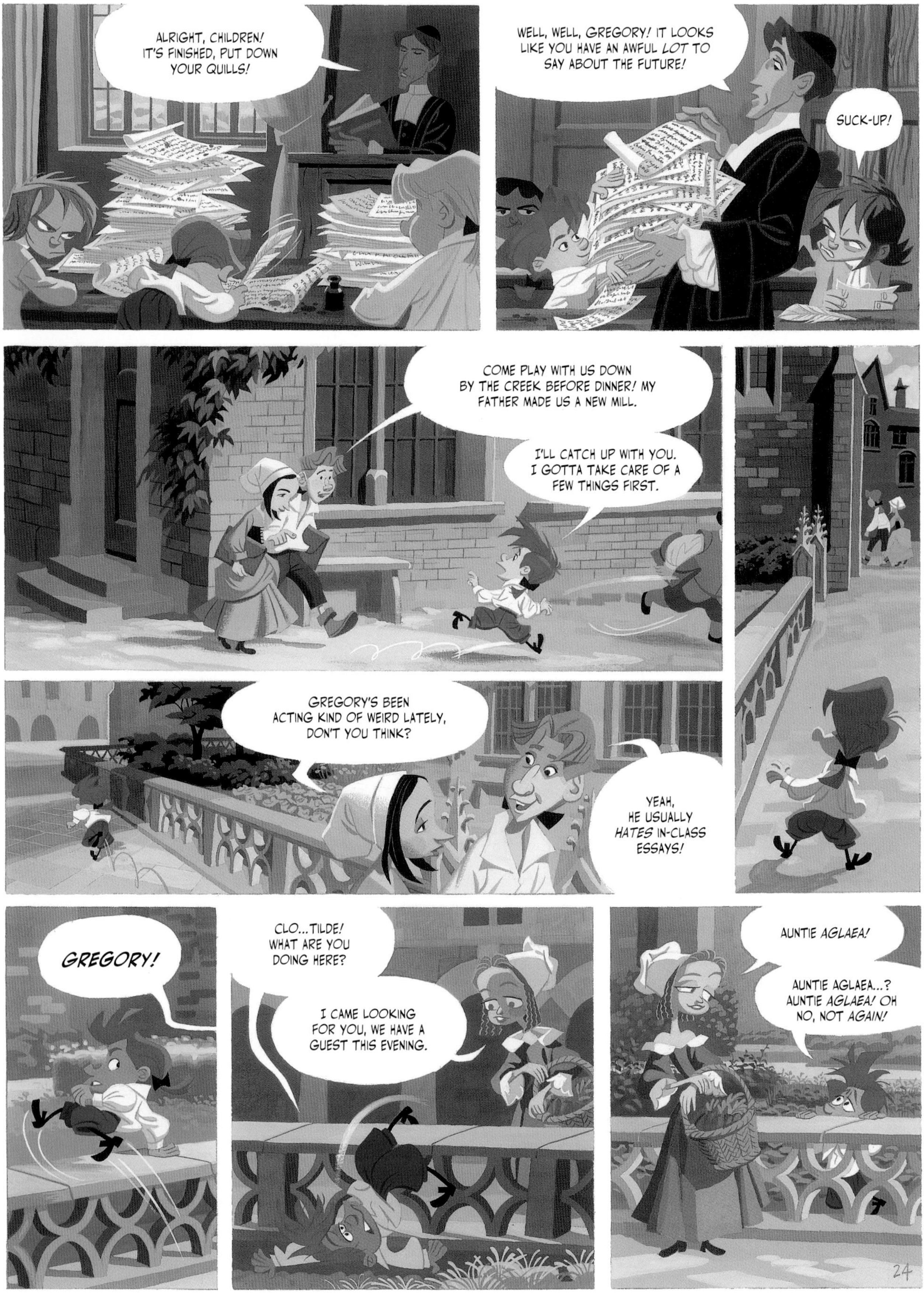
ALRIGHT, CHILDREN! IT'S FINISHED, PUT DOWN YOUR QUILLS!
WELL, WELL, GREGORY! IT LOOKS LIKE YOU HAVE AN AWFUL *LOT* TO SAY ABOUT THE FUTURE!
SUCK-UP!
COME PLAY WITH US DOWN BY THE CREEK BEFORE DINNER! MY FATHER MADE US A NEW MILL.
I'LL CATCH UP WITH YOU. I GOTTA TAKE CARE OF A FEW THINGS FIRST.
GREGORY'S BEEN ACTING KIND OF WEIRD LATELY, DON'T YOU THINK?
YEAH, HE USUALLY *HATES* IN-CLASS ESSAYS!
GREGORY!
CLO...TILDE! WHAT ARE YOU DOING HERE?
I CAME LOOKING FOR YOU, WE HAVE A GUEST THIS EVENING.
AUNTIE *AGLAEA!*
AUNTIE AGLAEA...? AUNTIE *AGLAEA!* OH NO, NOT AGAIN!
24

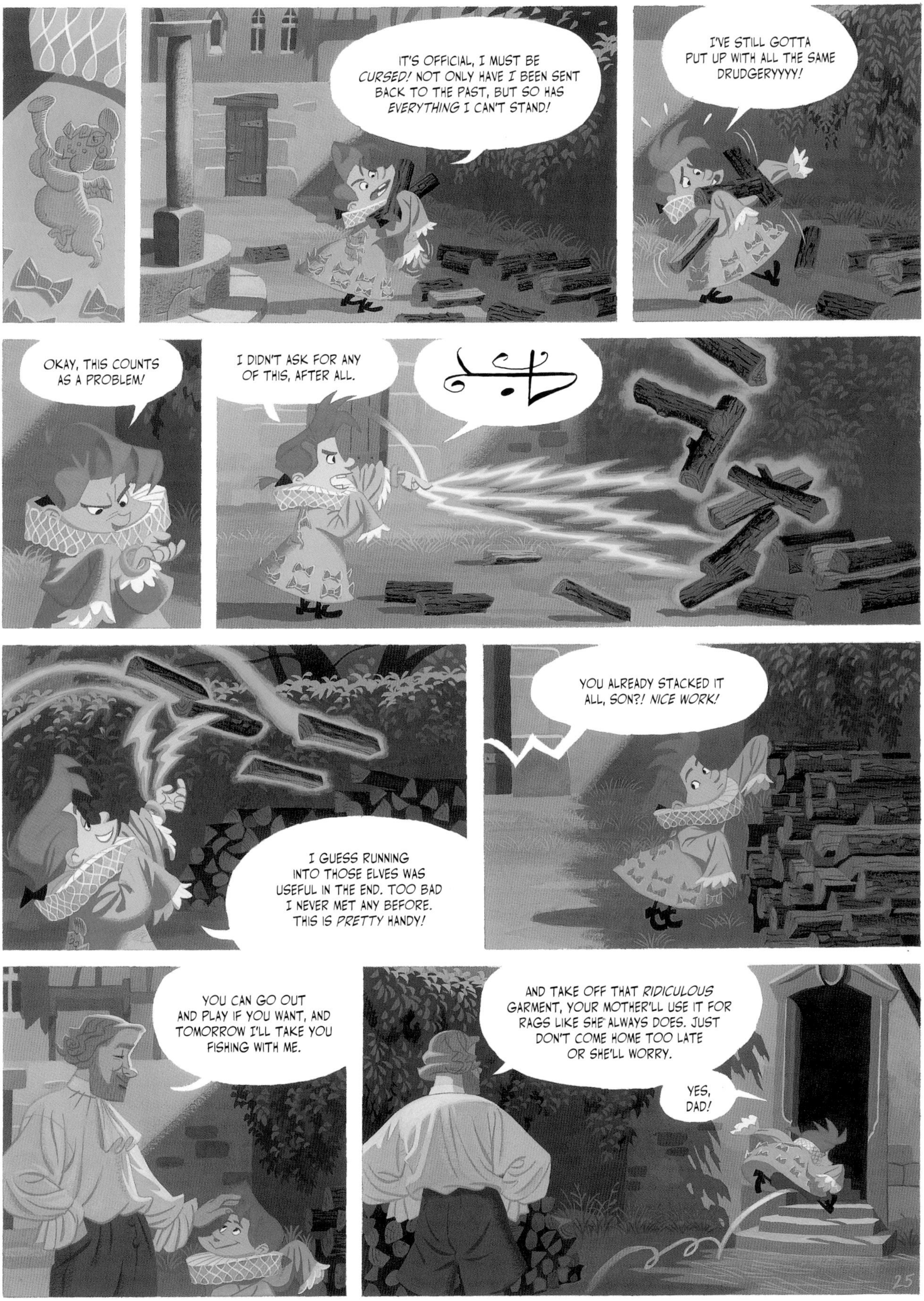
IT'S OFFICIAL, I MUST BE CURSED! NOT ONLY HAVE I BEEN SENT BACK TO THE PAST, BUT SO HAS EVERYTHING I CAN'T STAND!
I'VE STILL GOTTA PUT UP WITH ALL THE SAME DRUDGERYYYY!
OKAY, THIS COUNTS AS A PROBLEM!
I DIDN'T ASK FOR ANY OF THIS, AFTER ALL.
I GUESS RUNNING INTO THOSE ELVES WAS USEFUL IN THE END. TOO BAD I NEVER MET ANY BEFORE. THIS IS PRETTY HANDY!
YOU ALREADY STACKED IT ALL, SON?! NICE WORK!
YOU CAN GO OUT AND PLAY IF YOU WANT, AND TOMORROW I'LL TAKE YOU FISHING WITH ME.
AND TAKE OFF THAT RIDICULOUS GARMENT, YOUR MOTHER'LL USE IT FOR RAGS LIKE SHE ALWAYS DOES. JUST DON'T COME HOME TOO LATE OR SHE'LL WORRY.
YES, DAD!
25

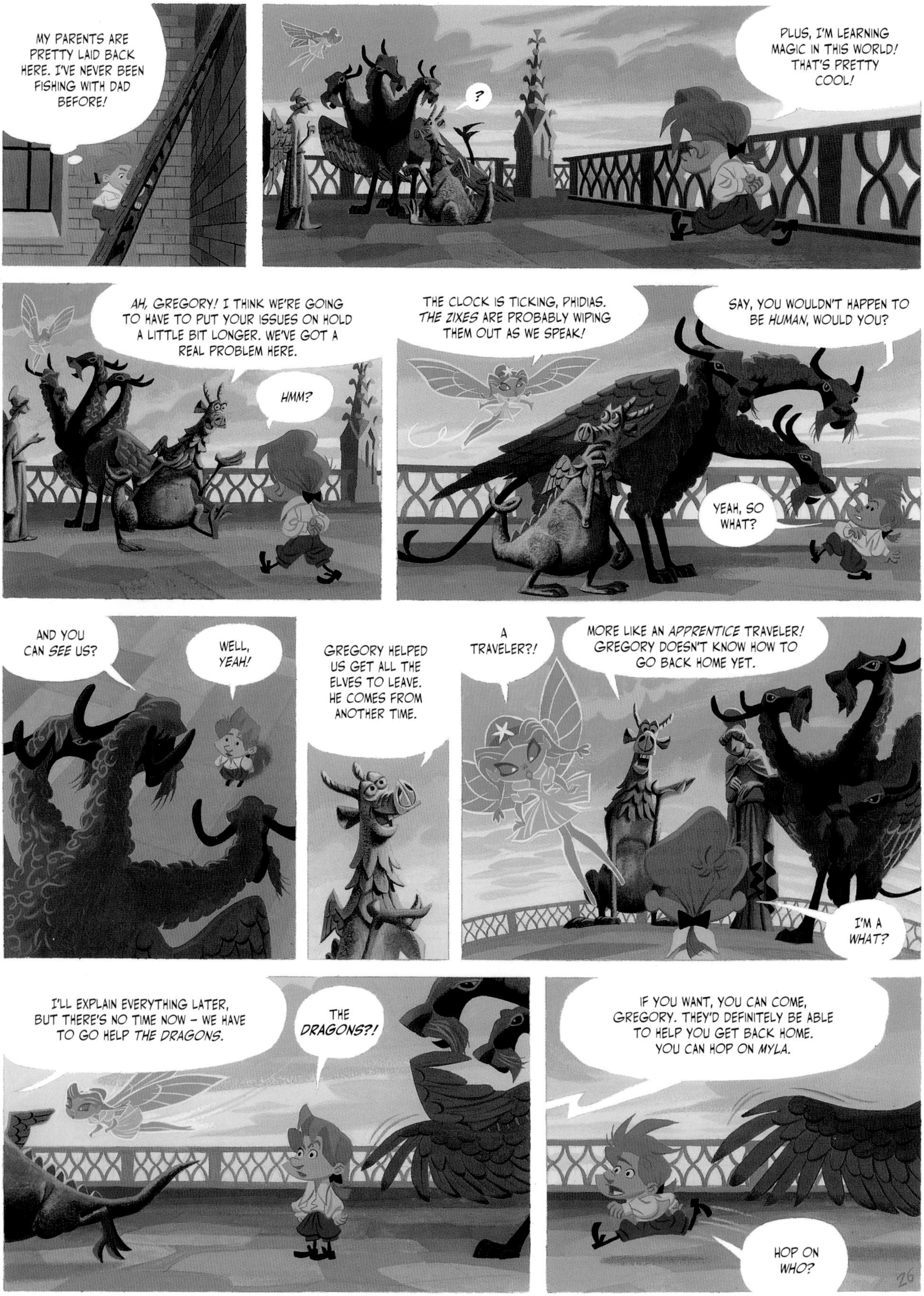
MY PARENTS ARE PRETTY LAID BACK HERE. I'VE NEVER BEEN FISHING WITH DAD BEFORE!
?
PLUS, I'M LEARNING MAGIC IN THIS WORLD! THAT'S PRETTY COOL!
AH, GREGORY! I THINK WE'RE GOING TO HAVE TO PUT YOUR ISSUES ON HOLD A LITTLE BIT LONGER. WE'VE GOT A REAL PROBLEM HERE.
HMM?
THE CLOCK IS TICKING, PHIDIAS. THE ZIXES ARE PROBABLY WIPING THEM OUT AS WE SPEAK!
SAY, YOU WOULDN'T HAPPEN TO BE HUMAN, WOULD YOU?
YEAH, SO WHAT?
AND YOU CAN SEE US?
WELL, YEAH!
GREGORY HELPED US GET ALL THE ELVES TO LEAVE. HE COMES FROM ANOTHER TIME.
A TRAVELER?!
MORE LIKE AN APPRENTICE TRAVELER! GREGORY DOESN'T KNOW HOW TO GO BACK HOME YET.
I'M A WHAT?
I'LL EXPLAIN EVERYTHING LATER, BUT THERE'S NO TIME NOW – WE HAVE TO GO HELP THE DRAGONS.
THE DRAGONS?!
IF YOU WANT, YOU CAN COME, GREGORY. THEY'D DEFINITELY BE ABLE TO HELP YOU GET BACK HOME. YOU CAN HOP ON MYLA.
HOP ON WHO?
26

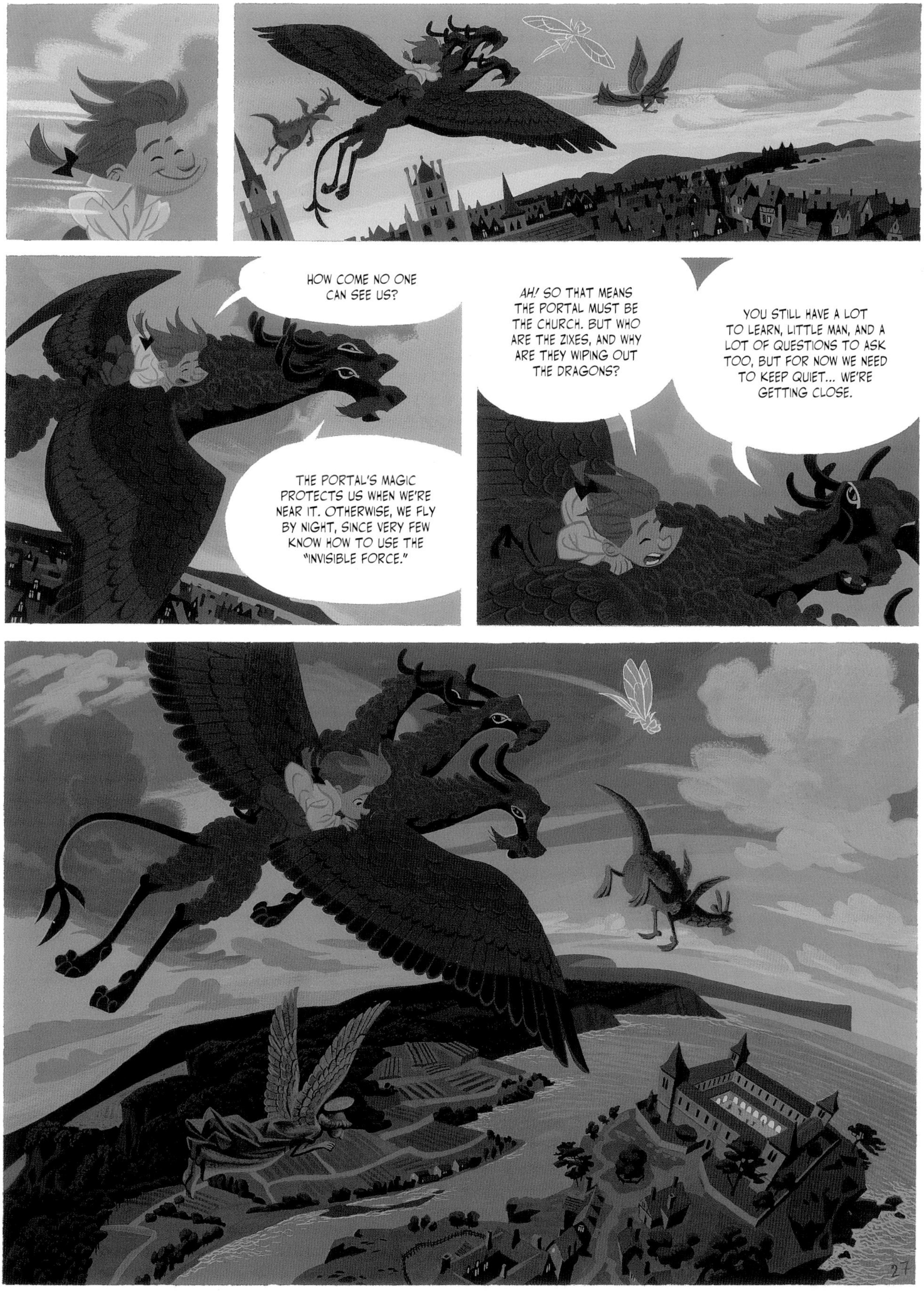
HOW COME NO ONE CAN SEE US?
THE PORTAL'S MAGIC PROTECTS US WHEN WE'RE NEAR IT. OTHERWISE, WE FLY BY NIGHT, SINCE VERY FEW KNOW HOW TO USE THE "INVISIBLE FORCE."
AH! SO THAT MEANS THE PORTAL MUST BE THE CHURCH. BUT WHO ARE THE ZIXES, AND WHY ARE THEY WIPING OUT THE DRAGONS?
YOU STILL HAVE A LOT TO LEARN, LITTLE MAN, AND A LOT OF QUESTIONS TO ASK TOO, BUT FOR NOW WE NEED TO KEEP QUIET... WE'RE GETTING CLOSE.
27

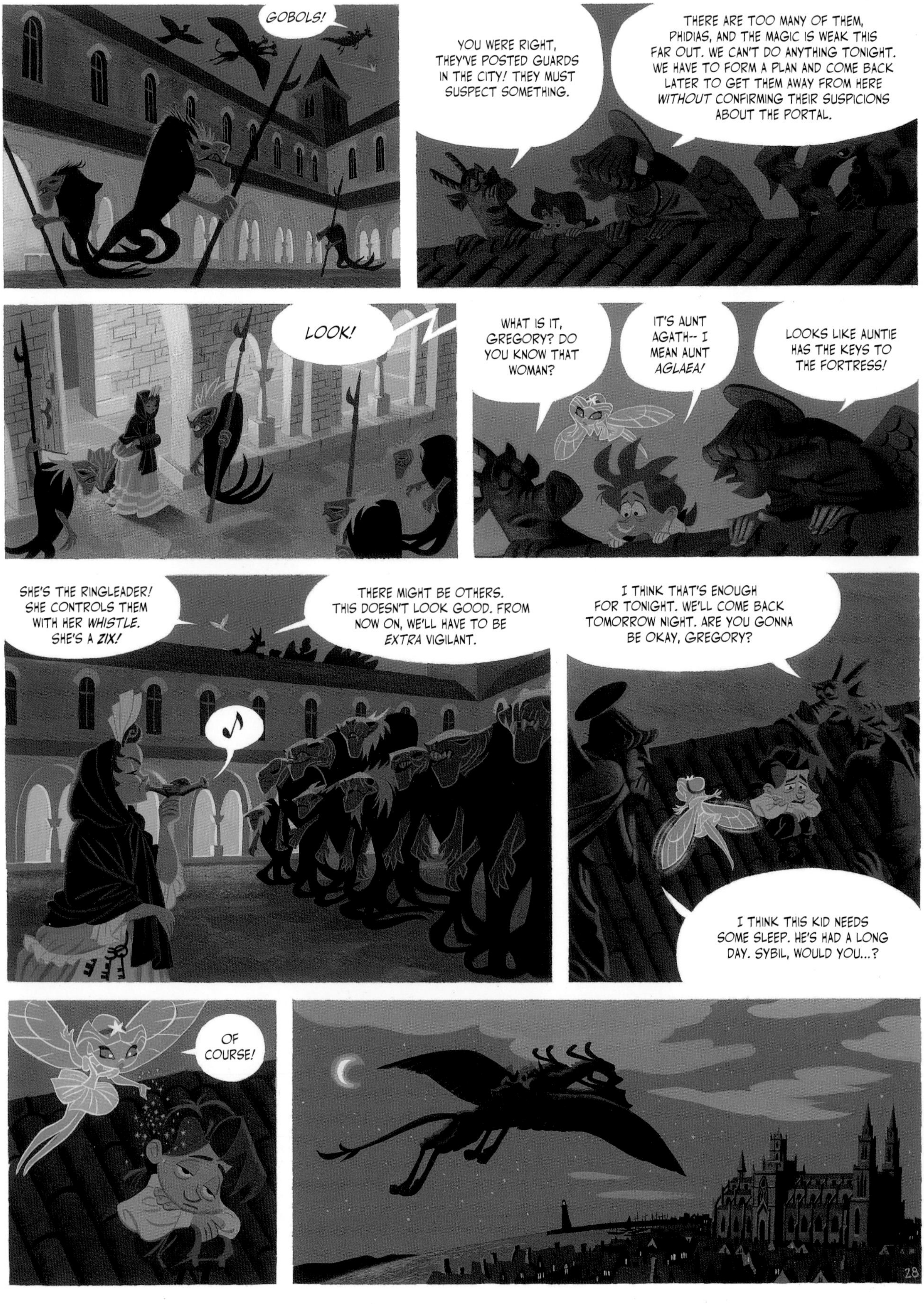
GOBOLS!
YOU WERE RIGHT, THEY'VE POSTED GUARDS IN THE CITY! THEY MUST SUSPECT SOMETHING.
THERE ARE TOO MANY OF THEM, PHIDIAS, AND THE MAGIC IS WEAK THIS FAR OUT. WE CAN'T DO ANYTHING TONIGHT. WE HAVE TO FORM A PLAN AND COME BACK LATER TO GET THEM AWAY FROM HERE WITHOUT CONFIRMING THEIR SUSPICIONS ABOUT THE PORTAL.
LOOK!
WHAT IS IT, GREGORY? DO YOU KNOW THAT WOMAN?
IT'S AUNT AGATH-- I MEAN AUNT AGLAEA!
LOOKS LIKE AUNTIE HAS THE KEYS TO THE FORTRESS!
SHE'S THE RINGLEADER! SHE CONTROLS THEM WITH HER WHISTLE. SHE'S A ZIX!
THERE MIGHT BE OTHERS. THIS DOESN'T LOOK GOOD. FROM NOW ON, WE'LL HAVE TO BE EXTRA VIGILANT.
♪
I THINK THAT'S ENOUGH FOR TONIGHT. WE'LL COME BACK TOMORROW NIGHT. ARE YOU GONNA BE OKAY, GREGORY?
I THINK THIS KID NEEDS SOME SLEEP. HE'S HAD A LONG DAY. SYBIL, WOULD YOU...?
OF COURSE!
28

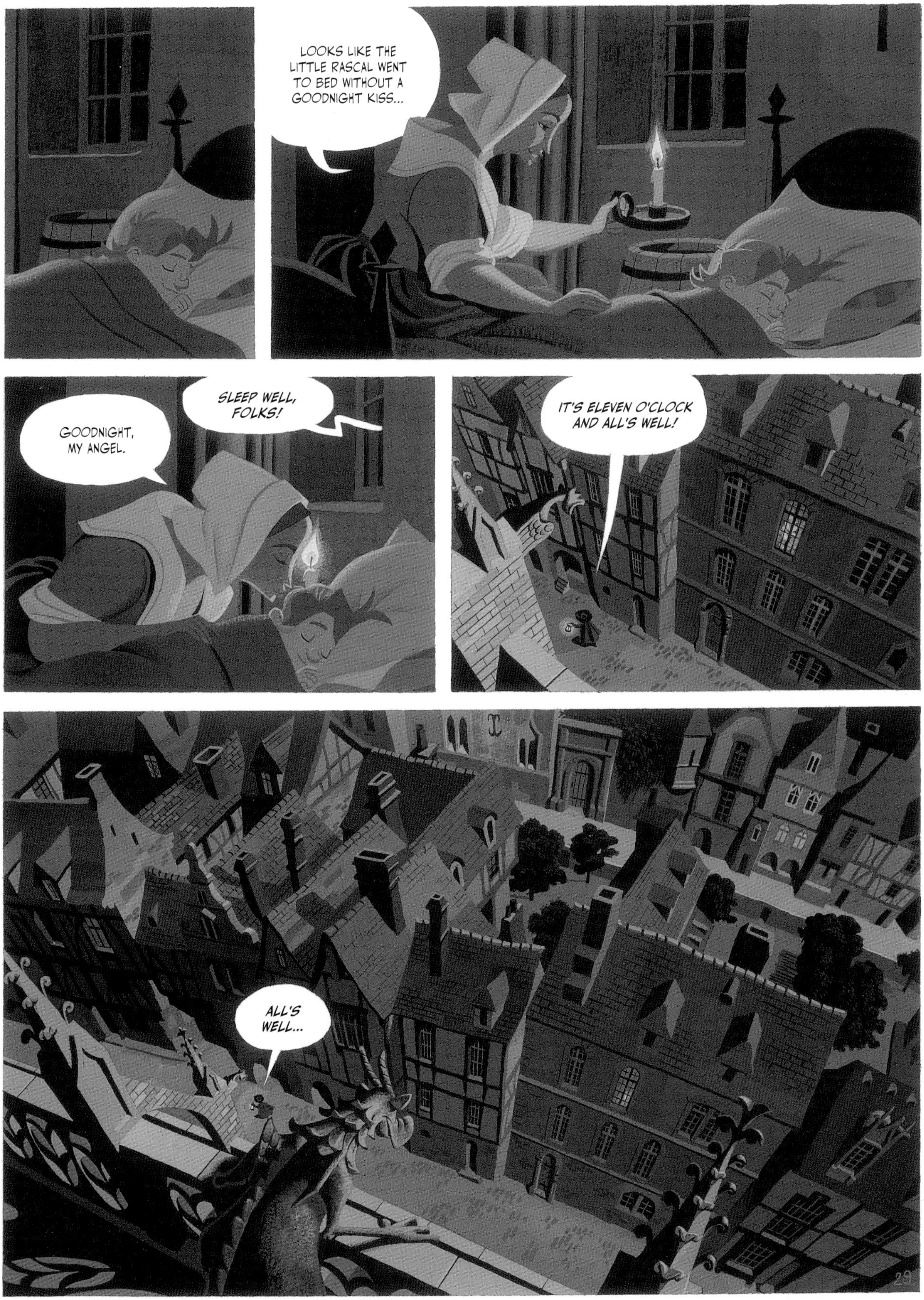
LOOKS LIKE THE LITTLE RASCAL WENT TO BED WITHOUT A GOODNIGHT KISS...
GOODNIGHT, MY ANGEL.
SLEEP WELL, FOLKS!
IT'S ELEVEN O'CLOCK AND ALL'S WELL!
ALL'S WELL...

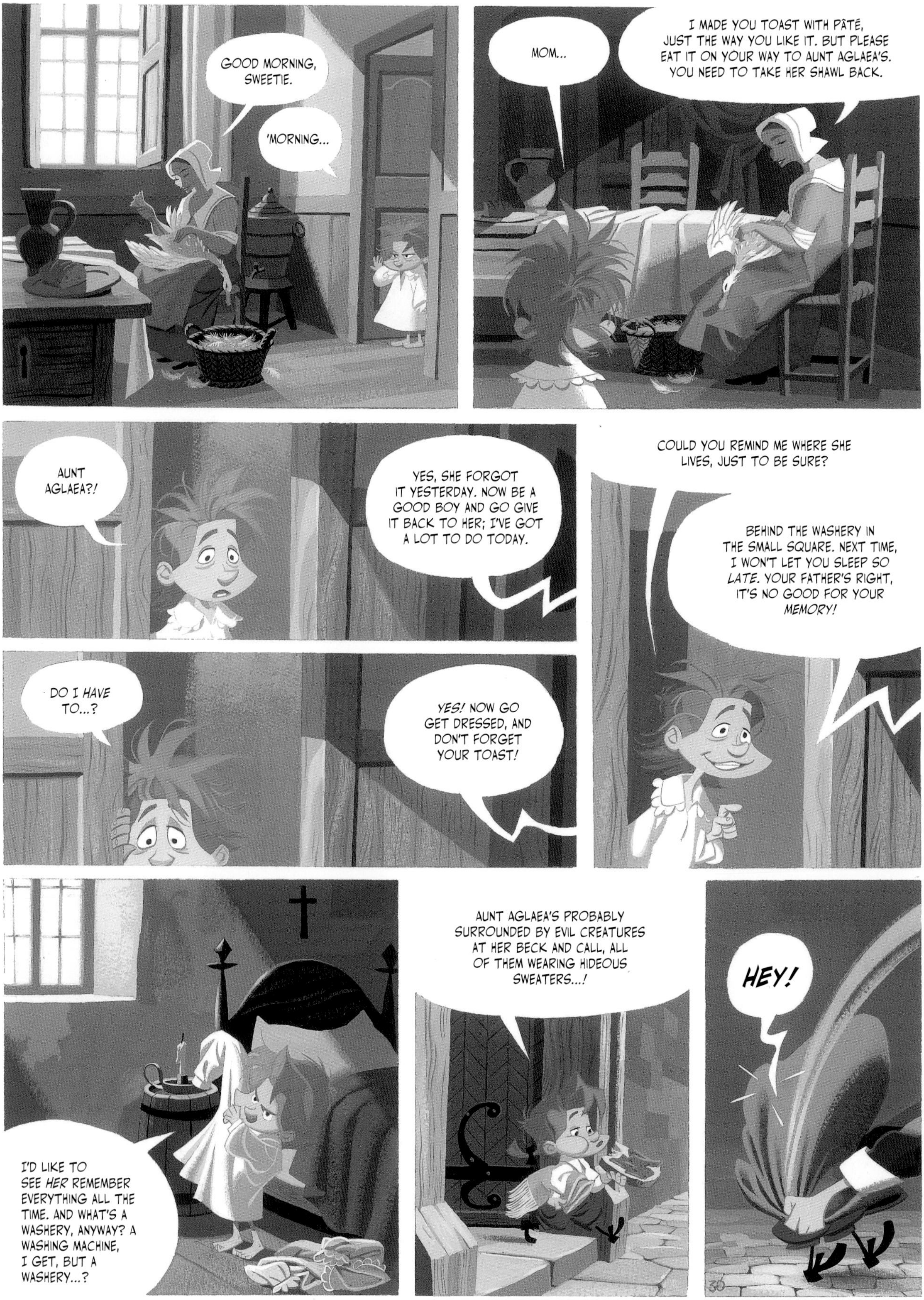
GOOD MORNING, SWEETIE.
'MORNING...
MOM...
I MADE YOU TOAST WITH PÂTÉ, JUST THE WAY YOU LIKE IT. BUT PLEASE EAT IT ON YOUR WAY TO AUNT AGLAEA'S. YOU NEED TO TAKE HER SHAWL BACK.
AUNT AGLAEA?!
YES, SHE FORGOT IT YESTERDAY. NOW BE A GOOD BOY AND GO GIVE IT BACK TO HER; I'VE GOT A LOT TO DO TODAY.
DO I *HAVE* TO...?
YES! NOW GO GET DRESSED, AND DON'T FORGET YOUR TOAST!
COULD YOU REMIND ME WHERE SHE LIVES, JUST TO BE SURE?
BEHIND THE WASHERY IN THE SMALL SQUARE. NEXT TIME, I WON'T LET YOU SLEEP SO *LATE*. YOUR FATHER'S RIGHT, IT'S NO GOOD FOR YOUR *MEMORY!*
I'D LIKE TO SEE *HER* REMEMBER EVERYTHING ALL THE TIME. AND WHAT'S A WASHERY, ANYWAY? A WASHING MACHINE, I GET, BUT A WASHERY...?
AUNT AGLAEA'S PROBABLY SURROUNDED BY EVIL CREATURES AT HER BECK AND CALL, ALL OF THEM WEARING HIDEOUS SWEATERS...!
HEY!

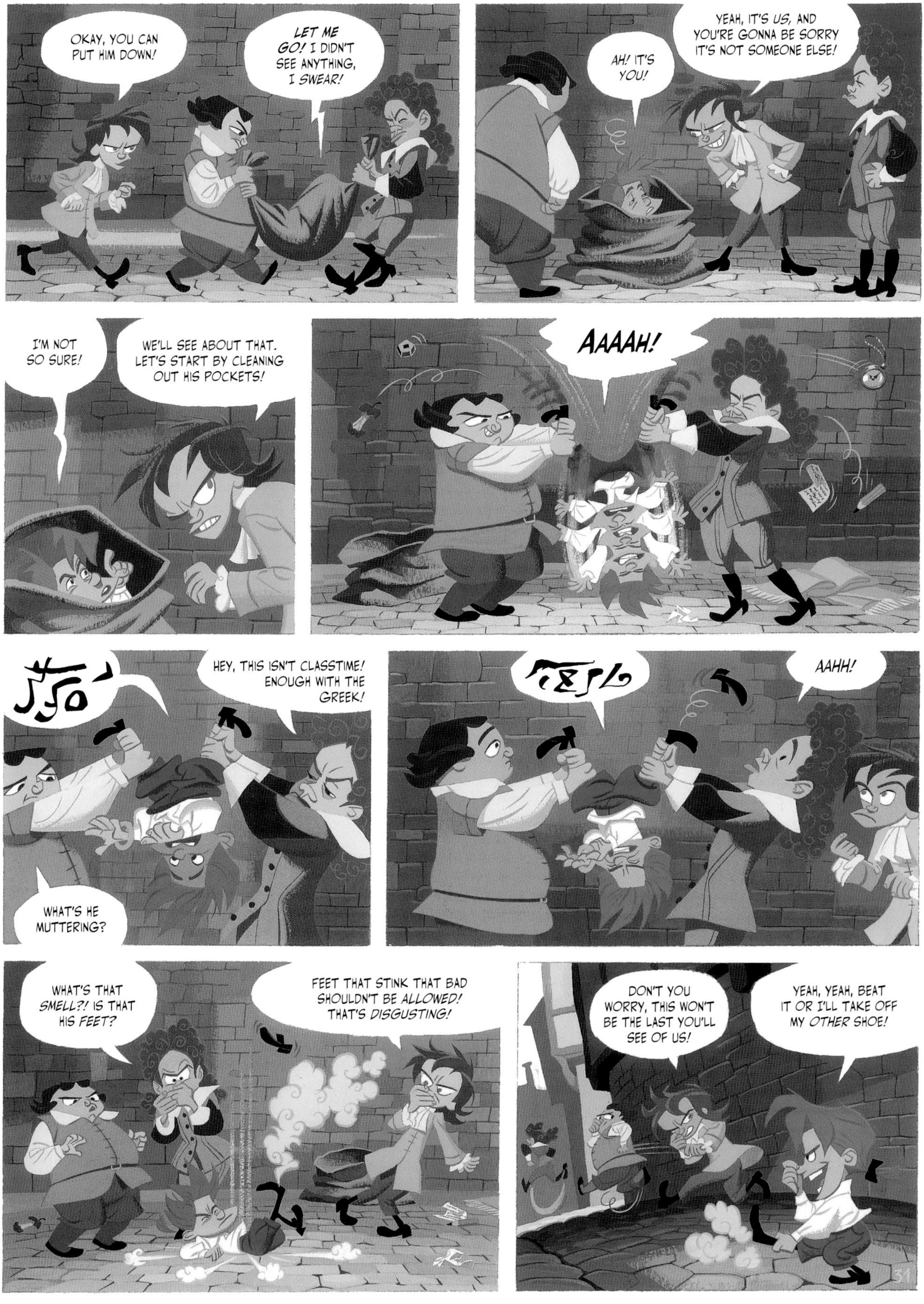
OKAY, YOU CAN PUT HIM DOWN!
LET ME GO! I DIDN'T SEE ANYTHING, I *SWEAR!*
AH! IT'S *YOU!*
YEAH, IT'S *US,* AND YOU'RE GONNA BE SORRY IT'S NOT SOMEONE ELSE!
I'M NOT SO SURE!
WE'LL SEE ABOUT THAT. LET'S START BY CLEANING OUT HIS POCKETS!
AAAAH!
HEY, THIS ISN'T CLASSTIME! ENOUGH WITH THE GREEK!
WHAT'S HE MUTTERING?
AAHH!
WHAT'S THAT *SMELL?!* IS THAT HIS *FEET?*
FEET THAT STINK THAT BAD SHOULDN'T BE *ALLOWED!* THAT'S *DISGUSTING!*
DON'T YOU WORRY, THIS WON'T BE THE LAST YOU'LL SEE OF US!
YEAH, YEAH, BEAT IT OR I'LL TAKE OFF MY *OTHER* SHOE!

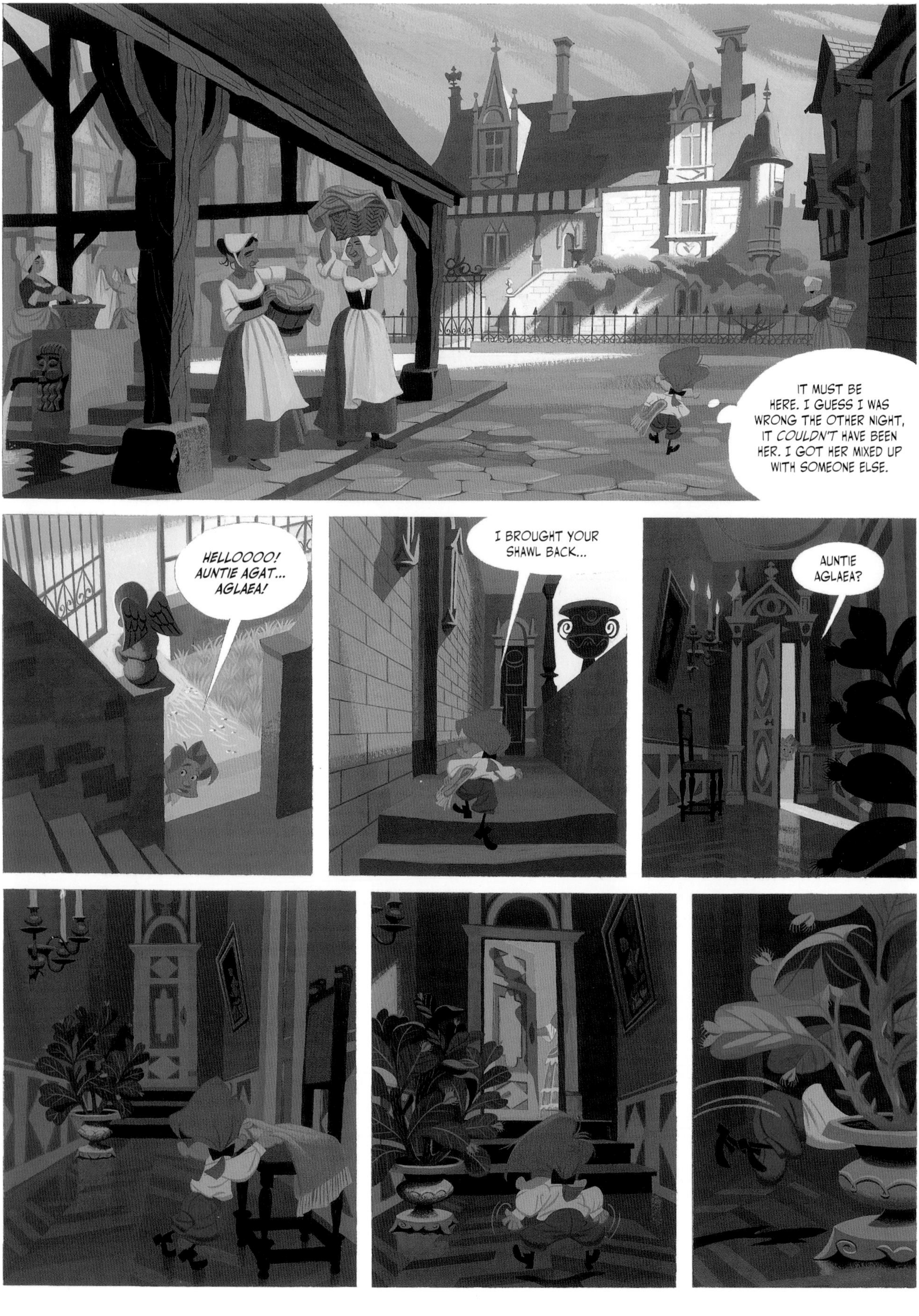
IT MUST BE HERE. I GUESS I WAS WRONG THE OTHER NIGHT, IT *COULDN'T* HAVE BEEN HER. I GOT HER MIXED UP WITH SOMEONE ELSE.
HELLOOOO! AUNTIE AGAT... AGLAEA!
I BROUGHT YOUR SHAWL BACK...
AUNTIE AGLAEA?

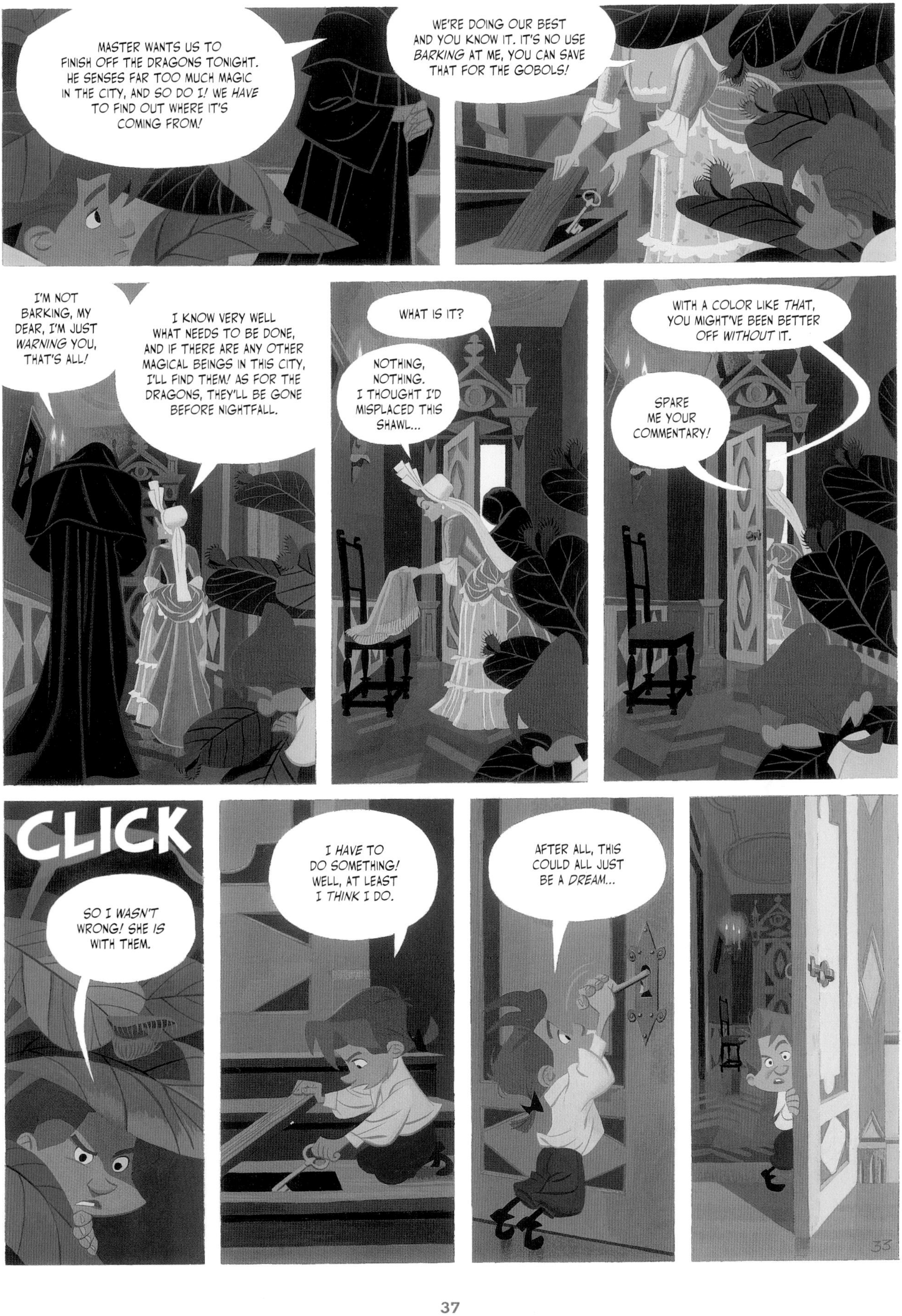
MASTER WANTS US TO FINISH OFF THE DRAGONS TONIGHT. HE SENSES FAR TOO MUCH MAGIC IN THE CITY, AND SO DO I! WE *HAVE* TO FIND OUT WHERE IT'S COMING FROM!
WE'RE DOING OUR BEST AND YOU KNOW IT. IT'S NO USE *BARKING* AT ME, YOU CAN SAVE THAT FOR THE GOBOLS!
I'M NOT BARKING, MY DEAR, I'M JUST *WARNING* YOU, THAT'S ALL!
I KNOW VERY WELL WHAT NEEDS TO BE DONE, AND IF THERE ARE ANY OTHER MAGICAL BEINGS IN THIS CITY, I'LL FIND THEM! AS FOR THE DRAGONS, THEY'LL BE GONE BEFORE NIGHTFALL.
WHAT IS IT?
NOTHING, NOTHING. I THOUGHT I'D MISPLACED THIS SHAWL...
WITH A COLOR LIKE *THAT*, YOU MIGHT'VE BEEN BETTER OFF *WITHOUT* IT.
SPARE ME YOUR COMMENTARY!
CLICK
SO I *WASN'T* WRONG! SHE *IS* WITH THEM.
I *HAVE* TO DO SOMETHING! WELL, AT LEAST I *THINK* I DO.
AFTER ALL, THIS COULD ALL JUST BE A *DREAM*...

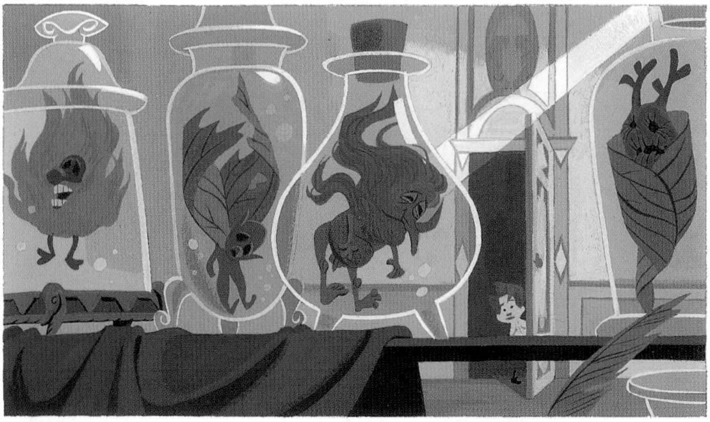
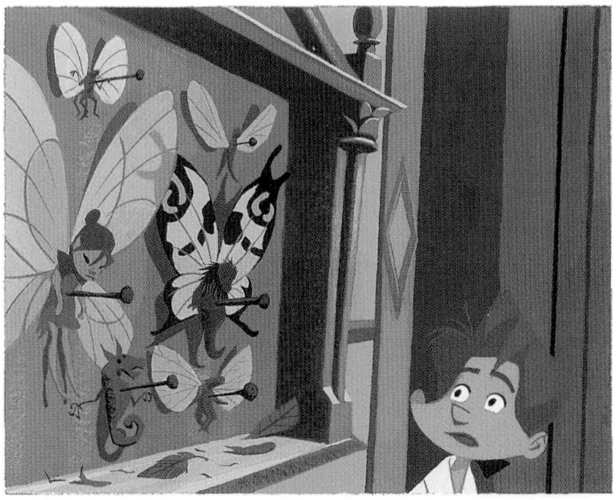
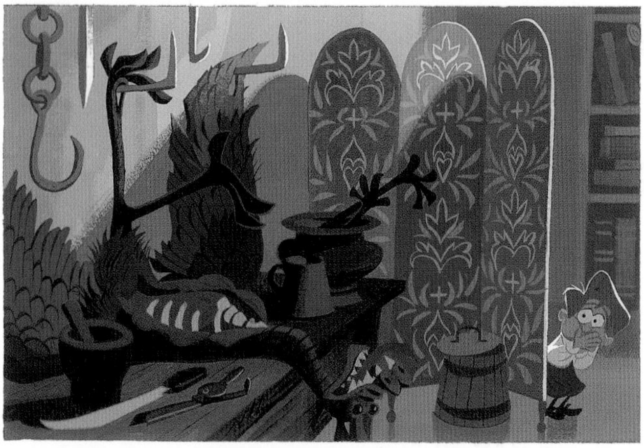
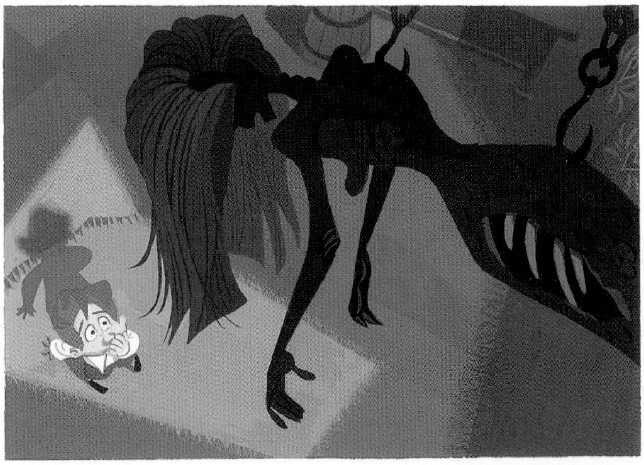
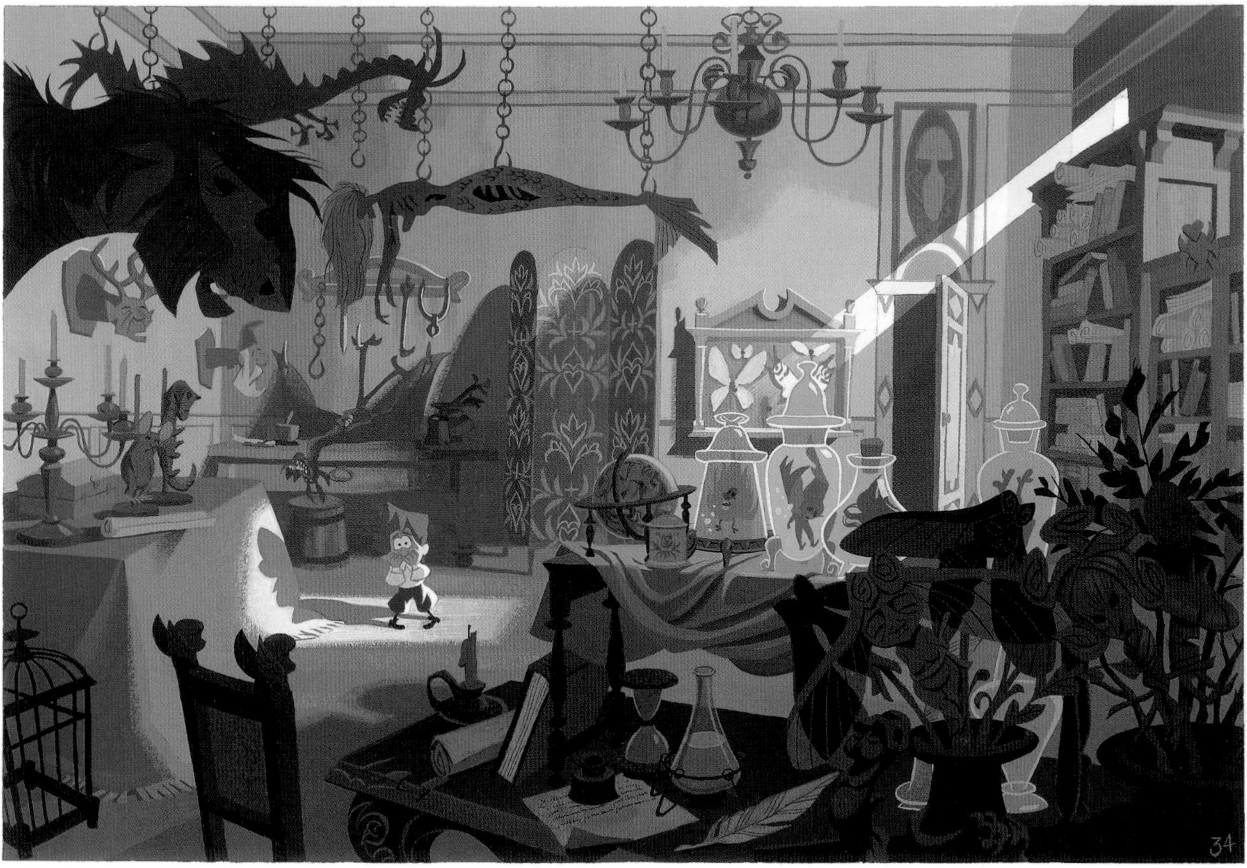
34

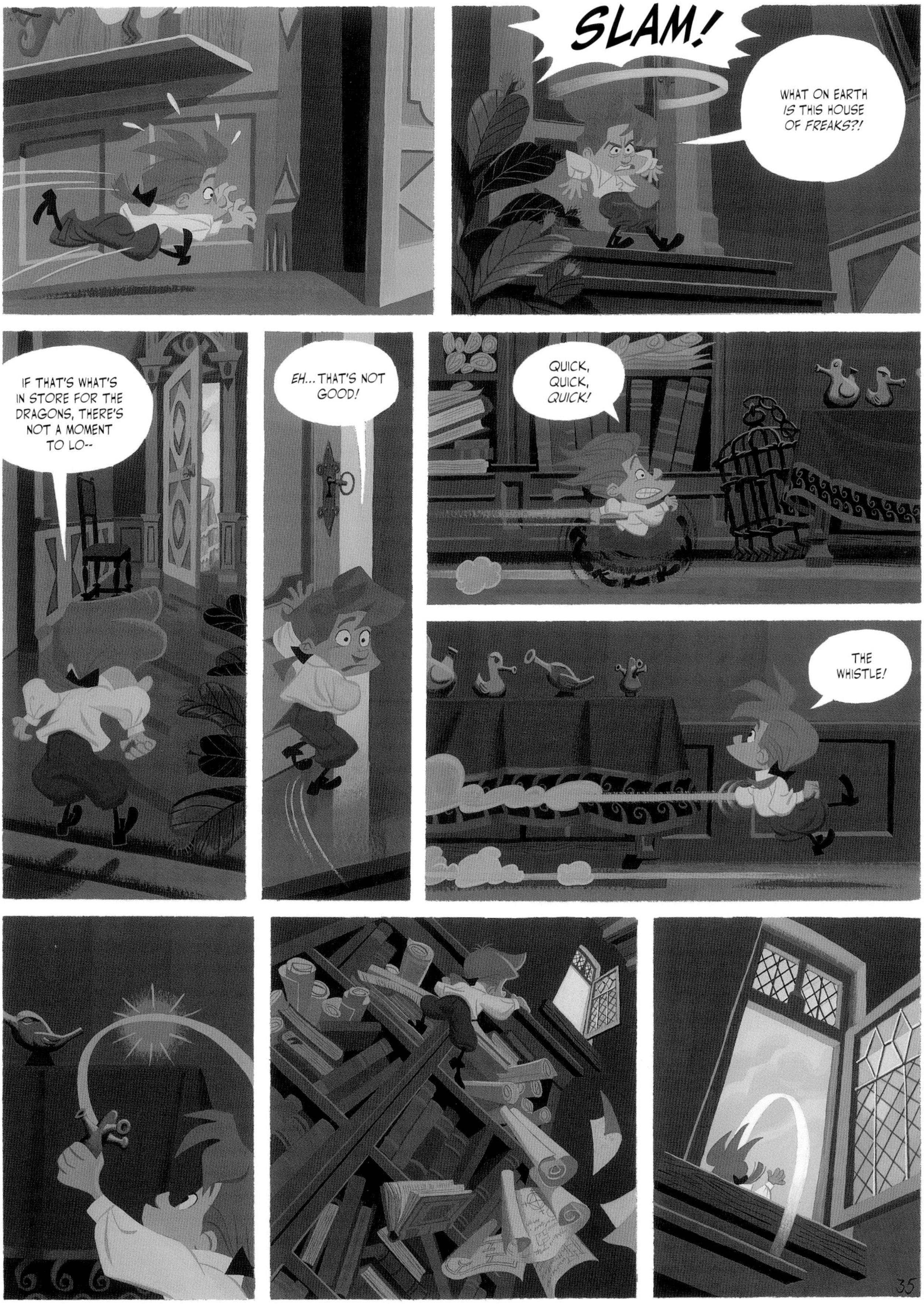
SLAM!
WHAT ON EARTH IS THIS HOUSE OF FREAKS?!
IF THAT'S WHAT'S IN STORE FOR THE DRAGONS, THERE'S NOT A MOMENT TO LO--
EH... THAT'S NOT GOOD!
QUICK, QUICK, QUICK!
THE WHISTLE!
35

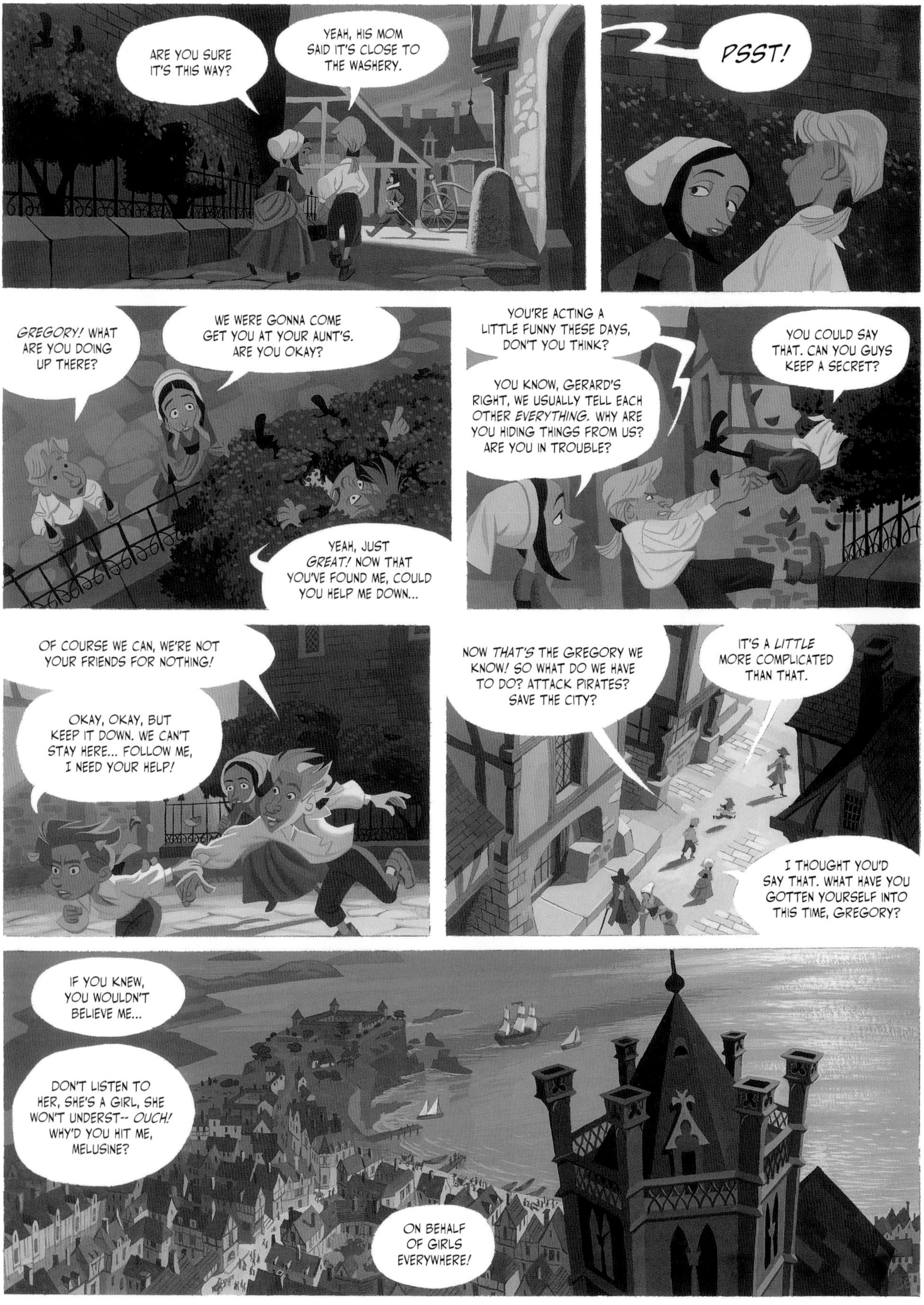
ARE YOU SURE IT'S THIS WAY?
YEAH, HIS MOM SAID IT'S CLOSE TO THE WASHERY.
PSST!
GREGORY! WHAT ARE YOU DOING UP THERE?
WE WERE GONNA COME GET YOU AT YOUR AUNT'S. ARE YOU OKAY?
YEAH, JUST *GREAT!* NOW THAT YOU'VE FOUND ME, COULD YOU HELP ME DOWN...
YOU'RE ACTING A LITTLE FUNNY THESE DAYS, DON'T YOU THINK?
YOU KNOW, GERARD'S RIGHT, WE USUALLY TELL EACH OTHER *EVERYTHING.* WHY ARE YOU HIDING THINGS FROM US? ARE YOU IN TROUBLE?
YOU COULD SAY THAT. CAN YOU GUYS KEEP A SECRET?
OF COURSE WE CAN, WE'RE NOT YOUR FRIENDS FOR NOTHING!
OKAY, OKAY, BUT KEEP IT DOWN. WE CAN'T STAY HERE... FOLLOW ME, I NEED YOUR HELP!
NOW *THAT'S* THE GREGORY WE KNOW! SO WHAT DO WE HAVE TO DO? ATTACK PIRATES? SAVE THE CITY?
IT'S A *LITTLE* MORE COMPLICATED THAN THAT.
I THOUGHT YOU'D SAY THAT. WHAT HAVE YOU GOTTEN YOURSELF INTO THIS TIME, GREGORY?
IF YOU KNEW, YOU WOULDN'T BELIEVE ME...
DON'T LISTEN TO HER, SHE'S A GIRL, SHE WON'T UNDERST-- *OUCH!* WHY'D YOU HIT ME, MELUSINE?
ON BEHALF OF GIRLS EVERYWHERE!

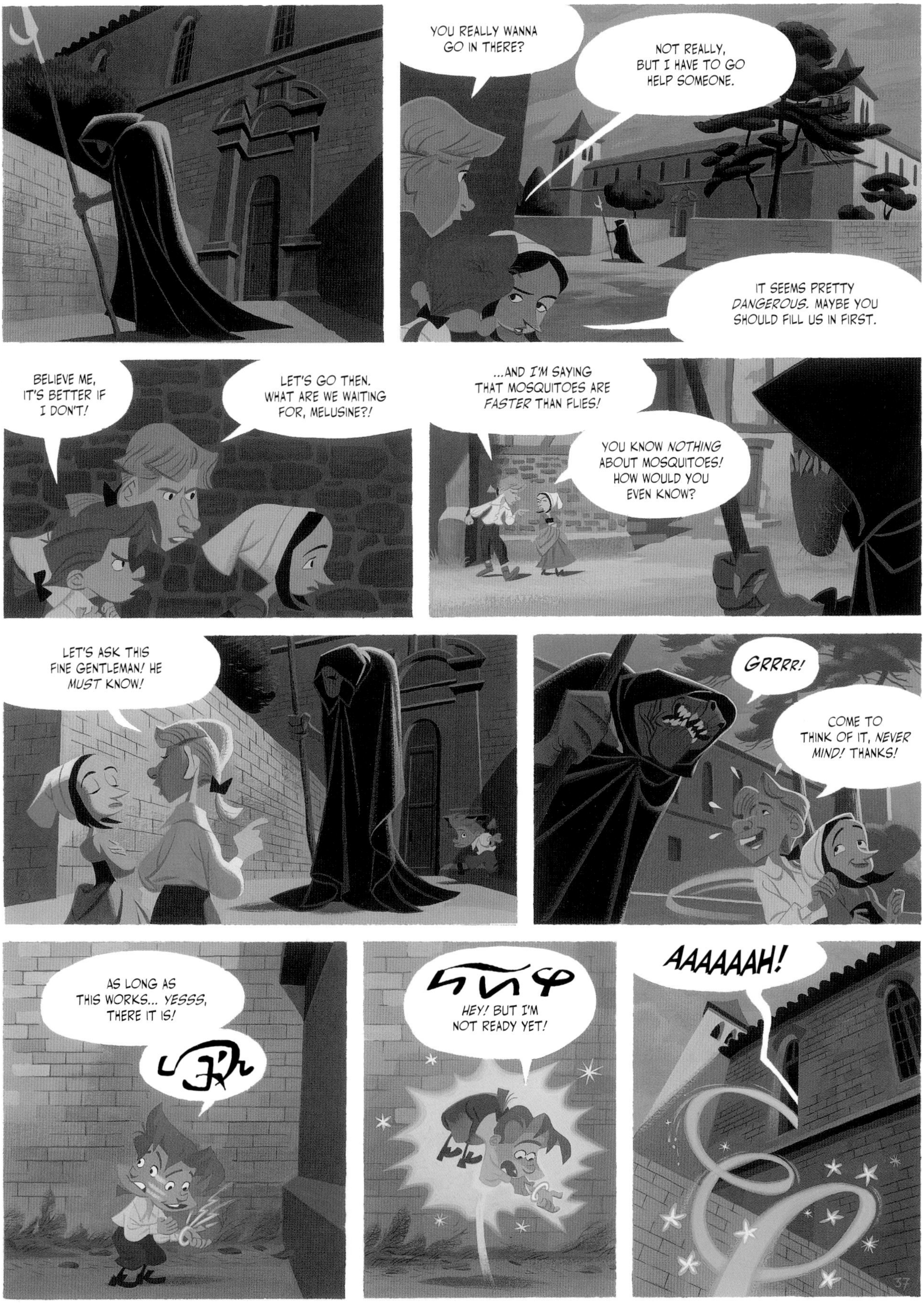
YOU REALLY WANNA GO IN THERE?
NOT REALLY, BUT I HAVE TO GO HELP SOMEONE.
IT SEEMS PRETTY DANGEROUS. MAYBE YOU SHOULD FILL US IN FIRST.
BELIEVE ME, IT'S BETTER IF I DON'T!
LET'S GO THEN. WHAT ARE WE WAITING FOR, MELUSINE?!
...AND I'M SAYING THAT MOSQUITOES ARE FASTER THAN FLIES!
YOU KNOW NOTHING ABOUT MOSQUITOES! HOW WOULD YOU EVEN KNOW?
LET'S ASK THIS FINE GENTLEMAN! HE MUST KNOW!
GRRRR!
COME TO THINK OF IT, NEVER MIND! THANKS!
AS LONG AS THIS WORKS... YESSS, THERE IT IS!
HEY! BUT I'M NOT READY YET!
AAAAAAH!

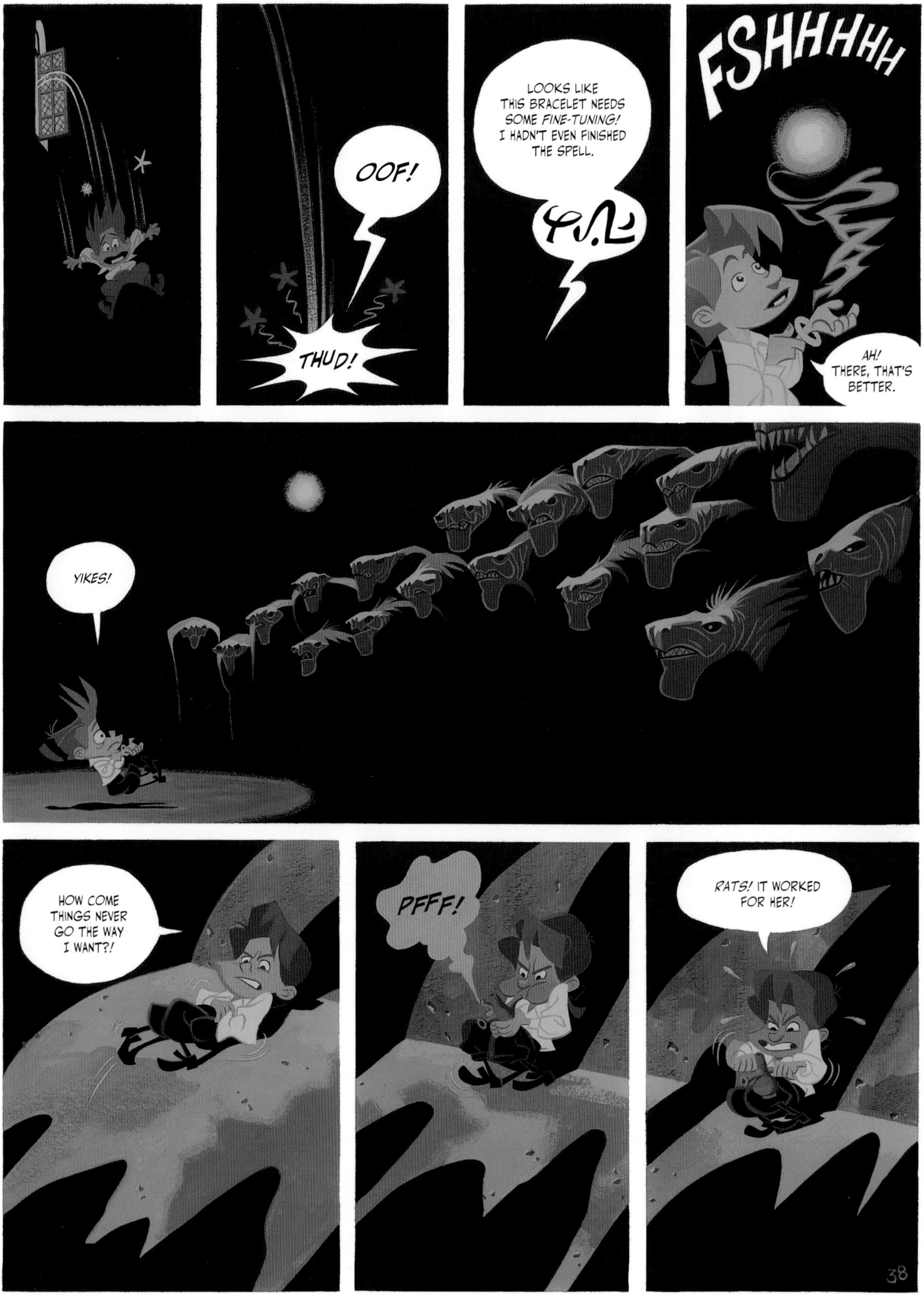
OOF!
THUD!
LOOKS LIKE THIS BRACELET NEEDS SOME *FINE-TUNING!* I HADN'T EVEN FINISHED THE SPELL.
FSHHHHH
AH! THERE, THAT'S BETTER.
YIKES!
HOW COME THINGS NEVER GO THE WAY I WANT?!
PFFF!
RATS! IT WORKED FOR HER!
38

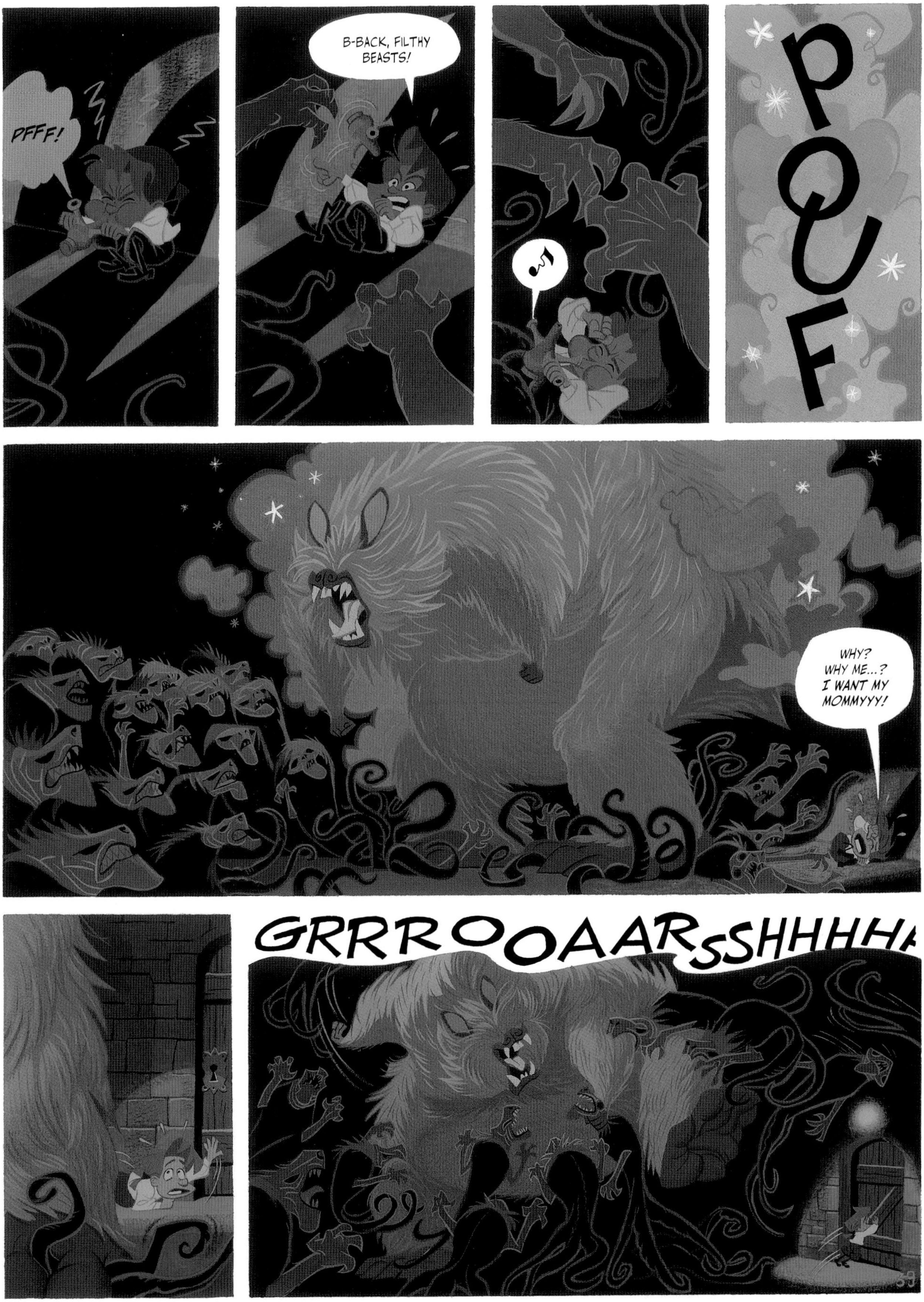
PFFF!
B-BACK, FILTHY BEASTS!
POUF
WHY? WHY ME...? I WANT MY MOMMYYY!
GRRROOAARSSHHHH

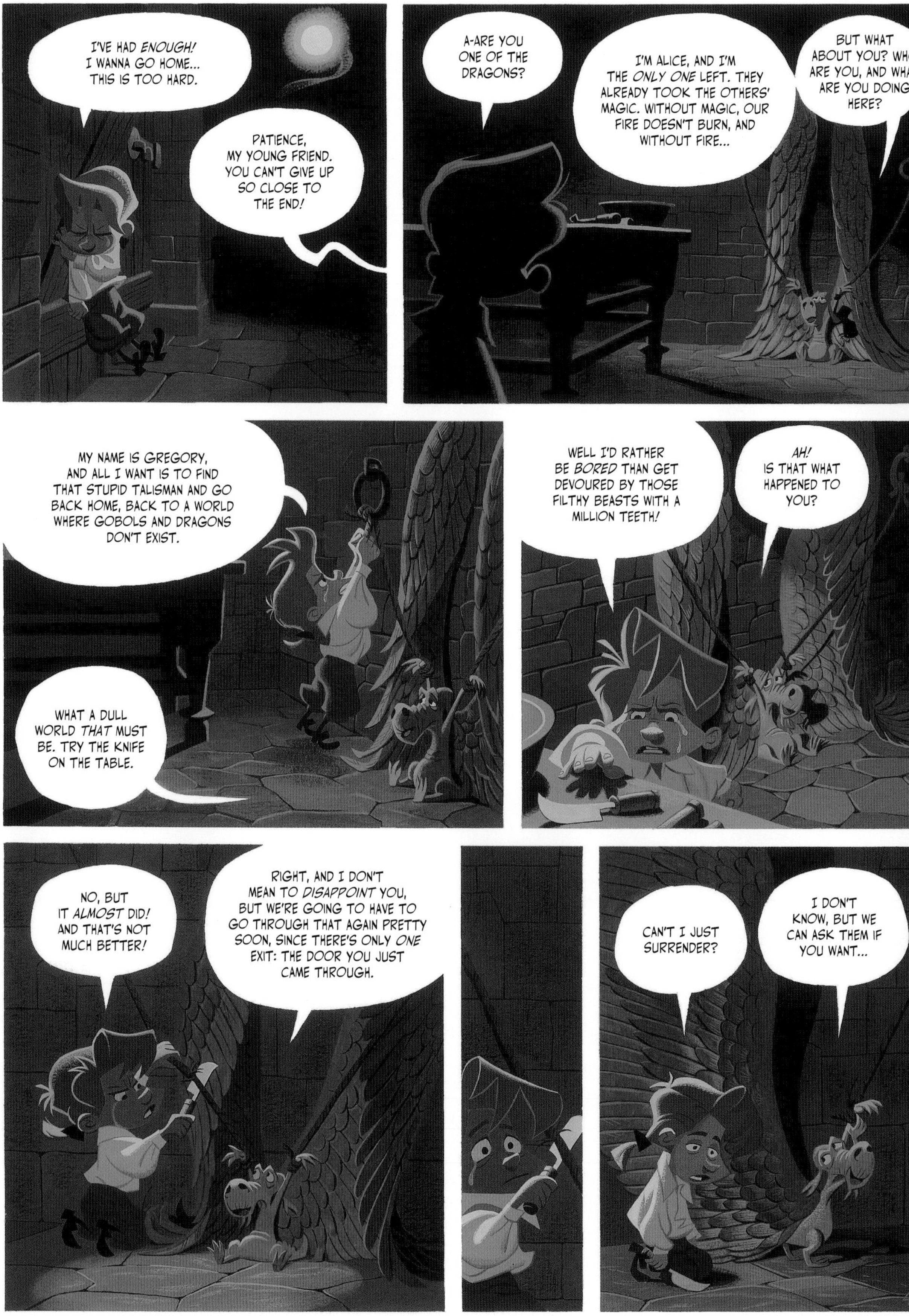
I'VE HAD *ENOUGH!* I WANNA GO HOME... THIS IS TOO HARD.
PATIENCE, MY YOUNG FRIEND. YOU CAN'T GIVE UP SO CLOSE TO THE END!
A-ARE YOU ONE OF THE DRAGONS?
I'M ALICE, AND I'M THE *ONLY ONE* LEFT. THEY ALREADY TOOK THE OTHERS' MAGIC. WITHOUT MAGIC, OUR FIRE DOESN'T BURN, AND WITHOUT FIRE...
BUT WHAT ABOUT YOU? WHO ARE YOU, AND WHAT ARE YOU DOING HERE?
MY NAME IS GREGORY, AND ALL I WANT IS TO FIND THAT STUPID TALISMAN AND GO BACK HOME, BACK TO A WORLD WHERE GOBOLS AND DRAGONS DON'T EXIST.
WHAT A DULL WORLD *THAT* MUST BE. TRY THE KNIFE ON THE TABLE.
WELL I'D RATHER BE *BORED* THAN GET DEVOURED BY THOSE FILTHY BEASTS WITH A MILLION TEETH!
AH! IS THAT WHAT HAPPENED TO YOU?
NO, BUT IT *ALMOST* DID! AND THAT'S NOT MUCH BETTER!
RIGHT, AND I DON'T MEAN TO *DISAPPOINT* YOU, BUT WE'RE GOING TO HAVE TO GO THROUGH THAT AGAIN PRETTY SOON, SINCE THERE'S ONLY *ONE* EXIT: THE DOOR YOU JUST CAME THROUGH.
CAN'T I JUST SURRENDER?
I DON'T KNOW, BUT WE CAN ASK THEM IF YOU WANT...
40

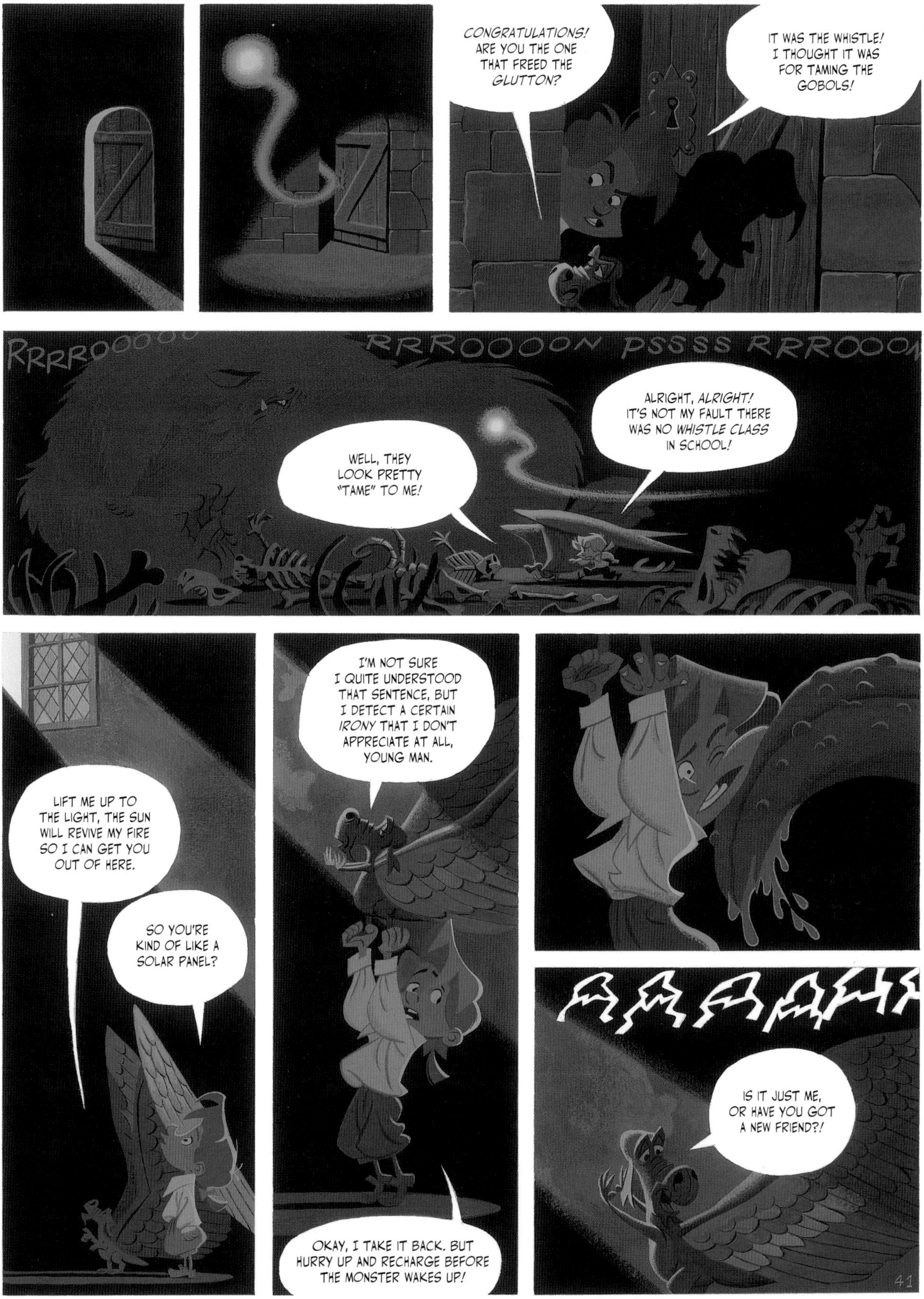
CONGRATULATIONS! ARE YOU THE ONE THAT FREED THE GLUTTON?
IT WAS THE WHISTLE! I THOUGHT IT WAS FOR TAMING THE GOBOLS!
RRRROOOOO
RRROOOOON PSSSS RRROOOON
WELL, THEY LOOK PRETTY "TAME" TO ME!
ALRIGHT, ALRIGHT! IT'S NOT MY FAULT THERE WAS NO WHISTLE CLASS IN SCHOOL!
LIFT ME UP TO THE LIGHT, THE SUN WILL REVIVE MY FIRE SO I CAN GET YOU OUT OF HERE.
SO YOU'RE KIND OF LIKE A SOLAR PANEL?
I'M NOT SURE I QUITE UNDERSTOOD THAT SENTENCE, BUT I DETECT A CERTAIN IRONY THAT I DON'T APPRECIATE AT ALL, YOUNG MAN.
OKAY, I TAKE IT BACK. BUT HURRY UP AND RECHARGE BEFORE THE MONSTER WAKES UP!
AAAAAH
IS IT JUST ME, OR HAVE YOU GOT A NEW FRIEND?!
41

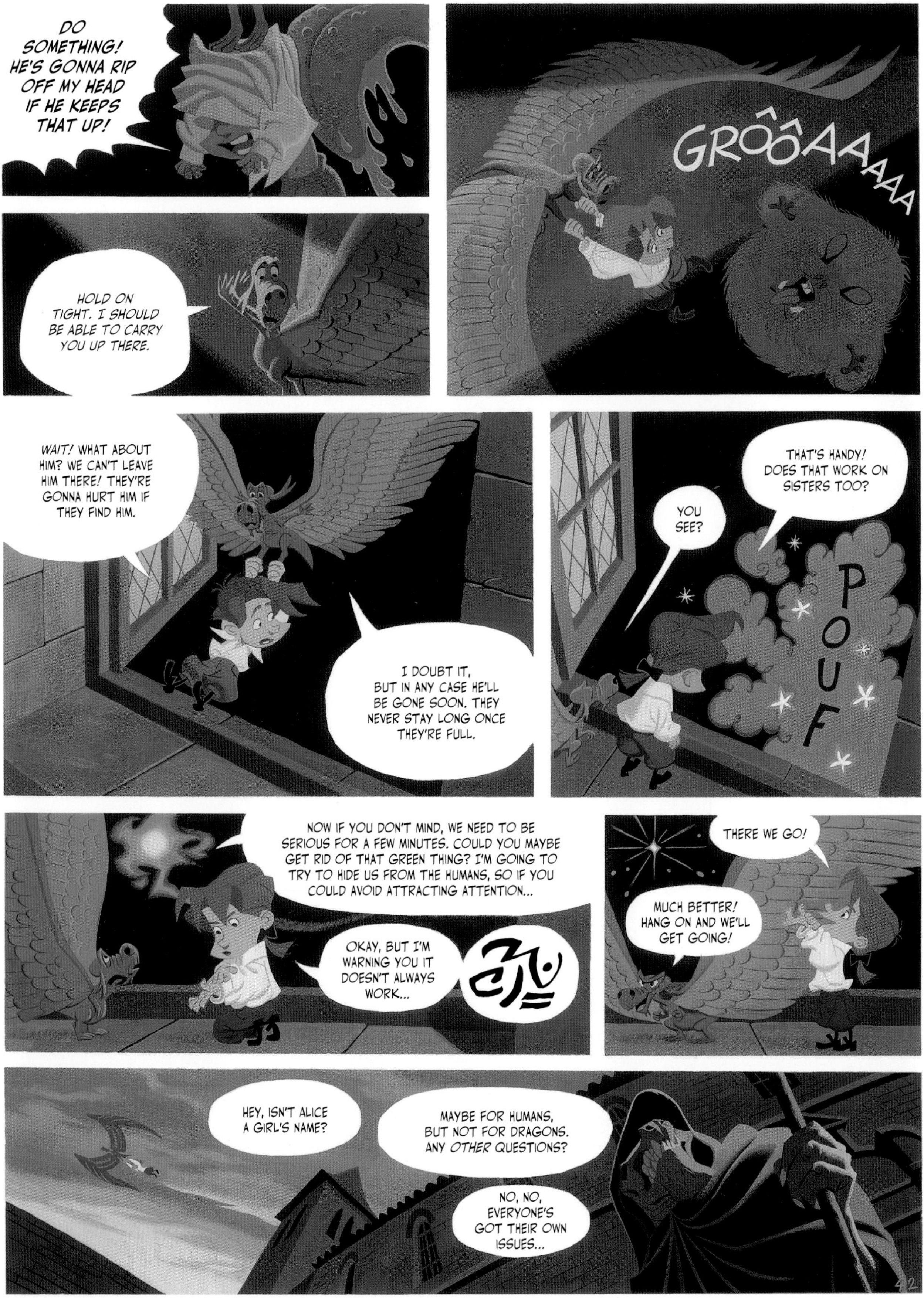
DO SOMETHING! HE'S GONNA RIP OFF MY HEAD IF HE KEEPS THAT UP!
GROÔÔAAAAAA
HOLD ON TIGHT. I SHOULD BE ABLE TO CARRY YOU UP THERE.
WAIT! WHAT ABOUT HIM? WE CAN'T LEAVE HIM THERE! THEY'RE GONNA HURT HIM IF THEY FIND HIM.
I DOUBT IT, BUT IN ANY CASE HE'LL BE GONE SOON. THEY NEVER STAY LONG ONCE THEY'RE FULL.
YOU SEE?
THAT'S HANDY! DOES THAT WORK ON SISTERS TOO?
POUF
NOW IF YOU DON'T MIND, WE NEED TO BE SERIOUS FOR A FEW MINUTES. COULD YOU MAYBE GET RID OF THAT GREEN THING? I'M GOING TO TRY TO HIDE US FROM THE HUMANS, SO IF YOU COULD AVOID ATTRACTING ATTENTION...
OKAY, BUT I'M WARNING YOU IT DOESN'T ALWAYS WORK...
THERE WE GO!
MUCH BETTER! HANG ON AND WE'LL GET GOING!
HEY, ISN'T ALICE A GIRL'S NAME?
MAYBE FOR HUMANS, BUT NOT FOR DRAGONS. ANY OTHER QUESTIONS?
NO, NO, EVERYONE'S GOT THEIR OWN ISSUES...

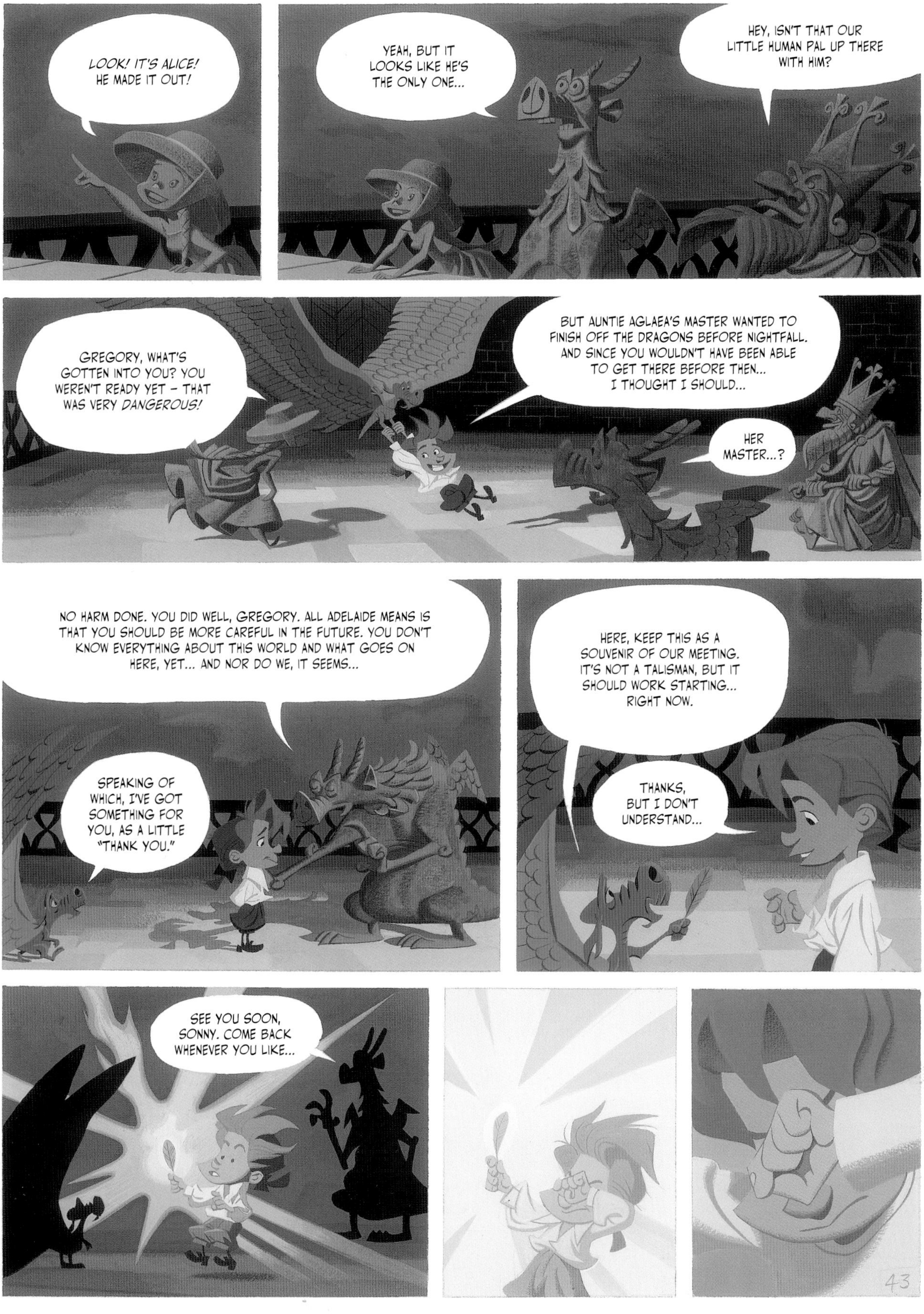
LOOK! IT'S ALICE! HE MADE IT OUT!
YEAH, BUT IT LOOKS LIKE HE'S THE ONLY ONE...
HEY, ISN'T THAT OUR LITTLE HUMAN PAL UP THERE WITH HIM?
GREGORY, WHAT'S GOTTEN INTO YOU? YOU WEREN'T READY YET – THAT WAS VERY DANGEROUS!
BUT AUNTIE AGLAEA'S MASTER WANTED TO FINISH OFF THE DRAGONS BEFORE NIGHTFALL. AND SINCE YOU WOULDN'T HAVE BEEN ABLE TO GET THERE BEFORE THEN... I THOUGHT I SHOULD...
HER MASTER...?
NO HARM DONE. YOU DID WELL, GREGORY. ALL ADELAIDE MEANS IS THAT YOU SHOULD BE MORE CAREFUL IN THE FUTURE. YOU DON'T KNOW EVERYTHING ABOUT THIS WORLD AND WHAT GOES ON HERE, YET... AND NOR DO WE, IT SEEMS...
SPEAKING OF WHICH, I'VE GOT SOMETHING FOR YOU, AS A LITTLE "THANK YOU."
HERE, KEEP THIS AS A SOUVENIR OF OUR MEETING. IT'S NOT A TALISMAN, BUT IT SHOULD WORK STARTING... RIGHT NOW.
THANKS, BUT I DON'T UNDERSTAND...
SEE YOU SOON, SONNY. COME BACK WHENEVER YOU LIKE...
43

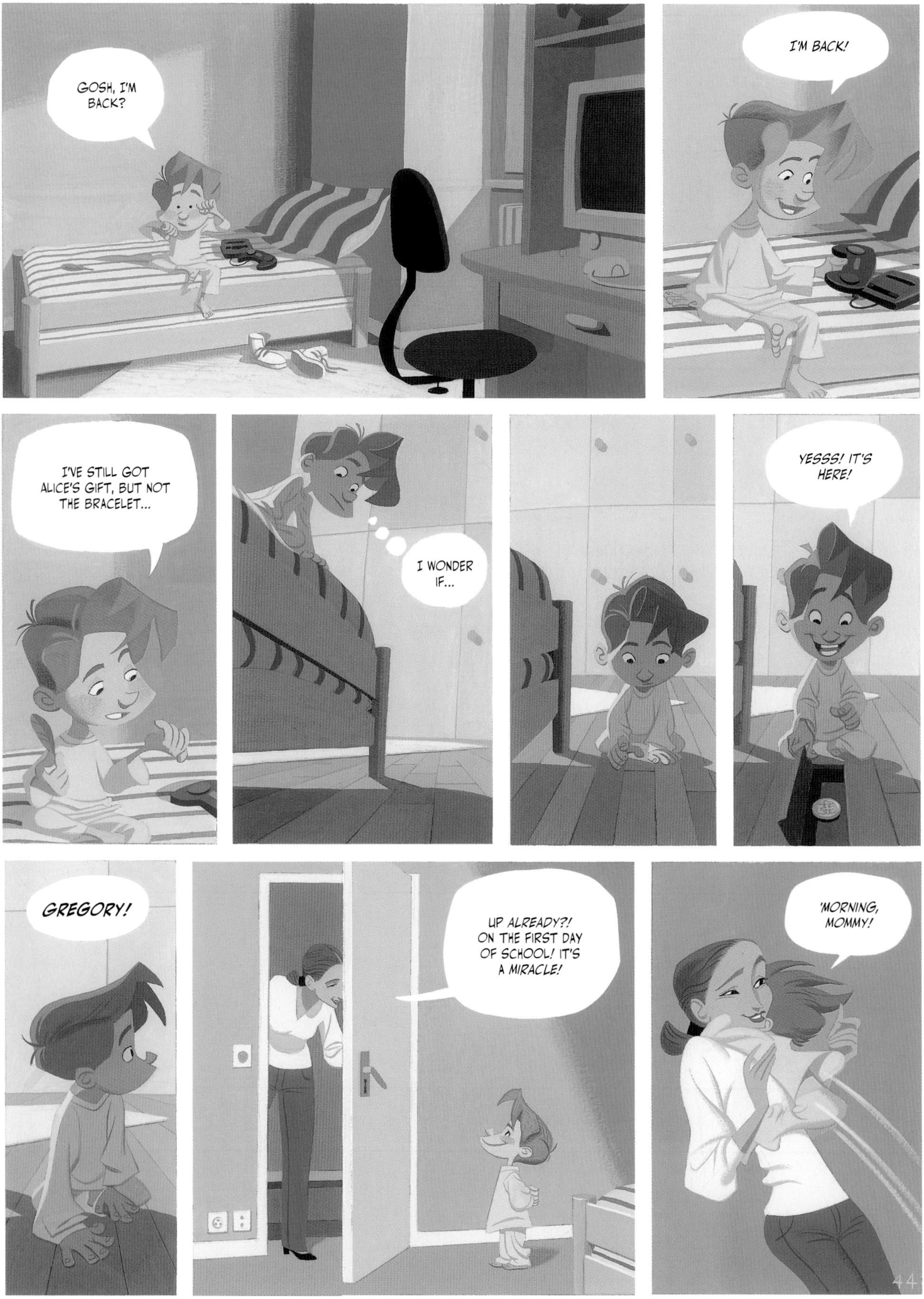
GOSH, I'M BACK?
I'M BACK!
I'VE STILL GOT ALICE'S GIFT, BUT NOT THE BRACELET...
I WONDER IF...
YESSS! IT'S HERE!
GREGORY!
UP ALREADY?! ON THE FIRST DAY OF SCHOOL! IT'S A MIRACLE!
'MORNING, MOMMY!

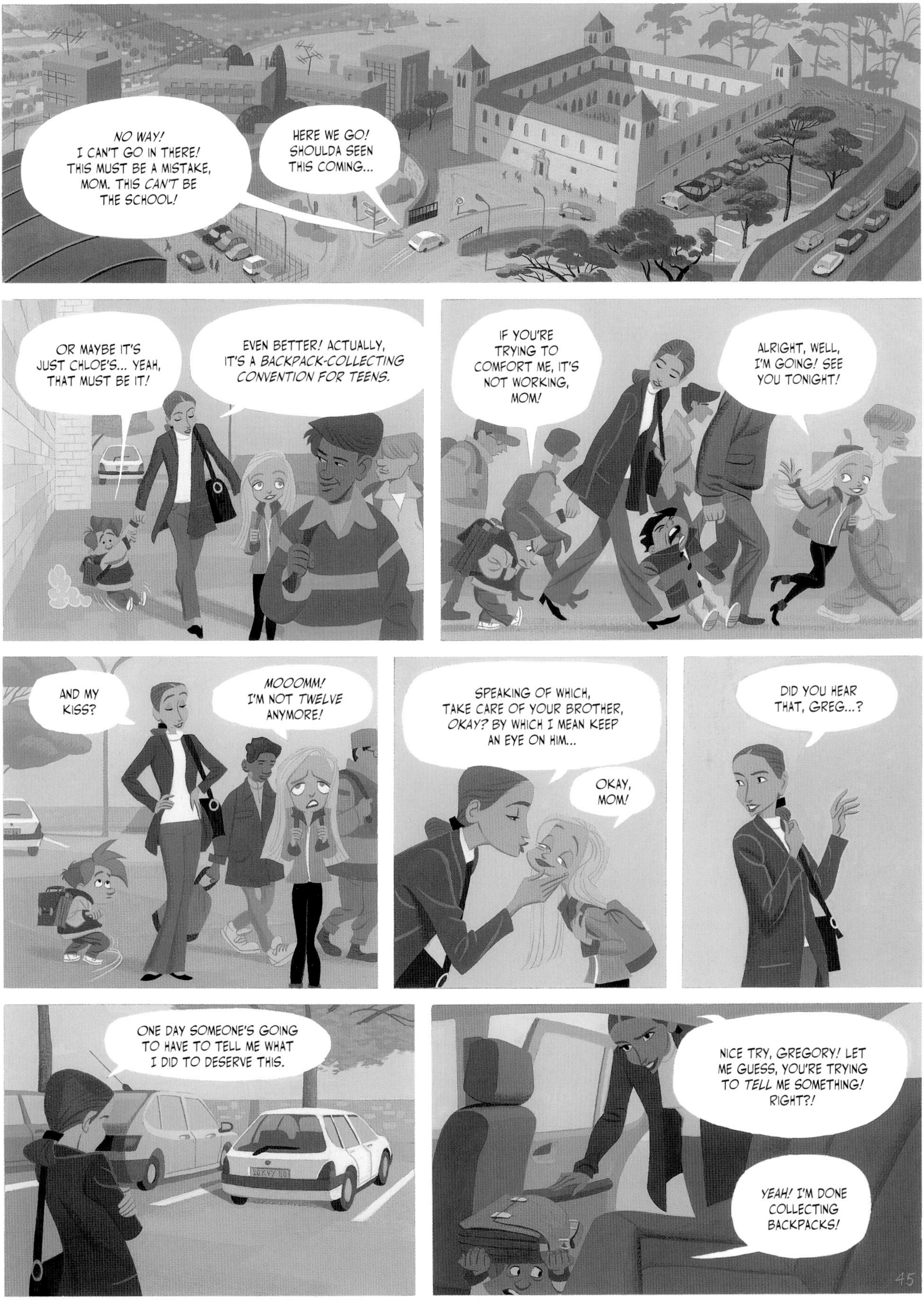
NO WAY! I CAN'T GO IN THERE! THIS MUST BE A MISTAKE, MOM. THIS CAN'T BE THE SCHOOL!
HERE WE GO! SHOULDA SEEN THIS COMING...
OR MAYBE IT'S JUST CHLOE'S... YEAH, THAT MUST BE IT!
EVEN BETTER! ACTUALLY, IT'S A BACKPACK-COLLECTING CONVENTION FOR TEENS.
IF YOU'RE TRYING TO COMFORT ME, IT'S NOT WORKING, MOM!
ALRIGHT, WELL, I'M GOING! SEE YOU TONIGHT!
AND MY KISS?
MOOOMM! I'M NOT TWELVE ANYMORE!
SPEAKING OF WHICH, TAKE CARE OF YOUR BROTHER, OKAY? BY WHICH I MEAN KEEP AN EYE ON HIM...
OKAY, MOM!
DID YOU HEAR THAT, GREG...?
ONE DAY SOMEONE'S GOING TO HAVE TO TELL ME WHAT I DID TO DESERVE THIS.
NICE TRY, GREGORY! LET ME GUESS, YOU'RE TRYING TO TELL ME SOMETHING! RIGHT?!
YEAH! I'M DONE COLLECTING BACKPACKS!

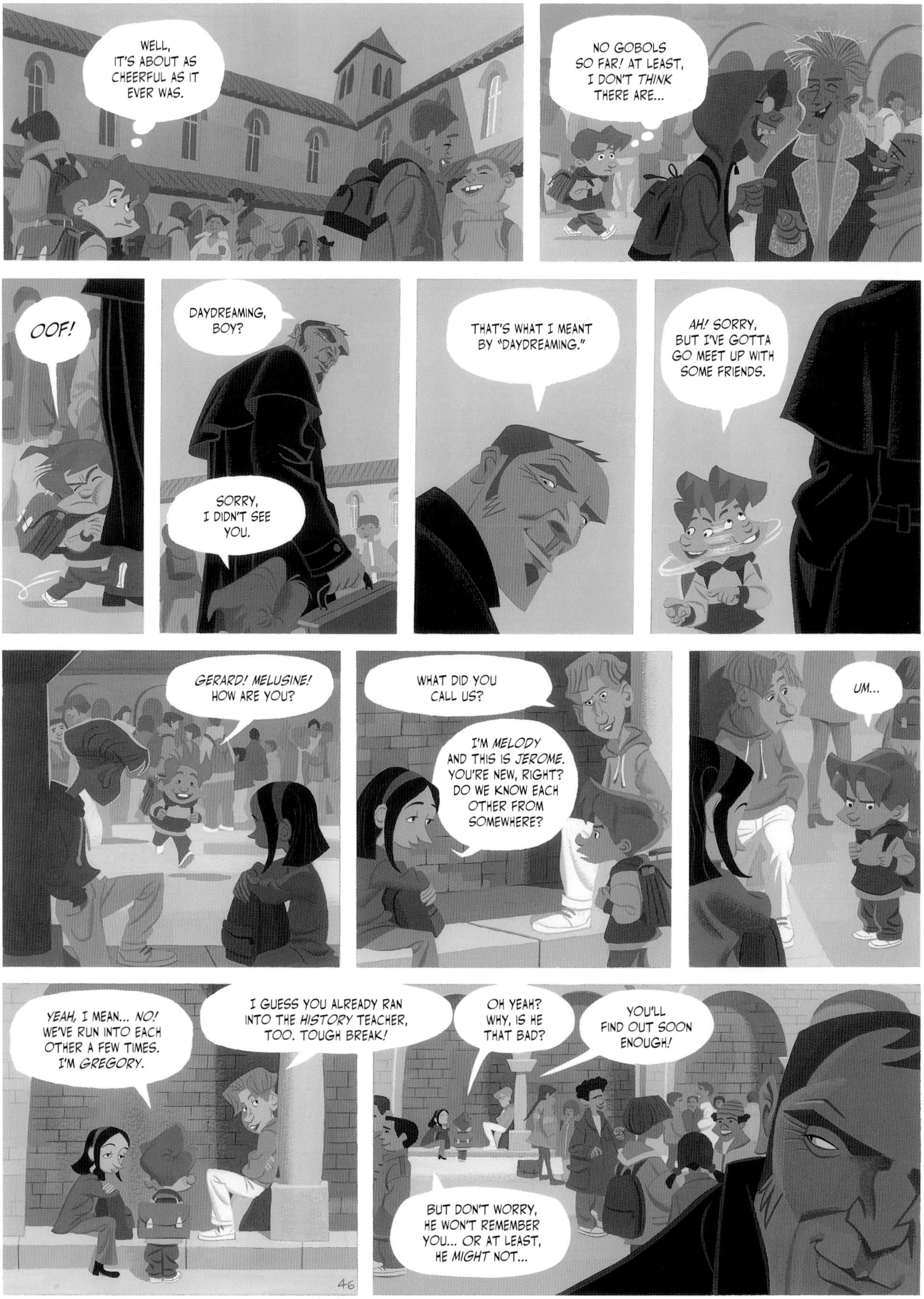
WELL, IT'S ABOUT AS CHEERFUL AS IT EVER WAS.
NO GOBOLS SO FAR! AT LEAST, I DON'T *THINK* THERE ARE...
OOF!
DAYDREAMING, BOY?
SORRY, I DIDN'T SEE YOU.
THAT'S WHAT I MEANT BY "DAYDREAMING."
AH! SORRY, BUT I'VE GOTTA GO MEET UP WITH SOME FRIENDS.
GERARD! MELUSINE! HOW ARE YOU?
WHAT DID YOU CALL US?
I'M *MELODY* AND THIS IS *JEROME*. YOU'RE NEW, RIGHT? DO WE KNOW EACH OTHER FROM SOMEWHERE?
UM...
YEAH, I MEAN... NO! WE'VE RUN INTO EACH OTHER A FEW TIMES. I'M *GREGORY*.
I GUESS YOU ALREADY RAN INTO THE *HISTORY* TEACHER, TOO. TOUGH BREAK!
OH YEAH? WHY, IS HE THAT BAD?
YOU'LL FIND OUT SOON ENOUGH!
BUT DON'T WORRY, HE WON'T REMEMBER YOU... OR AT LEAST, HE *MIGHT* NOT...
46

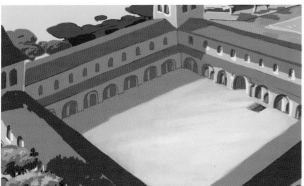

HEY, GREGORY, IS IT JUST ME OR ARE YOU A LITTLE ON *EDGE*...?

YEAH, STOP IT, YOU'RE *FREAKING* ME OUT!

HE'S NOT WEARING HIS CUTE LITTLE SWEATER TODAY. IS THAT WHAT'S MAKING THE BIG BABY SO NERVOUS?! HA HA HA!

I DON'T LIKE THIS PLACE! IT'S FULL OF *GOBOLS*!

FULL OF *WHAT*?!

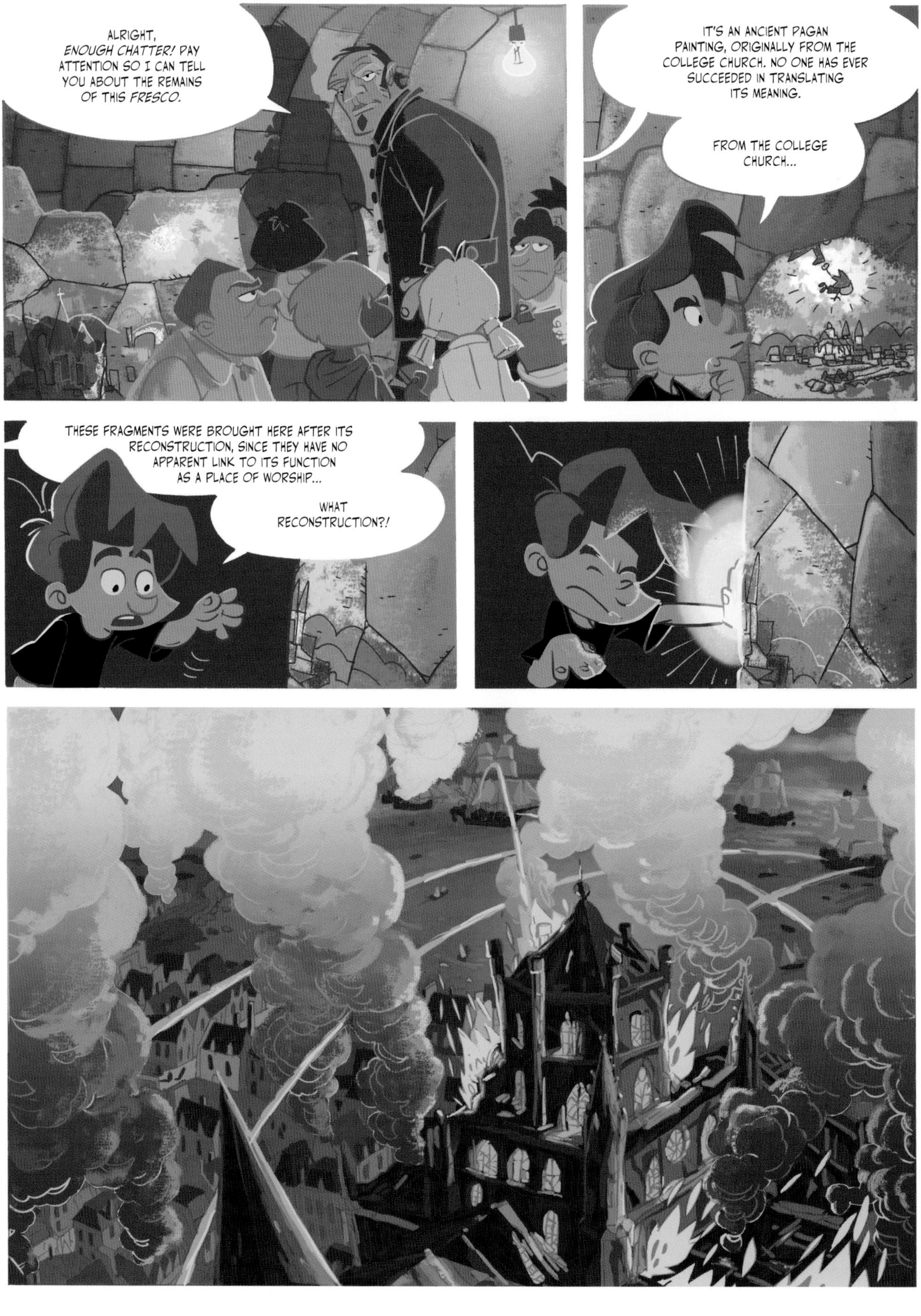
ALRIGHT, *ENOUGH CHATTER!* PAY ATTENTION SO I CAN TELL YOU ABOUT THE REMAINS OF THIS *FRESCO.*
IT'S AN ANCIENT PAGAN PAINTING, ORIGINALLY FROM THE COLLEGE CHURCH. NO ONE HAS EVER SUCCEEDED IN TRANSLATING ITS MEANING.
FROM THE COLLEGE CHURCH...
THESE FRAGMENTS WERE BROUGHT HERE AFTER ITS RECONSTRUCTION, SINCE THEY HAVE NO APPARENT LINK TO ITS FUNCTION AS A PLACE OF WORSHIP...
WHAT RECONSTRUCTION?!

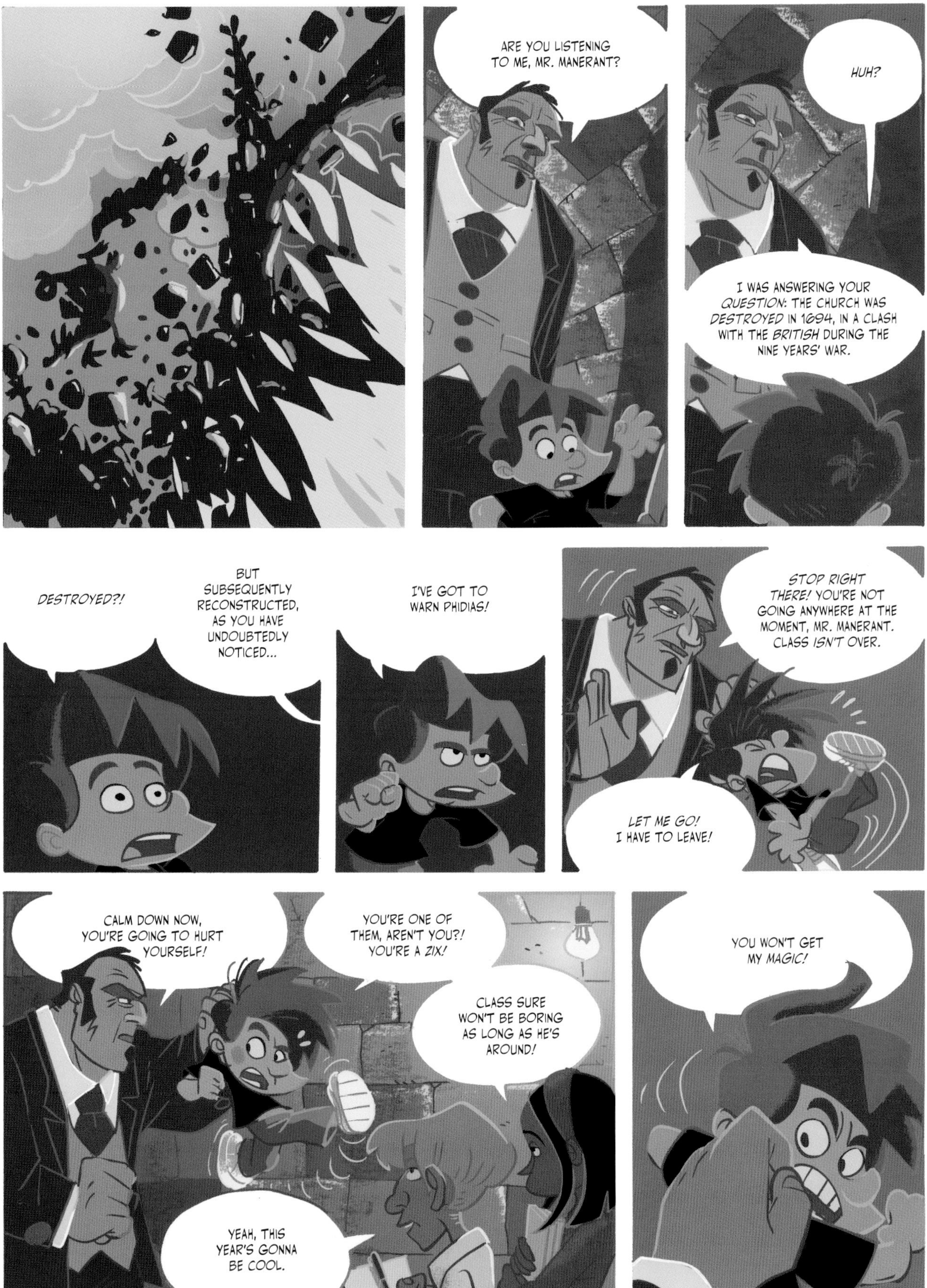
ARE YOU LISTENING TO ME, MR. MANERANT?
HUH?
I WAS ANSWERING YOUR QUESTION: THE CHURCH WAS DESTROYED IN 1694, IN A CLASH WITH THE BRITISH DURING THE NINE YEARS' WAR.
DESTROYED?!
BUT SUBSEQUENTLY RECONSTRUCTED, AS YOU HAVE UNDOUBTEDLY NOTICED...
I'VE GOT TO WARN PHIDIAS!
STOP RIGHT THERE! YOU'RE NOT GOING ANYWHERE AT THE MOMENT, MR. MANERANT. CLASS ISN'T OVER.
LET ME GO! I HAVE TO LEAVE!
CALM DOWN NOW, YOU'RE GOING TO HURT YOURSELF!
YOU'RE ONE OF THEM, AREN'T YOU?! YOU'RE A ZIX!
CLASS SURE WON'T BE BORING AS LONG AS HE'S AROUND!
YEAH, THIS YEAR'S GONNA BE COOL.
YOU WON'T GET MY MAGIC!

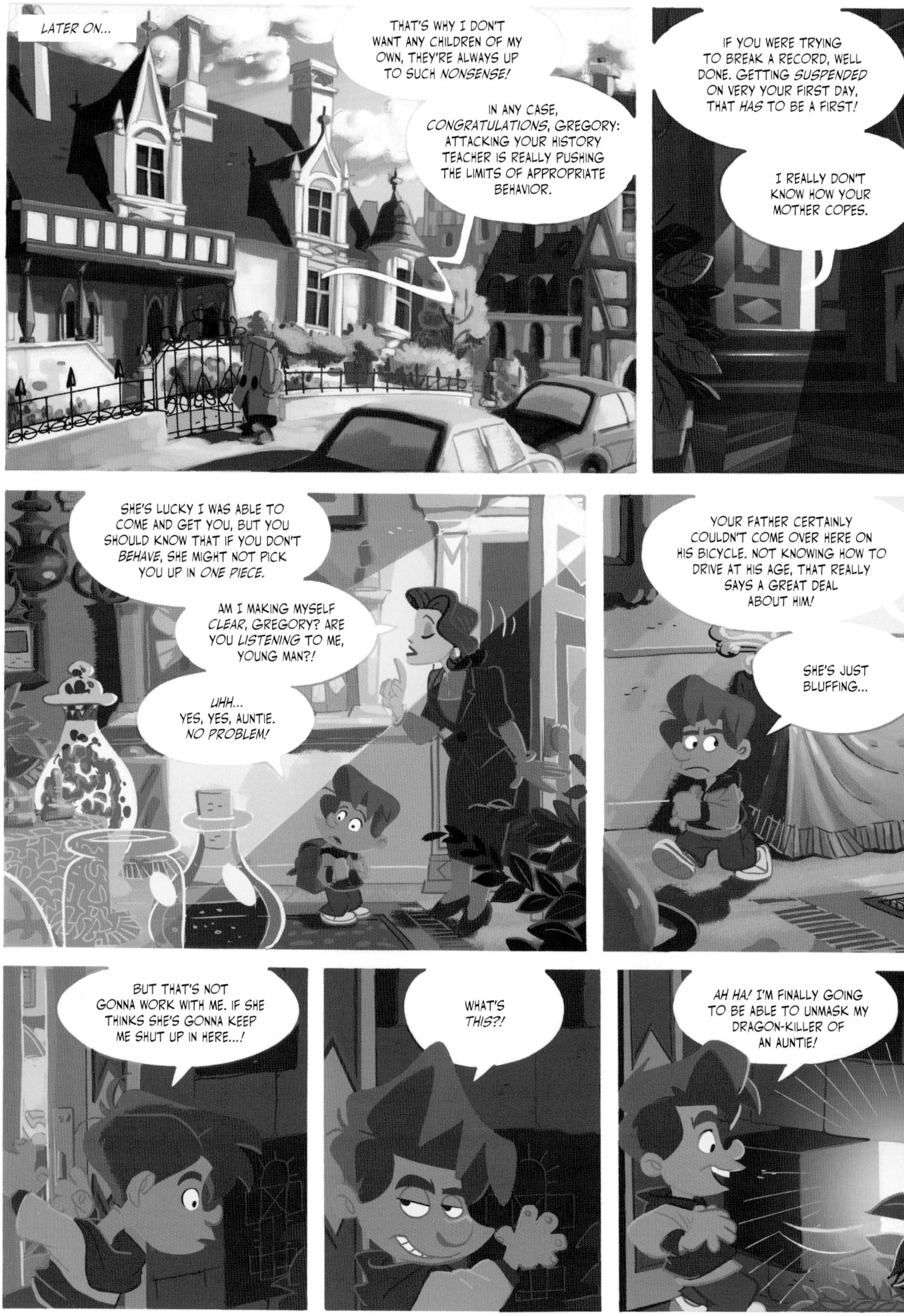
LATER ON...
THAT'S WHY I DON'T WANT ANY CHILDREN OF MY OWN, THEY'RE ALWAYS UP TO SUCH NONSENSE!
IN ANY CASE, CONGRATULATIONS, GREGORY: ATTACKING YOUR HISTORY TEACHER IS REALLY PUSHING THE LIMITS OF APPROPRIATE BEHAVIOR.
IF YOU WERE TRYING TO BREAK A RECORD, WELL DONE. GETTING SUSPENDED ON VERY YOUR FIRST DAY, THAT HAS TO BE A FIRST!
I REALLY DON'T KNOW HOW YOUR MOTHER COPES.
SHE'S LUCKY I WAS ABLE TO COME AND GET YOU, BUT YOU SHOULD KNOW THAT IF YOU DON'T BEHAVE, SHE MIGHT NOT PICK YOU UP IN ONE PIECE.
AM I MAKING MYSELF CLEAR, GREGORY? ARE YOU LISTENING TO ME, YOUNG MAN?!
UHH... YES, YES, AUNTIE. NO PROBLEM!
YOUR FATHER CERTAINLY COULDN'T COME OVER HERE ON HIS BICYCLE. NOT KNOWING HOW TO DRIVE AT HIS AGE, THAT REALLY SAYS A GREAT DEAL ABOUT HIM!
SHE'S JUST BLUFFING...
BUT THAT'S NOT GONNA WORK WITH ME. IF SHE THINKS SHE'S GONNA KEEP ME SHUT UP IN HERE...!
WHAT'S THIS?!
AH HA! I'M FINALLY GOING TO BE ABLE TO UNMASK MY DRAGON-KILLER OF AN AUNTIE!

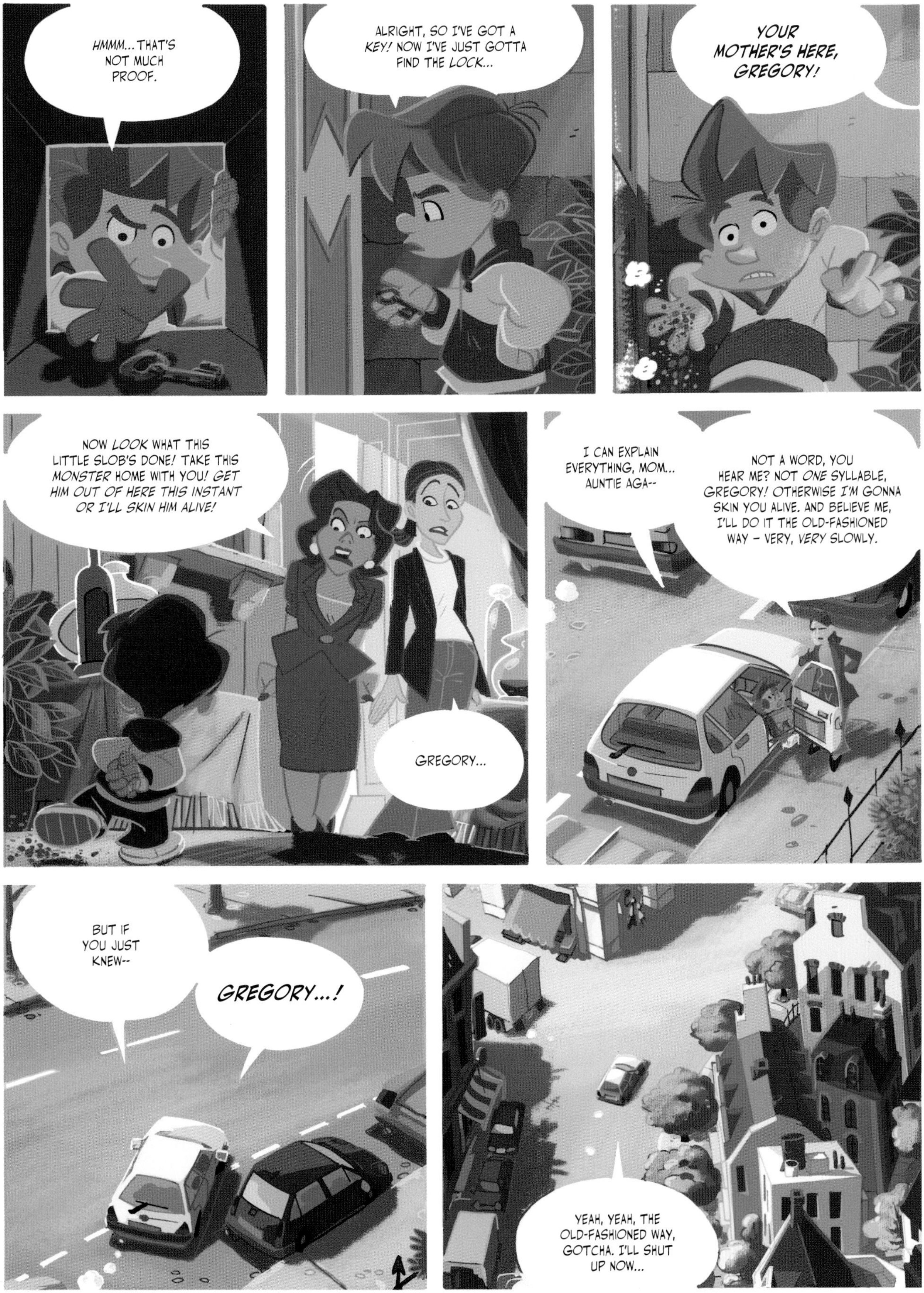
HMMM... THAT'S NOT MUCH PROOF.
ALRIGHT, SO I'VE GOT A KEY! NOW I'VE JUST GOTTA FIND THE LOCK...
YOUR MOTHER'S HERE, GREGORY!
NOW LOOK WHAT THIS LITTLE SLOB'S DONE! TAKE THIS MONSTER HOME WITH YOU! GET HIM OUT OF HERE THIS INSTANT OR I'LL SKIN HIM ALIVE!
GREGORY...
I CAN EXPLAIN EVERYTHING, MOM... AUNTIE AGA--
NOT A WORD, YOU HEAR ME? NOT ONE SYLLABLE, GREGORY! OTHERWISE I'M GONNA SKIN YOU ALIVE. AND BELIEVE ME, I'LL DO IT THE OLD-FASHIONED WAY – VERY, VERY SLOWLY.
BUT IF YOU JUST KNEW--
GREGORY...!
YEAH, YEAH, THE OLD-FASHIONED WAY, GOTCHA. I'LL SHUT UP NOW...

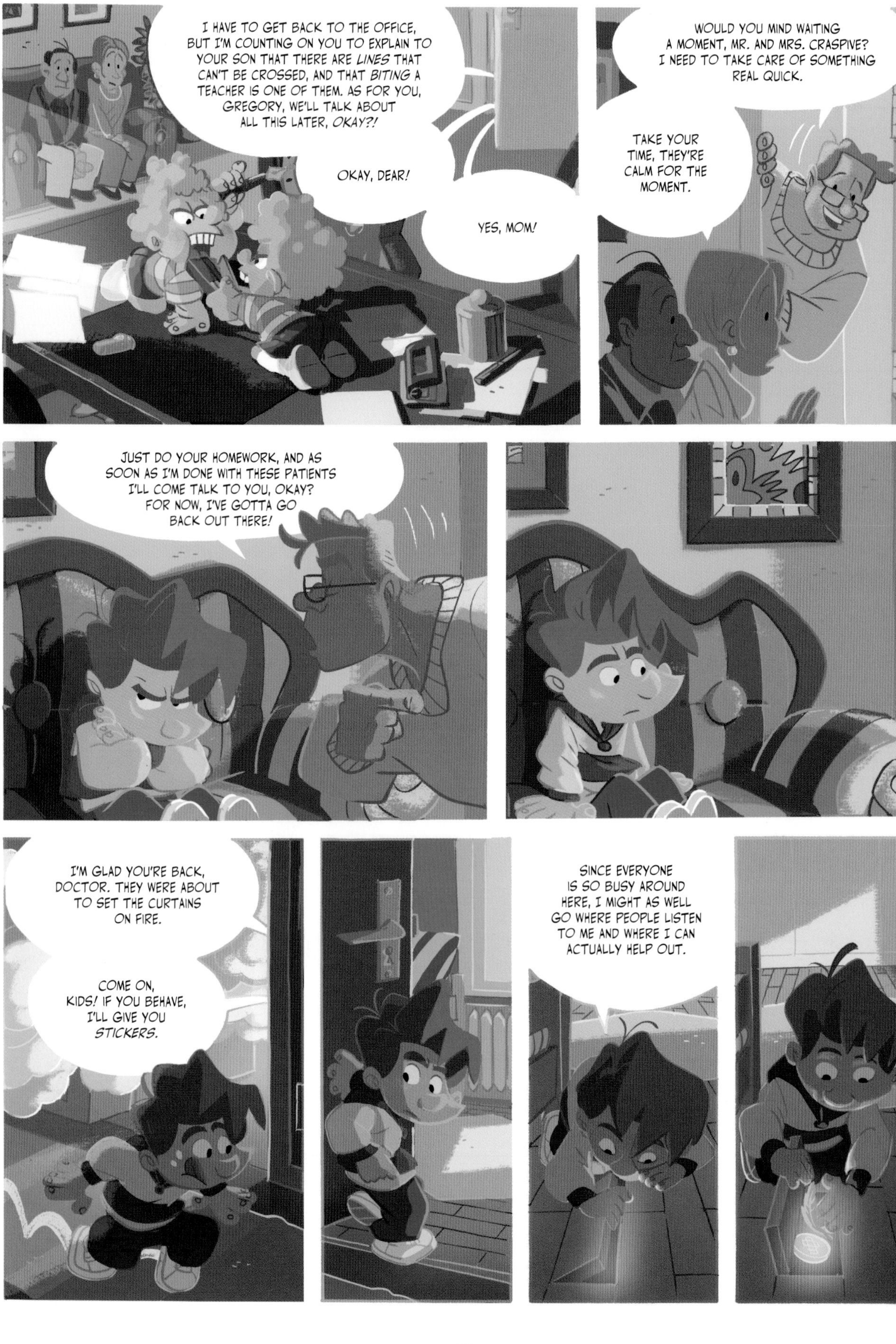
I HAVE TO GET BACK TO THE OFFICE, BUT I'M COUNTING ON YOU TO EXPLAIN TO YOUR SON THAT THERE ARE *LINES* THAT CAN'T BE CROSSED, AND THAT *BITING* A TEACHER IS ONE OF THEM. AS FOR YOU, GREGORY, WE'LL TALK ABOUT ALL THIS LATER, *OKAY?!*
OKAY, DEAR!
YES, MOM!
WOULD YOU MIND WAITING A MOMENT, MR. AND MRS. CRASPIVE? I NEED TO TAKE CARE OF SOMETHING REAL QUICK.
TAKE YOUR TIME, THEY'RE CALM FOR THE MOMENT.
JUST DO YOUR HOMEWORK, AND AS SOON AS I'M DONE WITH THESE PATIENTS I'LL COME TALK TO YOU, OKAY? FOR NOW, I'VE GOTTA GO BACK OUT THERE!
I'M GLAD YOU'RE BACK, DOCTOR. THEY WERE ABOUT TO SET THE CURTAINS ON FIRE.
COME ON, KIDS! IF YOU BEHAVE, I'LL GIVE YOU *STICKERS*.
SINCE EVERYONE IS SO BUSY AROUND HERE, I MIGHT AS WELL GO WHERE PEOPLE LISTEN TO ME AND WHERE I CAN ACTUALLY HELP OUT.

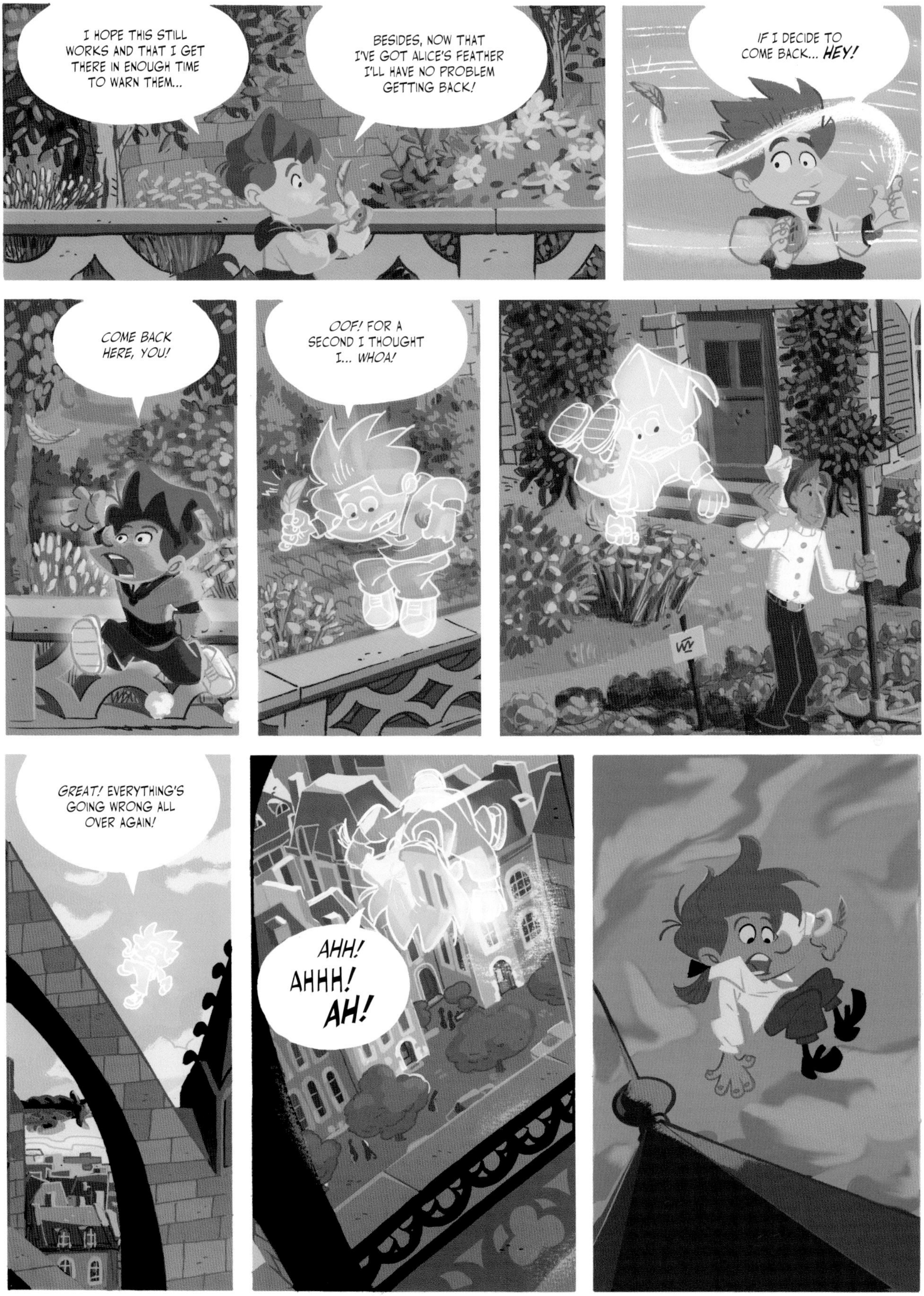
I HOPE THIS STILL WORKS AND THAT I GET THERE IN ENOUGH TIME TO WARN THEM...
BESIDES, NOW THAT I'VE GOT ALICE'S FEATHER I'LL HAVE NO PROBLEM GETTING BACK!
IF I DECIDE TO COME BACK... HEY!
COME BACK HERE, YOU!
OOF! FOR A SECOND I THOUGHT I... WHOA!
GREAT! EVERYTHING'S GOING WRONG ALL OVER AGAIN!
AHH! AHHH! AH!

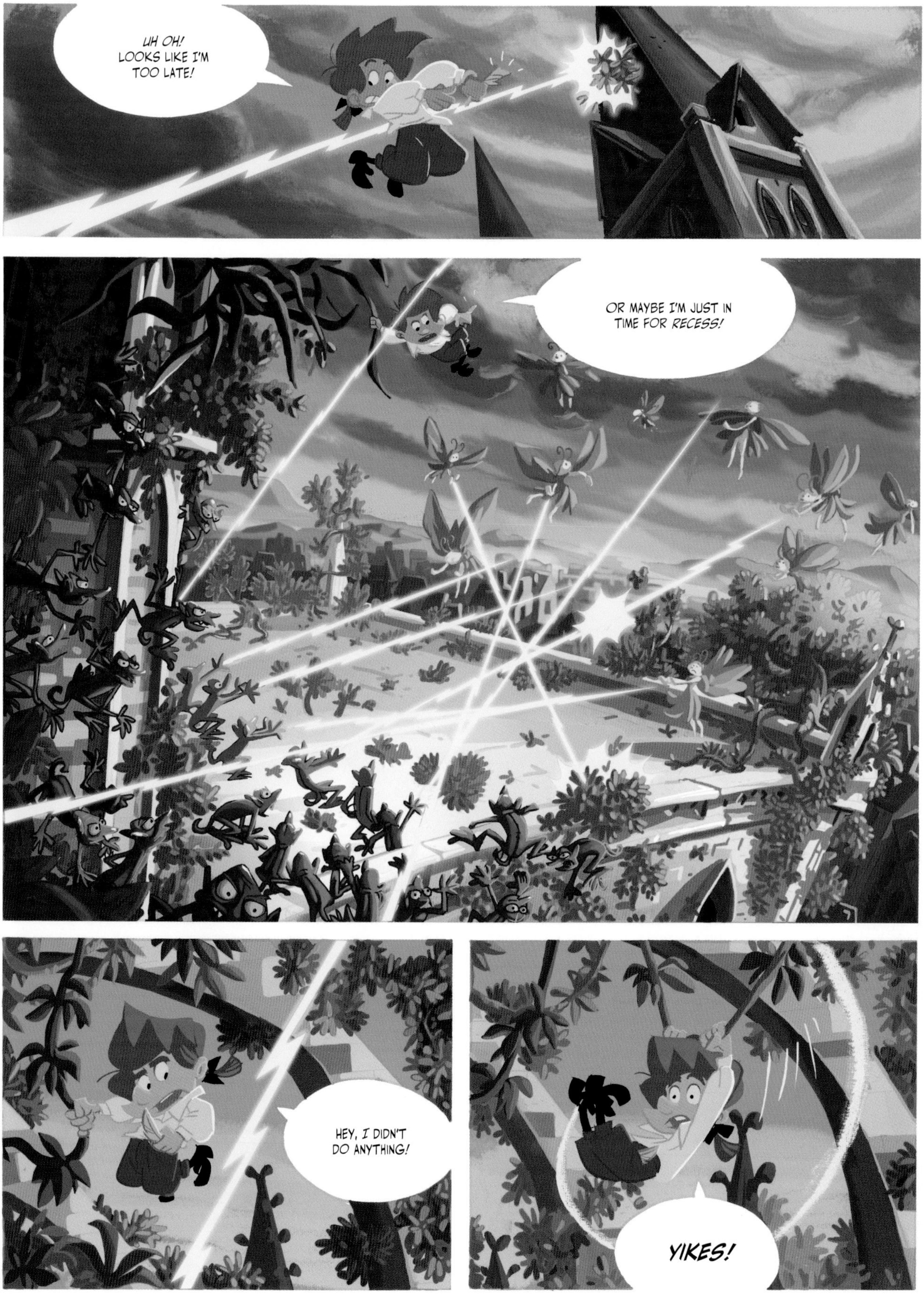
UH OH!
LOOKS LIKE I'M
TOO LATE!
OR MAYBE I'M JUST IN
TIME FOR *RECESS!*
HEY, *I* DIDN'T
DO ANYTHING!
YIKES!

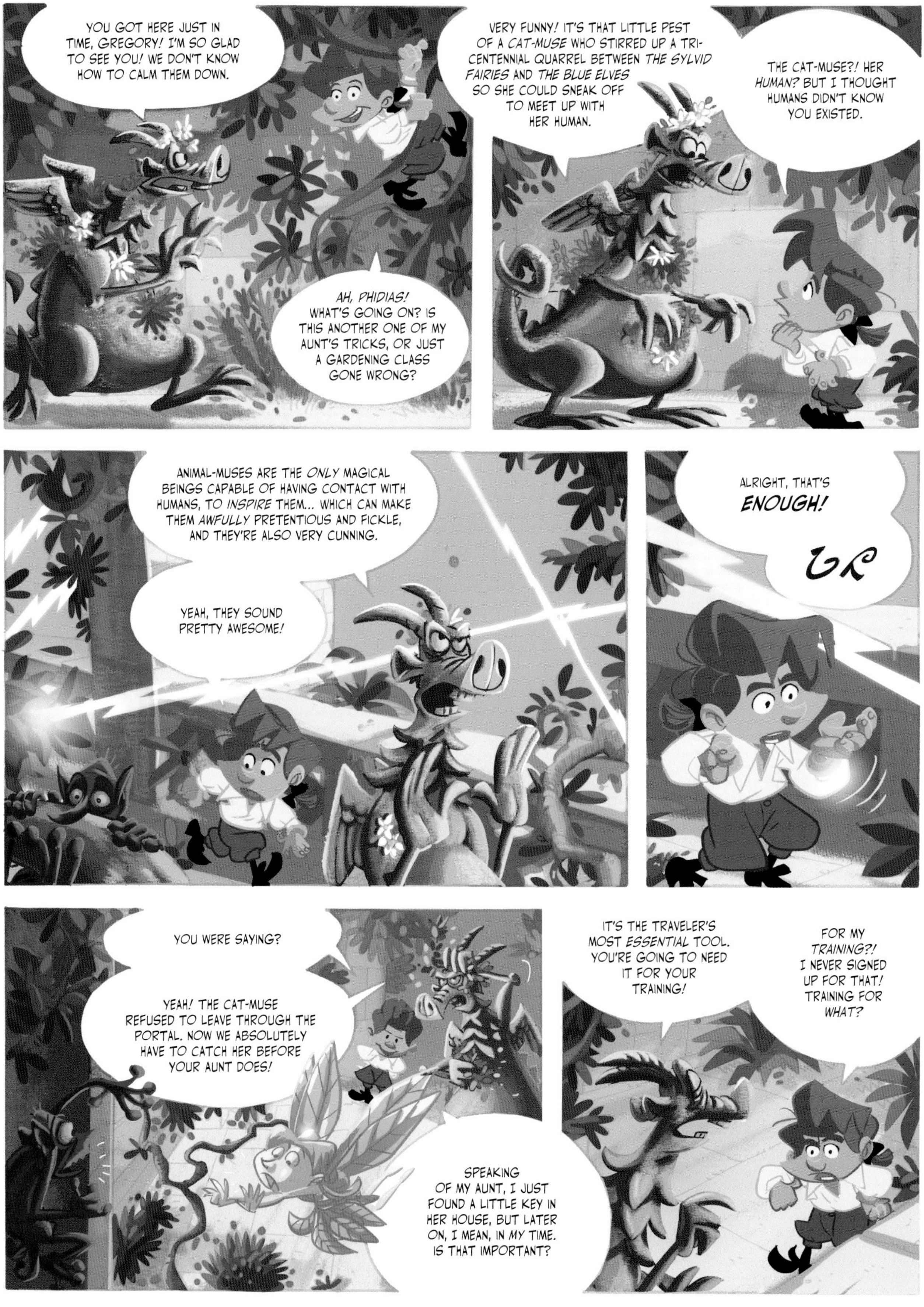

YOU GOT HERE JUST IN TIME, GREGORY! I'M SO GLAD TO SEE YOU! WE DON'T KNOW HOW TO CALM THEM DOWN.
AH, PHIDIAS! WHAT'S GOING ON? IS THIS ANOTHER ONE OF MY AUNT'S TRICKS, OR JUST A GARDENING CLASS GONE WRONG?
VERY FUNNY! IT'S THAT LITTLE PEST OF A CAT-MUSE WHO STIRRED UP A TRI-CENTENNIAL QUARREL BETWEEN THE SYLVID FAIRIES AND THE BLUE ELVES SO SHE COULD SNEAK OFF TO MEET UP WITH HER HUMAN.
THE CAT-MUSE?! HER HUMAN? BUT I THOUGHT HUMANS DIDN'T KNOW YOU EXISTED.
ANIMAL-MUSES ARE THE ONLY MAGICAL BEINGS CAPABLE OF HAVING CONTACT WITH HUMANS, TO INSPIRE THEM... WHICH CAN MAKE THEM AWFULLY PRETENTIOUS AND FICKLE, AND THEY'RE ALSO VERY CUNNING.
YEAH, THEY SOUND PRETTY AWESOME!
ALRIGHT, THAT'S ENOUGH!
YOU WERE SAYING?
YEAH! THE CAT-MUSE REFUSED TO LEAVE THROUGH THE PORTAL. NOW WE ABSOLUTELY HAVE TO CATCH HER BEFORE YOUR AUNT DOES!
SPEAKING OF MY AUNT, I JUST FOUND A LITTLE KEY IN HER HOUSE, BUT LATER ON, I MEAN, IN MY TIME. IS THAT IMPORTANT?
IT'S THE TRAVELER'S MOST ESSENTIAL TOOL. YOU'RE GOING TO NEED IT FOR YOUR TRAINING!
FOR MY TRAINING?! I NEVER SIGNED UP FOR THAT! TRAINING FOR WHAT?

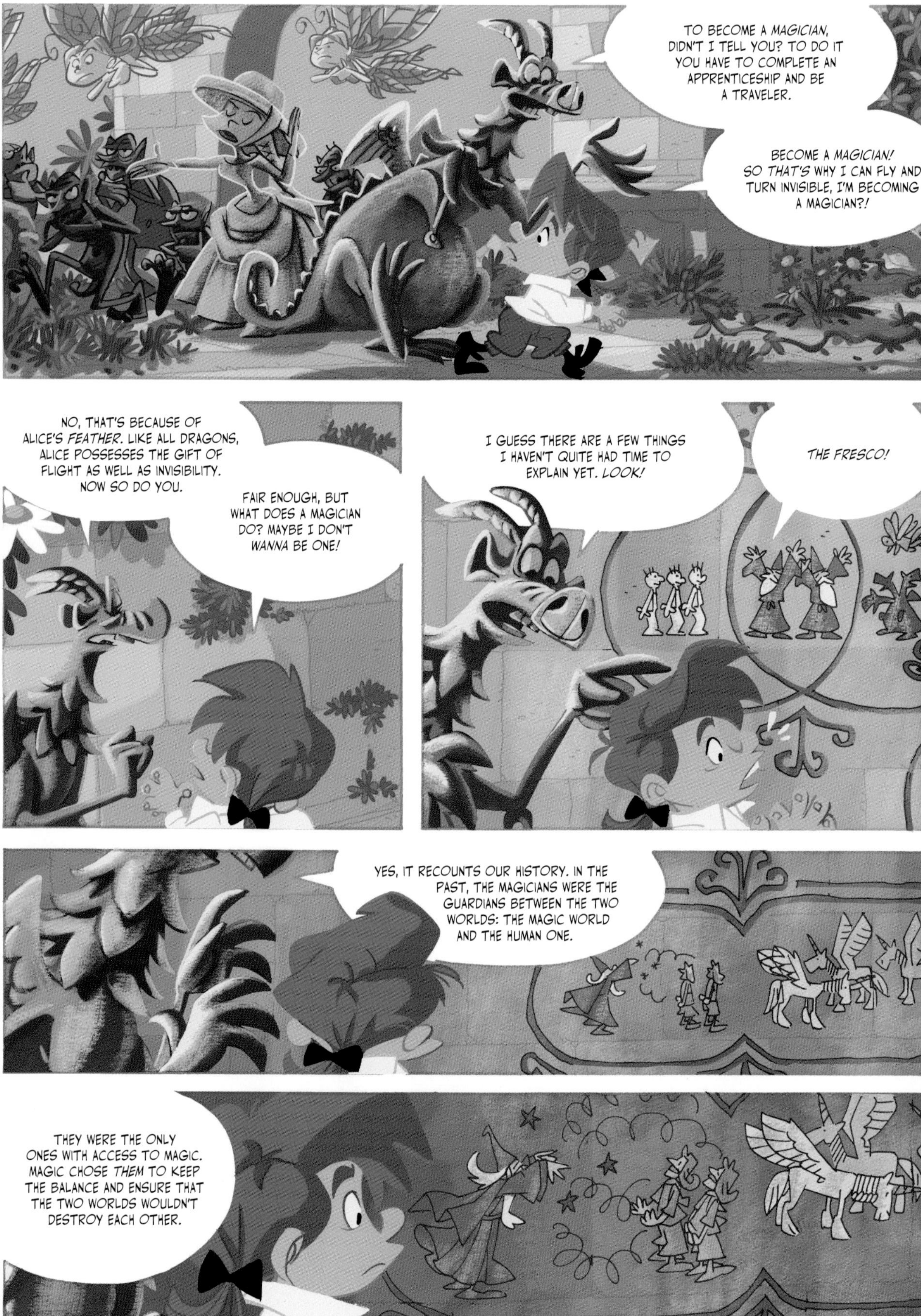

TO BECOME A *MAGICIAN*, DIDN'T I TELL YOU? TO DO IT YOU HAVE TO COMPLETE AN APPRENTICESHIP AND BE A TRAVELER.
BECOME A *MAGICIAN!* SO *THAT'S* WHY I CAN FLY AND TURN INVISIBLE, I'M BECOMING A MAGICIAN?!
NO, THAT'S BECAUSE OF ALICE'S *FEATHER*. LIKE ALL DRAGONS, ALICE POSSESSES THE GIFT OF FLIGHT AS WELL AS INVISIBILITY. NOW SO DO YOU.
FAIR ENOUGH, BUT WHAT DOES A MAGICIAN DO? MAYBE I DON'T *WANNA* BE ONE!
I GUESS THERE ARE A FEW THINGS I HAVEN'T QUITE HAD TIME TO EXPLAIN YET. *LOOK!*
THE FRESCO!
YES, IT RECOUNTS OUR HISTORY. IN THE PAST, THE MAGICIANS WERE THE GUARDIANS BETWEEN THE TWO WORLDS: THE MAGIC WORLD AND THE HUMAN ONE.
THEY WERE THE ONLY ONES WITH ACCESS TO MAGIC. MAGIC CHOSE *THEM* TO KEEP THE BALANCE AND ENSURE THAT THE TWO WORLDS WOULDN'T DESTROY EACH OTHER.

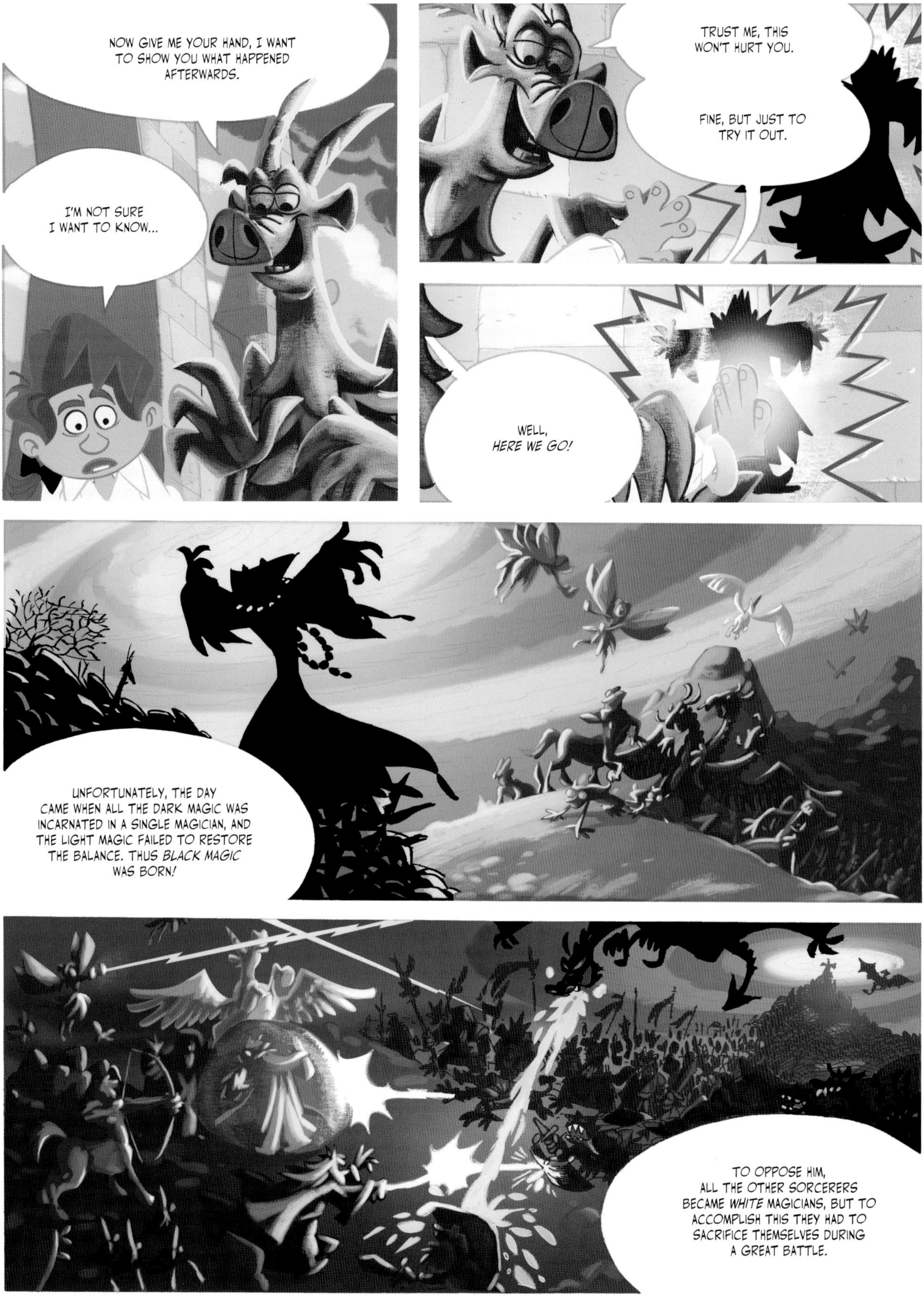
NOW GIVE ME YOUR HAND, I WANT TO SHOW YOU WHAT HAPPENED AFTERWARDS.
I'M NOT SURE I WANT TO KNOW...
TRUST ME, THIS WON'T HURT YOU.
FINE, BUT JUST TO TRY IT OUT.
WELL, *HERE WE GO!*
UNFORTUNATELY, THE DAY CAME WHEN ALL THE DARK MAGIC WAS INCARNATED IN A SINGLE MAGICIAN, AND THE LIGHT MAGIC FAILED TO RESTORE THE BALANCE. THUS *BLACK MAGIC* WAS BORN!
TO OPPOSE HIM, ALL THE OTHER SORCERERS BECAME *WHITE* MAGICIANS, BUT TO ACCOMPLISH THIS THEY HAD TO SACRIFICE THEMSELVES DURING A GREAT BATTLE.

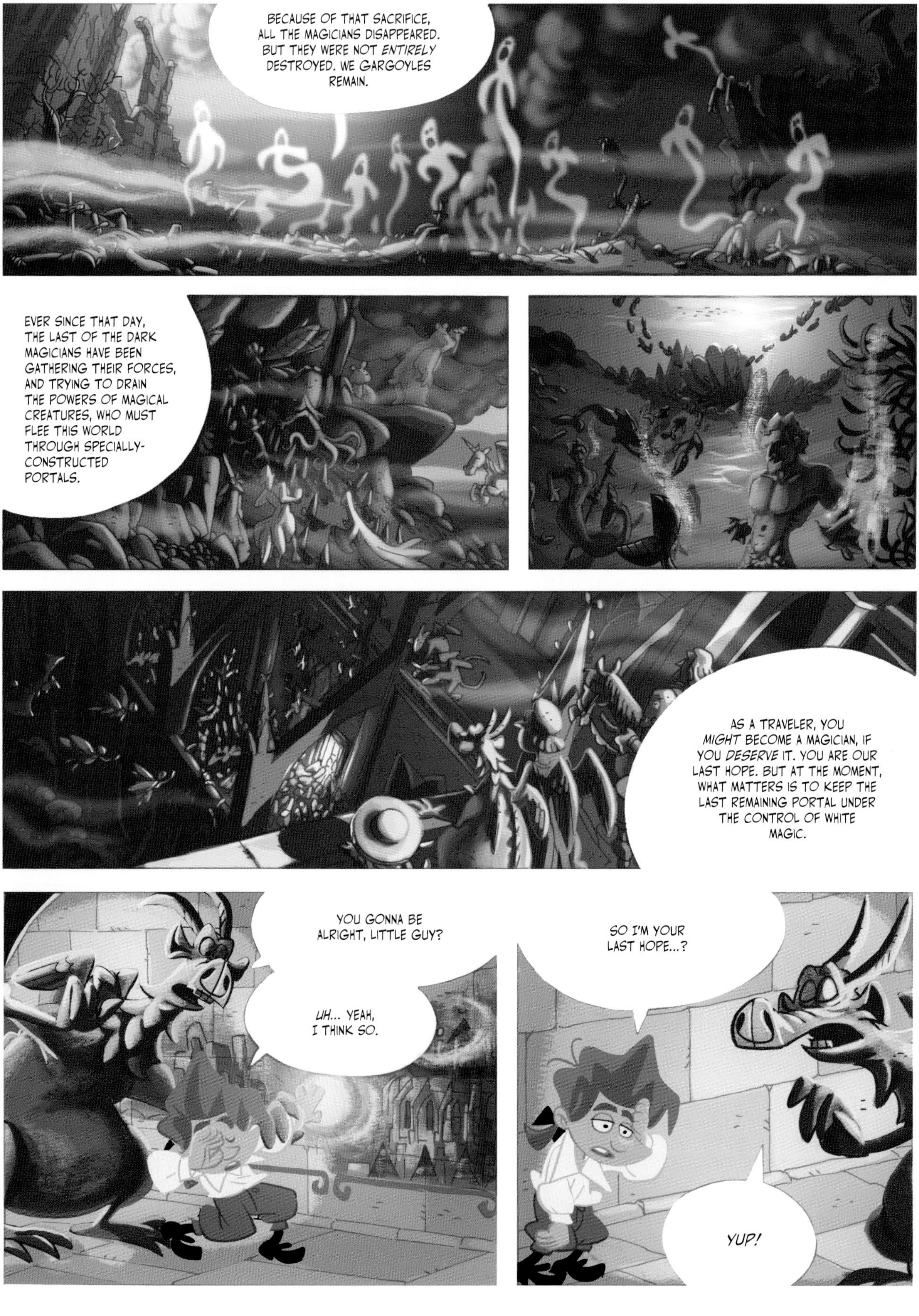
BECAUSE OF THAT SACRIFICE, ALL THE MAGICIANS DISAPPEARED. BUT THEY WERE NOT *ENTIRELY* DESTROYED. WE GARGOYLES REMAIN.
EVER SINCE THAT DAY, THE LAST OF THE DARK MAGICIANS HAVE BEEN GATHERING THEIR FORCES, AND TRYING TO DRAIN THE POWERS OF MAGICAL CREATURES, WHO MUST FLEE THIS WORLD THROUGH SPECIALLY-CONSTRUCTED PORTALS.
AS A TRAVELER, YOU *MIGHT* BECOME A MAGICIAN, IF YOU *DESERVE* IT. YOU ARE OUR LAST HOPE. BUT AT THE MOMENT, WHAT MATTERS IS TO KEEP THE LAST REMAINING PORTAL UNDER THE CONTROL OF WHITE MAGIC.
YOU GONNA BE ALRIGHT, LITTLE GUY?
UH... YEAH, I THINK SO.
SO I'M YOUR LAST HOPE...?
YUP!

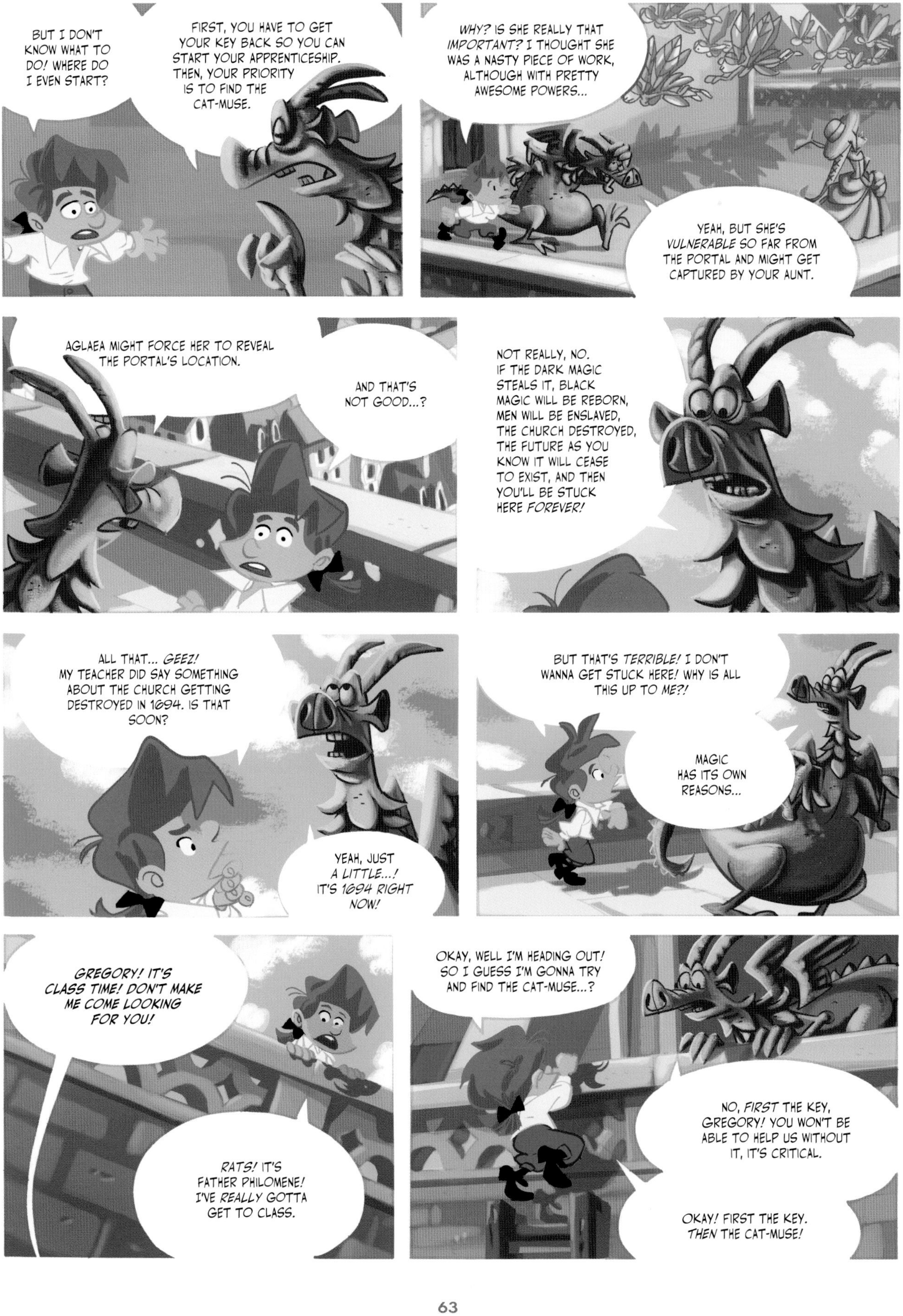

BUT I DON'T KNOW WHAT TO DO! WHERE DO I EVEN START?
FIRST, YOU HAVE TO GET YOUR KEY BACK SO YOU CAN START YOUR APPRENTICESHIP. THEN, YOUR PRIORITY IS TO FIND THE CAT-MUSE.
WHY? IS SHE REALLY THAT IMPORTANT? I THOUGHT SHE WAS A NASTY PIECE OF WORK, ALTHOUGH WITH PRETTY AWESOME POWERS...
YEAH, BUT SHE'S VULNERABLE SO FAR FROM THE PORTAL AND MIGHT GET CAPTURED BY YOUR AUNT.
AGLAEA MIGHT FORCE HER TO REVEAL THE PORTAL'S LOCATION.
AND THAT'S NOT GOOD...?
NOT REALLY, NO. IF THE DARK MAGIC STEALS IT, BLACK MAGIC WILL BE REBORN, MEN WILL BE ENSLAVED, THE CHURCH DESTROYED, THE FUTURE AS YOU KNOW IT WILL CEASE TO EXIST, AND THEN YOU'LL BE STUCK HERE FOREVER!
ALL THAT... GEEZ! MY TEACHER DID SAY SOMETHING ABOUT THE CHURCH GETTING DESTROYED IN 1694. IS THAT SOON?
YEAH, JUST A LITTLE...! IT'S 1694 RIGHT NOW!
BUT THAT'S TERRIBLE! I DON'T WANNA GET STUCK HERE! WHY IS ALL THIS UP TO ME?!
MAGIC HAS ITS OWN REASONS...
GREGORY! IT'S CLASS TIME! DON'T MAKE ME COME LOOKING FOR YOU!
RATS! IT'S FATHER PHILOMENE! I'VE REALLY GOTTA GET TO CLASS.
OKAY, WELL I'M HEADING OUT! SO I GUESS I'M GONNA TRY AND FIND THE CAT-MUSE...?
NO, FIRST THE KEY, GREGORY! YOU WON'T BE ABLE TO HELP US WITHOUT IT, IT'S CRITICAL.
OKAY! FIRST THE KEY. THEN THE CAT-MUSE!

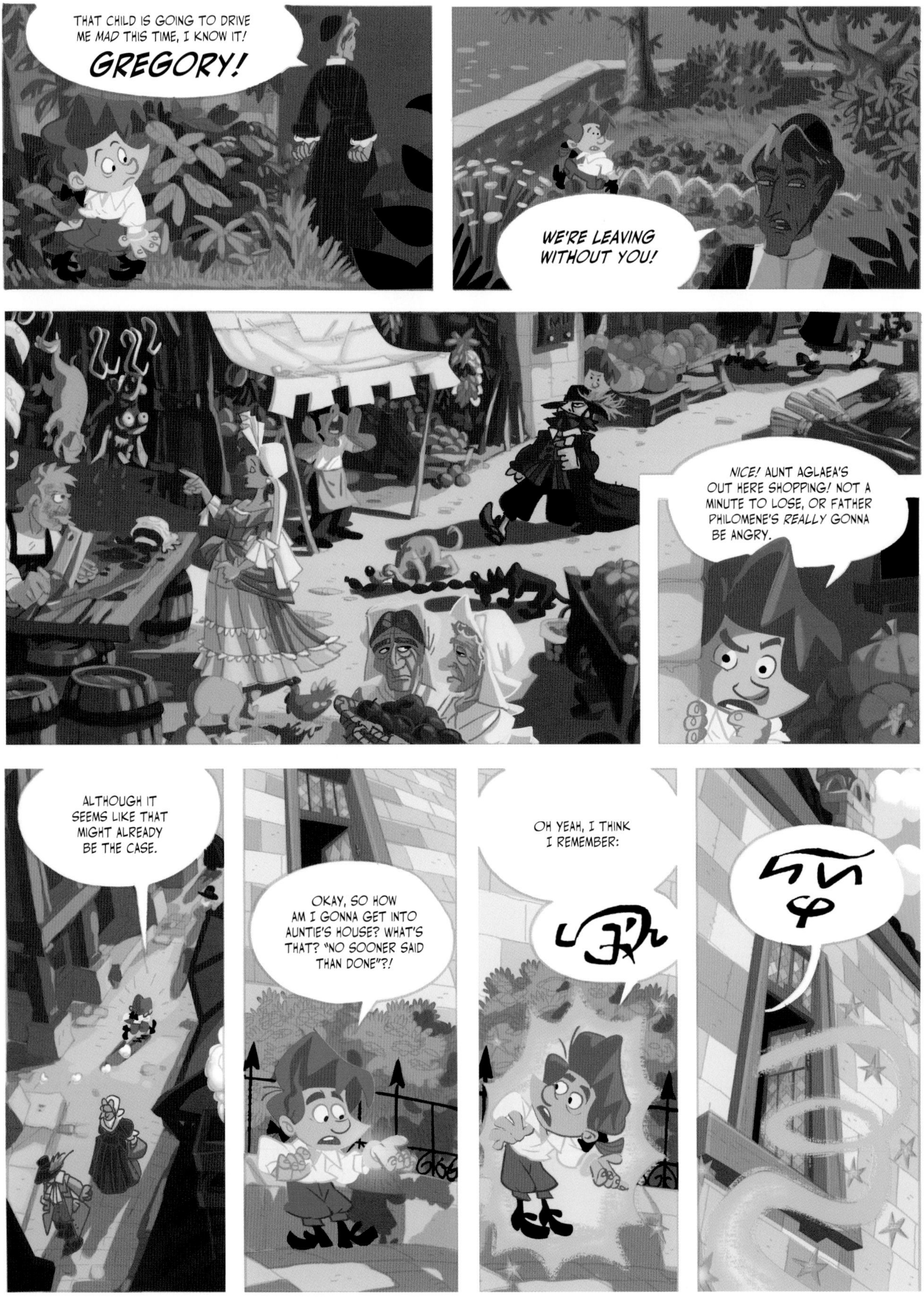
THAT CHILD IS GOING TO DRIVE ME MAD THIS TIME, I KNOW IT!
GREGORY!
WE'RE LEAVING WITHOUT YOU!
NICE! AUNT AGLAEA'S OUT HERE SHOPPING! NOT A MINUTE TO LOSE, OR FATHER PHILOMENE'S REALLY GONNA BE ANGRY.
ALTHOUGH IT SEEMS LIKE THAT MIGHT ALREADY BE THE CASE.
OKAY, SO HOW AM I GONNA GET INTO AUNTIE'S HOUSE? WHAT'S THAT? "NO SOONER SAID THAN DONE"?!
OH YEAH, I THINK I REMEMBER:

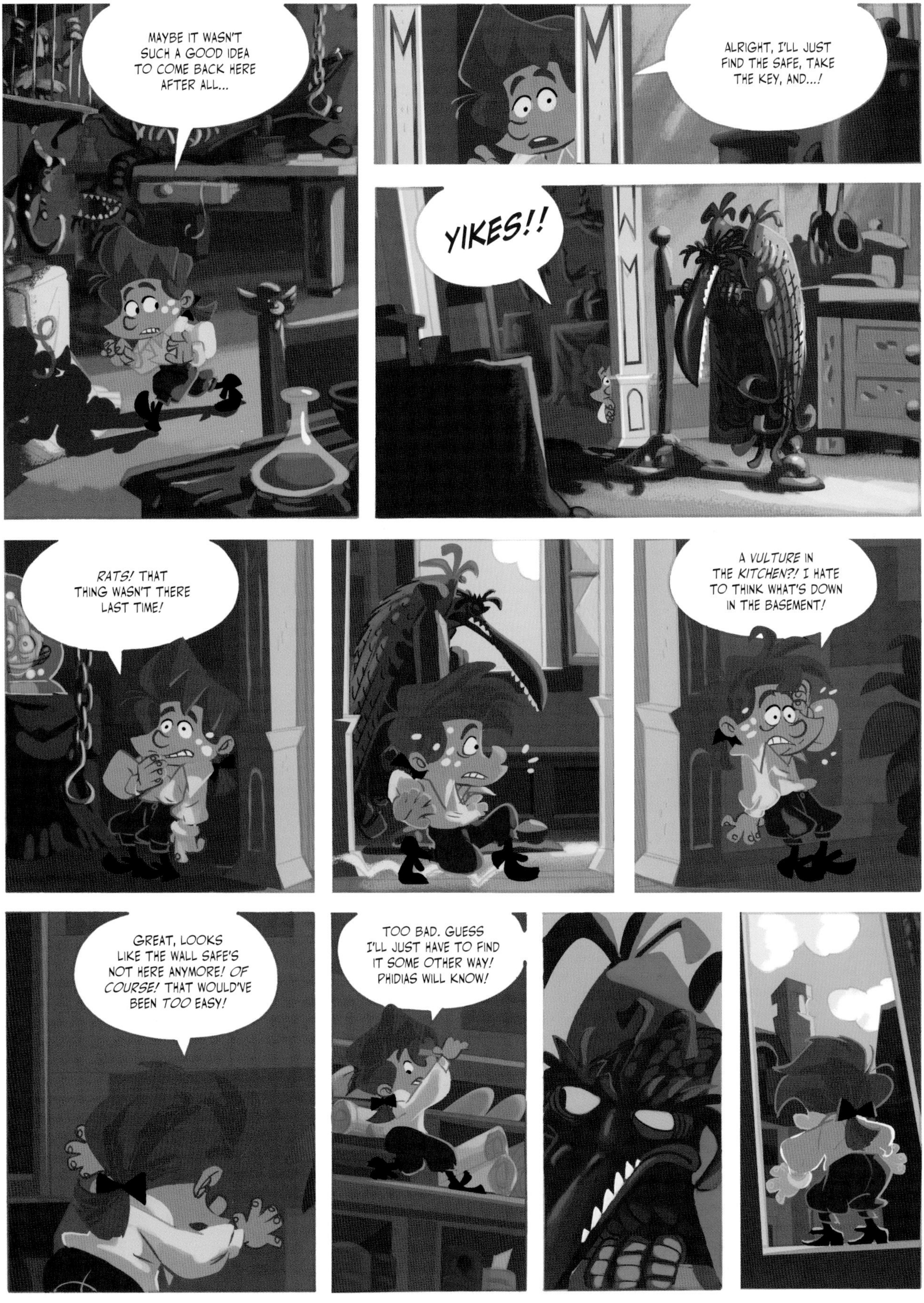
MAYBE IT WASN'T SUCH A GOOD IDEA TO COME BACK HERE AFTER ALL...
ALRIGHT, I'LL JUST FIND THE SAFE, TAKE THE KEY, AND...!
YIKES!!
RATS! THAT THING WASN'T THERE LAST TIME!
A *VULTURE* IN THE *KITCHEN?!* I HATE TO THINK WHAT'S DOWN IN THE BASEMENT!
GREAT, LOOKS LIKE THE WALL SAFE'S NOT HERE ANYMORE! *OF COURSE!* THAT WOULD'VE BEEN *TOO* EASY!
TOO BAD. GUESS I'LL JUST HAVE TO FIND IT SOME OTHER WAY! PHIDIAS WILL KNOW!

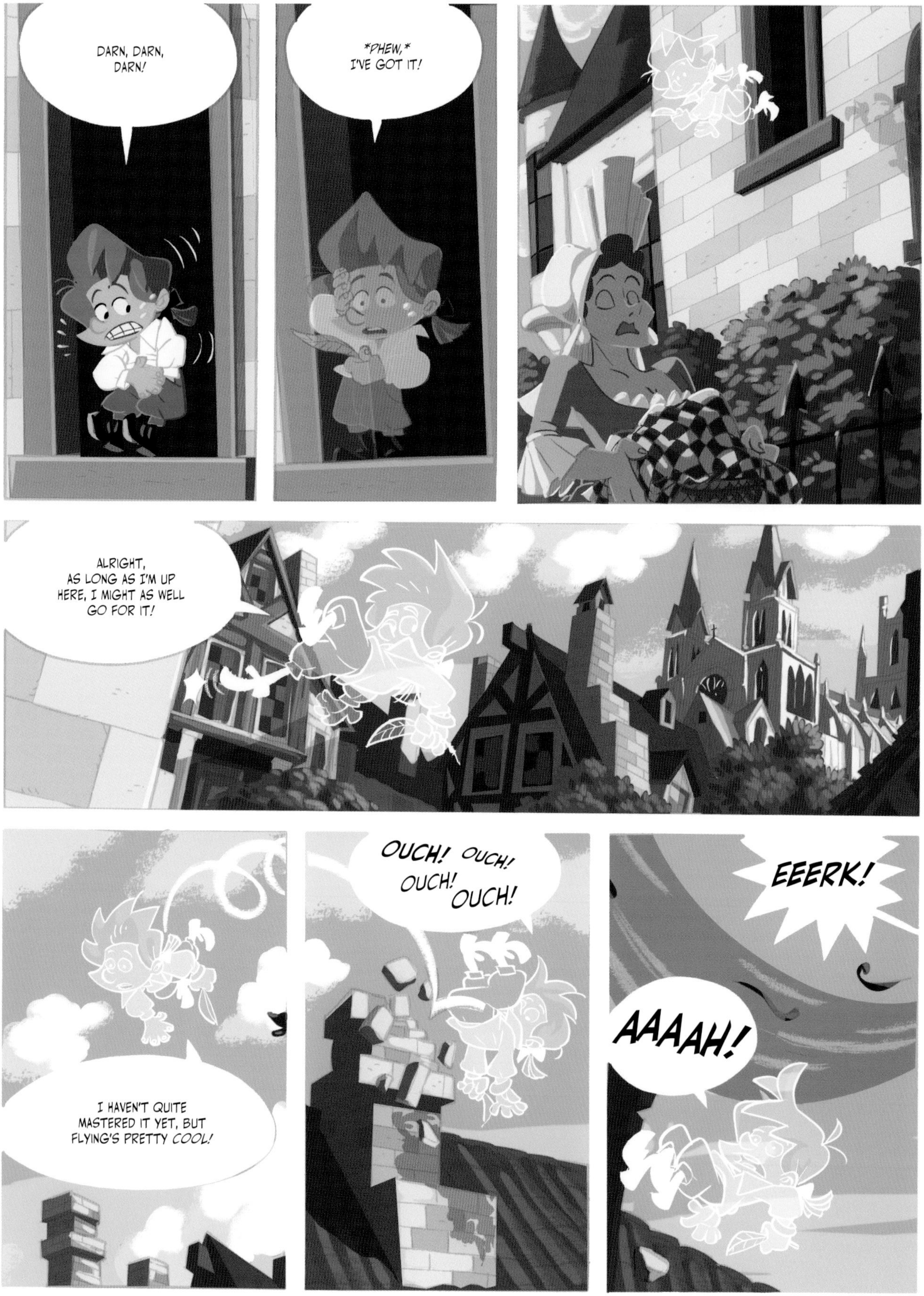
DARN, DARN, DARN!
PHEW, I'VE GOT IT!
ALRIGHT, AS LONG AS I'M UP HERE, I MIGHT AS WELL GO FOR IT!
I HAVEN'T QUITE MASTERED IT YET, BUT FLYING'S PRETTY COOL!
OUCH! OUCH! OUCH! OUCH!
EEERK!
AAAAH!

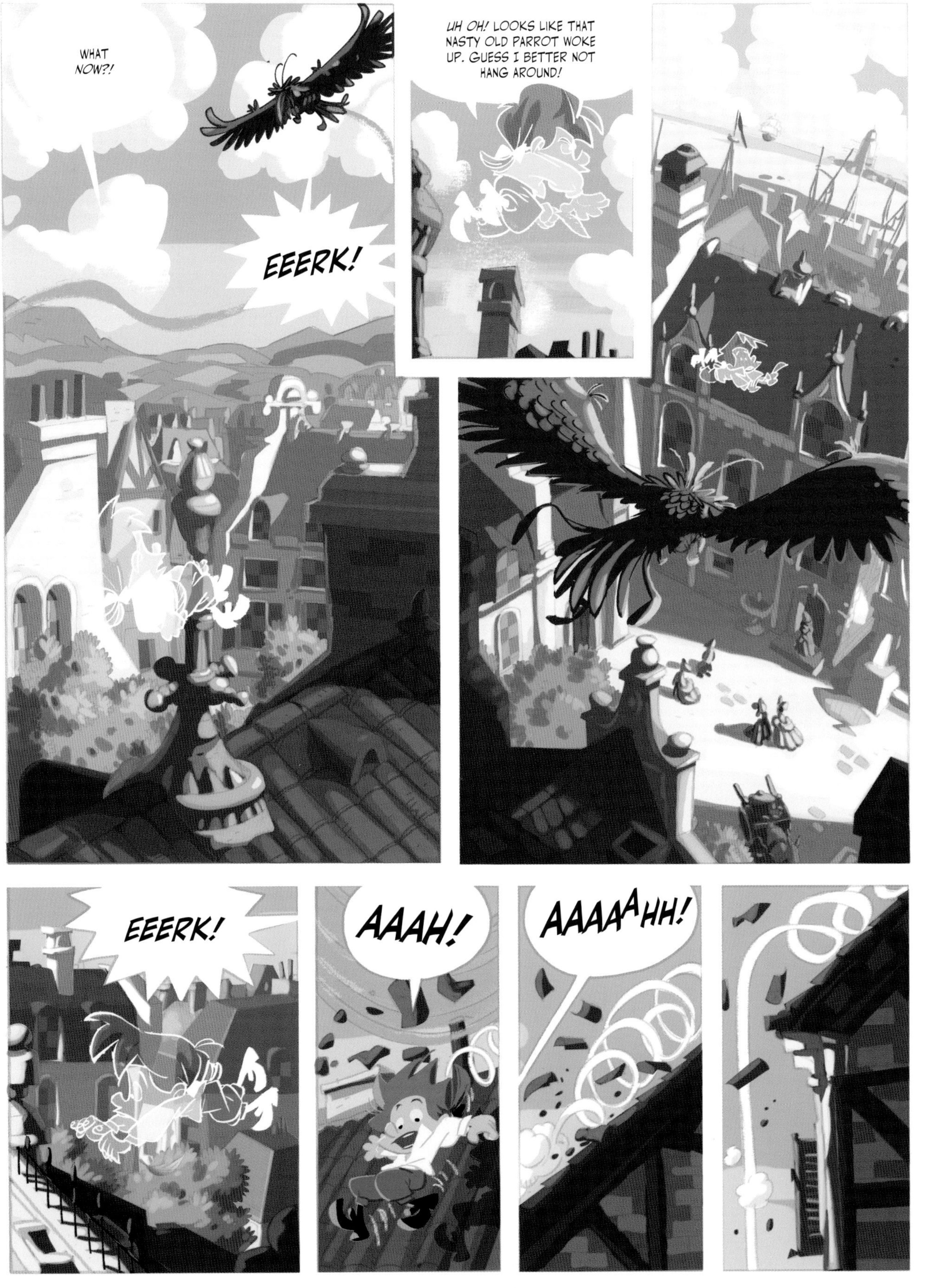
WHAT NOW?!
EEERK!
UH OH! LOOKS LIKE THAT NASTY OLD PARROT WOKE UP. GUESS I BETTER NOT HANG AROUND!
EEERK!
AAAH!
AAAAAHH!

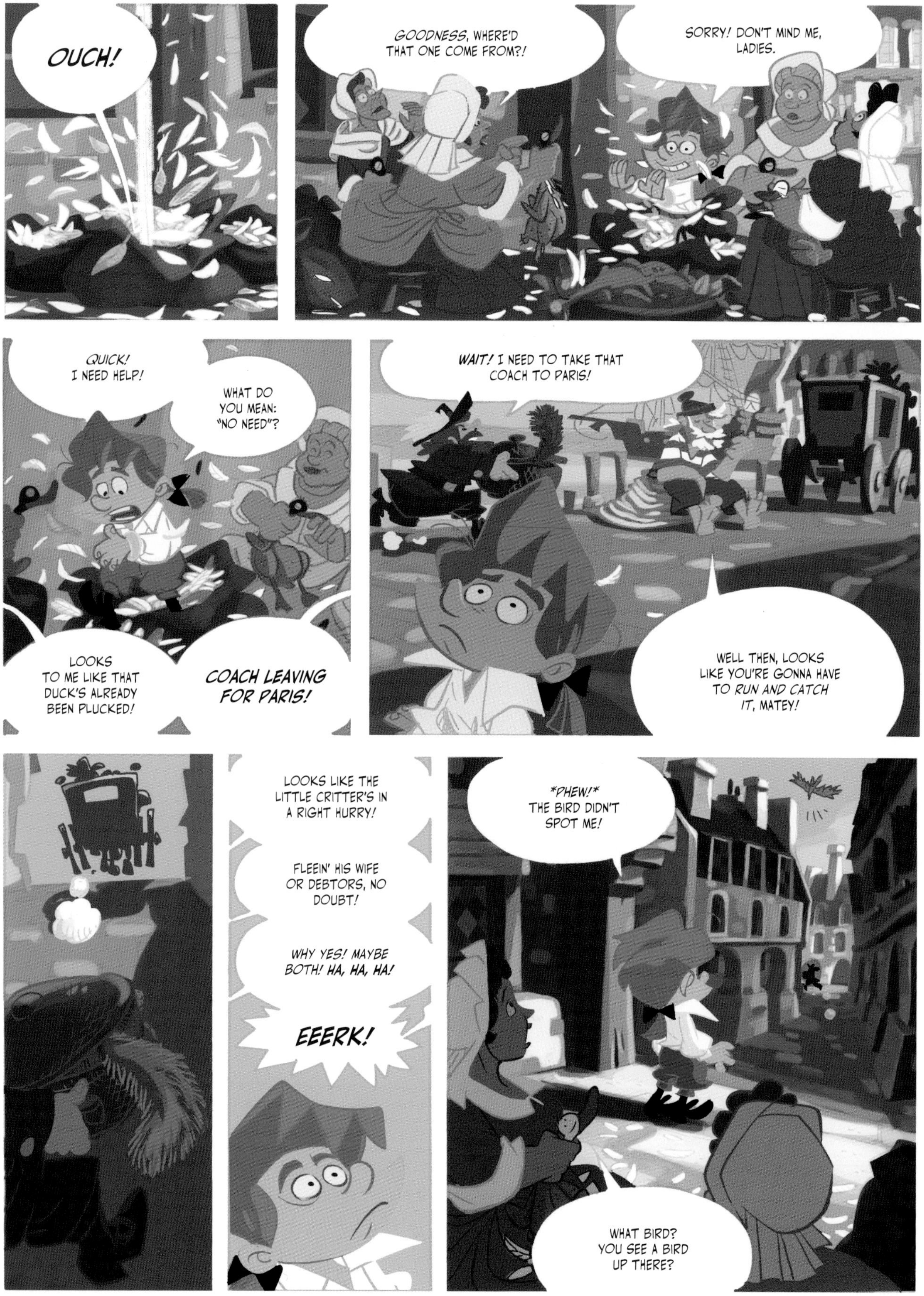

OUCH!
GOODNESS, WHERE'D THAT ONE COME FROM?!
SORRY! DON'T MIND ME, LADIES.
QUICK! I NEED HELP!
WHAT DO YOU MEAN: "NO NEED"?
LOOKS TO ME LIKE THAT DUCK'S ALREADY BEEN PLUCKED!
COACH LEAVING FOR PARIS!
WAIT! I NEED TO TAKE THAT COACH TO PARIS!
WELL THEN, LOOKS LIKE YOU'RE GONNA HAVE TO RUN AND CATCH IT, MATEY!
LOOKS LIKE THE LITTLE CRITTER'S IN A RIGHT HURRY!
FLEEIN' HIS WIFE OR DEBTORS, NO DOUBT!
WHY YES! MAYBE BOTH! HA, HA, HA!
EEERK!
PHEW! THE BIRD DIDN'T SPOT ME!
WHAT BIRD? YOU SEE A BIRD UP THERE?

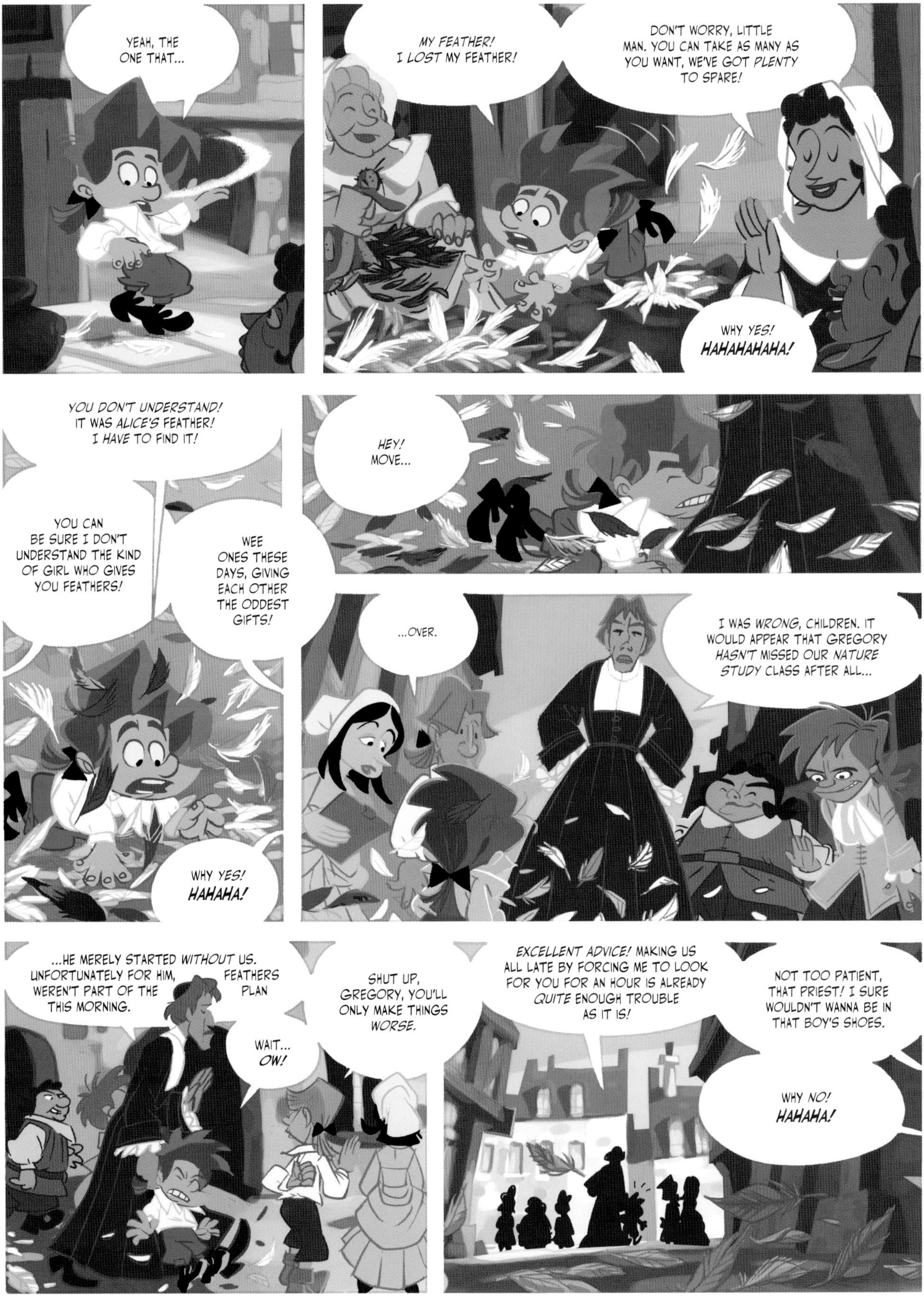
YEAH, THE ONE THAT...
MY FEATHER! I LOST MY FEATHER!
DON'T WORRY, LITTLE MAN. YOU CAN TAKE AS MANY AS YOU WANT, WE'VE GOT PLENTY TO SPARE!
WHY YES! HAHAHAHAHA!
YOU DON'T UNDERSTAND! IT WAS ALICE'S FEATHER! I HAVE TO FIND IT!
YOU CAN BE SURE I DON'T UNDERSTAND THE KIND OF GIRL WHO GIVES YOU FEATHERS!
WEE ONES THESE DAYS, GIVING EACH OTHER THE ODDEST GIFTS!
WHY YES! HAHAHA!
HEY! MOVE...
...OVER.
I WAS WRONG, CHILDREN. IT WOULD APPEAR THAT GREGORY HASN'T MISSED OUR NATURE STUDY CLASS AFTER ALL...
...HE MERELY STARTED WITHOUT US. UNFORTUNATELY FOR HIM, FEATHERS WEREN'T PART OF THE PLAN THIS MORNING.
SHUT UP, GREGORY, YOU'LL ONLY MAKE THINGS WORSE.
WAIT... OW!
EXCELLENT ADVICE! MAKING US ALL LATE BY FORCING ME TO LOOK FOR YOU FOR AN HOUR IS ALREADY QUITE ENOUGH TROUBLE AS IT IS!
NOT TOO PATIENT, THAT PRIEST! I SURE WOULDN'T WANNA BE IN THAT BOY'S SHOES.
WHY NO! HAHAHA!

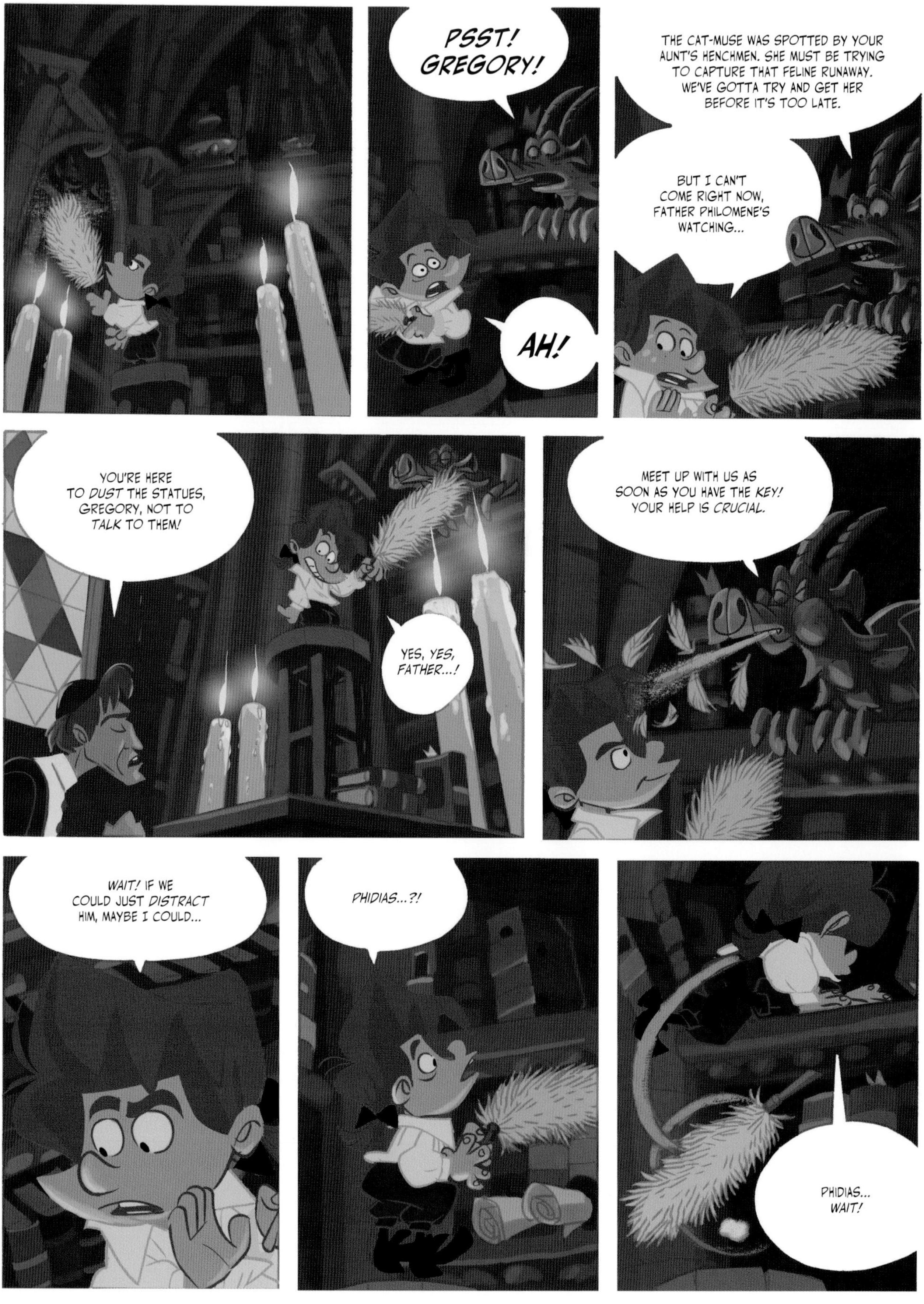
PSST! GREGORY!
AH!
THE CAT-MUSE WAS SPOTTED BY YOUR AUNT'S HENCHMEN. SHE MUST BE TRYING TO CAPTURE THAT FELINE RUNAWAY. WE'VE GOTTA TRY AND GET HER BEFORE IT'S TOO LATE.
BUT I CAN'T COME RIGHT NOW, FATHER PHILOMENE'S WATCHING...
YOU'RE HERE TO *DUST* THE STATUES, GREGORY, NOT TO *TALK* TO THEM!
YES, YES, FATHER...!
MEET UP WITH US AS SOON AS YOU HAVE THE *KEY!* YOUR HELP IS *CRUCIAL.*
WAIT! IF WE COULD JUST *DISTRACT* HIM, MAYBE I COULD...
PHIDIAS...?!
PHIDIAS... *WAIT!*

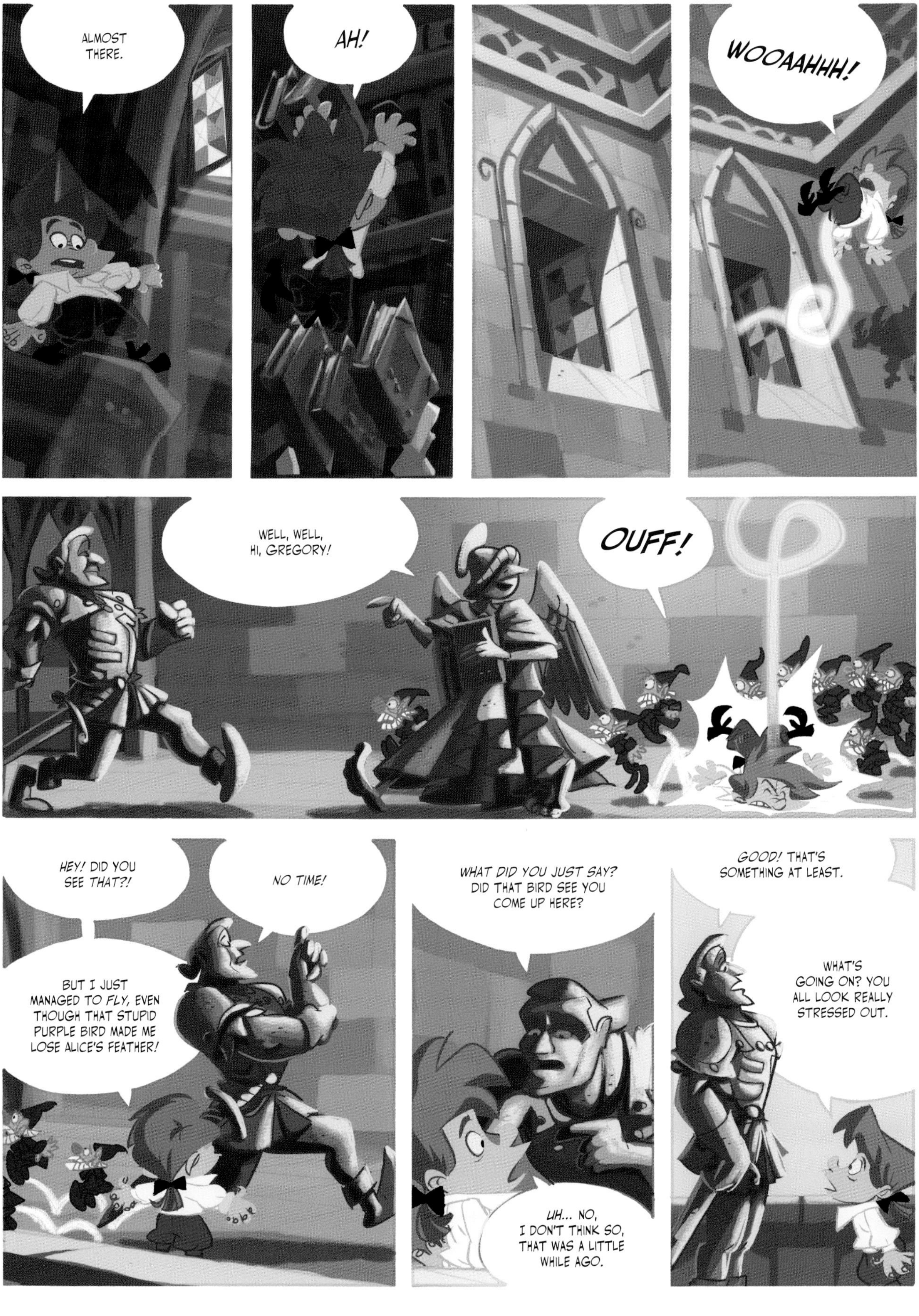
ALMOST THERE.
AH!
WOOAAHHH!
WELL, WELL, HI, GREGORY!
OUFF!
HEY! DID YOU SEE THAT?!
NO TIME!
BUT I JUST MANAGED TO FLY, EVEN THOUGH THAT STUPID PURPLE BIRD MADE ME LOSE ALICE'S FEATHER!
WHAT DID YOU JUST SAY? DID THAT BIRD SEE YOU COME UP HERE?
UH... NO, I DON'T THINK SO, THAT WAS A LITTLE WHILE AGO.
GOOD! THAT'S SOMETHING AT LEAST.
WHAT'S GOING ON? YOU ALL LOOK REALLY STRESSED OUT.

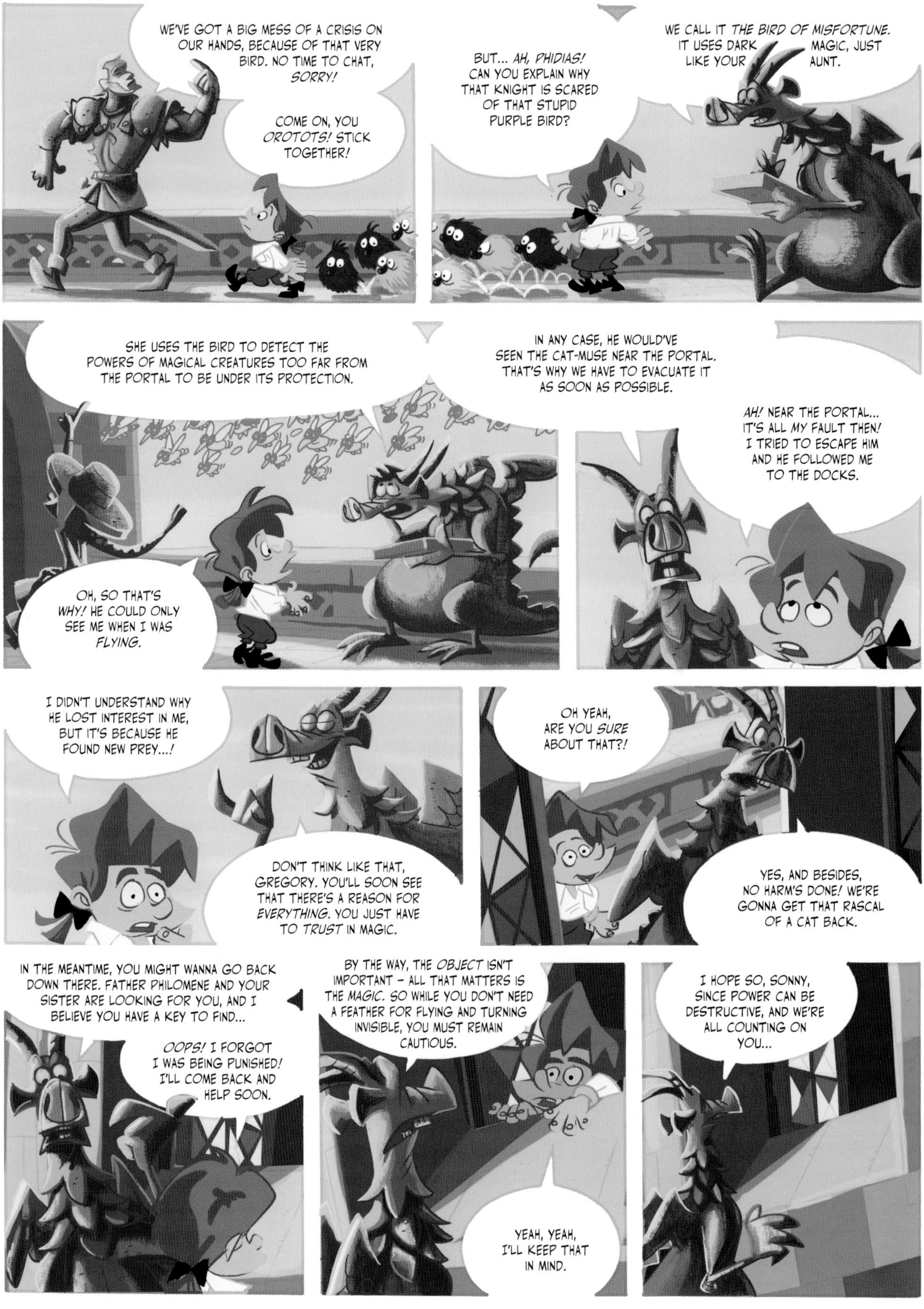
WE'VE GOT A BIG MESS OF A CRISIS ON OUR HANDS, BECAUSE OF THAT VERY BIRD. NO TIME TO CHAT, SORRY!
COME ON, YOU OROTOTS! STICK TOGETHER!
BUT... AH, PHIDIAS! CAN YOU EXPLAIN WHY THAT KNIGHT IS SCARED OF THAT STUPID PURPLE BIRD?
WE CALL IT THE BIRD OF MISFORTUNE. IT USES DARK MAGIC, JUST LIKE YOUR AUNT.
SHE USES THE BIRD TO DETECT THE POWERS OF MAGICAL CREATURES TOO FAR FROM THE PORTAL TO BE UNDER ITS PROTECTION.
IN ANY CASE, HE WOULD'VE SEEN THE CAT-MUSE NEAR THE PORTAL. THAT'S WHY WE HAVE TO EVACUATE IT AS SOON AS POSSIBLE.
OH, SO THAT'S WHY! HE COULD ONLY SEE ME WHEN I WAS FLYING.
AH! NEAR THE PORTAL... IT'S ALL MY FAULT THEN! I TRIED TO ESCAPE HIM AND HE FOLLOWED ME TO THE DOCKS.
I DIDN'T UNDERSTAND WHY HE LOST INTEREST IN ME, BUT IT'S BECAUSE HE FOUND NEW PREY...!
DON'T THINK LIKE THAT, GREGORY. YOU'LL SOON SEE THAT THERE'S A REASON FOR EVERYTHING. YOU JUST HAVE TO TRUST IN MAGIC.
OH YEAH, ARE YOU SURE ABOUT THAT?!
YES, AND BESIDES, NO HARM'S DONE! WE'RE GONNA GET THAT RASCAL OF A CAT BACK.
IN THE MEANTIME, YOU MIGHT WANNA GO BACK DOWN THERE. FATHER PHILOMENE AND YOUR SISTER ARE LOOKING FOR YOU, AND I BELIEVE YOU HAVE A KEY TO FIND...
OOPS! I FORGOT I WAS BEING PUNISHED! I'LL COME BACK AND HELP SOON.
BY THE WAY, THE OBJECT ISN'T IMPORTANT – ALL THAT MATTERS IS THE MAGIC. SO WHILE YOU DON'T NEED A FEATHER FOR FLYING AND TURNING INVISIBLE, YOU MUST REMAIN CAUTIOUS.
YEAH, YEAH, I'LL KEEP THAT IN MIND.
I HOPE SO, SONNY, SINCE POWER CAN BE DESTRUCTIVE, AND WE'RE ALL COUNTING ON YOU...

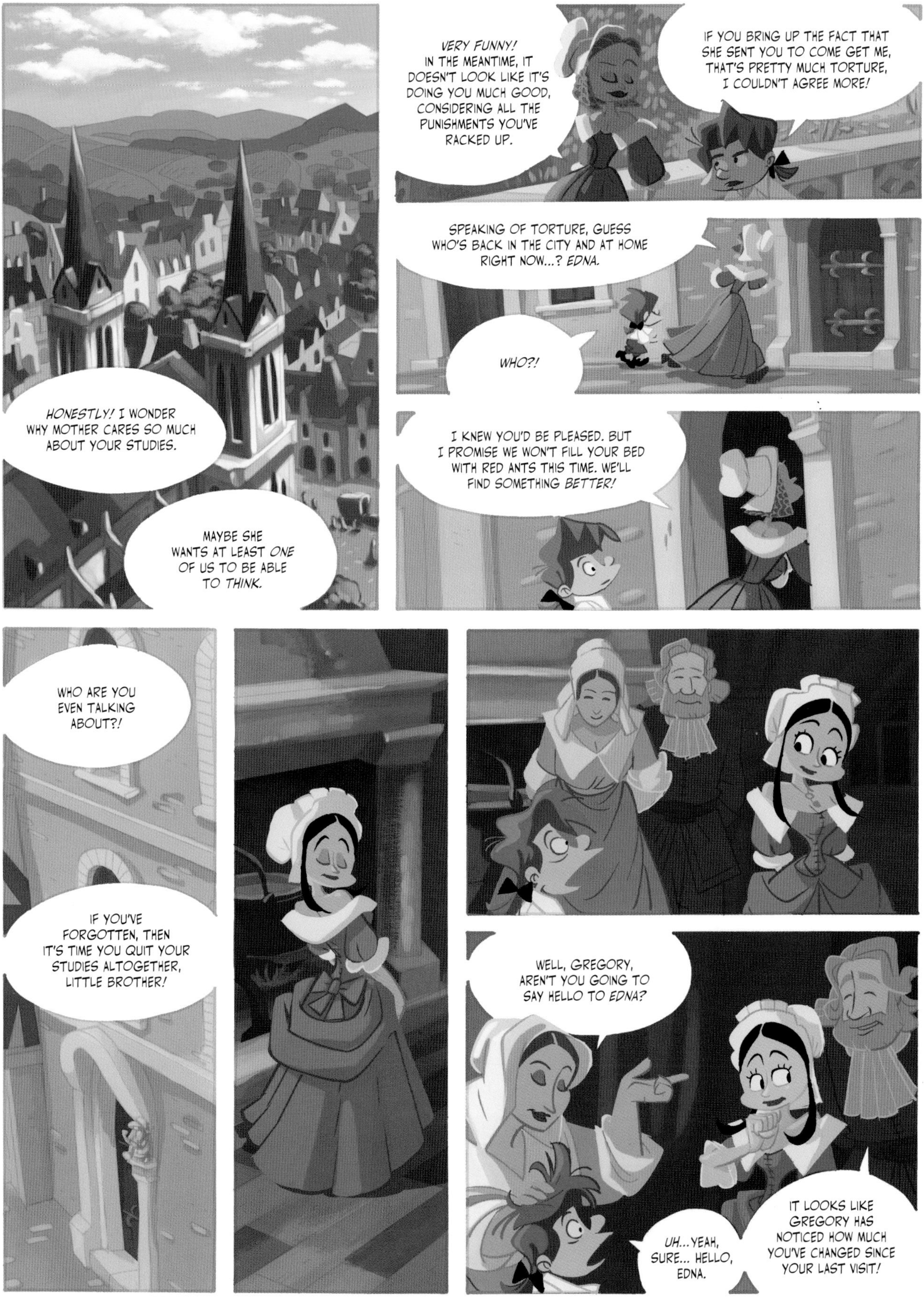
HONESTLY! I WONDER WHY MOTHER CARES SO MUCH ABOUT YOUR STUDIES.
MAYBE SHE WANTS AT LEAST ONE OF US TO BE ABLE TO THINK.
VERY FUNNY! IN THE MEANTIME, IT DOESN'T LOOK LIKE IT'S DOING YOU MUCH GOOD, CONSIDERING ALL THE PUNISHMENTS YOU'VE RACKED UP.
IF YOU BRING UP THE FACT THAT SHE SENT YOU TO COME GET ME, THAT'S PRETTY MUCH TORTURE, I COULDN'T AGREE MORE!
SPEAKING OF TORTURE, GUESS WHO'S BACK IN THE CITY AND AT HOME RIGHT NOW...? EDNA.
WHO?!
I KNEW YOU'D BE PLEASED. BUT I PROMISE WE WON'T FILL YOUR BED WITH RED ANTS THIS TIME. WE'LL FIND SOMETHING BETTER!
WHO ARE YOU EVEN TALKING ABOUT?!
IF YOU'VE FORGOTTEN, THEN IT'S TIME YOU QUIT YOUR STUDIES ALTOGETHER, LITTLE BROTHER!
WELL, GREGORY, AREN'T YOU GOING TO SAY HELLO TO EDNA?
UH...YEAH, SURE... HELLO, EDNA.
IT LOOKS LIKE GREGORY HAS NOTICED HOW MUCH YOU'VE CHANGED SINCE YOUR LAST VISIT!

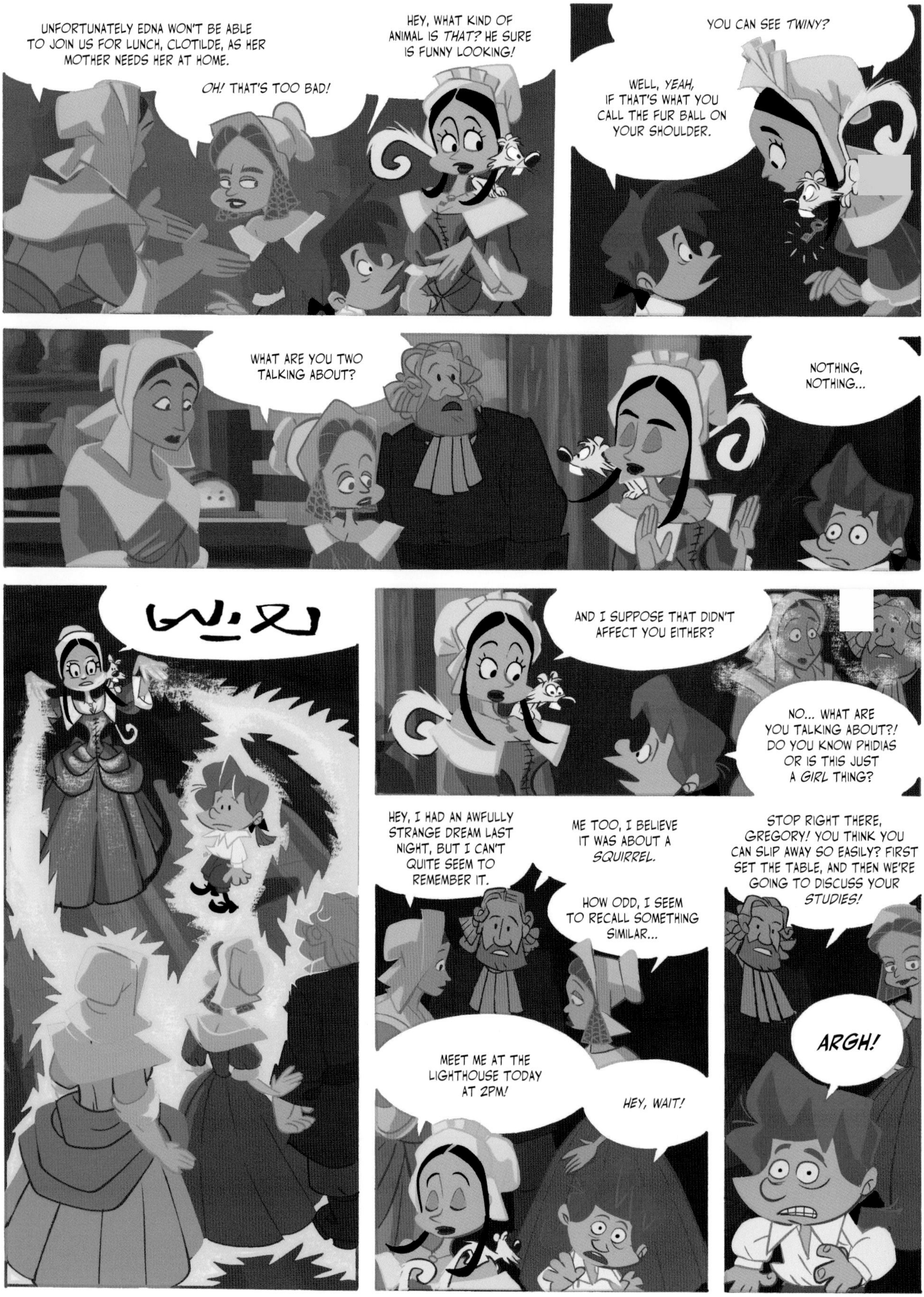
UNFORTUNATELY EDNA WON'T BE ABLE TO JOIN US FOR LUNCH, CLOTILDE, AS HER MOTHER NEEDS HER AT HOME.
OH! THAT'S TOO BAD!
HEY, WHAT KIND OF ANIMAL IS THAT? HE SURE IS FUNNY LOOKING!
YOU CAN SEE TWINY?
WELL, YEAH, IF THAT'S WHAT YOU CALL THE FUR BALL ON YOUR SHOULDER.
WHAT ARE YOU TWO TALKING ABOUT?
NOTHING, NOTHING...
AND I SUPPOSE THAT DIDN'T AFFECT YOU EITHER?
NO... WHAT ARE YOU TALKING ABOUT?! DO YOU KNOW PHIDIAS OR IS THIS JUST A GIRL THING?
HEY, I HAD AN AWFULLY STRANGE DREAM LAST NIGHT, BUT I CAN'T QUITE SEEM TO REMEMBER IT.
ME TOO, I BELIEVE IT WAS ABOUT A SQUIRREL.
HOW ODD, I SEEM TO RECALL SOMETHING SIMILAR...
MEET ME AT THE LIGHTHOUSE TODAY AT 2PM!
HEY, WAIT!
STOP RIGHT THERE, GREGORY! YOU THINK YOU CAN SLIP AWAY SO EASILY? FIRST SET THE TABLE, AND THEN WE'RE GOING TO DISCUSS YOUR STUDIES!
ARGH!

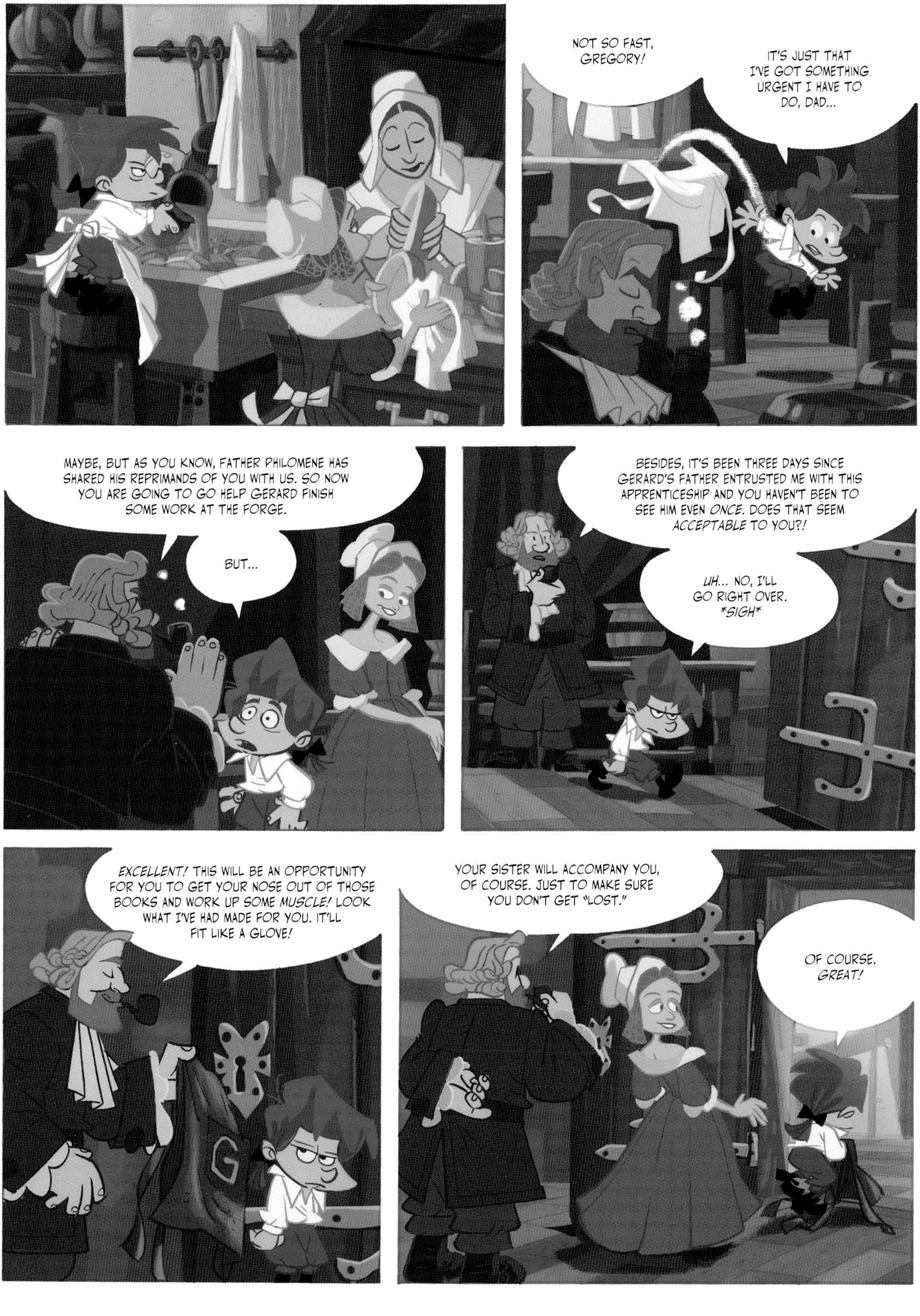
NOT SO FAST, GREGORY!
IT'S JUST THAT I'VE GOT SOMETHING URGENT I HAVE TO DO, DAD...
MAYBE, BUT AS YOU KNOW, FATHER PHILOMENE HAS SHARED HIS REPRIMANDS OF YOU WITH US. SO NOW YOU ARE GOING TO GO HELP GERARD FINISH SOME WORK AT THE FORGE.
BUT...
BESIDES, IT'S BEEN THREE DAYS SINCE GERARD'S FATHER ENTRUSTED ME WITH THIS APPRENTICESHIP AND YOU HAVEN'T BEEN TO SEE HIM EVEN *ONCE*. DOES THAT SEEM *ACCEPTABLE* TO YOU?!
UH... NO, I'LL GO RIGHT OVER. **SIGH**
EXCELLENT! THIS WILL BE AN OPPORTUNITY FOR YOU TO GET YOUR NOSE OUT OF THOSE BOOKS AND WORK UP SOME *MUSCLE!* LOOK WHAT I'VE HAD MADE FOR YOU. IT'LL FIT LIKE A GLOVE!
G
YOUR SISTER WILL ACCOMPANY YOU, OF COURSE. JUST TO MAKE SURE YOU DON'T GET "LOST."
OF COURSE. *GREAT!*

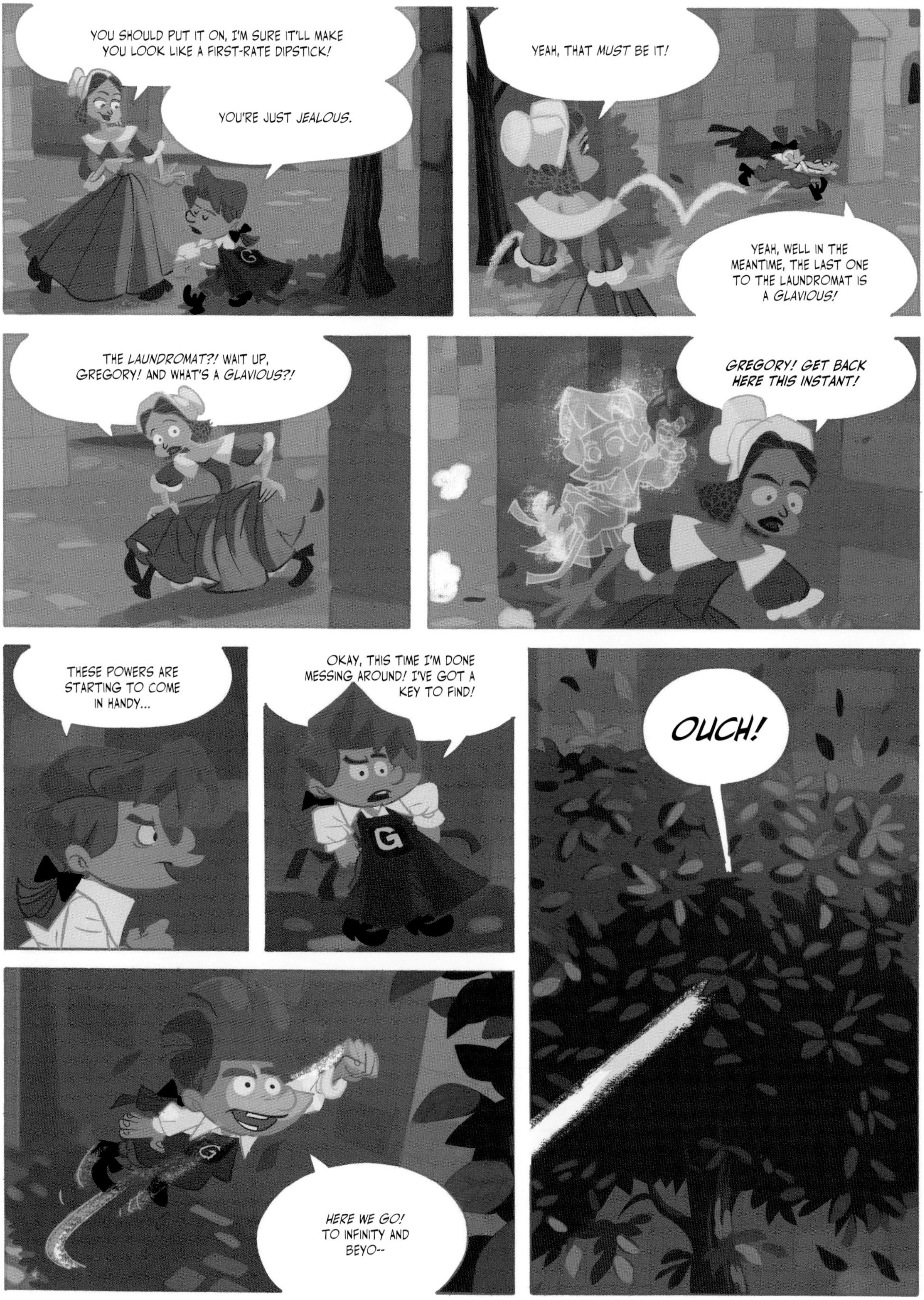
YOU SHOULD PUT IT ON, I'M SURE IT'LL MAKE YOU LOOK LIKE A FIRST-RATE DIPSTICK!
YOU'RE JUST *JEALOUS*.
YEAH, THAT *MUST* BE IT!
YEAH, WELL IN THE MEANTIME, THE LAST ONE TO THE LAUNDROMAT IS A *GLAVIOUS!*
THE *LAUNDROMAT?!* WAIT UP, GREGORY! AND WHAT'S A *GLAVIOUS?!*
GREGORY! GET BACK HERE THIS INSTANT!
THESE POWERS ARE STARTING TO COME IN HANDY...
OKAY, THIS TIME I'M DONE MESSING AROUND! I'VE GOT A KEY TO FIND!
HERE WE GO! TO INFINITY AND BEYO--
OUCH!

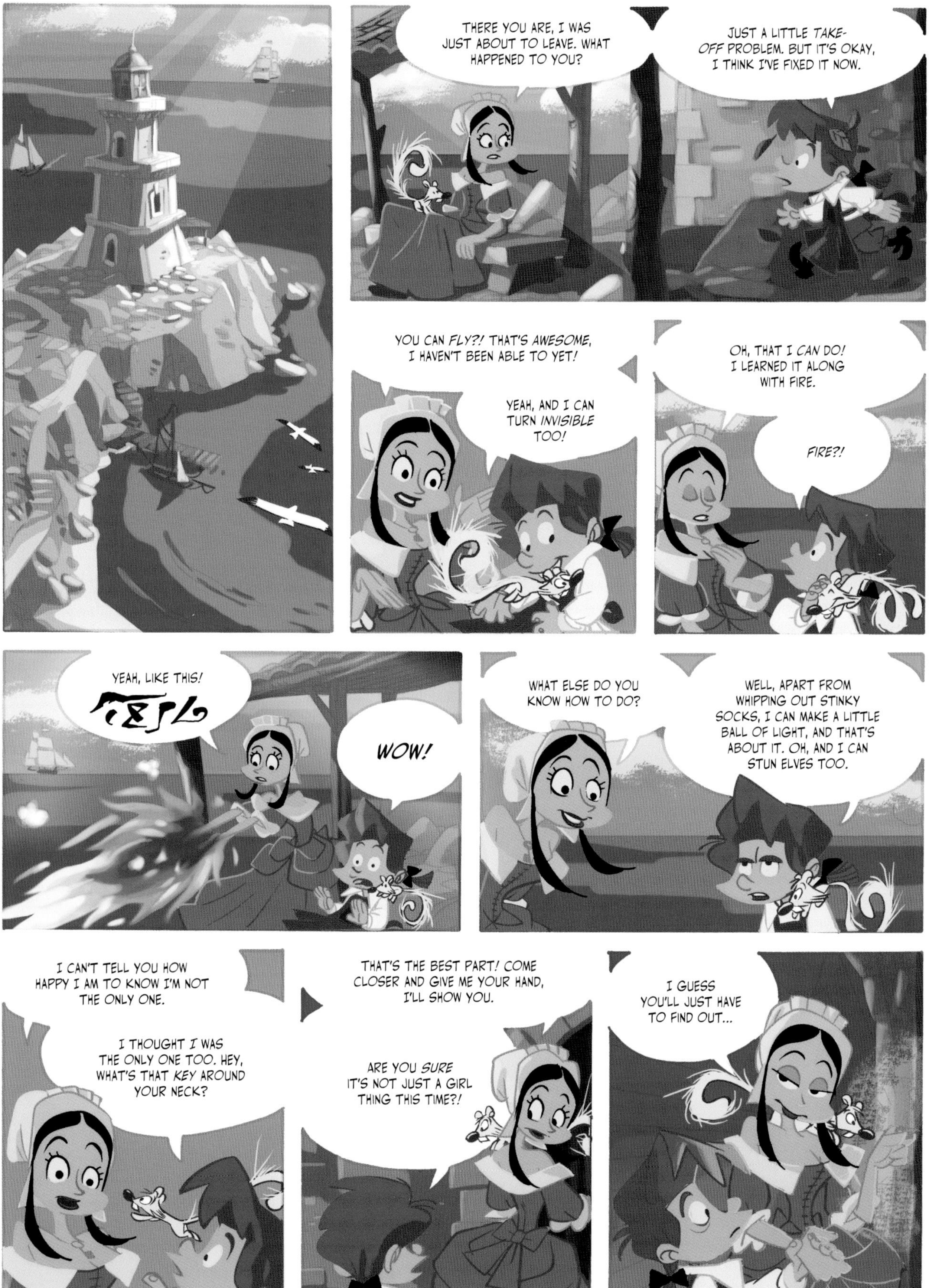
THERE YOU ARE, I WAS JUST ABOUT TO LEAVE. WHAT HAPPENED TO YOU?
JUST A LITTLE *TAKE-OFF* PROBLEM. BUT IT'S OKAY, I THINK I'VE FIXED IT NOW.
YOU CAN *FLY?!* THAT'S *AWESOME*, I HAVEN'T BEEN ABLE TO YET!
YEAH, AND I CAN TURN *INVISIBLE* TOO!
OH, THAT I *CAN DO!* I LEARNED IT ALONG WITH FIRE.
FIRE?!
YEAH, LIKE THIS!
WOW!
WHAT ELSE DO YOU KNOW HOW TO DO?
WELL, APART FROM WHIPPING OUT STINKY SOCKS, I CAN MAKE A LITTLE BALL OF LIGHT, AND THAT'S ABOUT IT. OH, AND I CAN STUN ELVES TOO.
I CAN'T TELL YOU HOW HAPPY I AM TO KNOW I'M NOT THE ONLY ONE.
I THOUGHT *I* WAS THE ONLY ONE TOO. HEY, WHAT'S THAT *KEY* AROUND YOUR NECK?
THAT'S THE BEST PART! COME CLOSER AND GIVE ME YOUR HAND, I'LL SHOW YOU.
ARE YOU *SURE* IT'S NOT JUST A GIRL THING THIS TIME?!
I GUESS YOU'LL JUST HAVE TO FIND OUT...

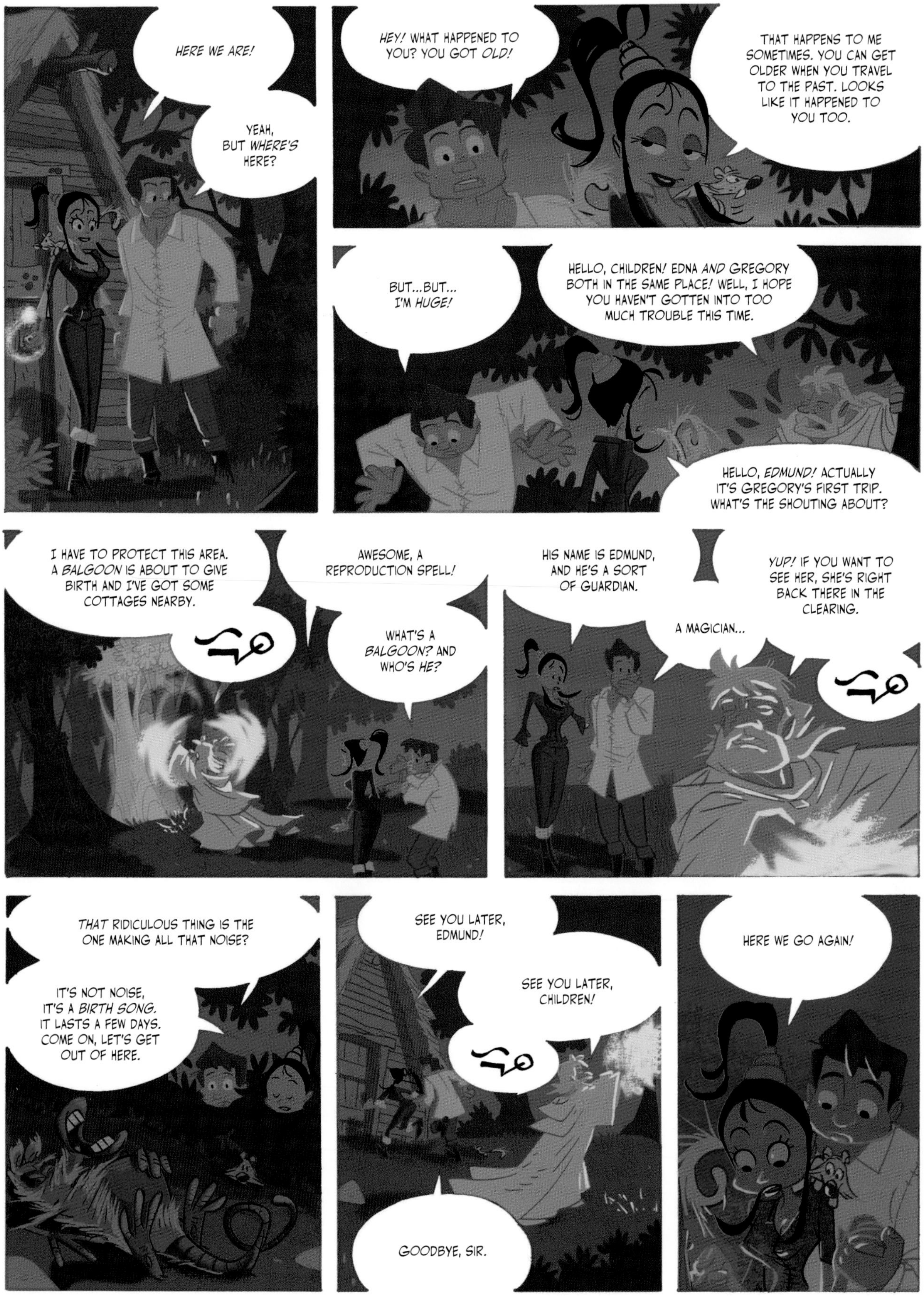
HERE WE ARE!
YEAH, BUT WHERE'S HERE?
HEY! WHAT HAPPENED TO YOU? YOU GOT OLD!
THAT HAPPENS TO ME SOMETIMES. YOU CAN GET OLDER WHEN YOU TRAVEL TO THE PAST. LOOKS LIKE IT HAPPENED TO YOU TOO.
BUT...BUT... I'M HUGE!
HELLO, CHILDREN! EDNA AND GREGORY BOTH IN THE SAME PLACE! WELL, I HOPE YOU HAVEN'T GOTTEN INTO TOO MUCH TROUBLE THIS TIME.
HELLO, EDMUND! ACTUALLY IT'S GREGORY'S FIRST TRIP. WHAT'S THE SHOUTING ABOUT?
I HAVE TO PROTECT THIS AREA. A BALGOON IS ABOUT TO GIVE BIRTH AND I'VE GOT SOME COTTAGES NEARBY.
AWESOME, A REPRODUCTION SPELL!
WHAT'S A BALGOON? AND WHO'S HE?
HIS NAME IS EDMUND, AND HE'S A SORT OF GUARDIAN.
A MAGICIAN...
YUP! IF YOU WANT TO SEE HER, SHE'S RIGHT BACK THERE IN THE CLEARING.
THAT RIDICULOUS THING IS THE ONE MAKING ALL THAT NOISE?
IT'S NOT NOISE, IT'S A BIRTH SONG. IT LASTS A FEW DAYS. COME ON, LET'S GET OUT OF HERE.
SEE YOU LATER, EDMUND!
SEE YOU LATER, CHILDREN!
GOODBYE, SIR.
HERE WE GO AGAIN!

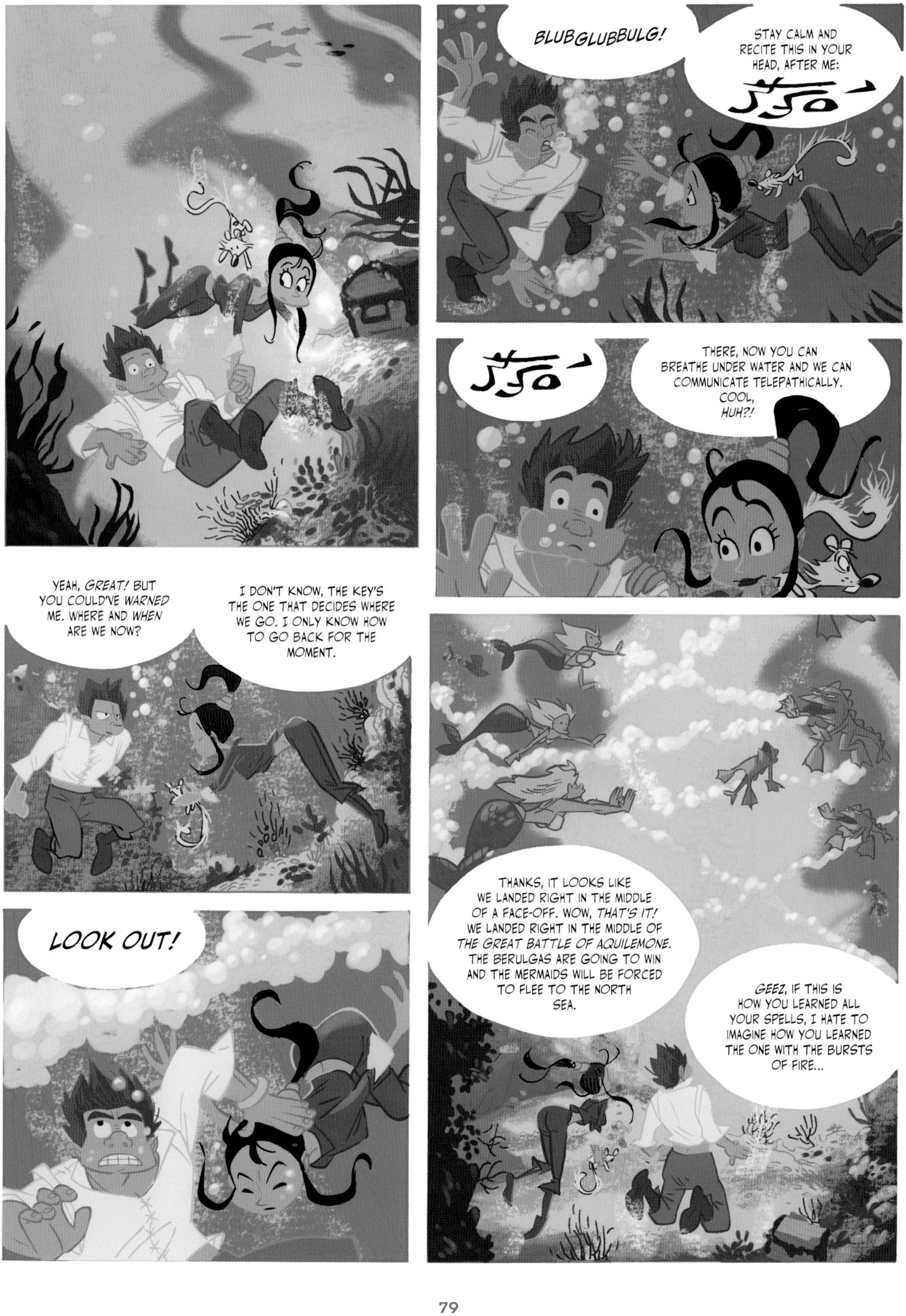
BLUBGLUBBULG!
STAY CALM AND RECITE THIS IN YOUR HEAD, AFTER ME:
THERE, NOW YOU CAN BREATHE UNDER WATER AND WE CAN COMMUNICATE TELEPATHICALLY. COOL, *HUH?!*
YEAH, *GREAT!* BUT YOU COULD'VE *WARNED* ME. WHERE AND *WHEN* ARE WE NOW?
I DON'T KNOW, THE KEY'S THE ONE THAT DECIDES WHERE WE GO. I ONLY KNOW HOW TO GO BACK FOR THE MOMENT.
LOOK OUT!
THANKS, IT LOOKS LIKE WE LANDED RIGHT IN THE MIDDLE OF A FACE-OFF. WOW, *THAT'S IT!* WE LANDED RIGHT IN THE MIDDLE OF *THE GREAT BATTLE OF AQUILEMONE.* THE BERULGAS ARE GOING TO WIN AND THE MERMAIDS WILL BE FORCED TO FLEE TO THE NORTH SEA.
GEEZ, IF THIS IS HOW YOU LEARNED ALL YOUR SPELLS, I HATE TO IMAGINE HOW YOU LEARNED THE ONE WITH THE BURSTS OF FIRE...

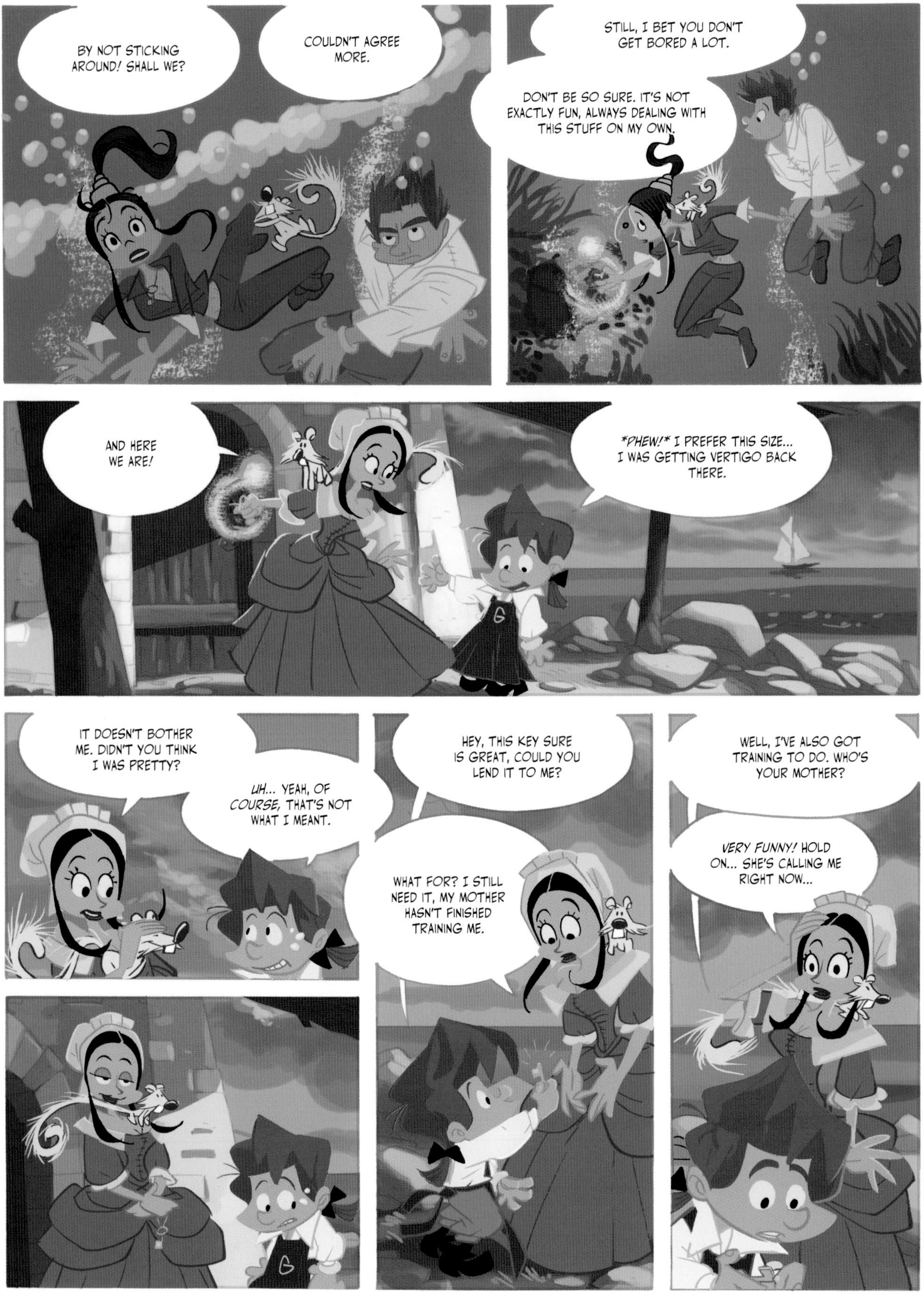

BY NOT STICKING AROUND! SHALL WE?
COULDN'T AGREE MORE.
STILL, I BET YOU DON'T GET BORED A LOT.
DON'T BE SO SURE. IT'S NOT EXACTLY FUN, ALWAYS DEALING WITH THIS STUFF ON MY OWN.
AND HERE WE ARE!
PHEW! I PREFER THIS SIZE... I WAS GETTING VERTIGO BACK THERE.
IT DOESN'T BOTHER ME. DIDN'T YOU THINK I WAS PRETTY?
UH... YEAH, OF COURSE, THAT'S NOT WHAT I MEANT.
HEY, THIS KEY SURE IS GREAT, COULD YOU LEND IT TO ME?
WHAT FOR? I STILL NEED IT, MY MOTHER HASN'T FINISHED TRAINING ME.
WELL, I'VE ALSO GOT TRAINING TO DO. WHO'S YOUR MOTHER?
VERY FUNNY! HOLD ON... SHE'S CALLING ME RIGHT NOW...

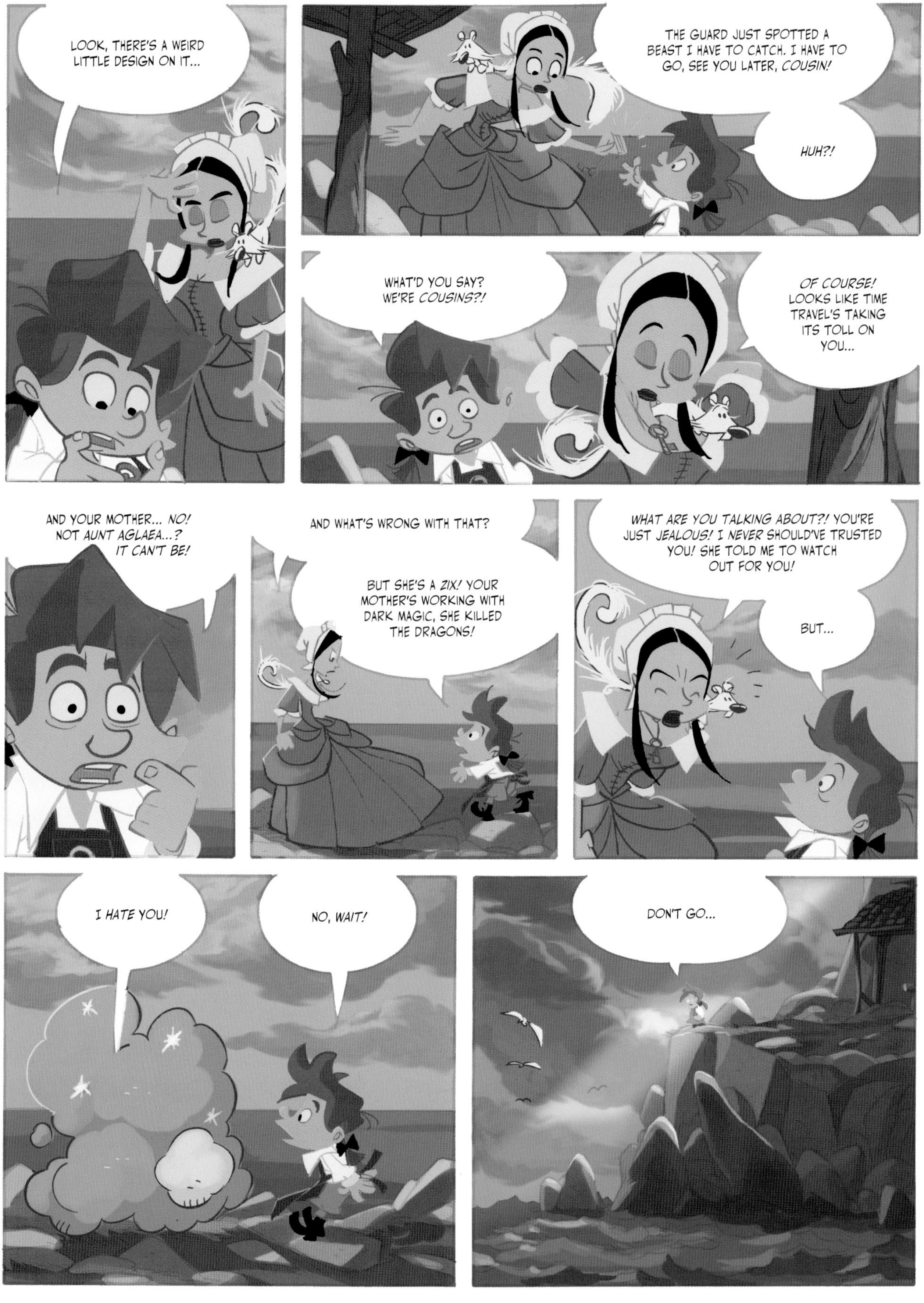
LOOK, THERE'S A WEIRD LITTLE DESIGN ON IT...
THE GUARD JUST SPOTTED A BEAST I HAVE TO CATCH. I HAVE TO GO, SEE YOU LATER, *COUSIN!*
HUH?!
WHAT'D YOU SAY? WE'RE *COUSINS?!*
OF COURSE! LOOKS LIKE TIME TRAVEL'S TAKING ITS TOLL ON YOU...
AND YOUR MOTHER... *NO!* NOT *AUNT AGLAEA...?* *IT CAN'T BE!*
AND WHAT'S WRONG WITH THAT?
BUT SHE'S A *ZIX!* YOUR MOTHER'S WORKING WITH DARK MAGIC, SHE KILLED THE DRAGONS!
WHAT ARE YOU TALKING ABOUT?! YOU'RE JUST *JEALOUS! I NEVER* SHOULD'VE TRUSTED YOU! SHE TOLD ME TO WATCH OUT FOR YOU*!*
BUT...
I HATE YOU!
NO, *WAIT!*
DON'T GO...

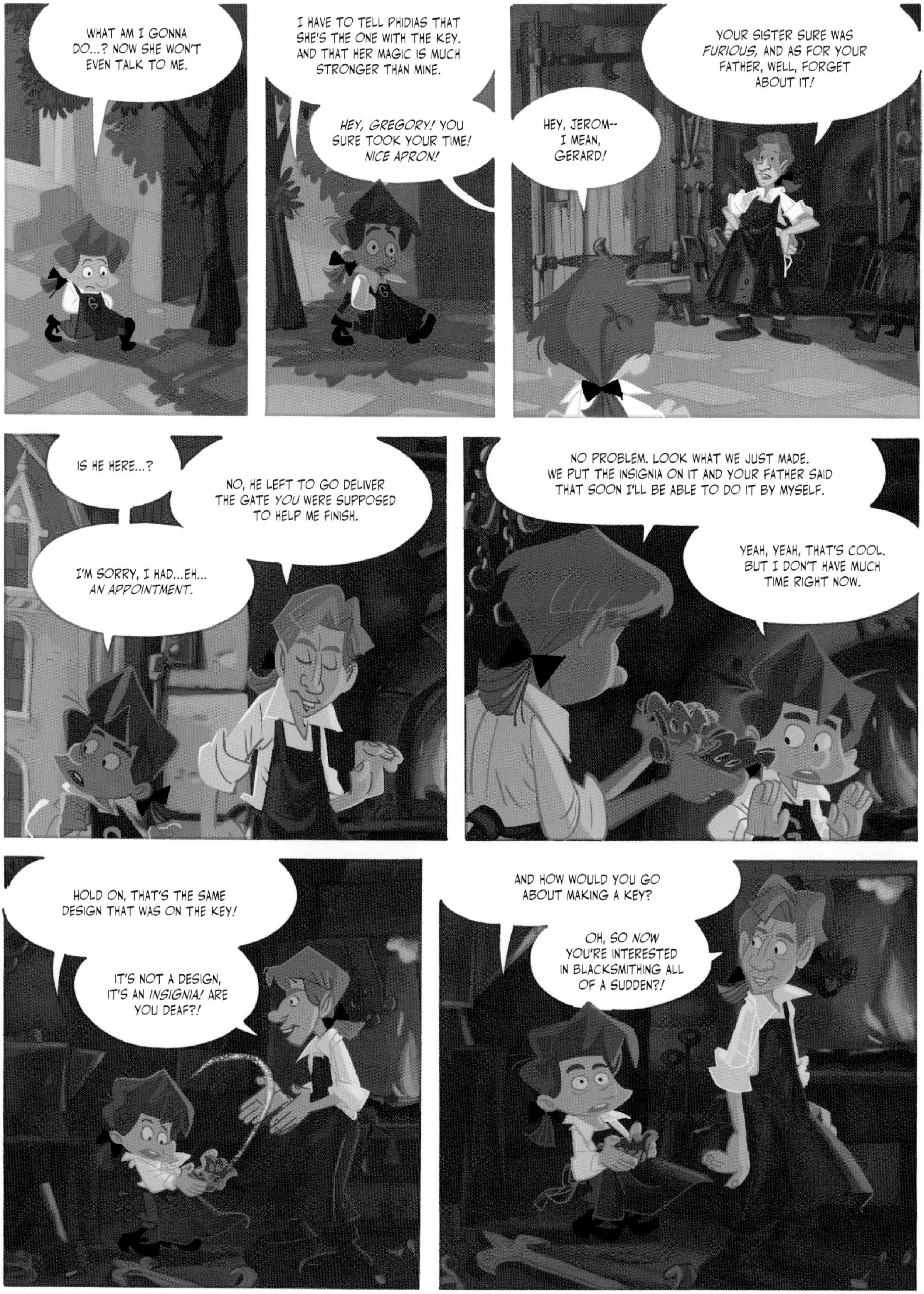
WHAT AM I GONNA DO...? NOW SHE WON'T EVEN TALK TO ME.
I HAVE TO TELL PHIDIAS THAT SHE'S THE ONE WITH THE KEY. AND THAT HER MAGIC IS MUCH STRONGER THAN MINE.
HEY, GREGORY! YOU SURE TOOK YOUR TIME! NICE APRON!
HEY, JEROM-- I MEAN, GERARD!
YOUR SISTER SURE WAS FURIOUS, AND AS FOR YOUR FATHER, WELL, FORGET ABOUT IT!
IS HE HERE...?
NO, HE LEFT TO GO DELIVER THE GATE YOU WERE SUPPOSED TO HELP ME FINISH.
I'M SORRY, I HAD...EH... AN APPOINTMENT.
NO PROBLEM. LOOK WHAT WE JUST MADE. WE PUT THE INSIGNIA ON IT AND YOUR FATHER SAID THAT SOON I'LL BE ABLE TO DO IT BY MYSELF.
YEAH, YEAH, THAT'S COOL. BUT I DON'T HAVE MUCH TIME RIGHT NOW.
HOLD ON, THAT'S THE SAME DESIGN THAT WAS ON THE KEY!
IT'S NOT A DESIGN, IT'S AN INSIGNIA! ARE YOU DEAF?!
AND HOW WOULD YOU GO ABOUT MAKING A KEY?
OH, SO NOW YOU'RE INTERESTED IN BLACKSMITHING ALL OF A SUDDEN?!

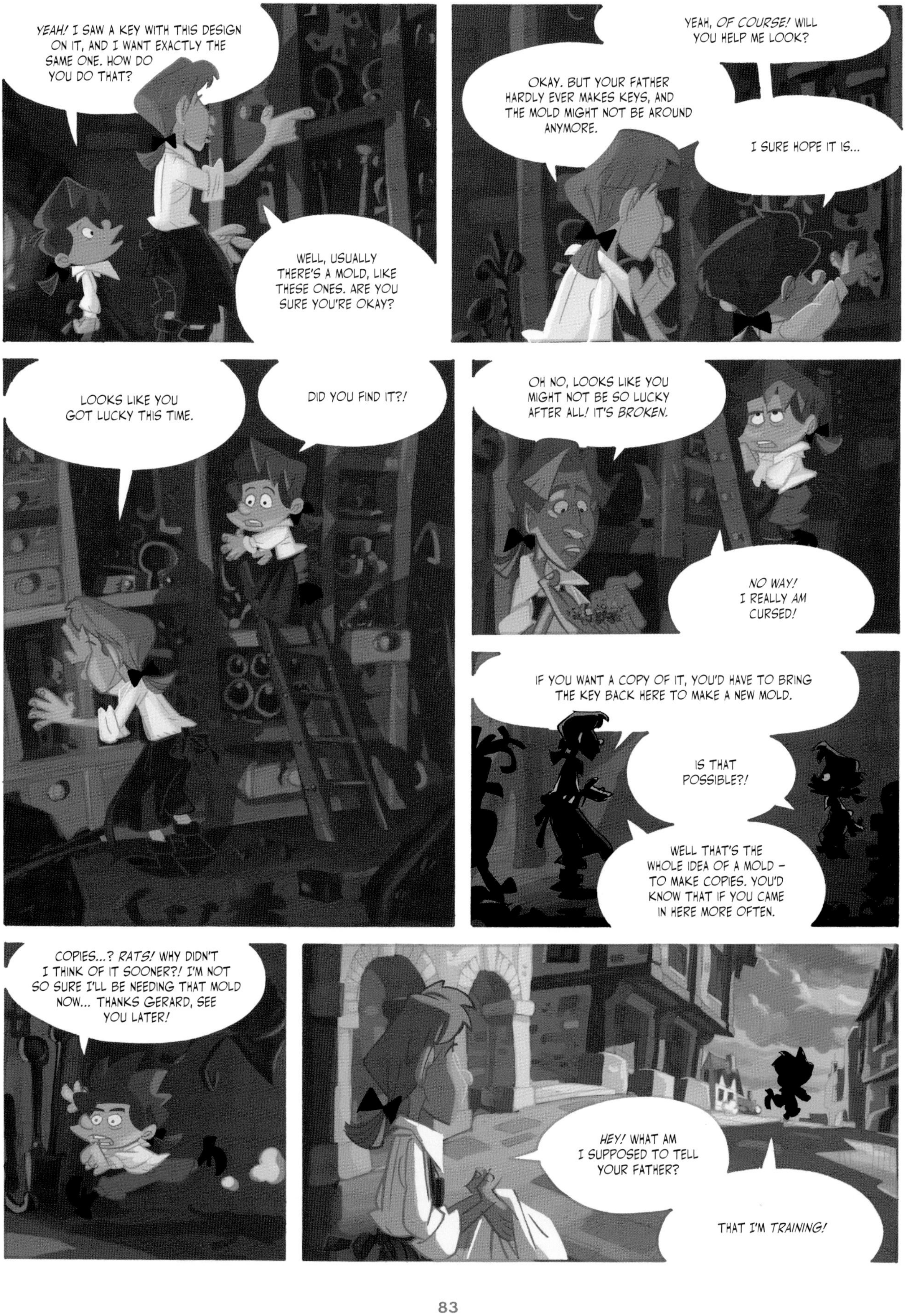

YEAH! I SAW A KEY WITH THIS DESIGN ON IT, AND I WANT EXACTLY THE SAME ONE. HOW DO YOU DO THAT?
WELL, USUALLY THERE'S A MOLD, LIKE THESE ONES. ARE YOU SURE YOU'RE OKAY?
YEAH, OF COURSE! WILL YOU HELP ME LOOK?
OKAY. BUT YOUR FATHER HARDLY EVER MAKES KEYS, AND THE MOLD MIGHT NOT BE AROUND ANYMORE.
I SURE HOPE IT IS...
LOOKS LIKE YOU GOT LUCKY THIS TIME.
DID YOU FIND IT?!
OH NO, LOOKS LIKE YOU MIGHT NOT BE SO LUCKY AFTER ALL! IT'S BROKEN.
NO WAY! I REALLY AM CURSED!
IF YOU WANT A COPY OF IT, YOU'D HAVE TO BRING THE KEY BACK HERE TO MAKE A NEW MOLD.
IS THAT POSSIBLE?!
WELL THAT'S THE WHOLE IDEA OF A MOLD – TO MAKE COPIES. YOU'D KNOW THAT IF YOU CAME IN HERE MORE OFTEN.
COPIES...? RATS! WHY DIDN'T I THINK OF IT SOONER?! I'M NOT SO SURE I'LL BE NEEDING THAT MOLD NOW... THANKS GERARD, SEE YOU LATER!
HEY! WHAT AM I SUPPOSED TO TELL YOUR FATHER?
THAT I'M TRAINING!

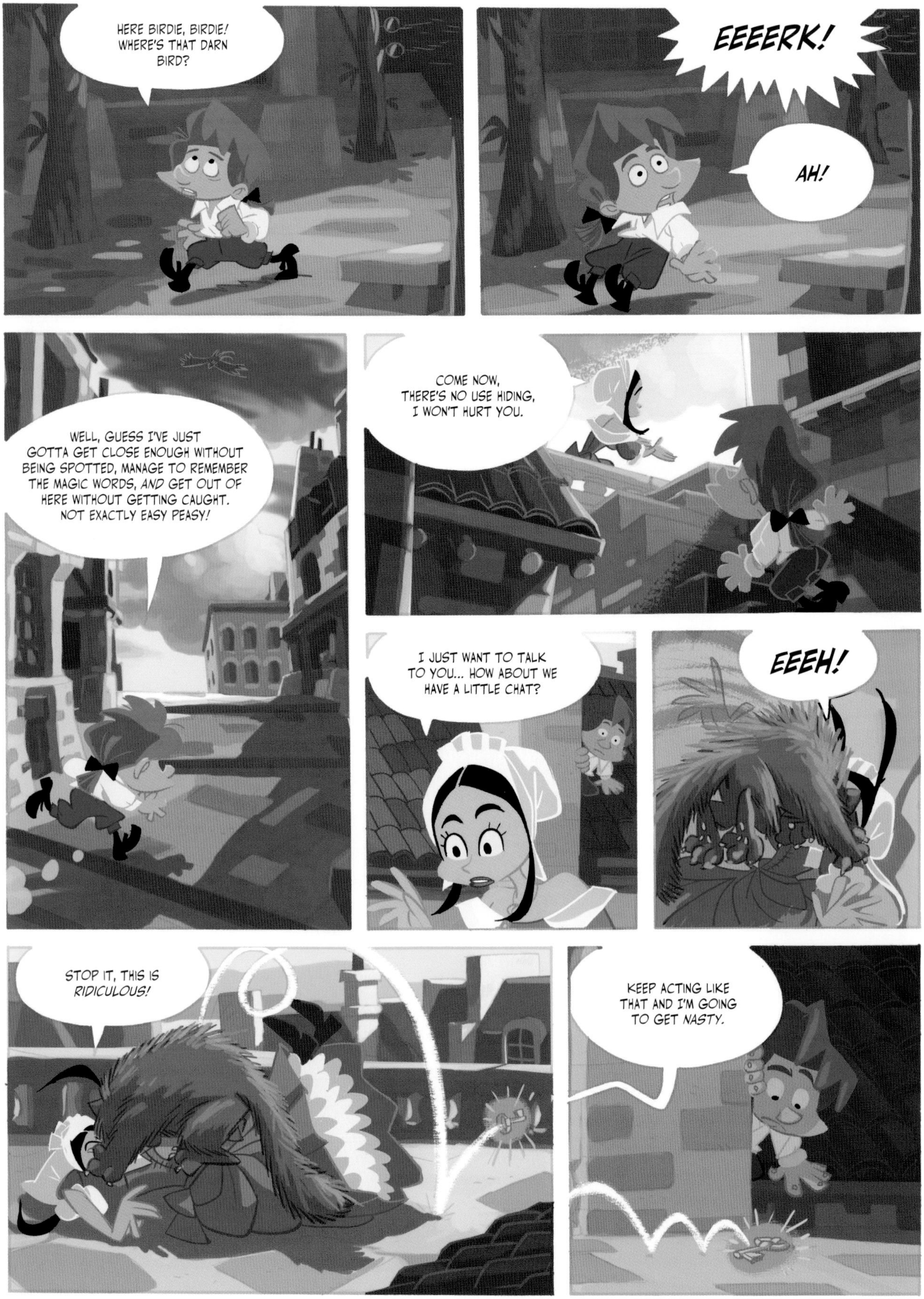
HERE BIRDIE, BIRDIE! WHERE'S THAT DARN BIRD?
EEEERK!
AH!
WELL, GUESS I'VE JUST GOTTA GET CLOSE ENOUGH WITHOUT BEING SPOTTED, MANAGE TO REMEMBER THE MAGIC WORDS, AND GET OUT OF HERE WITHOUT GETTING CAUGHT. NOT EXACTLY EASY PEASY!
COME NOW, THERE'S NO USE HIDING, I WON'T HURT YOU.
I JUST WANT TO TALK TO YOU... HOW ABOUT WE HAVE A LITTLE CHAT?
EEEH!
STOP IT, THIS IS RIDICULOUS!
KEEP ACTING LIKE THAT AND I'M GOING TO GET NASTY.

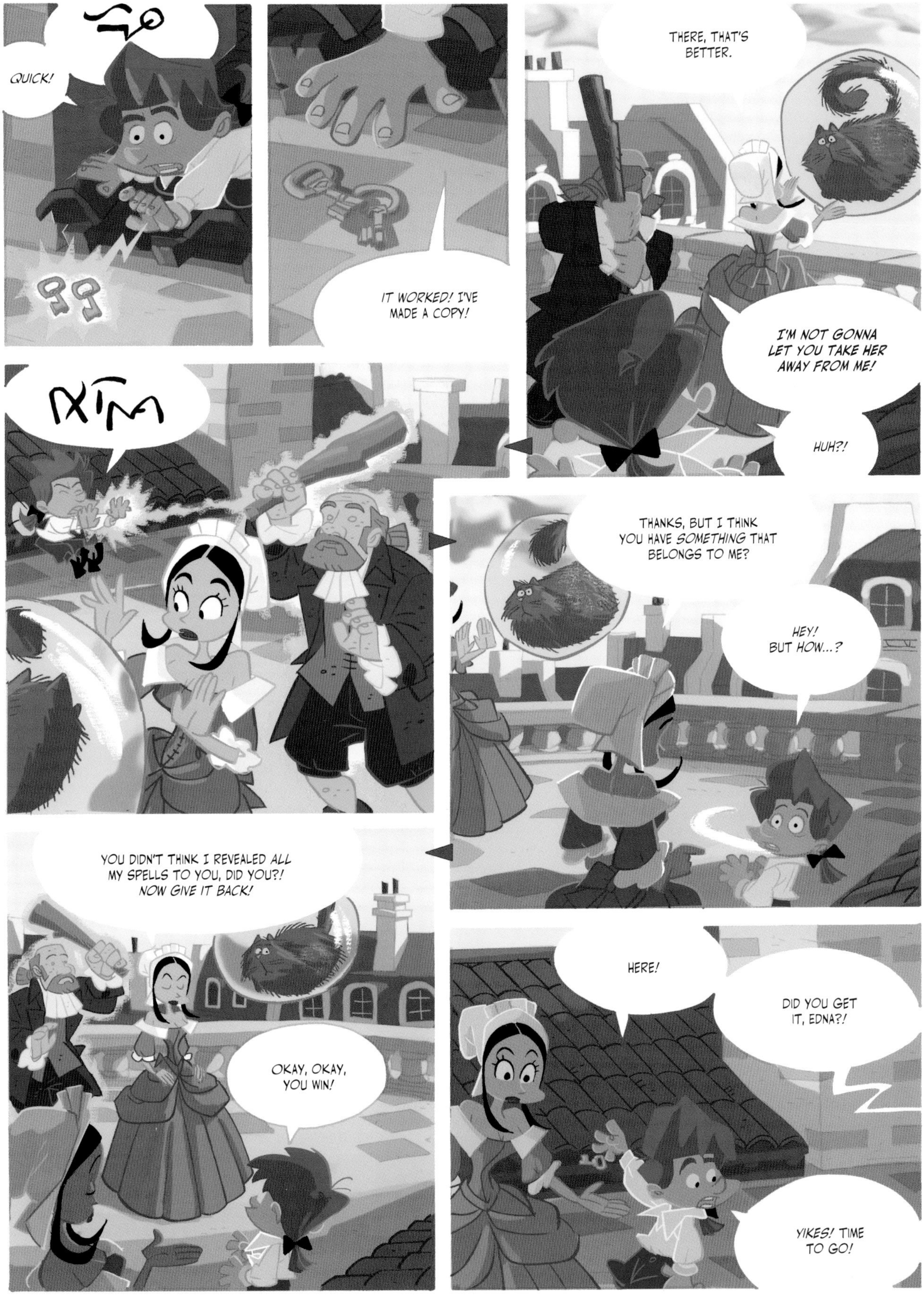
QUICK!
IT WORKED! I'VE MADE A COPY!
THERE, THAT'S BETTER.
I'M NOT GONNA LET YOU TAKE HER AWAY FROM ME!
HUH?!
THANKS, BUT I THINK YOU HAVE SOMETHING THAT BELONGS TO ME?
HEY! BUT HOW...?
YOU DIDN'T THINK I REVEALED ALL MY SPELLS TO YOU, DID YOU?! NOW GIVE IT BACK!
OKAY, OKAY, YOU WIN!
HERE!
DID YOU GET IT, EDNA?!
YIKES! TIME TO GO!

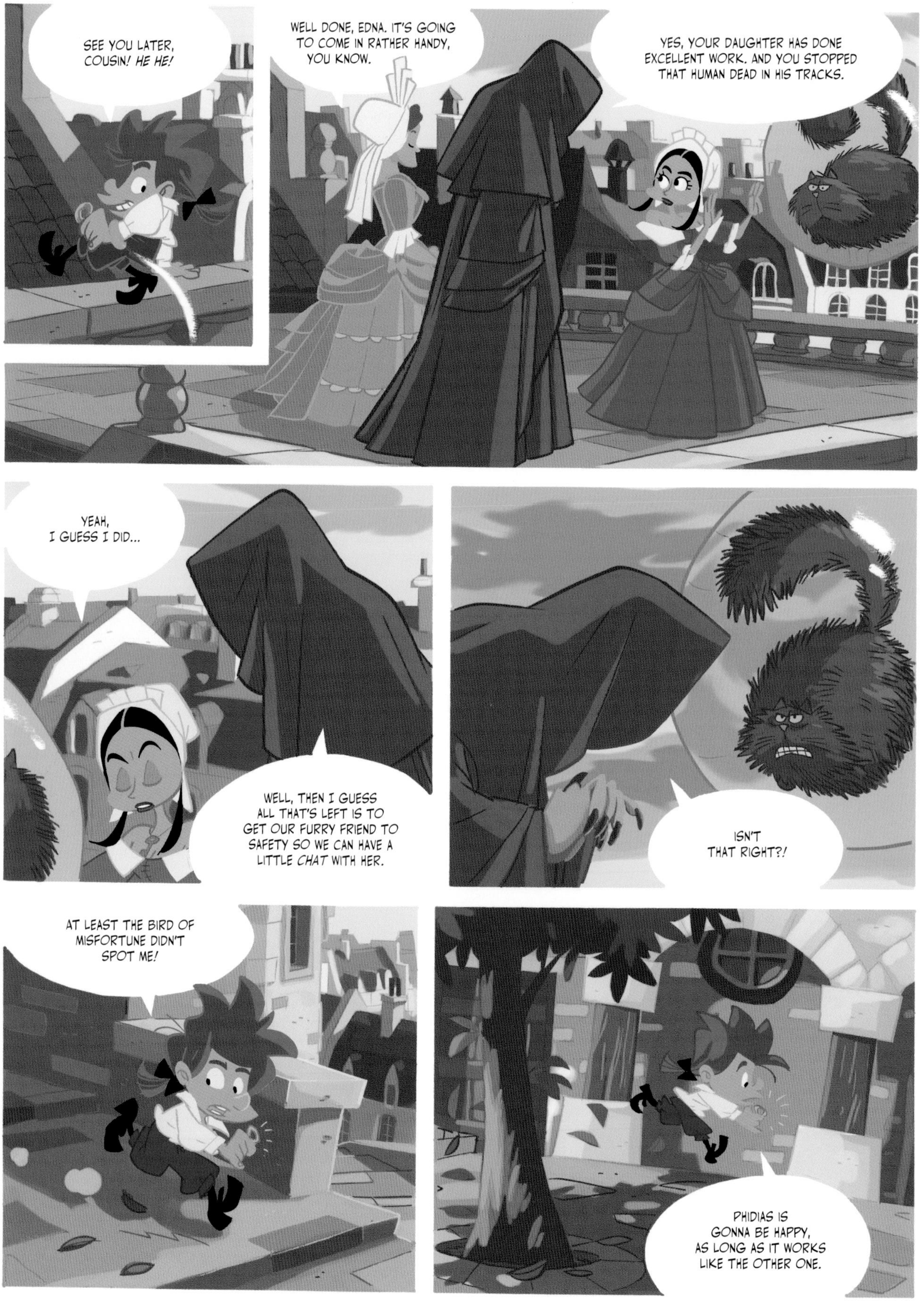
SEE YOU LATER, COUSIN! HE HE!
WELL DONE, EDNA. IT'S GOING TO COME IN RATHER HANDY, YOU KNOW.
YES, YOUR DAUGHTER HAS DONE EXCELLENT WORK. AND YOU STOPPED THAT HUMAN DEAD IN HIS TRACKS.
YEAH, I GUESS I DID...
WELL, THEN I GUESS ALL THAT'S LEFT IS TO GET OUR FURRY FRIEND TO SAFETY SO WE CAN HAVE A LITTLE CHAT WITH HER.
ISN'T THAT RIGHT?!
AT LEAST THE BIRD OF MISFORTUNE DIDN'T SPOT ME!
PHIDIAS IS GONNA BE HAPPY, AS LONG AS IT WORKS LIKE THE OTHER ONE.

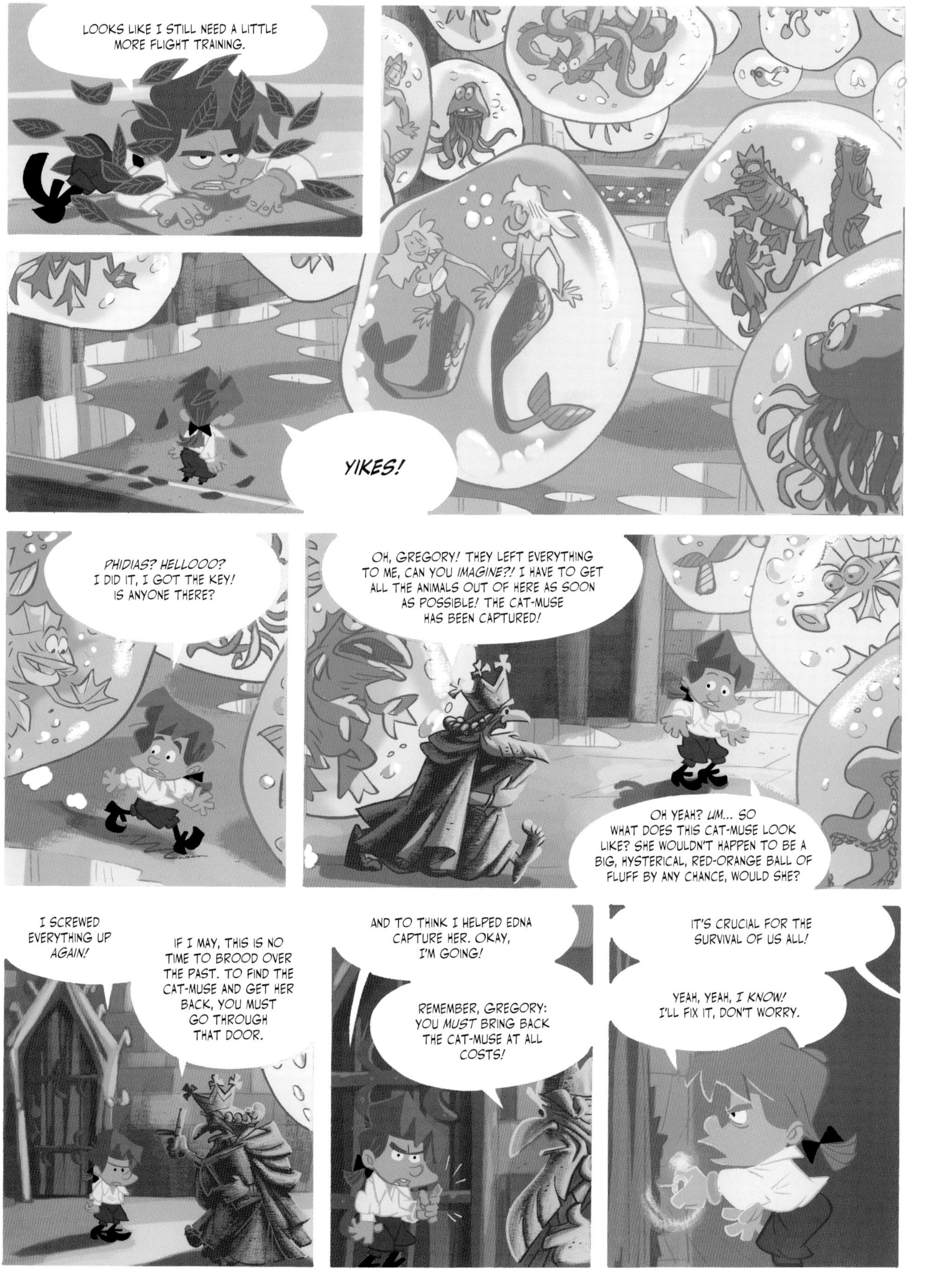
LOOKS LIKE I STILL NEED A LITTLE MORE FLIGHT TRAINING.
YIKES!
PHIDIAS? HELLOOO? I DID IT, I GOT THE KEY! IS ANYONE THERE?
OH, GREGORY! THEY LEFT EVERYTHING TO ME, CAN YOU IMAGINE?! I HAVE TO GET ALL THE ANIMALS OUT OF HERE AS SOON AS POSSIBLE! THE CAT-MUSE HAS BEEN CAPTURED!
OH YEAH? UM... SO WHAT DOES THIS CAT-MUSE LOOK LIKE? SHE WOULDN'T HAPPEN TO BE A BIG, HYSTERICAL, RED-ORANGE BALL OF FLUFF BY ANY CHANCE, WOULD SHE?
I SCREWED EVERYTHING UP AGAIN!
IF I MAY, THIS IS NO TIME TO BROOD OVER THE PAST. TO FIND THE CAT-MUSE AND GET HER BACK, YOU MUST GO THROUGH THAT DOOR.
AND TO THINK I HELPED EDNA CAPTURE HER. OKAY, I'M GOING!
REMEMBER, GREGORY: YOU MUST BRING BACK THE CAT-MUSE AT ALL COSTS!
IT'S CRUCIAL FOR THE SURVIVAL OF US ALL!
YEAH, YEAH, I KNOW! I'LL FIX IT, DON'T WORRY.

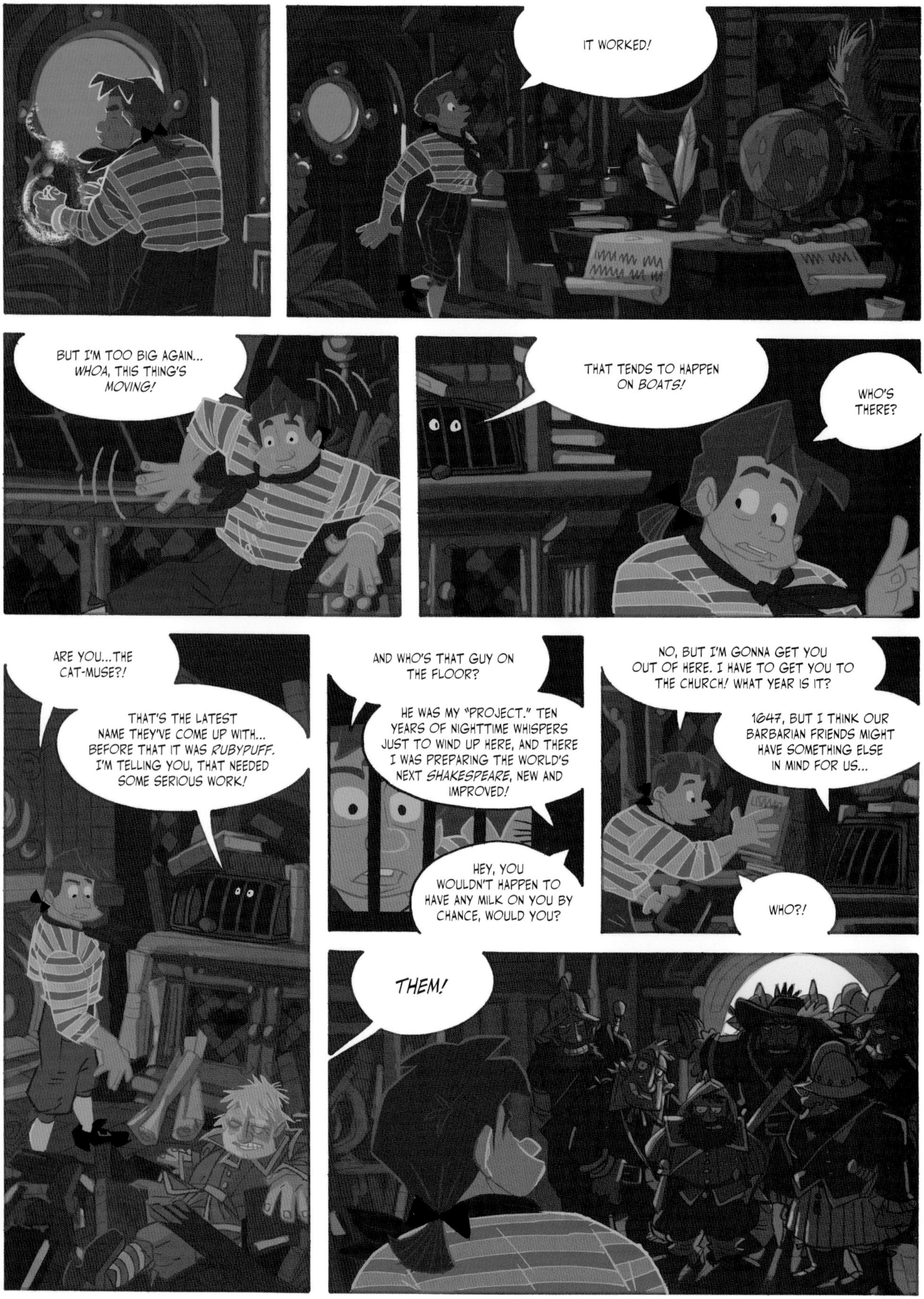
IT WORKED!
BUT I'M TOO BIG AGAIN... WHOA, THIS THING'S MOVING!
THAT TENDS TO HAPPEN ON BOATS!
WHO'S THERE?
ARE YOU...THE CAT-MUSE?!
THAT'S THE LATEST NAME THEY'VE COME UP WITH... BEFORE THAT IT WAS RUBYPUFF. I'M TELLING YOU, THAT NEEDED SOME SERIOUS WORK!
AND WHO'S THAT GUY ON THE FLOOR?
HE WAS MY "PROJECT." TEN YEARS OF NIGHTTIME WHISPERS JUST TO WIND UP HERE, AND THERE I WAS PREPARING THE WORLD'S NEXT SHAKESPEARE, NEW AND IMPROVED!
HEY, YOU WOULDN'T HAPPEN TO HAVE ANY MILK ON YOU BY CHANCE, WOULD YOU?
NO, BUT I'M GONNA GET YOU OUT OF HERE. I HAVE TO GET YOU TO THE CHURCH! WHAT YEAR IS IT?
1647, BUT I THINK OUR BARBARIAN FRIENDS MIGHT HAVE SOMETHING ELSE IN MIND FOR US...
WHO?!
THEM!

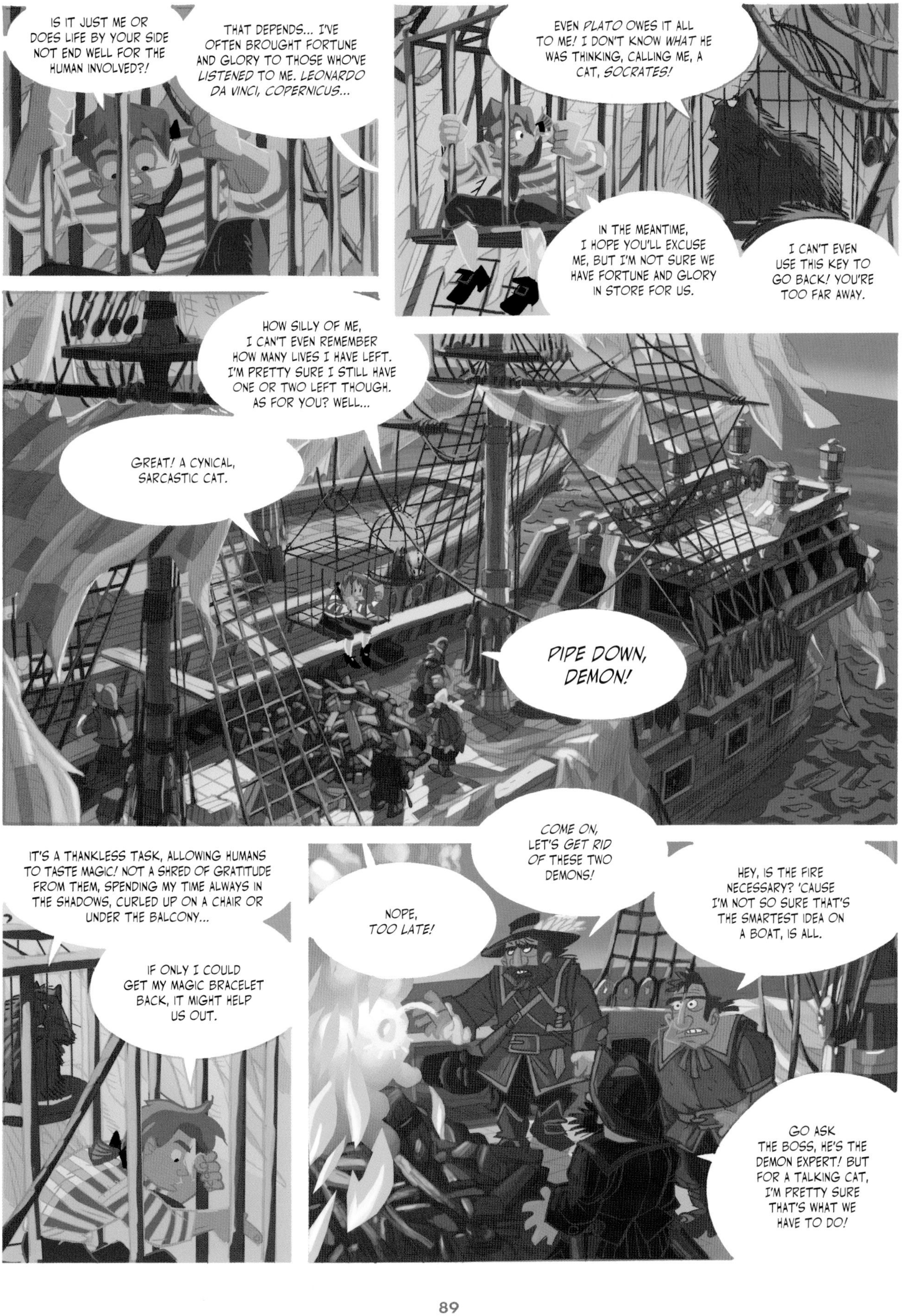
IS IT JUST ME OR DOES LIFE BY YOUR SIDE NOT END WELL FOR THE HUMAN INVOLVED?!
THAT DEPENDS... I'VE OFTEN BROUGHT FORTUNE AND GLORY TO THOSE WHO'VE LISTENED TO ME. LEONARDO DA VINCI, COPERNICUS...
EVEN PLATO OWES IT ALL TO ME! I DON'T KNOW WHAT HE WAS THINKING, CALLING ME, A CAT, SOCRATES!
IN THE MEANTIME, I HOPE YOU'LL EXCUSE ME, BUT I'M NOT SURE WE HAVE FORTUNE AND GLORY IN STORE FOR US.
I CAN'T EVEN USE THIS KEY TO GO BACK! YOU'RE TOO FAR AWAY.
HOW SILLY OF ME, I CAN'T EVEN REMEMBER HOW MANY LIVES I HAVE LEFT. I'M PRETTY SURE I STILL HAVE ONE OR TWO LEFT THOUGH. AS FOR YOU? WELL...
GREAT! A CYNICAL, SARCASTIC CAT.
PIPE DOWN, DEMON!
IT'S A THANKLESS TASK, ALLOWING HUMANS TO TASTE MAGIC! NOT A SHRED OF GRATITUDE FROM THEM, SPENDING MY TIME ALWAYS IN THE SHADOWS, CURLED UP ON A CHAIR OR UNDER THE BALCONY...
IF ONLY I COULD GET MY MAGIC BRACELET BACK, IT MIGHT HELP US OUT.
COME ON, LET'S GET RID OF THESE TWO DEMONS!
NOPE, TOO LATE!
HEY, IS THE FIRE NECESSARY? 'CAUSE I'M NOT SO SURE THAT'S THE SMARTEST IDEA ON A BOAT, IS ALL.
GO ASK THE BOSS, HE'S THE DEMON EXPERT! BUT FOR A TALKING CAT, I'M PRETTY SURE THAT'S WHAT WE HAVE TO DO!

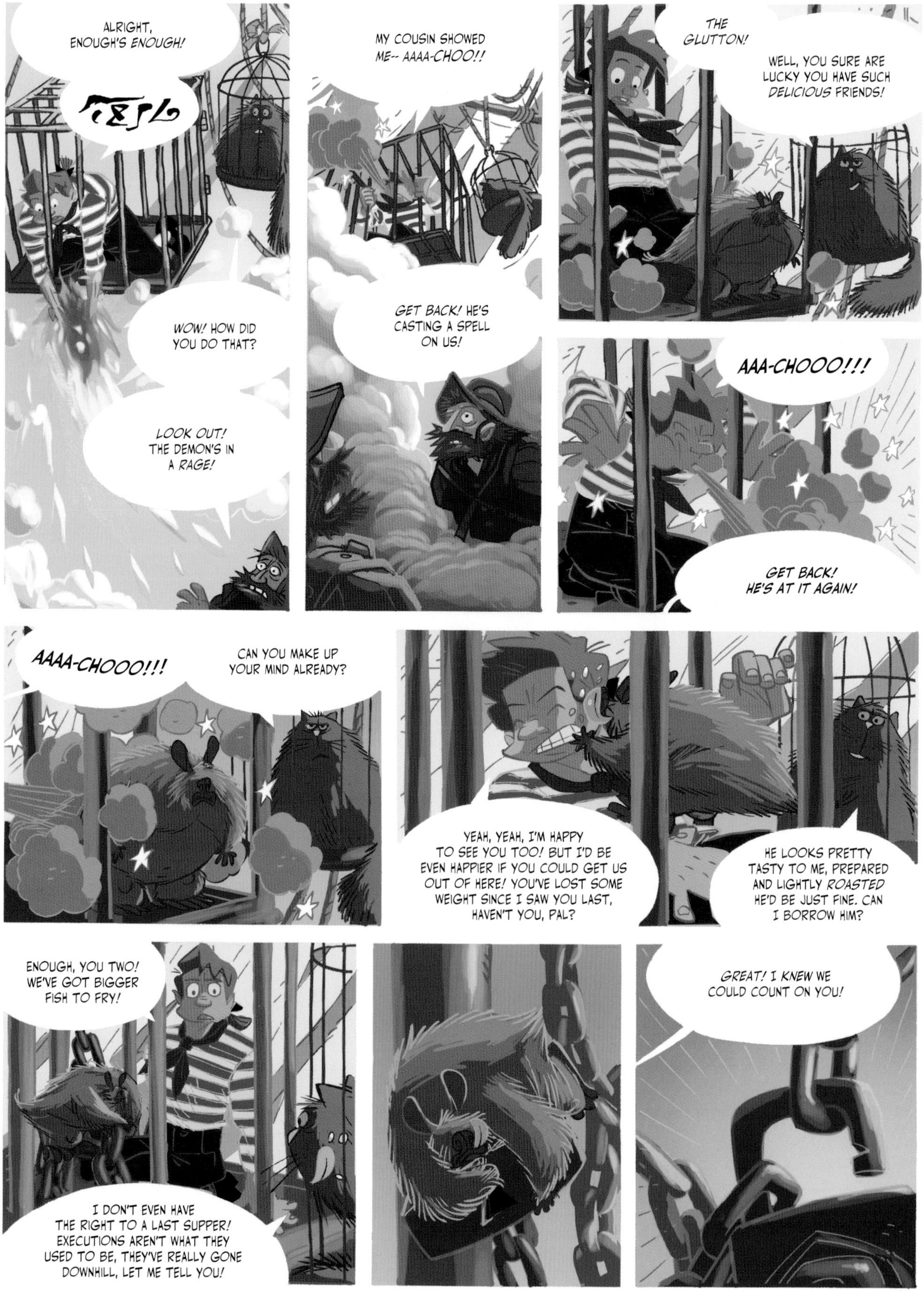

ALRIGHT, ENOUGH'S ENOUGH!
WOW! HOW DID YOU DO THAT?
LOOK OUT! THE DEMON'S IN A RAGE!
MY COUSIN SHOWED ME-- AAAA-CHOO!!
GET BACK! HE'S CASTING A SPELL ON US!
THE GLUTTON!
WELL, YOU SURE ARE LUCKY YOU HAVE SUCH DELICIOUS FRIENDS!
AAA-CHOOO!!!
GET BACK! HE'S AT IT AGAIN!
AAAA-CHOOO!!!
CAN YOU MAKE UP YOUR MIND ALREADY?
YEAH, YEAH, I'M HAPPY TO SEE YOU TOO! BUT I'D BE EVEN HAPPIER IF YOU COULD GET US OUT OF HERE! YOU'VE LOST SOME WEIGHT SINCE I SAW YOU LAST, HAVEN'T YOU, PAL?
HE LOOKS PRETTY TASTY TO ME, PREPARED AND LIGHTLY ROASTED HE'D BE JUST FINE. CAN I BORROW HIM?
ENOUGH, YOU TWO! WE'VE GOT BIGGER FISH TO FRY!
I DON'T EVEN HAVE THE RIGHT TO A LAST SUPPER! EXECUTIONS AREN'T WHAT THEY USED TO BE, THEY'VE REALLY GONE DOWNHILL, LET ME TELL YOU!
GREAT! I KNEW WE COULD COUNT ON YOU!

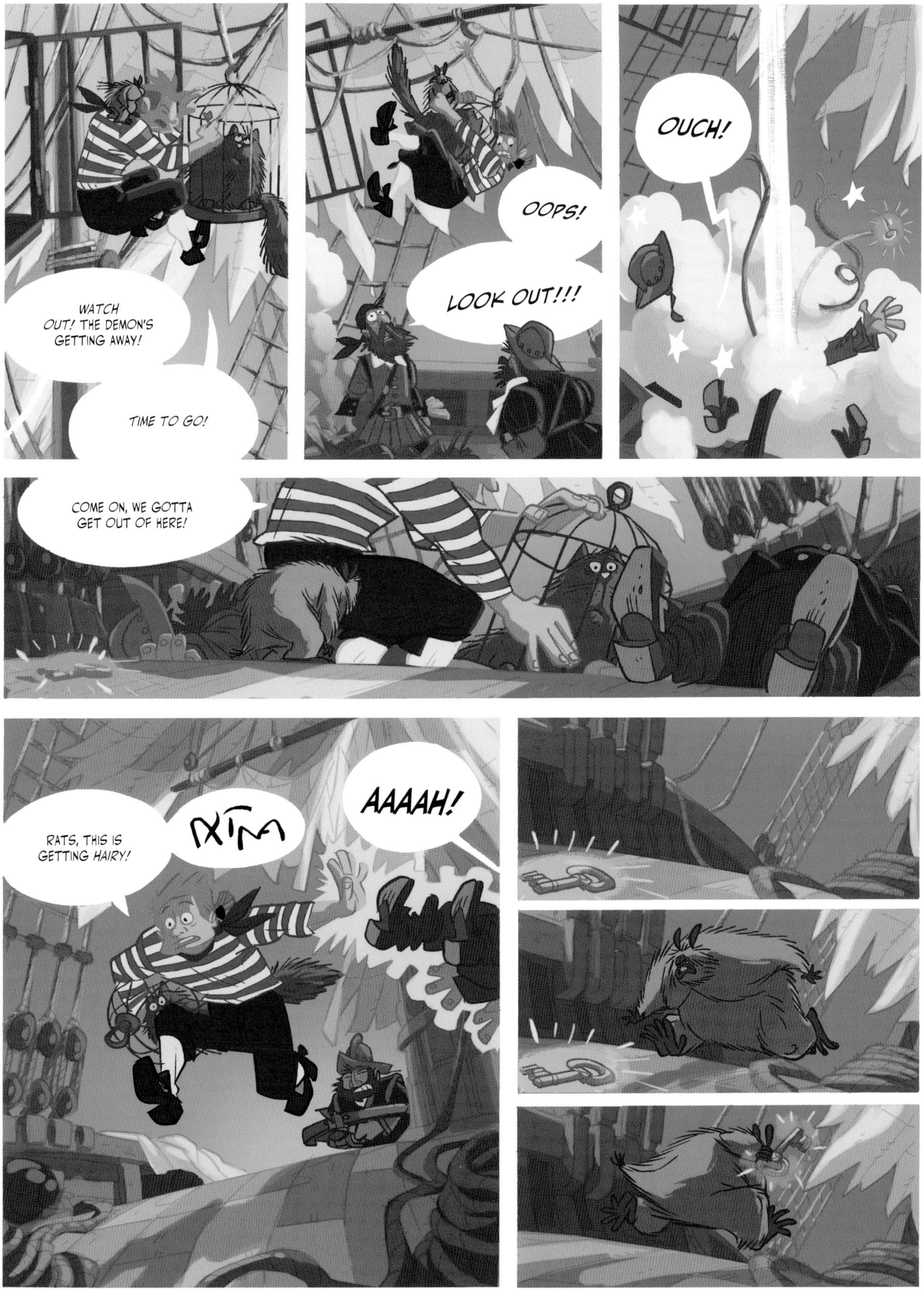
WATCH OUT! THE DEMON'S GETTING AWAY!
TIME TO GO!
OOPS!
LOOK OUT!!!
OUCH!
COME ON, WE GOTTA GET OUT OF HERE!
RATS, THIS IS GETTING HAIRY!
AAAAH!

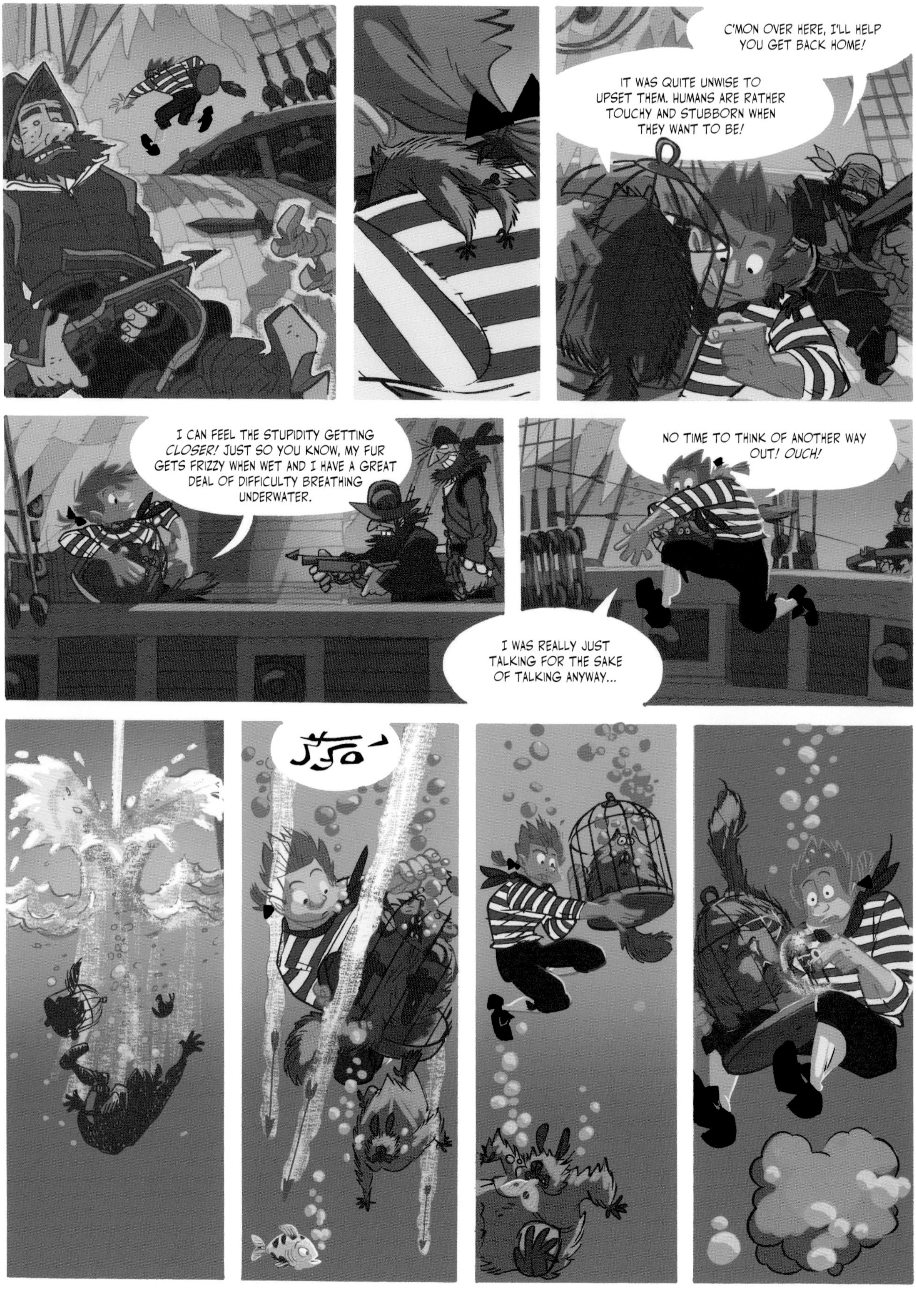
C'MON OVER HERE, I'LL HELP YOU GET BACK HOME!
IT WAS QUITE UNWISE TO UPSET THEM. HUMANS ARE RATHER TOUCHY AND STUBBORN WHEN THEY WANT TO BE!
I CAN FEEL THE STUPIDITY GETTING *CLOSER!* JUST SO YOU KNOW, MY FUR GETS FRIZZY WHEN WET AND I HAVE A GREAT DEAL OF DIFFICULTY BREATHING UNDERWATER.
NO TIME TO THINK OF ANOTHER WAY OUT! *OUCH!*
I WAS REALLY JUST TALKING FOR THE SAKE OF TALKING ANYWAY...

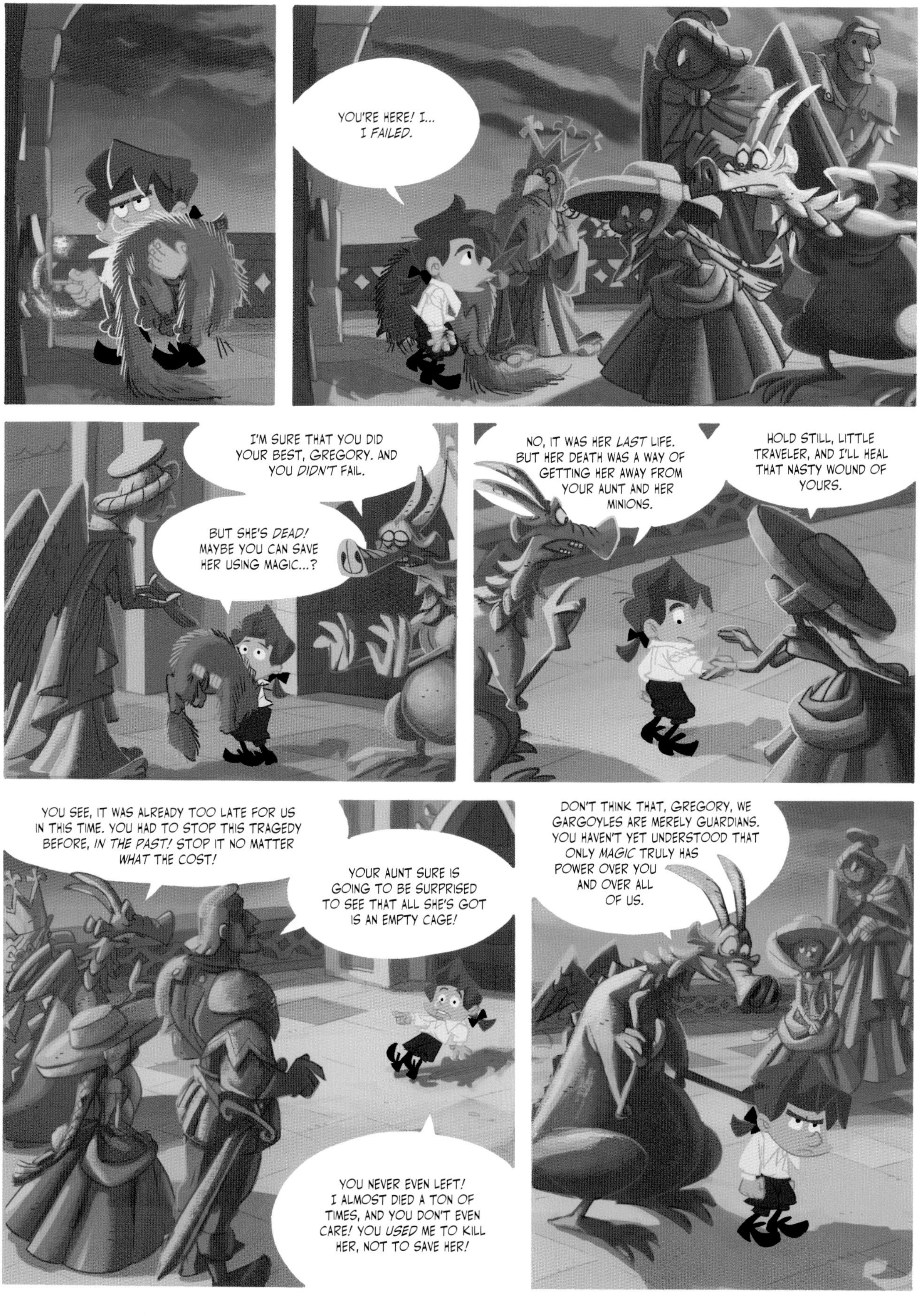
YOU'RE HERE! I... I FAILED.
I'M SURE THAT YOU DID YOUR BEST, GREGORY. AND YOU DIDN'T FAIL.
BUT SHE'S DEAD! MAYBE YOU CAN SAVE HER USING MAGIC...?
NO, IT WAS HER LAST LIFE. BUT HER DEATH WAS A WAY OF GETTING HER AWAY FROM YOUR AUNT AND HER MINIONS.
HOLD STILL, LITTLE TRAVELER, AND I'LL HEAL THAT NASTY WOUND OF YOURS.
YOU SEE, IT WAS ALREADY TOO LATE FOR US IN THIS TIME. YOU HAD TO STOP THIS TRAGEDY BEFORE, IN THE PAST! STOP IT NO MATTER WHAT THE COST!
YOUR AUNT SURE IS GOING TO BE SURPRISED TO SEE THAT ALL SHE'S GOT IS AN EMPTY CAGE!
YOU NEVER EVEN LEFT! I ALMOST DIED A TON OF TIMES, AND YOU DON'T EVEN CARE! YOU USED ME TO KILL HER, NOT TO SAVE HER!
DON'T THINK THAT, GREGORY, WE GARGOYLES ARE MERELY GUARDIANS. YOU HAVEN'T YET UNDERSTOOD THAT ONLY MAGIC TRULY HAS POWER OVER YOU AND OVER ALL OF US.

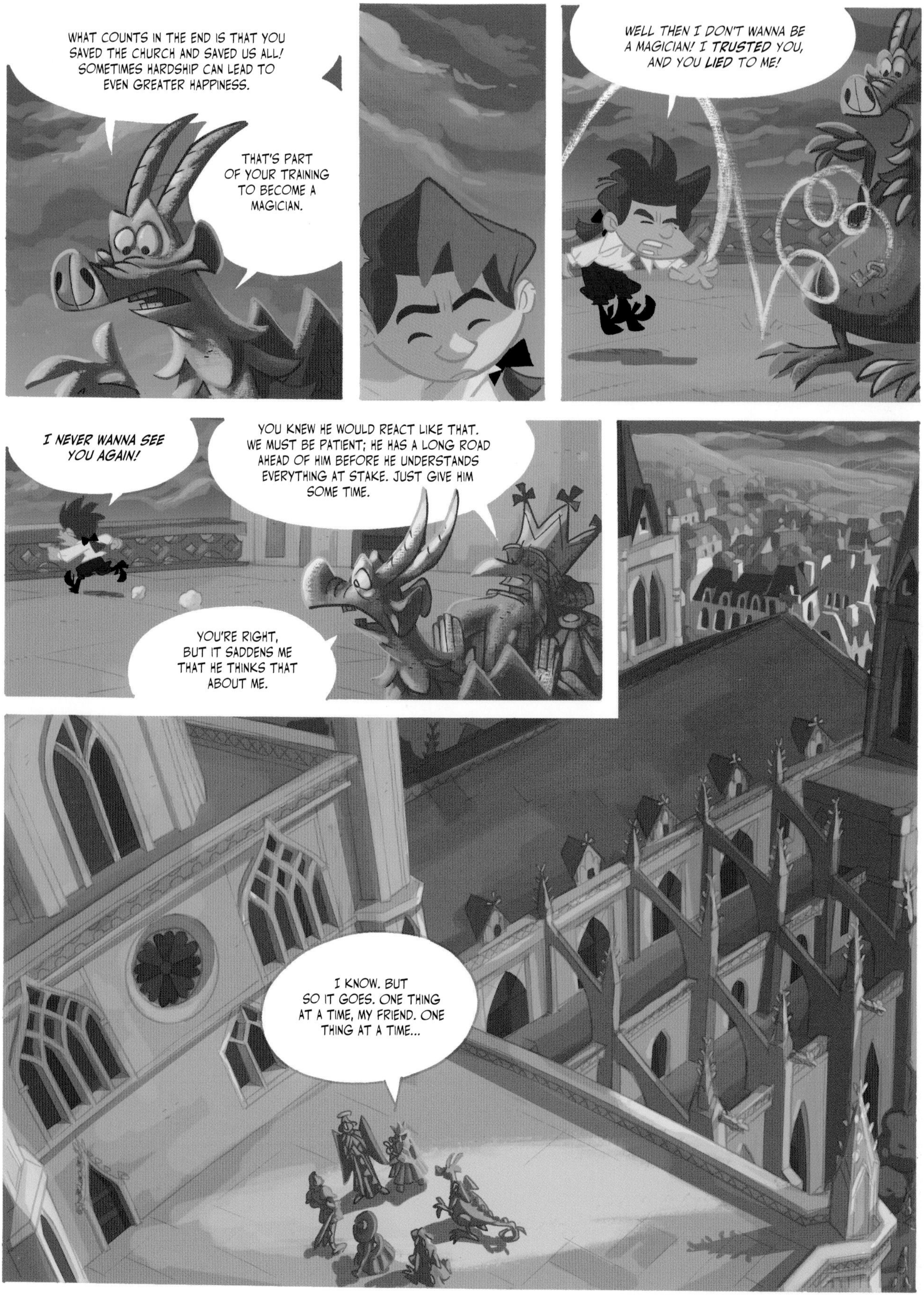
WHAT COUNTS IN THE END IS THAT YOU SAVED THE CHURCH AND SAVED US ALL! SOMETIMES HARDSHIP CAN LEAD TO EVEN GREATER HAPPINESS.
THAT'S PART OF YOUR TRAINING TO BECOME A MAGICIAN.
WELL THEN I DON'T WANNA BE A MAGICIAN! I TRUSTED YOU, AND YOU LIED TO ME!
I NEVER WANNA SEE YOU AGAIN!
YOU KNEW HE WOULD REACT LIKE THAT. WE MUST BE PATIENT; HE HAS A LONG ROAD AHEAD OF HIM BEFORE HE UNDERSTANDS EVERYTHING AT STAKE. JUST GIVE HIM SOME TIME.
YOU'RE RIGHT, BUT IT SADDENS ME THAT HE THINKS THAT ABOUT ME.
I KNOW. BUT SO IT GOES. ONE THING AT A TIME, MY FRIEND. ONE THING AT A TIME...

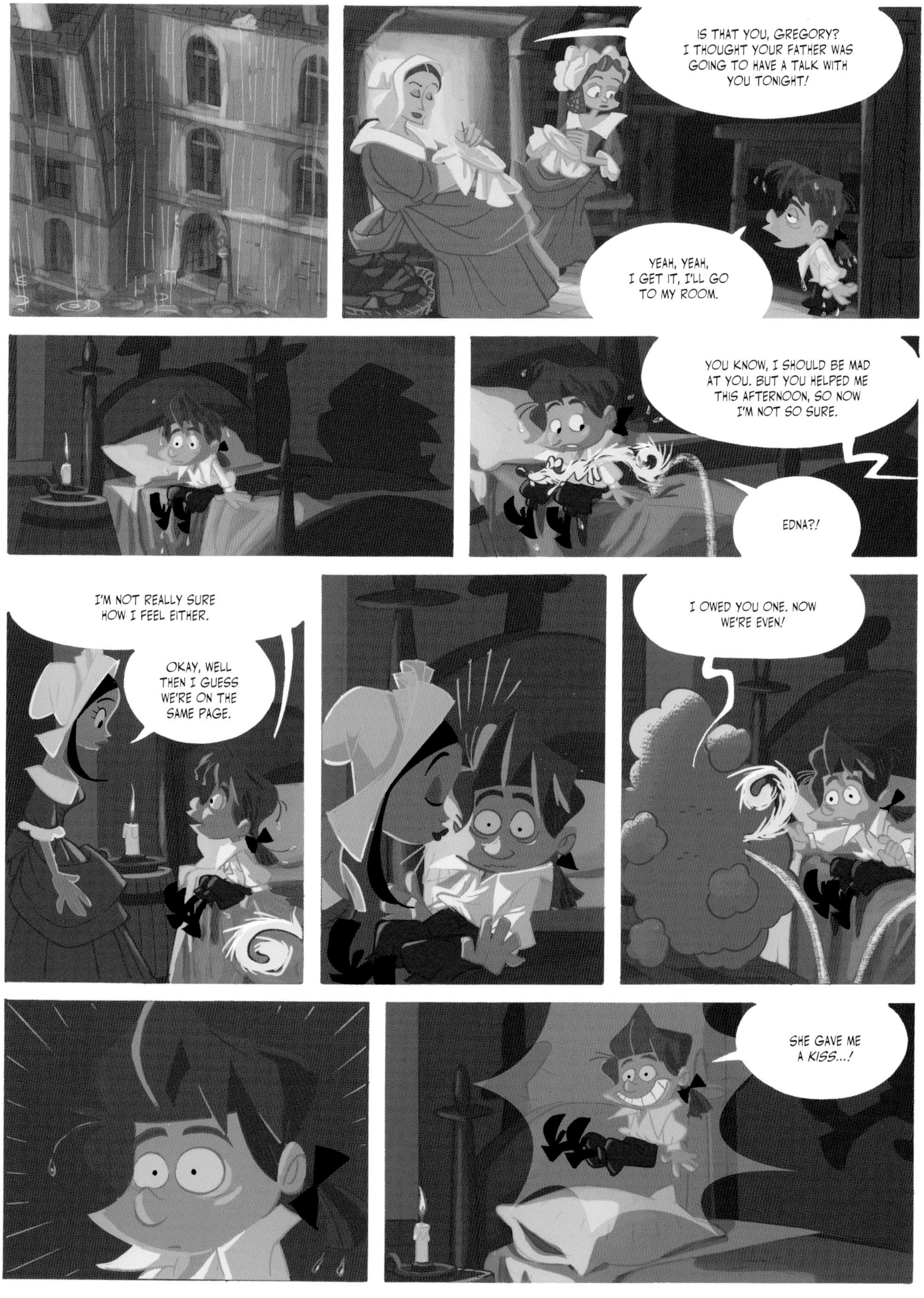
IS THAT YOU, GREGORY? I THOUGHT YOUR FATHER WAS GOING TO HAVE A TALK WITH YOU TONIGHT!
YEAH, YEAH, I GET IT, I'LL GO TO MY ROOM.
YOU KNOW, I SHOULD BE MAD AT YOU. BUT YOU HELPED ME THIS AFTERNOON, SO NOW I'M NOT SO SURE.
EDNA?!
I'M NOT REALLY SURE HOW I FEEL EITHER.
OKAY, WELL THEN I GUESS WE'RE ON THE SAME PAGE.
I OWED YOU ONE. NOW WE'RE EVEN!
SHE GAVE ME A *KISS*...!

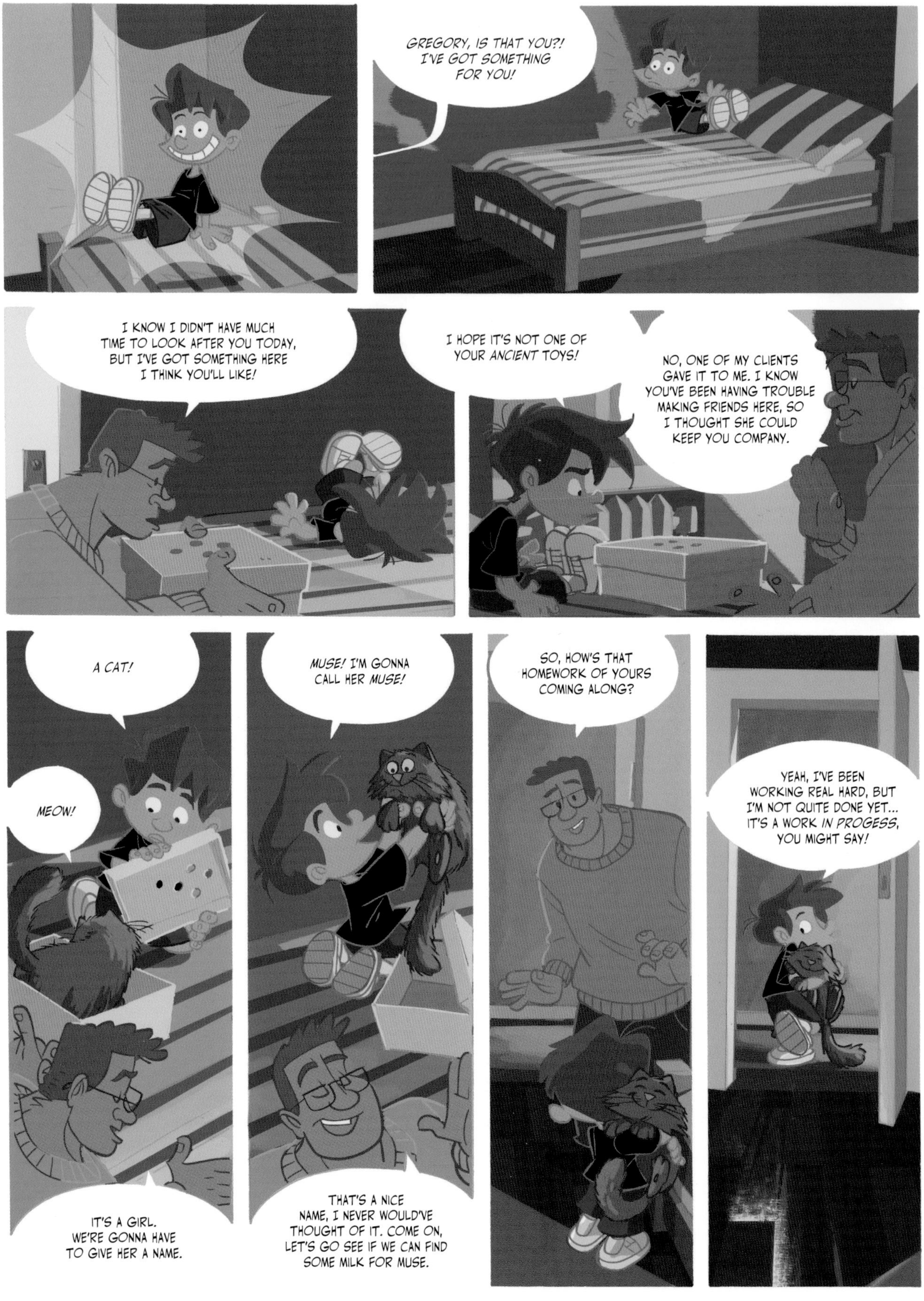
GREGORY, IS THAT YOU?! I'VE GOT SOMETHING FOR YOU!
I KNOW I DIDN'T HAVE MUCH TIME TO LOOK AFTER YOU TODAY, BUT I'VE GOT SOMETHING HERE I THINK YOU'LL LIKE!
I HOPE IT'S NOT ONE OF YOUR ANCIENT TOYS!
NO, ONE OF MY CLIENTS GAVE IT TO ME. I KNOW YOU'VE BEEN HAVING TROUBLE MAKING FRIENDS HERE, SO I THOUGHT SHE COULD KEEP YOU COMPANY.
A CAT!
MEOW!
IT'S A GIRL. WE'RE GONNA HAVE TO GIVE HER A NAME.
MUSE! I'M GONNA CALL HER MUSE!
THAT'S A NICE NAME, I NEVER WOULD'VE THOUGHT OF IT. COME ON, LET'S GO SEE IF WE CAN FIND SOME MILK FOR MUSE.
SO, HOW'S THAT HOMEWORK OF YOURS COMING ALONG?
YEAH, I'VE BEEN WORKING REAL HARD, BUT I'M NOT QUITE DONE YET... IT'S A WORK IN PROGESS, YOU MIGHT SAY!

THE ADVENTURE CONTINUES IN
GREGORY AND THE GARGOYLES BOOK 2!